National Bestselling Author

JILL MARIE LANDIS

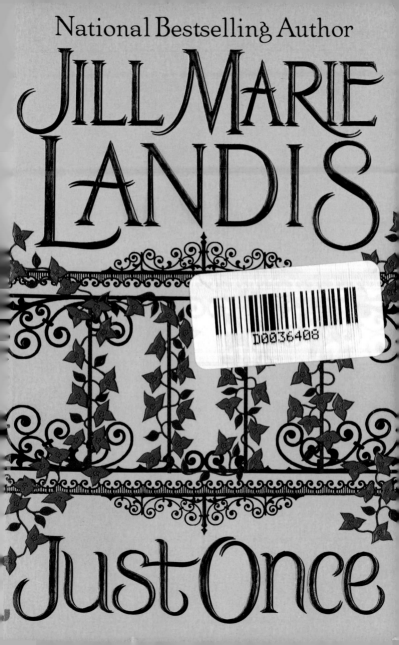

D0036408

Just Once

JOVE

$6.50 U.S.
$8.50 CAN

EAN

"JUST ONCE

is a superb reading experience, rich in poignancy and humor."
—*Romantic Times*

"Characters that come alive and make you cry—Jill Marie Landis
is a winner!!!"
—*Kat Martin*

Also by
Jill Marie Landis...

DAY DREAMER

*When Celine Winters exchanged cloaks—and futures—with a
stranger, she hoped to find a destiny greater than any daydream.*

"Not since *Jade* has Jill Marie Landis delved into romantic sus-
pense with as much verve and skillful storytelling as she has
done in *Day Dreamer*." —*Romantic Times*

LAST CHANCE

*Rachel McKenna shocked everyone when she danced with leg-
endary gunfighter Lane Cassidy. But she knew he could be her last
chance for happiness...*

"Readers who loved *After All* . . . will be overjoyed with this first-
rate spinoff." —*Publishers Weekly*

AFTER ALL

*The passionate and moving story of a dance hall girl trying to
change her life in the town of Last Chance, Montana.*

"Historical romance at its very best." —*Publishers Weekly*

UNTIL TOMORROW

*A soldier returning from war shows a backwoods beauty that every
dream is possible—even the dream of love...*

"Landis does what she does best by creating characters of great
dimension, compassion, and strength." —*Publishers Weekly*

PAST PROMISES

She was a brilliant paleontologist who came west in search of dinosaurs. But a rugged cowboy poet was determined to unearth the beauty and passion behind her bookish spectacles...

"Warmth, charm and appeal...*Past Promises* is guaranteed to satisfy romance readers everywhere." —Amanda Quick

COME SPRING
WINNER OF THE "BEST ROMANCE NOVEL OF THE YEAR" AWARD

Snowbound in a mountain man's cabin, beautiful Annika learned that unexpected love can grow as surely as the seasons change...

"A beautiful love story." —Julie Garwood

JADE

Her exotic beauty captured the heart of a rugged rancher. But could he forget the past—and love again?

"Guaranteed to enthrall...an unusual, fast-paced love story." —*Romantic Times*

ROSE

Across the golden frontier, her passionate heart dared to dream...

"A gentle romance that will warm your soul." —*Heartland Critiques*

WILDFLOWER

Amidst the untamed beauty of the Rocky Mountains, two daring hearts forged a perilous passion...

"A delight from start to finish!" —*Rendezvous*

SUNFLOWER
WINNER OF THE ROMANCE WRITERS OF AMERICA'S "GOLDEN MEDALLION FOR BEST HISTORICAL ROMANCE"

Jill Marie Landis's stunning debut novel, this sweeping love story astonished critics, earning glowing reviews including a FIVE STAR rating from *Affaire de Coeur*...

"A truly fabulous read! The story comes vibrantly alive, making you laugh and cry..." —*Affaire de Coeur*

Just Once

Jill Marie Landis

JOVE BOOKS, NEW YORK

JUST ONCE

A Jove Book / published by arrangement with
the author

PRINTING HISTORY
Jove edition / June 1997

The Putnam Berkley World Wide Web site address is
http://www.berkley.com

Jill Marie Landis's World Wide Web site address is
http://www.nettrends.com/jillmarielandis

ISBN: 0-515-12062-6

A JOVE BOOK®
Jove Books are published by The Berkley Publishing Group,
200 Madison Avenue, New York, New York 10016.
JOVE and the "J" design are trademarks
belonging to Jove Publications, Inc.

PRINTED IN THE UNITED STATES OF AMERICA

10 9 8 7 6 5 4 3 2 1

Dear Reader,

Sometimes you get what you wish for, only to discover that what you wished for isn't what you really wanted at all. *Just Once* is the story of two people, Hunter Boone and Jemma O'Hurley, an honorable, stubborn hero and an impetuous but determined heroine who insist on following their dreams, even when those dreams threaten to tear them apart.

During their adventures on the perilous streets of New Orleans and the Kentucky frontier, Hunter and Jemma learn the meaning of love, commitment, family, and self-worth; most of all, they realize that sometimes dreams are even better when you share them with someone you love.

Here's hoping *Just Once* brings you a few chuckles, a few tears, and a few hours of entertainment.

Keep dreaming!

Jill Marie Landis

To Mom

For sending me to all those Saturday CCD classes.

There's a reason for everything.

But who would have thought...

Just Once

chapter
1

One quick, final prayer to St. Joseph and Jemma O'Hurley was ready.

Poised in the foyer of her Boston town house, filled with high hopes, she began the long walk down the hall toward her father's study. A thick carpet runner beneath her feet muffled the sound of raspberry-silk slippers dyed to match her gown, the likes of which no one had seen since before the war. It was a frothy French creation her father had purchased on his last trip abroad.

The house, as always, was as quiet as a mausoleum. With every step, her heartbeat seemed to echo louder, as if it pounded against the cherrywood paneling and not inside her chest. Pausing outside the door, she lifted her hand and finger-combed her unruly blond curls. Her long, thick hair constantly resisted pins and combs but, knowing how much stock her father put in appearances, she tried to tame it, determined to look her best.

Jemma took a deep breath, knocked gently, and waited.

She rarely saw her father. She could count on her fingers and toes the sum total of all the hours he had ever spent with her. There was no time in his life for anything but business, not even for her, his only child.

But things were about to change.

When he called out for her to enter, Jemma pushed the door open and slipped inside; closing it without a sound, she leaned against its hard, glossy surface for support. Her father stood across the room, staring out the open window that fronted the street. The gleaming expanse of his burlwood desk separated them. Something always did.

Outside, the waning summer's heat beat down on the city. Not a breath of air stirred. Enormous thunderheads threatened rain as they gathered over the harbor. Traffic was light this afternoon, the sultry humidity forcing most sane Bostonians indoors.

While she waited for him to turn around, Jemma watched her father take out his handkerchief and wipe his brow. Replacing the kerchief after carefully matching its original folds, he straightened his already flawless cravat. Even the stifling heat did not keep him from appearing anything less than the meticulous, successful businessman he was.

She had requested this meeting and was surprised when he had actually left his office at the warehouse early in order to allow her a few minutes before dinner. Time was always of the essence for Thomas O'Hurley. He would appreciate it if she came right to the point, and she knew it, so Jemma screwed up her courage, clasped her hands in earnest, and began to argue her cause.

"Father, I've been thinking a lot about the future lately—"

"As have I, Jemma. As have I."

Slowly he turned and gave her his full attention. His eyes were the same shade of blue as her own, a deep Irish blue. He was fit and trim, bald, with thick muttonchops and round, cherub cheeks above a salt-and-pepper mustache. He exuded confidence and pride—indeed, for good reason. He had risen from humble beginnings to become one of the wealthiest men on the eastern seaboard.

Jemma breathed a sigh of relief. Things were off to a good start.

"I'm so glad to know we're of like mind," she began. "Now that I'm no longer at school, I think this is the perfect time to look to the future, don't you?"

"Smart girl. You've always had a good head on your shoulders, even though that old reprobate grandfather of yours tried to fill it with nonsense. Yes, indeed. I think it's high time to settle down, look to the future."

Settle down? The idea of settling down had never entered her mind. She felt a moment of concern, but forged quickly ahead.

"I've spent the week since we received news of Mr. Finlay's death trying to come up with something useful I could do for the company. I've a good head with figures, as you know, and I would be more than willing to travel with you, arrange your appointments, act as your personal secretary." She paused, her hopes high, her expectations grand. Surely it would sound as sensible to him as it did to her.

He was staring at her as if she had suddenly grown feathers.

"I already have a secretary." His tone was hesitant, almost evasive. Not like him at all.

"But Jefferson is getting older. Surely he is about to retire. Frequent crossings back and forth to the London office can't be easy for him anymore."

"Jemma, Jefferson is only five years older than I am."

She shrugged. "Whatever. I've never been good at ages." She glanced down at the tips of her favorite shoes. He valued courage. She met his gaze directly. "There must be something I can do at the office, Father. I can't sit here day after day doing embroidery. Mrs. Greene can run this household with her eyes closed. I need something worthwhile to fill my days. I want to feel useful, to be productive. I've thought of writing professionally, but I know you wouldn't look very favorably on that."

"To what end? You're a woman, Jemma."

She sighed again. "That *is* a problem for me, I'll admit." She smiled, recalling Sister Mary Martin's praise for her outstanding, imaginative works of fiction. "I have a rare gift for storytelling, you know."

His only comment was silent dismissal. He turned and walked to a side table where crystal decanters of various shapes and sizes caught the rays of the sun. Neatly lined up one by one, they stood like soldiers in sparkling rainbow coats. For years the housekeeper, Mrs. Greene, had seen to it that the grand house was kept perfect from top to bottom. There wasn't a single object that wasn't always in its place, starched, pressed, positioned, or shining like a newly minted coin.

Her father continued to ignore her as he poured a liberal splash of brandy into a Baccarat snifter. Jemma waited. He swirled the expensive French liquor. She watched it slick the sides of the glass like amber honey. His hand was shaking slightly. When she suddenly detected the hint of nervousness, his edginess quickly communicated itself to her.

She had never seen her father nervous. As a founding partner in O'Hurley and Finlay Imports, he had never been intimidated by any commercial challenge. He had spent the better portion of his life making lucrative business transactions, always besting his competitors. There was no reason on earth why this discussion should cause him any anxiety—none that she could think of, anyway.

He carefully set the snifter down on the corner of his desk, ran his hand over his cravat again, then along the front of his jacket. He patted his trim waist. When he cleared his throat, she was convinced that he had something very important on his mind. Something he was very hesitant to tell her.

Finally he said, "As a matter of fact, I do need your help, Jemma."

Thank you, St. Joseph!

Her worry vanished. "I *knew* you would see my point. I'm more than willing to do anything I can to learn the business."

She was hard-pressed to hide her joy, but it was short lived when she realized what he was saying.

"Teaching you the business wasn't exactly what I had in mind." He walked around behind his desk, unlocked a side drawer, and bent slightly so that he could reach inside. Straightening, he held an important-looking set of documents in his hand. He was not smiling. His forehead was marred with deep furrows beaded with perspiration.

"What *did* you have in mind?" Jemma's stomach began to flutter. Something momentous was about to occur. She could feel it as certainly as she could smell the salt tang on the sultry air in the stuffy room.

"All I ask is that you please hear me out."

Her stomach turned over. "I don't like the way that sounds."

"Before Finlay's death, I had already decided to relocate the company to New Orleans."

"But you'll still have to go to London to settle affairs, won't you? I had hoped that you would finally consent to taking me abroad." What he had said about relocation began to register. Her mind raced with endless possibilities. A move to New Orleans? "This seems so sudden. You just returned from New Orleans two months ago. Why didn't you say anything then?"

It was like him not to discuss his plans with her, but this move was so momentous that she couldn't believe he had waited until now to tell her. Excitement and anticipation replaced her anxiety. For years she had begged him to take her with him on his travels, but he had never agreed. Now, out of the blue, a whole new world was about to open up for her.

This is it, Jemma gal. Your chance for adventure!

She could almost hear her Grandpa Hall urging her to grasp hold of this unexpected opportunity for a grand new way of life in an exciting new place. She was only half-listening to her father as he went on.

"Since the end of the war, the Mississippi River Valley has been attracting commerce faster than anyone dared hope. I'm selling Finlay's London holdings and reopening as O'Hurley Imports in New Orleans as soon as I return from settling Finlay's affairs. I'll be moving to Louisiana permanently."

Jemma glanced around the study at the familiar surroundings: the wall of books, the wide bank of windows with their panoramic view of the bay, the gilt-framed portrait of the mother she had never known. This was the only house she had ever lived in, but she would say good-bye gladly if it meant a new beginning, new sights and sounds and experiences. She would no longer have to rely on her imagination or her memory of her grandfather's many tales to sweep her away to exotic lands.

"It'll be wonderful, Father. A gateway to another world." She paused, remembering that he had to see to Finlay's affairs first. "I know there will be a lot to do here to prepare for the move, but I would still love to go to London with you first."

"I'm afraid there's a bit more to all of it than that. Maybe you'd like to sit down."

She felt her intestines twist into a knot, and in a reflexive gesture gathered the raspberry silk of her skirt in her hands and hung on.

"I'd rather stand," she whispered, her gaze locked on the papers in his fist.

He took a deep breath, looked down at the documents in his hand and said on a rush of words, "On my last trip to New Orleans, I signed this marriage agreement between you and a Creole aristocrat, a rich young man named Alex Moreau—"

"*You did what?*" Her knees turned to jelly.

"He'll be able to keep you in grand style."

"I don't need grand style. I don't want—"

He silenced her with a wave of his hand.

"Hear me out. I've spent my life amassing a fortune so that you'll never know poverty. I've spoiled you with wealth and privilege and a fine education because I wanted you to have everything my father could never afford to give me. I should have arranged for your future long ago, but to tell you the truth, the years got away from me. Somehow, overnight, you're through with convent school and you've become a woman. It's high time I see you settled. Naturally, I want you to have the very best. Where's the crime in that?"

Panic struck her hard. The tears that stung her eyes threatened to spill over her lower lashes. The sight of her father holding a copy of the cursed wedding agreement shimmered and swam, his image wavering, distorted.

How could he have done this to her? Jemma swiped away traitorous tears with the back of her hand. "All I've ever wanted was for us to be closer. I'd like to travel with you and see the world. Why can't I take part in opening the new office with you instead of marrying this . . . this Alex Moreau?"

When she realized she was begging, she reminded herself that he hated crying as much as he disliked any other sign of weakness. She bit her lips to keep them from trembling and stood firm, aching to run to him, longing to have him take her in his arms and hold her close to his heart. She wished he would tell her that she was his girl and that he loved her, that he would never force her to marry a stranger.

Why should she expect him to be any different than he ever was, she wondered. Thomas O'Hurley had never openly shown her one moment of affection, never told her he loved her. For him, it was enough that he spent money on things, that he gave her lavish gifts and provided her with the very best that money could buy. Simple acts of caring, of voicing his affection, were beyond him.

She had more than enough *things*. What she longed for

was for him to listen to her, just once, the way Grandpa Hall had before he died. She wanted her father to see her as something more than a pretty showpiece. She wanted him to believe in her. She wanted to be someone he could believe in.

Jemma wiped away her tears and waited for him to make the next move, staring at him from across the room, needing his love and understanding but at a loss as to how to win it.

"Believe me, Jemma. I didn't do this without thought. This alliance is for your own good."

Alliance. Business. She was nothing but a pawn.

Something inside her broke. She was deeply hurt, but the pain didn't prevent her temper from simmering.

"My own good? Father, you're too adept at business to sign a marriage contract and get nothing out of it."

Sweating profusely, Thomas yanked his handkerchief out and patted his brow again. "That's true. When I said I needed your help, I meant it. Those Creoles are as close as nits on a comb. Your marrying into one of their prominent families will help tremendously when I go down there to make business connections. I want this new branch of O'Hurley Imports established before river trade expands. Americans are already flooding into New Orleans in droves."

"You *sold* me," she whispered. "To the highest bidder."

"I did no such thing. It's a marriage arrangement and damn it, girl, it's for your own good."

She stared up at the decorative scrollwork that bordered the ceiling, so upset that she couldn't even think of a single saint's name. Never had she felt so desperate or so alone. She clasped her hands together at her waist until her knuckles went white, and faced him again. She tried to steady her voice, raising her chin a notch.

"With his last breath, Grandpa Hall made me promise

I would sample as much as I could at the banquet of life before I married."

He slapped the papers against his palm. "I rue the day I let that penniless old windbag move in here and fill your head with that complete and utter nonsense. Don't you know that all of his stories were nothing but a lot of tall tales? Why is it he's been dead and buried over nine years and he still has more of an influence over you than I *ever* did?"

Her breath hitched. She was almost nineteen. Definitely not a child anymore. It was time he knew the truth. Time she told him of the aching need that had lingered in the shadows of her heart for years.

"Maybe because he and I spent more hours together in what little time he had left than you've ever spared me in my whole life."

"I've been breaking my back to give you everything—"

"Everything but what I wanted most. Your time, your love. To be part of your life, not merely another of your precious possessions."

His expression darkened as his lips firmed into a hard line. She hadn't thought it possible, but his frown deepened. He looked at her as if she were suddenly speaking in tongues. Jemma knew that infuriating her father was no way to beat him at his own game. She had asked for this meeting to convince him that she was mature enough, wise enough to become a partner in business with him—not to argue.

The tension in the room was as thick as the humidity. There was only one way to convince him to break the wedding agreement and that was to reason with him calmly, to make him think the decision had been his own idea.

Jemma pressed her palms together the way Sister Agatha Lucille always did before she was going to make an important point. She took a deep breath.

"You know I would do anything you ask of me—"

"Then do this, Jemma. Please."

She turned aside in order to wipe away more tears before they spilled down her cheeks. She had never let him see her cry, not since she had learned as a child that even the slightest show of tears caused him to immediately turn her over to her nanny.

Her father used the heavily silent pause to put down the agreement and pick up the snifter. He made his way back to the liquor table. His hand shook when he lifted the decanter and removed the heavy crystal stopper. When he finally turned around, Jemma had gained some control. Before she could speak, he started in again.

"As soon as the young men around here find out you're home, the offers of marriage will start to come in. Marriage and family are your only options."

Don't forget your promise, Jemma gal. Don't let him see you tied down.

When Grandpa's admonition came back to her, as loud and clear as if he were alive and in the room, Jemma shook her head, beginning to wonder if she was losing her mind.

"I want to see some of the world before I silently slip from one household to another, into another man's keeping," she said.

"I can't *believe* we are even having this conversation." With a lost look in his eyes, Thomas stared up at Marjorie Hall O'Hurley's portrait, shook his head, and hastily downed the brandy.

Jemma felt increasingly desperate. "Don't you see? I don't want to be tied down by marriage yet. I've just spent nine years at convent school. I don't know anything about the world. I want to see things, do things I've only imagined. I have my own dreams, Father. I want a taste of adventure."

"Don't be ridiculous."

His cold reaction to her heartfelt plea was like a slap in the face.

"Ridiculous? Why is it all right for a man to want to

experience the world, but a woman must quickly settle down and give up her freedom?''

''Damn your grandfather's eyes!'' Thomas slammed the snifter down on the desk so hard that the remaining liquor sloshed all the way to the rim.

He had not been enthusiastic about taking in her maternal grandfather when the old man had come knocking on the door nine years ago, but she hadn't realized the depth of her father's resentment until today. Theodore Hall had come to Boston to live out the last few months of his life, forced to accept his son-in-law's charity or die alone on the streets. A penniless adventurer, Grandpa Hall had spent most of his life at sea or roaming through foreign ports. Since her father measured a person by his wealth, in his eyes Theodore Hall had been worth nothing. To Jemma, Grandpa was a hero, a spinner of tall tales who owned more than riches. He possessed a treasure trove of memories and he had shared them all with her before he died.

''If I were a son, not a daughter, you'd *expect* me to sow wild oats, wouldn't you? But no . . . I'm cursed. I'm a woman, so you've gone ahead without consulting me. Did you know that Grandpa once told me that his one regret was that Mama died so young, without having really lived, without having seen anything but this one little corner of the world?''

At first she thought he was not going to say anything, but when he did respond, the words were so softly uttered that she barely heard them.

''We were young and in love, your mother and I. She died having you. I don't think she would have traded one moment of her life for adventure.''

It was the first time Jemma had ever heard even a touch of love and reverence in his voice. She watched Thomas set the empty snifter on the desk. His eyes seemed incredibly bright. Jemma caught her breath. Perhaps this was the miraculous moment she had been praying for, for so very long. She had finally reached his heart and he had heard her.

Now he would ask her to forgive him and tell her the marriage contract was all a big mistake. That she didn't have to marry a stranger. They would work together. She would be his right hand. He would be the father she had always wanted.

Now he would open his arms to her and show his fatherly love.

But when he looked back up and met her gaze, there was nothing but cool determination in his hard, uncompromising stare.

The moment for miracles had vanished.

"Jemma, don't make this any harder than it has to be," he told her. "I've done this for you. In time, you'll see I'm right. You'll come to love Alexandre Moreau. I hear he's handsome, charming, and quite an honorable man."

"So, you honestly expect me to marry a virtual stranger? Some man you had to *pay* to marry me?"

"I didn't have to pay him," he sputtered.

"There is no dowry involved?"

Cornered, he shrugged. "A small one."

"Knowing you, this small dowry could probably keep an entire family living modestly for years."

"I'm not about to back down. I can't. I made this agreement with the Moreaus and I need your cooperation. I've never asked anything of you before, have I?" He took a deep breath and let out a long, ragged sigh. "I've never begged anyone for anything in my life, but I'm begging you now, Jemma. If you love me, help me keep my good name and secure the future of the company. Please do this for me. Promise me that you'll marry Alex Moreau."

This was a nightmare. A bad dream she prayed would end. Jemma dug her nails into her palms, hoping the pain would awaken her. It only proved she wasn't dreaming. Her father was still standing there with perspiration beading his forehead, waiting expectantly for an answer.

He'd said he had never begged anyone for anything in his life, and she knew that was true, just as he had never asked anything so important of her either, until now. But this—

"Well, Jemma?"

His voice called her back. "What, Father?"

"Please make me a solemn vow that you'll marry Alexandre Moreau."

Don't do it, Jemma gal!

"I—" The words stuck in her throat.

"I need this. I need you to uphold the O'Hurley name and see this through."

He *had* made a promise to the Moreaus, had signed his good name to an official document. He could be ruined before he even began in New Orleans. No matter how much she wished the circumstances away, she could never be the cause of his dishonor.

Fight it, Jemma gal. Don't give in.

Her grandfather was only a memory. Her father was flesh and blood and he was standing there expectantly, waiting for her to do as he asked, willing her to do the honorable thing.

"But I promised Grandpa Hall. . . ."

"He would only want what's best for you, too, Jemma. You know that, as a woman, this is really the only course you can follow. Do this for me and I promise you'll never regret it."

Deep down, she knew there was no way she could refuse; still, he was asking her to pour her hopes and dreams onto thirsty sand and watch them evaporate.

"Must I give you an answer today?" She knew it would only prolong the agony; still, she hoped—

"I've booked passage for you on a ship bound for New Orleans at the end of the week."

"But *you're* sailing to London in two days."

He looked away. "I can't be there to see you wed. You know the settlement of the London assets can't wait. Fin-

lay was deep in personal debt. I have to try to save what
I can of his portion of the partnership; everything I have
depends on that. I'm counting on you to sail to New Orleans without me and see this marriage through, Jemma.''

So torn. A refusal was on her lips until he did the one
thing she had never expected. He slowly reached out and
laid his hand on her shoulder. With a feather-light touch,
he gave her an awkward but gentle pat.

Jemma broke. She felt her lower lip begin to tremble
and bit down hard to keep it still. Once more her father's
image was blurred by shimmering tears. The same love
that had kept her hoping he would one day show his affection bubbled up from the wellspring of love that bound
her to him and bid her to obey.

Don't give in!

She could still hear Grandpa urging her to refuse, but
the memory of the sound of his voice had begun to fade
to a muffled hint of a whisper.

''I'll do it,'' she said quickly, softly, as if muting the
words might lessen the strength of her promise.

Her father lifted his hand and smiled in relief. She had
given him what he wanted, had given in, knowing as she
did so that she would never go back on her word. Obviously, he wasn't as certain of her honor. He pressed for
more.

''*Swear* to me you'll do it, Jemma.''

''Do you know how much this hurts me, Father?''

''I have to have your solemn vow.''

She met his gaze and swore. ''I promise on St. Lucy's
eyes that I'll marry Alex Moreau.''

Even with all the windows open, the air on the second
floor was stifling. Jemma closed the door to her room and
leaned against it, eyes shut, her heart hammering as if it
were a creature trying to escape her chest. Her earlier bravado had evaporated the minute she left the study. Never
had she known such confusion. She opened her eyes and

pressed a hand over her lips, afraid an uncontrollable sob might escape. Slowly, by taking deep, even breaths, she eventually calmed herself—trying not to think of what she had just agreed to, but failing.

Often, when she had felt frightened and alone as a child, she would sneak down to the kitchen, sit on a stool near the hearth, and spin stories for the help that kept them all enthralled. There had been a closeness, a camaraderie among the servants that was now missing from her life. At times she had even pretended they were her family, until Mrs. Greene came to announce that her nanny was looking for her or that it was almost time for her father to come home and that she had best get back upstairs where she belonged.

Shortly after her return from school she had wandered into the kitchen looking for company, only to find that the one familiar face there was Mrs. Greene's. The new staff saw her as an adult, as their mistress. She could tell that her presence made them uncomfortable. She wasn't accepted among them.

Where did she fit in? Surely not in some swamp in Louisiana. What if she hated Alex Moreau? What if she hated Louisiana? By the time she discovered whether either one suited her, it would be too late to escape.

She crossed to the wide bank of windows. Unlatching them one by one, she swung them open, hoping to attract any stray wisp of breeze. Then, she walked over to the *prie-dieu* standing before a small altar on a side table. Votive candles burned in various shapes and sizes of stemware purloined from the pantry, all lined up before a collection of small likenesses of saints portrayed in various poses. The framed miniatures were hung in a gathering on the wall above the table.

She had collected the portraits at convent school. Some had been awarded to her for scholastic achievement. Others she had obtained as gratuities for her donations to the Save the Heathen Children collection. The familiar images had always been comforting, like a host of friends and family she could call on during times of need. In that way they were always with her, like the brothers and sisters she never had. She gazed up at the pictures of the men and women posed with their emblems, the symbols of each individual taken from stories of martyrdom or sacrifice.

Bowing her head, Jemma crossed herself and began a prayer devoted to a specific few, the virgin martyrs.

"Dear Ladies, if you could only find a way to save me from this marriage without breaking my word to my father, I would be truly grateful."

She hastily reminded the saints that she had led a life of obedience that even St. Francis could not have faulted. An ordered, predictable, boring life.

"Now I'm facing marriage to a man I've never laid eyes on—a man who will expect me to vow obedience, bear his children, and see to his household, somewhere in a swamp full of alligators. The guillotine would be more inviting."

Realizing what she had just said, she crossed herself and added hastily, "Forget that last statement. And if you're up there listening, Grandpa Hall, I'm sorry I can't keep my promise. I hope you'll understand that there was really no way out."

Jemma crossed herself, stood up and kicked off her slippers, then skimmed off her stockings before she went back to the window seat and sat down. Listlessly staring out at the heat clouds in the distance, she drew her skirt up until her hem rested across her thighs. She leaned back against the wall.

If her saints could not save her, then she had two months before she would arrive in New Orleans to grow accustomed to settling down and sharing a bed with a virtual stranger. After everything Sister Augusta Aleria had taught her students about the evils of lying with a man—any man, including a husband—the very thought of having to do anything of the sort made Jemma queasy. Yet, at the same time, it filled her with a titillating sense of curiosity and excitement. When it was time to sleep with her husband, would she be able to confine her desires to lovemaking for the sake of procreation, or would she cross the line into the evil realm of wanton sensuality? Would she run amok in the devil's playground that Sister Augusta Aleria had so often—and in such very colorful detail—warned her students about?

Jemma's gaze drifted from the open window to the wall opposite the framed saints. It was lined with the many framed samplers of proverbs and sayings she had embroidered. They showed a progression of her needlework skills from the age of six onward. Contemplating the varied pieces, she realized she had been groomed for nothing but marriage. She was educated, but had no real vocation. She was more than capable of overseeing a household staff, balancing household accounts, hostessing parties, and appearing on her husband's arm, but nothing more would ever be expected of her.

Since she had left convent school she had felt adrift, a ship without a rudder. Her life had no purpose, no meaning. Although she had no idea then what destiny held in store for her, she had been convinced it would be something greater than more of the staid, ordinary life she had already led.

Was she ready to raise children? She didn't know one thing about babies. Why, she had never even held one in her arms.

She bounded up off the window seat and went to one of two huge armoires that banked the far wall. The closet was filled to bursting, a cornucopia of silk and satin gowns with high waistlines and low-cut bodices. Capes and cloaks and riding attire. Fabrics embellished with the finest Belgian lace and shimmering ribbons. Casually tossed, mismatched piles of silk slippers dyed to match the various gowns, as well as an assortment of bonnets, gloves, parasols, and bags.

Her dresser held velvet-lined boxes of pearls and gem-stones set into drop earrings. There was probably not another young woman her age who would not change places with her. Now she was to be settled with a rich husband who would continue to keep her in style. She had spoken the truth earlier when she had told her father that she would trade all of it away if he could only spend more time with her.

As she stared at the abundance around her, she prayed for a miracle. Barring that, she prayed for strength and a sign from heaven. She even prayed that her father would change his mind, but deep in her heart she knew that he would not, that he *could* not go back on his word.

Just as she knew she could not go back on her own promise to him.

She stood before the armoire, trying to decide what to take and what to leave behind. One trunk would be enough for now. The rest could be sent later. One thing was certain in this time of uncertainty and doubt—she would have to decide what to pack, and act quickly to see that everything was ready.

As she sorted through the gowns, she felt no enthusiasm, no excitement. She felt more alone than ever. Even in this, her marriage, her father was distancing himself, putting O'Hurley and Finlay first.

He would not even be there on the most important day of her life.

chapter
2

Hunter Sinclair Boone knew he wouldn't find the woman he was looking for in the Swamp.

The unsavory district was a favorite haunt of ruffians and rivermen who traveled down the Mississippi—a hell-hole on Girod Street made up of slapdash structures of lumber salvaged from barges and flatboats that were broken up once they reached New Orleans. Twelve blocks from the French Quarter, the Swamp was a teeming den of iniquity that even the New Orleans police refused to enter after dark, a place where the only law was every man for himself. The dregs of the underworld—crooked gamblers, pimps and prostitutes, derelicts and criminals of every description—roamed the lawless streets and back alleys that provided the perfect setting for the gut-busting "frolics" the rivermen engaged in night after night without fail.

But Hunter Boone wasn't looking to frolic. He was looking for Amelia White and although *he* knew better, *she* thought she was above the Swamp. He headed for the French Quarter.

With an eye out for Amelia, he was soon strolling through the Vieux Carré, rubbing shoulders with the Creoles and American merchants, the men and women of wealth and privilege. As he passed by, occasional comments were whispered in French, some just loud enough for him to hear. Although he couldn't understand the words, he could tell by the tone that the utterances were about him and that they were none too complimentary.

It didn't matter one bit to the damn Frenchies that he and others like him had served in detachments from Tennessee and Kentucky fighting alongside General Andrew Jackson to save this crowded, stinking city from the redcoats. To the Creoles, all of the backwoodsmen who came down the Mississippi by flatboat, keelboat, or barge were "Kaintucks," uncultured barbarians.

Granted, in his well-greased buckskin coat and leggings, a low-crowned, wide-brimmed felt hat, and moccasins, he certainly looked less than civilized. But most "Kaintucks" signed on as boatmen just to make sixty dollars working the perilous journey downriver so they could spend it on a hell of a drinking spree and a night of debauchery.

Hunter had come to New Orleans for two reasons: one was to sell off his brother's latest batch of whiskey, and the other was personal. He had hoped by a wild twist of fate that he might run into the woman to whom he had quite a few things to say—none of them kind. After that, he would be free to get on with his life for the first time in all of his twenty-eight years.

A slight mist had begun to fall, illumined by the lamplight, creating a veil of damp gossamer that settled over the sidewalks and muddy streets. Now and again he paused before the open doors of the crowded coffeehouses and cafés and let his gaze scan the rooms, hoping to catch a glimpse of the woman to whom he had opened his home and his heart; the woman who had stolen his savings and disappeared without a word, leaving behind her own daughter by another man, a man she couldn't even name.

Amelia White had the morals of an alley cat. He hoped fate might bring them together tonight; but on this one night he would spend in town, he wasn't about to waste more than a few hours looking for her.

At midnight, a performance of the popular *Two Hunters and the Dairy Maid* at the Theatre d'Orleans let out. The glittering crowd of theater patrons joined others on the street to enjoy the evening's usual pastimes. Women with parasols hurried along, trying to save their elaborate gowns and silk slippers from the effects of the rain.

Hunter stood head and shoulders above most of the crowd as he scanned the milling throng. Quickly becoming adept at ignoring offensive stares, he kept his long rifle in one hand and his lethally sharp knife sheathed at his side, and knew he presented a formidable figure. If Amelia caught a glimpse of him first, there would be no chance of an encounter.

The street in front of the theater was congested as dark-skinned carriage drivers vied for curb space and the audience hurried to seek shelter from the light rain. Not far away, the cathedral bell tolled, deep and ominous, the peals reverberating over shrill whistles and the crack of a driver's whip.

Hunter was close to giving up and heading back toward the river when he spotted a tall, slim brunette, flanked by two gentlemen dressed in black, headed in the opposite direction.

In a glance he took in the nape of the woman's long, elegant neck, the upswept dark hair that swirled in a smooth, modish style, the richness of her ebony satin cloak. Hunter cut the distance between them by half in three long strides. Without thinking, he barged through the crowd until he was directly behind them, then reached out and laid his hand on the woman's shoulder.

"Amelia!"

"*Monsieur?*" The woman turned abruptly, affronted by the intrusion. She was near thirty. Her tone was icy cold, but her faded hazel eyes could not hide her piqued interest.

Hunter was more relieved than frustrated.
It wasn't Amelia.

Nothing had gone smoothly since Jemma had left Boston.
The dismal rain only made things worse as she stood beneath a streetlamp on the levee clutching her umbrella, her
ruby-velvet hooded cloak fast becoming soaked. She had
no maid to see to her care. The young girl whom Mrs.
Greene had chosen to accompany her had taken ill at the
last moment, and none of the other servants wanted to
leave Boston. Determined to see to her own needs, Jemma
made the decision to travel alone with Wheaton, her father's most trusted bodyguard.

The hulking, slow-witted man had just returned from
hiring a carriage; he stood beside her grumbling about the
dark, the rain, and the unseasonable heat in a high-pitched
whine that didn't match his physical stature. The distinct
odor of liquor emanated from him, no doubt supplied by
the telltale bottle-shaped bulge in the pocket of his coat.

"There's nothing we can do about our late arrival,
Wheaton, so you might as well stop grousing."

"Someone from the Moreaus' shoulda been here to
meet us, what with the wedding set for tonight."

She wished he hadn't reminded her. "We're a week late
and it's already near midnight. I doubt they could actually
be planning on carrying out the wedding tonight, do you?"
She wondered how anyone could be so dense.

Jemma wondered what her father would have suggested.
She had tried to persuade him that Finlay wasn't getting
any deader, hoping he would postpone his trip to London,
but he had not sailed with her and had gone on to England
instead. Over the past few years, Finlay had taken out so
many personal loans against the business that Thomas
O'Hurley stood to lose much if he ignored his duties.

Jemma remained bitterly disappointed, but was still determined to hold up her end of the marriage arrangement
without her father at her side. A promise is a promise.

"Maybe we should find out how to get to the plantation. Should I load up the trunk?" Wheaton asked.

"It's that or continue to stand out here in the rain like two brainless idiots." Jemma looked around the nearly deserted dock. The passengers had all disembarked. Only a few stragglers remained. Beside them, her trunk and Wheaton's small bag were getting soaked.

"Miss O'Hurley?"

She turned at the sound of the familiar voice behind her and found the ship's captain politely waiting to address her.

"What is it, Captain Connor?" She had found the man eager to help make the voyage as comfortable as possible, even when the ship had run into the terrible gale that had blown it off course.

"This was delivered when we docked. I'm sorry, but the purser forgot to give it to you." He handed her a sealed letter.

"Thank you," she said absently, concentrating on the missive in her hand. As the captain departed, she handed Wheaton the umbrella. He held it over both of them while Jemma broke the wax seal and turned the page up to the streetlamp.

"Oh, my God." She closed her eyes, awed by the absolute power of prayer.

"What is it, miss?" Wheaton was suspended in a half-hovering stance, as if he had been cast in bronze while waiting for direction.

She had offered novenas to each and every saint the nuns had ever mentioned since the moment she had sworn to marry Alex Moreau. She had kept a votive candle burning in her room in Boston, an offering to St. Jude, the patron of hopeless causes. Aboard ship she had suspended the practice because of the danger of fire, but she continually prayed to all of her saints.

Someone up there had worked a miracle.

"This letter is from Henri Moreau. He regretfully states

that his grandson, Alex Moreau, was killed in a duel a month ago. He goes on to add that I am not to worry, that we are to proceed to the plantation where another grandson, the one who is now his heir, will marry me in Alex's place.'' She held out a separate piece of paper for him. ''Here's a map.''

''Then let's be off.''

The letter crumpled as Jemma closed her fist around it and blinked away a sudden gust of mist that hit her lashes. It was a miracle. Alex Moreau had died before she could be forced to marry him. Now, in all good conscience, she could tell the Moreaus that the wedding was off. She had given her father a sworn oath that she would marry *Alex* Moreau, not his cousin. In her mind, the promise no longer stood.

Before her, the carriage door stood open. The darkness inside loomed, as did her uncertain future. Wheaton stood beside the door, waiting patiently for her to climb aboard. Like a faithful retriever, he would stand there all night if need be.

Her mind spinning, Jemma lifted her skirt and let Wheaton help her into the high-sprung vehicle. Once she was inside and the latch clicked with terrifying finality, she had a sobering thought.

What if the Moreaus would not hear of calling off the wedding? Once she reached the plantation, they might force her to go through with it, and there would be no one to stand up for her. She glanced out the window at Wheaton, who continued to stand in the rain with a blank look on his face. No help from that quarter.

After another three seconds of heart-palpitating panic, Jemma forced herself to think. It would be months before her father returned to Boston, then weeks before he could relocate to New Orleans. She had at least four months to do whatever she liked before he found out that the wedding had never even taken place.

Balling her hands into fists, she pressed them against

each other, held them to her lips, and closed her eyes tight. What would Grandpa Hall say?

Do it, Jemma gal! Run!

She whispered a hasty prayer to St. Thecla, a young girl who had called off her engagement so she could remain a virgin, and then had miraculously escaped death by fire, stood up to beasts, and dressed as a man to escape persecution. Faced with ravishment, Thecla was delivered to safety when the back of a cave opened and she disappeared. If anyone could help her in this hour of need, Thecla could.

Suddenly the cathedral bells pealed the quarter hour. Jemma's eyes flew open.

"Wheaton!"

"Miss?"

"Before we go to the Moreaus' I would like to stop at that cathedral across the square. During the storm at sea, I promised to light a candle and offer up a prayer just as soon as I reached dry land."

He shook his head. "I dunno. We're late enough as it is—"

"What's a few minutes more? You won't even have to climb down off the box. It won't take me but a minute. Maybe less."

He lifted his hat, unmindful of the water that cascaded off the brim, and scratched his head. His thick forehead bunched like a cauliflower.

"You aren't plannin' sompthin' tricky, are you?"

"Of course not. I pray *very* fast."

The good Lord knew she was becoming adept at it. She'd done nothing but pray for the past two months.

Finally, Wheaton nodded. His jowls danced.

"One second, no more," he warned.

"Thank you." She smiled. "Is my trunk secure?"

She might never again see the trousseau she had thrown together.

"Everything's ready."

Beneath her ruby cloak she wore an ice-blue silk gown and matching slippers fit for drawing-room wear. She wished she had worn something suitable for the street, but with the five gold pieces Mrs. Harris had sewn into the hem of her underskirt for emergencies, she could soon outfit herself more appropriately.

Barely able to contain her excitement, Jemma sat back and dropped the window shade. Wheaton shouted to the team of horses, and a very serious jolt sent her sprawling onto the floor of the closed carriage, nearly knocking the wind out of her. Bracing her hands on the leather seat, Jemma pulled herself up and held on to the strap dangling beside the window. She drew aside the shade and was immediately hit in the face with a spray of water.

Sputtering as the shade slapped back into place, Jemma wiped her eyes and then carefully took another peek. The carriage rumbled to a halt in front of the cathedral.

Drawing a deep breath, Jemma waited a moment to see if Wheaton was going to climb down and open the door for her, but when nothing happened, she opened it a mere crack. As she had suggested, he remained on the box.

The lamplight shone on St. Louis Cathedral, highlighting its imposing majesty. The church was but a stone's throw away. All she had to do was negotiate the muddy thoroughfare. By the time Wheaton became suspicious, she would have slipped out a back door and lost herself on the dark city streets.

Grandpa Hall would have been so very proud!

When Wheaton belched—a loud and obnoxious rumble that made her wince—Jemma shoved the door open so fiercely that it banged against the side of the carriage. She held her breath, but the bodyguard did not comment, so she gathered up her hem, tucked her ruby cloak around her, and carefully stepped down. Holding her gown out of the mud, she headed toward the front door of the cathedral.

You're on your way now, gal!

Her slippers were soaked through. One shoe was nearly

sucked off by the mud before she had taken more than four steps, but her heart was singing.

Deliverance was within her grasp.

The heels of her shoes pounded dire warnings on the wet banquette in front of the silent, ominously dark building. In her mad dash to safety, she thought her mind was playing tricks on her when she saw a shadowy image lurking in a dark alcove. It was another cloaked figure, a woman near her own height. Afraid Wheaton might mistake the woman for her and come to see what she was about, Jemma reached out and snagged the girl as she whipped past. She dragged the struggling girl along behind her as she flung open the door to the vestibule and hurried inside.

The one tall taper lit near the collection box sputtered as the draft eddied about the room. The heavy door swung shut with a bang. Incense permeated the air, reminding Jemma of countless masses she had attended as a child. Her unwilling companion had not yet uttered a sound, but continued to fight her tight hold.

Jemma let go of the other girl's wrist and, close to shedding tears of joy, she smiled. God and the saints had been listening after all. It was another miracle that standing before her now was a young woman of nearly the same age and height, with a riot of flowing ebony hair and piercing amethyst eyes shadowed with pain and worry. Here, obviously, was someone else who was desperate. Shoving back the hood of her velvet cloak, Jemma almost danced for joy.

If she could persuade this girl to take her place in the carriage, she could buy even more time. Wheaton would not send up a hue and cry until he reached the Moreaus' with the wrong passenger. By then, Jemma figured she would have had more than enough time to find shelter and think about her options.

Wanting to put her newfound companion at ease before

the harried stranger escaped, Jemma spoke softly, her whisper echoing in the deserted chamber.

"I can't believe it. God finally answered one of my prayers, and in the nick of time, too. I was beginning to give up." She unfastened the gold clasp at her throat, drew her cloak off her shoulders, and held it out to the dark-haired girl.

"Here. Take this and be quick. I'll need yours," she said.

"What are you talking about?" Her savior glanced frantically about, as if she expected someone to leap at them from the shadowed corners of the church.

"I don't have all night." Jemma glanced at the door, afraid Wheaton would become suspicious and come looking for her. She had intended to be long gone by now. She had to either exchange places with this girl or leave immediately by another entrance. Jemma shook the ruby velvet at her stunned companion.

"Take it and give me yours."

"But—"

"Look, I know there is some reason you were hiding out there all alone at this time of night, and my guess is that you are on the run. Am I right?"

The black-haired girl glanced around again, refusing to answer.

Jemma saw her well-laid plan beginning to crumble. "Please, I'm begging you," she implored. "You have to help me. I'm trying to get away, too."

"I'm in no position to help anyone." The girl seemed to be sizing Jemma up, weighing the possibilities. She was soaked through, her hair limp and tangled. Her strange eyes were haunted, centuries-old eyes in a young face. "You are right. I am in a hurry to get away from here." It was all the stranger would admit.

"Good. Give me your cloak," Jemma demanded.

The dark-haired girl glanced into the recesses of the

church, into the cavernous building where continuous rituals of birth, life, and death were celebrated.

Certain that things were about to go her way, Jemma forced herself to stay calm and not frighten the girl any more than she already had. Finally, the mysterious stranger untied the plain cord that held a forest-green wool cloak closed at her throat.

She gathered the worn fabric against her heart before she handed it over to Jemma. "Why are you so willing to help me?"

"I'm offering you a way out of here in exchange for my own freedom," Jemma shook the cloak at her again.

They quickly traded wraps. Donning the threadbare wet wool, Jemma whipped the tie tight, poised to flee, waiting to give the other girl instructions. When the gold clasp on Jemma's velvet cape was latched, the girl pulled the hood up. Jemma shoved the fugitive toward the door.

"Keep the hood up, run across the street, and get into the carriage."

"But the driver—"

"He can't wait to be rid of me. *You*, that is," she lied. "Just don't let him see your hair or your face. He's a lout who won't even bother to help you aboard. Just climb in and slam the door."

"Surely I could never pass as you—"

"Where you are headed, no one has ever laid eyes on me. You will have a whole new life if you decide to take it. Just go along with all of it—or not—but by the time they find out you are not me, it'll be too late by then and I'll have gotten away."

It was the perfect out. After all, she was not exactly sending this beautiful, exotic stranger to her doom.

"Will I be safe?"

The question took Jemma aback. She hadn't thought for a moment that she might be setting the girl up for harm; still, she reckoned the worst that could happen was that the Moreaus would rant and rave a while when they learned the truth. Her father might have sold her into marriage, but he would have never signed the agreement if he had not approved of the Moreaus in the first place.

"I would never send anyone into danger. So, you will do it?" She could feel precious seconds evaporating with every frantic heartbeat. Jemma grabbed the door handle and opened the door a few inches. Planting her hand on the stranger's waist, she urged her out into the rain.

Wheaton was still hunched on the driver's box. She watched him tip his head back as he pressed the mouth of a bottle to his lips.

Just when Jemma thought the girl was about to run for the carriage, she paused once more, turned back, and with a worried sincerity in her eyes asked, "If I take your place tonight, what will you do?"

Jemma could see that the girl was about to falter. She needed just the right answer, something that would convince the fugitive that going along with the plan was the right thing to do.

"I will fulfill my wildest dream. I want to be a nun."

It was a bald-faced lie, but it worked. Relief and acceptance washed over the dark-haired girl, as if she had been waiting for some sign that it was all right to agree with the scheme. The thought of freeing Jemma to follow a religious calling had done the trick.

Jemma stiffened when she saw Wheaton pocket the bottle and glance over at the church. He placed one hand on the back of the seat, about to climb down.

"Hurry!" Jemma shoved the girl again. "Keep the hood over your face."

"But—"

"Go!"

The dark-haired girl pulled the edges of the cloak close and drew the hood around her face. Jemma could not afford to waste time to see whether Wheaton would discover the switch. She turned and ran for the side door. The vestibule floor was slick with the muddy water they had tracked in. She took care not to slip.

Heading for a side door near the altar, she ran down the center aisle of the church, rounded the front pew, and skidded to a stop. She ran back to genuflect hastily before the altar, crossing herself with a wave of her hand before she was off again. The door banged shut behind her.

The cold rain was a shock. She took a deep breath to clear her head. The heady scent of incense had given her a headache. Her heart was pounding. She was alone on the streets of one of the most exotic, crowded, dangerous cities in the world.

It was positively exciting. It was absolutely thrilling.

"I hope you're watching over me, Grandpa," she whispered as she started running up a busy street behind the church.

Go, girl, go.

Quickly she lost herself amid the crowd, mingling with the well-dressed pedestrians. Snatches of conversation hummed about her, a lyrical sound, a strange combination of French and English and something more. Beneath many of the balconies overhanging the street, dark-eyed beauties took shelter from the rain on the arms of their escorts.

Jemma kept the hood of her cloak up as she zigzagged between the couples and small clusters of pedestrians who vied for space on the wooden walkway that kept them out of the quagmire on the muddy street. She slipped between two groups, hoping each would think she was with the other.

The street was crowded with carriages. Daring a glance over her shoulder, Jemma breathed an audible sigh of relief. There was no sign of Wheaton or the hired carriage.

Sheltered from the rain beneath a balcony, her interest was piqued when she noticed a crowd gathered around a very tall man in a black hat. His leather clothing appeared to be adapted from the style of an Indian tribesman, made of pieces of well-tanned hide stitched together.

Intrigued by the woodsman, frustrated because she was behind him and couldn't see the big man's face, Jemma edged along the front of the building, keeping in the shadows but drawing closer to hear what was being said.

The man was apologizing to a dark-haired, sloe-eyed Creole gentleman who was apparently very angry. In a move Jemma thought more than foolish, the Creole struck the giant backwoodsman squarely across the jaw with a white kid glove. Jemma decided the shorter man was either very stupid or very foolhardy.

The man in buckskins had a voice that carried over the crowd. "I told you I was sorry. I stopped your lady friend here because I thought she was someone else. What the hell was that slap for?"

Even Jemma knew what the slap meant, and she suspected the woodsman did too. It seemed ridiculous, such a bold challenge coming from a quaking little Creole with a rapier-thin mustache and oiled hair. He was so much shorter than his opponent that he had to bend backward just to meet the taller man's eye.

Jemma crept closer to listen and heard the Creole say, "I am calling you out, *monsieur*. We will meet under the oaks at dawn. I'm sure you can find someone of your kind to stand as second."

Incredibly homely, the lady the woodsman had mistaken for an acquaintance possessed a long horseface and uneven teeth. While her escort fumed, the brunette stared curiously at the woodsman, carefully looking him up and down.

"Look, mister," the tall man began, "I'm sorry, but I don't get up before dawn for anybody, not even you. If you're smart, you'll accept my apology and forget it. I didn't mean the lady any harm."

Jemma could see that the man in buckskins was trying to win the others over with a smile. At least six foot three, he far outmatched the Creole.

"*Never* will I forget such an insult to my Colette!" The young man's eyes glittered as he wove unsteadily on his feet. Too much drink gave him false courage. "Choose your weapon, *monsieur*."

The crowd around them gasped—all but Jemma, who hung on every word and action. It was the most exciting scene she had ever witnessed.

The unattractive woman had become the center of attention. She gazed at the crowd and almost preened, apparently thrilled that one of her companions would even consider dueling to defend her honor.

The huge man in backwoods dress sighed so loudly that everyone heard it. "I choose fists."

The two smaller gentlemen burst into a spate of Creole French, one obviously arguing a case of common sense to the other. The brunette whipped up the fan at her wrist and snapped it open. Holding it above her head, she used it to shield her face from the rain.

When the woodsman drawled, "Excuse me, *monsewer*," Jemma almost giggled aloud. The man was well aware of the crowd pressed around them. He shifted his stance and flexed his wide shoulders to make a point of emphasizing his stature and build before he said, "The last man who challenged me to a fistfight never lived to tell about it. If I were you, I'd take that apology and call it a night." As a *coup de grâce*, he cradled his long rifle in his arms like a babe. The trigger was level with the little Creole's nose.

Finally, the challenger backed down and dismissed the giant with a nod. The crowd sighed with relief.

"That's mighty neighborly of you. No hard feelings?" The huge American finally smiled.

"I accept your apology, *monsieur*." The offended Creole was beet-red.

The Creole linked arms with his disappointed admirer and, along with his male companion, began to hustle the brunette away through the crowd. Titters of laughter and conversation filled the night air as the tension was broken and the theater patrons began to move on.

Jemma edged around the crowd, more compelled to see what the face of the amazing man in leather looked like than she was to stay dry. Squeezing between two burly gentlemen who smelled of bay rum and musty wool, she nudged forward.

Jemma blinked once and then again. The backwoods giant had turned around and she could see him clearly. He had tied a headful of wild blond hair into a queue, but most of it had escaped to hang over his shoulders. The thick shadow of a new beard couldn't hide his strong jaw and emphasized his moss-green eyes. The long, well-oiled barrel of his rifle caught the lamplight as he cradled it with a practiced nonchalance.

His entire being radiated adventure, daring, the call of the wilderness.

Not so much as a flicker of emotion crossed the woodsman's face. The crowd was nearly disbanded. Jemma realized her vulnerability. She ducked back into the shadows, unwilling to let the man in the tanned leather see her until she could formulate a plan. He turned and headed off alone in the direction of the cathedral.

"Damn!" she whispered under her breath, dogging his steps while she hugged the buildings. Praying that Wheaton was well on the way to the Moreau plantation, Jemma took a chance and followed the backwoodsman down the street.

She couldn't help but notice how confidently he strode along, his shoulders as wide as a door, his back as straight as an oak. The people he passed paused to take a second glance at his imposing presence before they moved on. Everything about him appeared savage, from his dress to his unkempt hair and the long, lethal knife strapped to his thigh.

Here was a man who laughed in the face of danger. Here was a man whose middle name was adventure.

Here was a man of honor. She could tell by the way he'd refused to participate in a duel he obviously would have won, no matter what weapons were chosen. Here was a man who could get her out of New Orleans, a man she would feel safe with. All she had to do now was convince this savage-looking stranger that he wanted nothing more than to help save her from a fate worse than death.

She had to find out where he was going and ask him to take her along. She needed to convince him that he was the only one who could help her.

Jemma waited until they had traveled another block and were virtually alone on the street. No one else was moronic enough to stay out in the rain. As she hurried along, trying not to let the woodsman out of her sight, Jemma shoved her splayed fingers into her hair and tugged the wet curls in all directions until her hair stood out around her head like a madwoman's.

After loosening the string on the worn, sodden cape so that it hung limply off one shoulder, she took hold of the pale silk fabric of her gown at the shoulder and tugged until she heard the stitches pop. With one final jerk, she separated the shoulder seam until there was a wide tear. Her skin showed between the ragged edges.

She gathered up her skirt and started running headlong down the street, her footsteps pounding against the wooden banquette. Launching herself at her objective, she grabbed hold of the stranger's leather sleeve and tugged on his left arm.

The instant she touched him, he somehow managed to whip out the knife that had been sheathed at his right side. The long rifle clattered against the boardwalk. He had grasped a hank of her hair and had whipped her around, effectively pinning her against him while he held the knife to her throat.

Jemma gasped, afraid to move, yet afraid to hold her tongue and have him slit her throat before she could even utter an explanation.

''I need help,'' she whispered, holding her teeth clenched, afraid if she opened her mouth that the cold, lethal steel at her throat would slide into her skin.

She felt the pressure on the blade ease, but the giant continued to hold her clasped against him. He was glaring down at her, his eyes glittering like emerald shards in the lamplight.

His image began to swim before her eyes. Rainwater dripped off the brim of his hat, down into her face. Jemma blinked rapidly. He let go of her long enough to drag her with him until they stood beneath an overhang.

''What's this all about?'' he demanded.

When he spoke, his voice was strong and deep, just as it had been when he apologized to the Creoles on the street. She forced herself to remember how he had offered those men an apology to avoid a confrontation. She prayed she had not been hasty. Surely such a man would not harm her.

Wincing as his hand tightened on her hair, Jemma grabbed the front of his fringed coat. She screwed up her courage and shouted, ''You've got to save me!''

chapter
3

"SHIT."

Hunter groaned aloud. He didn't need this. He really didn't.

Doubting his own sanity, he stared down at the disheveled blond with bewitching china-blue eyes and twin dimples and knew that plenty of the "Kaintucks" roaming the streets of New Orleans would not have hesitated to drag her off to a crib in the Swamp district first and ask questions later. Her breath was coming fast and shallow, her face smooth and pale as moonlight except for twin spots of high color on her cheeks and the shadows in her dimples.

"Save you from what?"

"Put the knife away and I'll tell you," she ordered.

"Lady, you're the one who flew out of nowhere and grabbed *me*. Start talking." To appease her, he lowered the knife, but didn't relax his guard. His gaze flicked to his rifle. It was lying on the boardwalk where he'd dropped it. Then he glanced up and down the street. There was not a soul in sight.

"They're still after me, trying to track me down and capture me." A tremor shot through her as her eyes widened in fear.

"Who?" He looked down the street again. There was no one around.

"I've sworn not to let them take me, even if I have to *kill* myself." Her small hands tightened on his fringed coat.

"*Who's* trying to track you down?" Certain she was mad, he spoke slowly and distinctly.

"Do you think you could please let go of my hair? You're hurting me."

He could see he was not going to get to the bottom of this very quickly, and his rifle was getting soaked. He let go of her hair, kept one hand on her arm, and sheathed his knife. Hunter dragged her over to the weapon and picked it up before ducking back beneath the overhang. Then he pulled the wool cloak over her exposed shoulder.

"I asked who was after you," he repeated.

"The emir's men, the palace guards. They've chased me half way round the world . . . from Algiers."

"Algiers?"

"It's on the coast of northern Africa."

"I know where it is." He *really* didn't need this.

"You do?" She looked him up and down.

"What were you doing there?"

"I'd just left the convent."

"The convent?"

"You certainly ask a lot of questions." She took a deep breath. "My father had been forced to send me there after he lost the family fortune. By the time I received the letter carried by special envoy, it was too late. The nuns wouldn't let me go." She paused long enough to smile and cast her gaze heavenward. "They believed I had a special calling, certain I was destined for sainthood. Like St. Theresa."

"Christ," he mumbled.

"No, St. Theresa."

"How did you get out of the convent?" Despite his well-greased buckskins, Hunter was nearly soaked through. This was a night he would not remember fondly.

She shrugged. "Why, the way any sane person would. I tunneled under the garden wall." Her eyes took on a faraway glow. "It took months."

"And the emir's men?"

"What I didn't know, as I made my escape, was that the convent was under siege. It seems there was a fortune in jewels hidden in the old chapel. The emir's Berber guard had the place surrounded. I tunneled right into their hands. When they saw my hair—you know, blond hair is quite an oddity in Algiers—they realized I had not yet taken my solemn vows. The guards became determined to deliver me to their master for his harem. They expected he would pay a huge sum for a . . . well, you know." Her cheeks stained with color and she quickly looked away.

He had no idea what the emir would pay more for, or what hair had to do with taking vows. "But somehow, you managed to escape."

She nodded. "Barely. And only by slipping into a huge empty oil jar. I stowed away and that's how I ended up here in New Orleans tonight. Those men will stop at nothing to find me again."

She paused for breath. Hunter had forgotten he was holding her, until he realized she was actually leaning against him. He abruptly let her go. Although he was fairly certain she was a crazy lunatic and just as unpredictable, she was too small to do him any physical harm. The poor wit-scrambled girl was running from something all right, but he was willing to bet everything he owned that it was from an insane asylum.

"Will you help me?"

Somebody always wanted something.

Hunter took a step back, intent on going his own way. Amelia White had already made a bigger fool of him than any woman had a right to. Not only that, but she had run off and left behind her daughter Lucy, who was no kin to him at all. Even though Amelia had done him a big favor by leaving, he wasn't about to let any woman talk her way into his life again, especially this addlepated blue-eyed blond with the face of an angel and twin dimples.

"I'm afraid I'm getting out of the savior business. You'll have to find somebody else." He tipped the brim of his hat and succeeded in sending a stream of water down over his hand. Without a backward glance, Hunter started down the street, fighting to ignore the girl's startled expression of disbelief.

"Are you just going to walk off and leave me standing out here alone like this?" Her voice came to him through the rain, reed-thin and shaky.

"Yep." He told himself to keep walking. He didn't want to dwell on her standing there soaked through, shivering with fright. With those eyes and that figure, she was most likely a whore trying to escape her pimp, not some convent escapee on the run from Berber tribesmen.

For half a block she followed him. He could hear her light, rapid footsteps dogging his on the boardwalk; then there was silence. Hunter warned himself not to turn around, not to get involved. She had come from someplace and she would end up somewhere else. She could damn well get there on her own. He didn't need to worry about what happened to her.

He put a few blocks between them and was about to step off the end of the walk and negotiate the muddy street when he heard the scream. The sound tore through the night air. He spun around.

In the distance, two shadowy figures struggled beneath a lamppost. The yellow glow from the lantern radiated around the silhouettes locked in a frenetic tussle. Raindrops glistened in a shimmering halo around a head of wild, curly blond hair. Hunter picked up his pace, his moccasins slapping hard thumps against the wooden walk.

A gent dressed like a card shark in a tall hat, cutaway coat, and natty stirrup pants was accosting St. Theresa of Algiers.

The gambler was so intent on attacking his helpless victim that he didn't see or hear Hunter until it was too late. Six paces from the gambler, Hunter got a strong whiff of whiskey. In two paces he reached out and whipped the man away from the frantic blond, drew back his arm, and sent his fist crashing into his victim's chin before the gambler knew what hit him. The man's waistcoat was spattered with blood. The sateen shone in the glow of the lamp as the man lay face up in the pelting rain.

The girl threw herself against Hunter, nearly toppling them both. He drew her under cover of an overhanging balcony once more.

"Good God! I could have been killed . . . or worse! You just can't leave me alone like this," she said, clutching him tight. A sob caught in her throat and she shuddered. Genuine fear was reflected in the tears shimmering in her eyes.

He thought of Lucy, Amelia's girl, who wasn't much younger than this one. What if Lucy were out alone on the streets and no one helped her? Not that shy little Lucy would ever find herself in such a fix, but still, he couldn't help but compare the two. Years of being responsible won out.

"I'm headed for Tchoupitoulas Street. I'll put you up in a hotel, but you're on your own from there."

"Tchoupitoulas?" She worked the word around on her tongue.

"Fronts the river. You might have seen it when you climbed out of your oil jar at the wharf."

She looked confused and then sniffed. "I was only in the oil jar until it was carried aboard ship." Trembling as she glanced over at the still-inert gambler, she rubbed her arms and shivered.

"There are some places to bed down, none of them decent, but you'll be safer than you would be in the Swamp."

"The Swamp?" Her eyes were huge.

Enough time had been wasted. He started to drag her down the street. "Plenty of other whores down there, too."

"*Other* whores?" She stopped abruptly, refusing to budge.

"You heard me."

"I, sir, am *no* whore."

She had thrust her chin at him in defiance until he looked her up and down and had the satisfaction of seeing her quell beneath his glare. Giving her a tug, he started her moving again.

"Then what the hell are you? This time I want the truth."

She sniffed. "How can you be so cruel? I'm a defenseless young woman alone . . . trying to . . . to get to her long lost father . . . and brother."

"And where might they be?"

Her gaze touched on his and then quickly slipped away. "Where are you headed?"

Her ability to turn the tables was giving him a headache. "Upriver, but what's that got to do with anything?"

"Aha! Don't you *see*?"

"Lady, I don't see anything but two fools jawin' out in the rain." They were passing the cathedral. The river was not far away.

"It just so happens that *I'm* desperate to go upriver too. Up the mighty Mississippi to join my father and . . . and my older brother. They are on a mapping expedition in the wilds of Canada. You and I are headed in the very same direction. That's quite a coincidence, don't you think?"

"I don't know what to think," he mumbled.

When they stepped out from behind the cathedral and started across the square, they were set upon by four policemen rounding the corner of the building. Shoving Hunter aside, one of the men quickly took his weapons while another held a gun on him. The second pair of uniformed officers grabbed the girl. Hunter's stomach lurched as he watched an officer snatch the hood off her shining hair, grasp her chin, and tilt her pretty face toward the lamp-light.

"I swear I never saw her before." Hunter struggled against the men's holds, nearly broke free, and earned a sharp blow to his temple for his efforts.

"She's not the one." The policeman abruptly let the blond go and then nodded toward Hunter. "Let him go, too."

As Hunter shook the men free, he couldn't help but note the intense look of relief upon his petite companion's face.

"Who are you looking for?" she managed.

"A girl named Celine Winters. Have either of you run into a black-haired young woman in a dark cape?"

Hunter shook his head. The blond was trembling like a leaf. He threaded her arm through the crook of his.

"We haven't seen her." He held out his hand to the men holding his weapons. "Now, I'd like to get her out of the rain," he told them.

He was handed his knife and he sheathed it, then he took his rifle. The officers quickly apologized and hurried off, headed across the square.

"Thank you," she said, then added, "Will you help me now? My God, there are murderers actually running these streets." She frowned at the shadows around the cathedral and then glanced up and down the street.

"As well as lunatics," he mumbled.

"I can pay you handsomely."

"You don't look like you have a dixie on you."

"What's a dixie?"

"It's a ten-dollar note that says *dix* on one side. That's French for 'ten.' "

She probably wasn't from New Orleans, he decided, or she would know that rivermen had named the place *Dixie* after the paper money issued in English on one side and French on the other.

They were splashing along the quay now, headed toward the cheap hotels and floating gaming flatboats moored along Tchoupitoulas. She had to run to match his stride.

"What's your name?" She called out.

"Hunter Boone. What makes you think you can trust me? How do you know I'm not going to cut your throat and take your money?" he puzzled aloud.

"If you were going to harm me, you've already had ample chance. Besides, I was watching you on the street long before I approached you. I heard you apologize to that dandy with the oily hair and that ridiculous mustache. You're just the level-headed sort of escort I'm looking for. That knife you're wearing convinced me I should enlist your help."

They had reached a ramshackle hotel built of unpainted, mismatched planks salvaged from parts of crude river craft. A hand-lettered sign that said ROTGUT hung over the door. Hunter pushed her up the steps and then through the swinging doors of the tavern that fronted the rowdy establishment.

"What *is* this place?" There was more curiosity than fear in her eyes.

"This, St. Theresa, is where we part company."

Jemma took stock of the small tavern in horrified wonder. The place was beyond shabby, the patrons cutthroats and scoundrels. There wasn't a woman in the room. It was dangerous and sinfully thrilling.

Grandpa would have loved it.

Across the room, two long planks had been laid across tall oak-stave barrels to form a bar. Half a dozen men were swilling the liquor that gave the place its distinctive odor, not to mention its name. Here and there, rickety tables with mismatched chairs dotted the floor. Most of them were occupied, but not all of the occupants were conscious.

The man called Hunter Boone had paused inside the door. She could tell he was taking stock of his surroundings, judging each man, sending them threatening glances. She was convinced she had made the right choice.

"Come on," he said softly and walked away, headed toward the bar.

She made the mistake of staring too long at a shady-looking character in a black hat seated at the nearest table. He was smiling at her quite menacingly and flashed the few yellow teeth he still had beneath a thick black mustache with curled ends. Enveloped in a long, black great-coat, he looked like evil incarnate.

When the man pushed out of his chair and came toward her, she froze as if her stained slippers had suddenly been nailed to the floor. She opened her mouth to cry out to Hunter, who was now halfway across the room, but nothing more than a pitiful, inaudible squeak escaped her.

"What's a purty lady like you doing with an ugly cuss like that?" The yellow-toothed man indicated her companion with a jerk of his head.

"I . . . I'm . . . he . . ."

She couldn't form a cohesive thought as she stared into the blackest, most evil eyes she had ever seen. The fires of hell burned inside them. Jemma shivered. What in heaven's name had ever, *ever* possessed her to take to the streets?

The man had his hand on her arm. His fingers bit into her flesh through the threadbare wool cloak. When she winced and tried to wrest her arm from his hold, his eyes lit up with a perverse glow.

"Please. I . . ."

"What's the matter? Ain't I better than that no-good son of a polecat you walked in with? I can show you a better time without tryin'." His breath was rancid. Up close she could see the pores of his oily skin.

Hunter was almost at the bar. Her attacker pulled her up against him, so close she could feel the rough scratchy wool of his shirtfront and smell his fetid breath. Jemma decided not to wait for her newfound escort to save her.

She lifted her knee, planning to ram her foot down on the man's shoe, but in the process she hit him hard in the crotch. The result was almost instantaneous. He let out a yowl of pain and lurched back as he grabbed himself with both hands and began to spew curses the likes of which she had never heard before.

Jemma was awestruck, determined to remember the move and the curses. Every man in the room burst into gales of laughter—every man but Boone, who was bearing down on her with quiet rage simmering in his eyes. He grabbed her arm and whipped her up against the nearest wall before she knew what was happening.

She began to argue. "I'm getting a little tired of men grabbing me—"

"Keep your mouth shut," he said, pressing closer. "Look up at me as if you're going to kiss me."

After what had just happened, she had no idea what to expect next. Shoved against the rough plank wall, Jemma stared up at the big man hunched over her. In the haunting glow of the oil lamps hanging from the rafters, he looked even more forbidding than he had outside. His eyes were an intense, liquid green, his lips full, set in a hard line, but he was fairly clean and didn't smell at all bad. And he had all of his teeth.

Somehow she knew it had been the sun and not laughter that had creased the skin at the corners of his eyes. His hair, light blond, was wet.

"You don't look like you want to kiss me very much," she said, fully aware of the precarious predicament she had foolishly put herself in. Had this man suddenly turned on her, too?

"I *don't* want to kiss you," he muttered, leaning close enough to be almost nose-to-nose. "Put your arms around me."

She slipped her arms around his neck. "Now what—"

"I'm going to kiss you."

"But you don't want to?"

"No. We'll just be doing it for the audience."

"Why?"

He closed his eyes and sighed heavily, then stared down at her again. "They're all just like your friend over there." He nodded toward the mustachioed man with his eyes glazed with pain and his hands hugging his private parts. Hunter was so close now that he was whispering against her lips. A very queer tingling sensation quivered through her, one that ran right down to her toes with his every word.

"There are men in this room who would just as soon cut your throat for a picayune as look at you, not to mention all the colorful things they'd like to do to you first. Raise up a bit more on your tiptoes."

When she did as he bid her and raised herself up onto her toes, her breasts pressed against his chest. She could see the slashes of emerald against the lighter green of his irises. He really did have magnificent eyes for a man.

Flattened full against him, she barely had time to adjust to the very strange sensations that were leapfrogging from her breasts to her belly to unmentionable places below that, when he lowered his lips to hers and their mouths touched.

The kiss was feather-light, no more than a meeting of lips. He slowly pressed his mouth to hers. His lips were warm, softer than she had ever imagined a man's mouth would be, and surprisingly gentle. Even though this didn't seem to be the most utterly sinful kind of kiss imaginable, for he hadn't done the unspeakable and tried to slip his tongue into her mouth, this definitely was not what Sister Augusta Aleria would have called a sanctioned spiritual union. No indeed. It if had been, her blood wouldn't have begun to simmer so quickly.

After a moment or two she lost track of time. Hunter lifted his head. He quickly straightened away from her. Disoriented, Jemma had a hard time concentrating. Her head was spinning.

He'd given her her very first kiss. She could hardly believe it. Tonight was to have been her wedding night; but the intended groom was dead, and here she was with a stranger who had just given her the first kiss of her life in a place called the Rotgut.

Truly, the saints worked in strange and wonderful ways.

Hunter was staring at her with an odd, calculating look.

"Keep your eyes down, stay with me, and let me do the talking." He started to walk away again.

"Wait!" Jemma grabbed his arm.

"What now?"

She lowered her voice to a whisper. "I forgot to tell you my name—"

"I didn't ask because that's the way I wanna keep it," he shot back. "Look, I'm getting you a room for the night and then we part ways." As he turned around he mumbled, "At least I've gotten you out of the rain."

Jemma refused to budge and whispered frantically, "I told you, I've got money. I'm not a charity case."

"Come on."

This time when he walked away she stuck close, pulled the edges of the wool cloak together, and tried to keep her gaze lowered. Her surly escort with the soft lips stepped to the bar and spoke to the barkeep.

"I need a crib for the night."

Jemma glanced up in time to discover another slovenly man, this one obviously in charge, standing behind the plank bar staring at her. From the looks of his shirt, he had spilled more liquor down the front of himself than he had poured into glasses. She felt his disgusting leer even as she forced herself to look away from his gap-toothed smile.

"You got the devil's own luck," he told Hunter. "Purty woman and one room left at the inn. Two bits," the barkeep said.

Hunter opened his coat and reached into a fur pouch lashed to his waist. He flipped up the cover flap, drew out a coin, and laid it on the bar.

The barkeep's filthy hand snaked out and closed over

the coin. "Back there," he said, thumbing his hand toward the back.

Hunter Boone tugged her across the room, this time toward a door that sagged on its hinges. As they made their way toward the dim recesses of the tavern, she noticed that her guide continued to flash unsavory glances in every direction. She looked up at his broad shoulders and massive arms and thought that any man who challenged him would have to be out of his mind.

Once inside a squalid, dark room no bigger than both of her armoires shoved together, he barred the door. Once more he reached into the small bag at his waist, this time to withdraw flint to light the smoky oil lamp on a stand in the corner.

As the lamp flared to life, the crude interior of the room was further revealed. A thin, lumpy mattress had been unceremoniously tossed in the middle of the floor along with two blankets of very troubled origin. Sobering reality careened into her thoughts.

She was alone in a filthy room with a complete stranger; just outside the door hovered even more of a threat. She tried to calm her nerves by telling herself that this was what she had wanted. This was *her* choice, not her father's or anyone else's. Had she gone through with the marriage as arranged, she would still be locked in a bedroom with a complete stranger right about now.

At least she had picked this one out herself.

As Hunter Boone walked across the room to open a window high in the wall, Jemma decided to calm down and stay put. The devil she barely knew was better than any of those lounging in the other room.

"Keep the door locked and you'll be safe enough until morning. Just leave before most of them get up." He nodded in the direction of the outer room.

"Where are *you* going?" His statement took her by such surprise that she could barely form the question.

"Out the window."

"You really do mean to just leave me here? I . . . I thought you might be joking."

"Look, lady, this is no joke. I'm not beholden to you in any way and I don't intend to be."

"But—"

His easy dismissal rendered her speechless. She reached up and tried to make some order out of her limp, soggy hair. She realized she must look a sight. Sister had told the girls never to be vain enough to use beauty or flirtatious ways on men, for it would stir a man's blood and cause him to lose his head and lead an unsuspecting girl into sinful acts.

Jemma wondered if maybe, just maybe, she tried batting her lashes at Hunter Boone—and that was *all* she would try in the way of flirtation—he might be cajoled into staying and watching over her. And skip the sinful acts.

"Surely you realize I need a male escort to escape the city." She fluttered her lashes furiously and found it very difficult to see.

"You're going to get a headache doing that. I've told you before, I'm not taking you along." He was frowning intently at her, obviously unmoved. For a moment she thought he might have developed a tic, for his lips were twitching.

She decided to try to buy him off again. She bent over and drew up the hem of her once lovely ice-blue gown. Like her slippers, it was hopelessly ruined. A good third of a yard from the hem up was stained by mud and water. Even more disturbing, the weight of the five gold pieces that had been sewn inside her underskirt felt suspiciously lighter.

"Oh, no!"

He stepped close, bending down to see what she was upset about.

"There's a rip in the hem." She moaned as she held the edge of the undergarment up for closer inspection. "I've only one gold piece left."

Working the remaining coin along the hem, she pushed it over to the tear and slipped it out. It shone brightly, the only sparkle in the dim light and squalor.

"Take this in exchange for guiding me upriver as far as you can."

The sight of the coin surprised him, she could see that. He actually seemed to be considering her offer. Jemma stared at the coin in her palm, wondering how she was going to survive after she turned all of her money over to this man. It was one thing to run off with enough gold to finance a grand adventure, but it was quite another to set out virtually penniless. After two hours and as many attacks on her person, she was beginning to question the idea of heading anywhere but toward safety.

There was still time to confess the entire truth to Boone and have him hire someone to take her to the Moreau plantation. But what if the Moreaus tried to force her to go through with the marriage?

Think of the adventure, Jemma gal. Don't turn back now.

Her grandfather's voice again. She practically groaned aloud. She really would be letting Grandpa Hall down if she faltered now. Things were bound to get better.

Hunter Boone was staring down at the gold piece. He looked as wet and tired as she felt. He didn't appear to be a man who could afford to turn down her offer.

"Well?" she pressed. "Will you do it?"

Hunter sighed, mentally tallying what it would take to outfit the girl for the journey and how much he would have left over in the bargain. Perhaps enough to by Nette a whole bolt of new cloth for her quilting. Lately he had done little enough for the widow woman who cooked and cleaned for him and all the river travelers who stopped at the tavern and trading post at Sandy Shoals. Then too, Nette had also been raising Lucy since Amelia had left him. The old woman deserved a little surprise.

He glanced up and caught St. Theresa watching him closely and thought he saw something in her eyes he hadn't seen all evening—a trace of fear. The idea that she might be frightened moved him more than any of her silly eyelash wiggling or the sight of the money. He shook himself like a great bear, but it didn't dispel the concern he was beginning to feel, no matter how hard he tried to fight it.

He knew himself well enough to know that he couldn't leave St. Theresa to the mercy of just anyone who happened along. Not after kissing her. That kiss had been enough to convince him that she wasn't the whore he had first suspected her to be. This girl had no idea *what* to do when a man asked for a kiss, and she wasn't a good enough liar *or* actress to have carried off such complete innocence.

Again he thought of Lucy. He hoped to God someone would see fit to take care of her if she were ever stranded and in need of help. Someone trustworthy. Someone like him.

It made him mad as hell for even contemplating hauling the girl upriver. He should have walked away when she first approached him. He should know better by now.

If he took her along, it would be for the gold piece she offered and what he could buy with it. It certainly wouldn't be because she had fluttered her lashes at him or because, if he let himself, he might still be thinking about that damned kiss. He didn't even know her name.

And he couldn't very well think of her as St. Theresa forever.

"What's your name?"

"Jemma O'—" Her eyes widened. "I would prefer not to tell you my last name just yet. At least until we're out of New Orleans."

"You wanted for anything, Jemma-O?"

She shook her head and smiled that infernal angelic smile. "It's just Jemma. And no, I'm not wanted for anything. But . . . with the threat of the emir's men always hanging over my head, I feel the less you know, the better for both of us.''

If nothing else, she was one hell of a storyteller. Thinking of the glittering gold piece, he offered, ''I'll take you as far as Sandy Shoals in Kentucky. From there you can join another party traveling up to Canada.''

He cursed himself even as he made the offer. She was bound to slow him down, just when he was set on getting back with his brother's whiskey money, determined to announce to everyone in his family circle that he was finally heading west.

He was such a damn idiot.

''Here, then.'' She held out the gold piece.

''I'll have to use part of it for your traveling supplies,'' he told her. His fingers slipped across her palm as he took the coin. Hunter shoved it into the possibles bag at his waist. The small leather pouch held an assortment of life's necessary items: flints, money, a chaw of tobacco, the lucky arrowhead he'd dug out of the old bear who had tried to eat Jed Taylor before Hunter came along to kill it, the money he'd made from Luther's whiskey.

Turning away from her, he nudged the stained, moss-filled mattress with the toe of his moccasin. He would have preferred making a lean-to in the open to sleeping in this flea-bitten room that was no doubt crawling with bedbugs, too. He hated towns—hated the crowds and the noise and the filth that came from so many people congregated in one place, but he couldn't very well have had the girl bed down on the street.

''Are you related to Daniel Boone?''

He didn't miss the awe in her voice; when he looked up, he found her staring at him with something akin to hero worship in her eyes.

''He's a distant cousin. Real distant. Never met him.''

''My grandfather met him once,'' she said.

''Your grandfather ever live in Algiers, too?'' He

couldn't resist, but the question didn't bother her at all.

"For a while. There's only one bed here," she reminded him unnecessarily.

Hunter sighed. "*I'll* sleep on the floor."

"Oh, no. I'll sleep on the floor," she quickly volunteered.

He looked at the mattress again and guessed there was more than kindness behind her gesture of goodwill. He didn't want the damn mattress either.

It was amicably decided that both of them would sleep on the floor on either side of the pallet. He gave her one of the blankets. She wrinkled her nose at it but didn't complain as she spread it on the floor. Wrapping herself in her damp cape, she lay down on the hard planks and closed her eyes. Within seconds after she had stopped talking—which in itself, he thought, was a miracle—she had fallen asleep.

Before he blew out the lamp, Hunter retrieved his Kentucky long rifle and loaded it with dry powder. He would keep it beside him while he slept. A breeze wafted through the window. The lamplight fluttered. The rain had become a full-fledged storm, but it didn't seem to bother the girl. She was still asleep with her head cradled on her arm.

He snuffed out the lamp and lay down. The noise outside the room had tapered off to an occasional shout or the crash of a bottle. Lightning flickered, illuminating the room in ghostly silver.

Hunter lay on his side, his shoulder already aching where it pressed against the hard floor, listening to the irritating, incessant *plop, plop, plop* of water as it dripped into various puddles around the room. They would be lucky if they didn't drown in their sleep.

He could hear Jemma's deep, even breathing over the sound of the rain. The storm was moving inland. Lightning continued to flash. Thunder echoed from afar. Hunter glanced over at his new charge, who looked even more like an angel-come-to-earth in her sleep than she had awake. Her blond curls teased one cheek. Her hand lay palm up, relaxed, soft and white. Like Amelia's, but not like anyone's at Sandy Shoals. This girl had never done a hard day's work in her life. She was either totally vulnerable or totally convincing.

He hated the fact that he was tempted to get up, walk around the mattress, and touch her hair to see if it felt as soft as it looked.

There was still time to forget the gold piece, leave it with her and climb out the window. He didn't owe this stranger anything, didn't have to spare her another thought.

Jemma-with-no-last-name would have to look out for herself.

Without making a sound, Hunter sat up, drew one knee to his chest, and draped his arm over it. He stared through the darkness, still intrigued, too pestered by his ruminations to sleep.

What respectable young girl would be out on the streets of New Orleans alone? Why did she want to get out of the city so badly that she would put her trust and her life in the hands of a man she'd never laid eyes on?

He glanced at the door. Things had quieted down some outside. If he was going to walk out, now was the time, while she was asleep. Before she could talk him into staying.

He thought of the man who had grabbed her in the tavern and the gambler who had wrestled with her beneath the streetlight. His conscience would plague him for weeks if he left her now.

The truth of the matter was that he had made an agreement with her and above all, he was a man of his word.

There was no going back on it now.

chapter
4

BY THE OVERCAST LIGHT OF A NEW DAWN, THE SQUALID
rented room looked worse than it had in the darkness. So
did the reality of her situation. Jemma furtively paced the
confines of the tiny room, familiar with every stain and
crack on the uneven planking. The hideous stench of the
place—a combination of fish, stale liquor, and something
else she didn't want to think about—was so thick she
could almost taste the very air.

As she skirted the mattress on the floor and crossed the
room for the hundredth time, she tugged the ripped shoulder of her gown and then she pressed her open palm to
her forehead.

Hunter Boone was gone, ostensibly after supplies. He
had left just before dawn, but not until she had sworn she
would not open the door until she heard his voice again.
The last she'd seen of him was his backside as he crawled
out the window, insisting he didn't want anyone to realize
she was in the room alone.

Now, what seemed an eternity later, her imagination was
proving to be a curse rather than a gift. Had Boone taken
her last coin and deserted her? She didn't know which
upset her more, the idea that he would not be coming back
or that at some point she was going to have to actually

open the door and face the creatures outside the room.

The seductive quiet outside the door lulled her into a sense of security. Her silk slippers, ruined by the mud and mire of the streets, made no sound as she crossed the room and paused with her ear to the rough wooden door. Closing her eyes, she tried to imagine opening it and stepping out into the unknown. Her options were limited by the mere fact that she was a woman. Thanks to her own foolhardiness, she was now penniless as well.

The hollow, ominous sound of the cathedral bells marked the hour. The church was not that far away. If she could safely leave this den of iniquity and somehow make her way alone through the streets, she might take sanctuary there, explain her situation and beg shelter at a convent, at least until her father arrived. Once there, she would have months to repent her impulsive, rash act.

Forgetting the fetid stench in the air, she took a deep breath and gagged as her empty stomach revolted. She had to get out. She whirled around and retrieved the musty wool cloak, still damp, and flung it around her shoulders. Drawing the hood up, she fastened the ties, reminded of the gold catch on the elegant velvet cloak she had traded for this ragbag piece. She could have used the ornate filigree ornament to buy her way out of this place.

Her hand was on the bolt that secured the door from within when a powder flash of memory of last night's sequence of events fell into place like dominoes. The Moreau letter, the dark-haired girl in the cathedral shadows, the heart-stopping terror of being accosted on the street, finding Hunter Boone. It had been so dramatic, so very thrilling—the stuff of Grandpa's tales and her wildest daydreams. But now, with no more substance than imagination, the dream had vanished. She was alone in this foul, hellish back room of the devil's own lair.

Just as Jemma was about to throw the bolt and run for it, a quick, gentle tap sounded on the other side of the door. Hunter's low whisper demanded that she open up. Now.

Jemma unlocked the door and barely had time to clear the doorway before Hunter strode into the room. His arms were full of a bundle of coarse fabrics, all of them drab and definitely unattractive, along with his ever-present rifle. He tossed the clothes at her.

"Take your clothes off." He propped the weapon in the corner of the room.

"I will do nothing of the sort. Where have you been? Do you realize I've been frantic with worry, thinking you had run off with my money with no intention of fulfilling your end of our bargain?"

"I'm glad to see you, too."

"I didn't think you would leave me in this... this sty... so long. I'm starving. What are you looking at?"

"A madwoman, I think."

He crossed his arms and stood there, silent, waiting for her to undress. He filled the room with his very presence, all leather and fringe with the sun stamped bronze on his skin, the essence of the outdoors evident in his untamed hair and the moss-green emerald of his eyes.

"I take it you want me to put these on," she said, indicating the bundle in her arms.

"You can't go waltzing up the Trace in that ball gown you're wearing."

Suddenly the ruined gown was important to her. It was a last, albeit soiled remnant of home. "This isn't a ball gown. It's—"

"Torn and flimsy and won't last a half a day more where we're going. It's cold up north." Hunter reached out for her sleeve and rubbed the expensive fabric between his rough fingers. He glanced down at her slippered feet.

"There are shoes wrapped up in the other things. Put them on, too."

Jemma clung to the bundle in her arms. Her chin went up a notch. "Step outside, please."

"Some of the drunks out there are beginning to stir. I'm staying right here."

"You actually intend to stand there while I change clothes?"

"I suggest you get started."

Her face was afire. She had already compromised herself by spending the night unchaperoned with this man, but to actually disrobe and engage in so intimate an act as dressing was unthinkable.

"I'm sorry, I can't do that."

"Maybe you're having second thoughts about this trip?"

"Just because I won't undress in front of you?"

"We're going to be in very close company for weeks. We're going to be eating together, riding together. I'm going to know more about you than you know about yourself by the time we get to Sandy Shoals."

"*Weeks?* I didn't know it would take that long. I—"

"You can still change your mind."

He was watching her closely. All the doubt she had experienced during his absence shimmied to the forefront of her mind. It would be so simple to agree, to call it off.

To miss the adventure.

"No. I'll not change my mind."

"Then you'll have to get used to doing what I say, when I say it. Your life will depend on it."

"I doubt that my life depends on my changing clothes in front of you."

He sighed. It was the wordless expression of a man at the end of his tether. Jemma knew better than to push him.

"All right. Have it your way, but please turn around."

Hunter turned, wishing he could ignore the sound as easily as he was avoiding the sight of her changing. As the silk rustled behind him he couldn't help but imagine the barely blue material sliding off her shoulders, over her ample breasts, into a sensuous pool at her feet. His fingertips still tingled from the feel of the silk. He was willing to bet that her skin would feel the same, if not smoother.

All morning, as he had gone about the business of outfitting her for the trail, he'd told himself he would regret it. The reality of at least four weeks alone with this beguiling, exasperating, infuriating, and definitely tempting young woman was daunting. Who was she really? Why did she insist on going upriver? He doubted she would ever tell him the truth.

"These are pants!"

"You'll stand a better chance of not being singled out on the Trace if you wear them."

"Just like Thecla." There was awe in her tone.

"Who?"

"St. Thecla. I pray to her all the time. She was a young virgin who was persecuted and dressed like a man to escape ravishment—"

"Are you dressed yet?"

"No. Could you have found *itchier* clothing?"

He almost smiled. "Are you ready?"

"No! Don't turn around."

The words were muffled. He pictured her tugging the shirt over her curly blond head, struggling into it. He had convinced himself that he was about to set out on a fool's errand, all because he had never been able to turn his back on someone in need. When was he going to learn?

"Were these the *only* shoes you could find?"

Hunter turned around. Jemma-with-no-last-name was standing there holding out the battered brown leather shoes he'd bought right off a cabin boy walking along the levee.

"They look to be your size," he commented offhandedly.

"They're hideous. They weigh more than a barrel of rocks. Even with these impossibly coarse socks they'll probably raise blisters." She looked down and wriggled her toes.

He wanted to laugh. Waiflike, her bewitching figure was

completely disguised. Standing there clutching the salt-stained, hard leather shoes, she was dwarfed by the baggy pants and billowing oversized shirt that came to her knees.

Beyond the door, the ominous sound of shattering wood rent the temporary peace. The girl dropped one shoe, her bright-eyed gaze darting to the door and then back.

"What was *that?*" she whispered.

"My guess is it was the sound of a chair meeting its end."

As she bent to retrieve the shoe, an inhumane growl followed by the sound of a body crashing against the wall drew their attention. The growl was followed by a long-winded threat.

"I'm the son of a three-headed buffalo raised up by a she-wolf and a grizzly! Try to pick my pocket again, you som'bitch, and I'll have your hide stripped off your worthless bastard's body before you know it's gone."

The voice could have belonged to anyone of the derelict rivermen in the outer room. Hunter glanced at the door when another resounding thud and then a tremor shook the flimsy wall.

"Are they trying to break in?" The girl's voice quivered with fright.

"Not yet, but it's only a matter of time before somebody sobers up enough to remember your entrance last night." He walked over to her and held out his hand.

"Give me your shoes."

Obviously too upset to argue, she handed over the shoes. He motioned to her to sit. When she lowered herself to the floor, Hunter hunkered down on one knee, put the one shoe down beside him, and pulled a bulky wool stocking out of the other.

"Here." He gave her the sock and she pulled it on, grimacing at the odor.

"I see you spared no expense," she said, wrinkling her nose.

"There weren't a lot of choices on the street this time of day."

"May I ask where you got these?" She extended her foot as casually as if he slipped shoes on them every morning.

"You don't want to know. Believe me." Her foot with its delicate high arch was smaller than his hand. He fitted the shoe over the bulky stocking and tapped the heel in place, but not without noticing her well-turned ankle and shapely calf. She shifted her bottom on the hard floor and gave him a blushing, grateful smile as she lifted her other foot.

Her innocence gave his tired heart a jolt. The room seemed to shrink to the space around them. So bright, so trusting, she appeared even more the angel in the foul room. Her skin was warm against his hands.

Hunter cursed and hurried his task. Realizing he was not as immune to her charms as he thought, he vowed to keep his distance from her on the trail. Female companionship wasn't something he needed or wanted in his life. Amelia had taught him as much. He was a self-avowed loner, determined to leave Sandy Shoals and explore the far reaches of the frontier as soon as he delivered Luther's money and told everyone good-bye.

The girl was staring up at him with her big blue eyes. He shoved her shoe on and let go of her as if she were a hot rock. Reaching around her, he picked up the black felt hat that had been wrapped inside the other clothing and began to pound his fist inside the crown, trying to shape it, but it still looked like a lump of coal. He shrugged and jammed it on her head until her face was almost hidden.

She immediately shoved the hat back and tilted it at a rakish angle. Hunter reached out, grabbed the overwide brim and pulled it back down until it was low on her brow, hiding all but the lower half of her face.

"Leave it there or you're on your own," he warned.

She frowned again and wrinkled her nose but didn't touch the hat. "No coat?"

"I left it with the other supplies and the horses at a stable a few blocks away."

She glanced around the room, then jumped as another loud crash thundered outside the door. Hunter scooped up her gown, paused when her white petticoat fell out of the silk folds, and then balled up the gown and undergarment and rolled them both inside her green wool cape.

"Here." He handed her the clothing. "Hang on to this and stay close behind me. I'm going to open the door and then we're going to cross the room without attracting any more attention than we have to. If we're lucky, we can sneak out while everyone is concentrating on the brawl." The sound of glass shattering against the wall in the barroom emphasized his point.

Hunter checked his knife and then picked up his long rifle, certain he would rather be crossing the raging Mississippi during a flood than wading through the Rotgut bar with St. Theresa in tow.

"If you've got any particular person you'd like to pray to just now, you'd best do it," he said over his shoulder. She immediately started mumbling a hushed prayer. He threw the latch and swung the door open, just enough to catch a glimpse of the free-for-all that was going on in the bar.

Three pairs of rivermen were engaged in a favorite pastime—hand-to-hand knife fighting. A whore clung to the back of the nearest combatant like an opossum baby riding its mother. The woman was shrieking at the top of her lungs, using curses Hunter had never even heard before as she alternately hit the man with a bottle and pulled out handfuls of hair.

It was definitely no place for a would-be nun.

He felt Jemma's hand tug the hem of his coat and glanced back at her.

"Just thought I'd hold on," she whispered. He saw that

she was clutching a fistful of the fringe that dangled from his jacket. "Not that I'm scared, mind you. It was far more perilous trying to escape the twenty mounted Berbers who had trailed me to the oasis, but—"

"Eyes down," he snapped, effectively shutting her up before he started across the bar. He zigzagged through the crowd, thankful that the boatmen were too occupied to notice them as they skirted tables, darted past the bar, and burst into the morning sunlight.

Hunter kept moving, his gaze cutting right and left, wishing he had eyes in the back of his head. Two blocks of muddy streets were behind them before he slowed down. The sun was busy baking the night's rain out of the rooftops. Smokelike wisps of steam snaked skyward, making the entire Tchoupitoulas district appear as if it were on fire.

As he hurried toward the stable, he felt a persistent drag on the back of his coat. Behind him, he could hear the girl's panting and the squish and thud of her heavy shoes as they plowed through the mud. She had not let go since taking hold of his jacket in the bar.

Finally, when they reached the relative safety of the livery stable, he drew her into the shadow of the big open building, put his hands on her shoulders and pressed her up against the wall. All he could see was the pitted crown of her hat. Her shoulders were heaving as she caught her breath, her eyes trained on the ground.

"You can look up now," he said when he realized she was still following his order. He expected to see her white-faced, frightened half out of her wits. He expected her blue eyes to be brimming with tears of relief. He thought he would hear a shaky admission that she had been terrified. Maybe she would finally call off this farce.

Her breath was coming fast but even. She clutched the rolled cape containing her soiled clothing to her breasts. When she tipped her head up and met his gaze, he was awestruck by the radiant glow of sheer delight mingled with gratitude that shone in her eyes. Her cheeks were flushed; her dimples accented her bright smile.

"Mr. Boone," she said with an unmistakably ecstatic sigh, *"that was wonderful!"*

Natchez Trace, One Week Later

The sable mantle of night cloaked the wild landscape along the nearly invisible Indian track that sojourners heading north called the Trace. With nothing more than a blanket between her body and the hard ground, Jemma lay on her side, staring through the flickering flames of the low campfire, listening to the sounds of unseen night creatures that rustled the underbrush and pine needles.

She was truly on her way, miles from New Orleans, civilization, and her quiet, ordered life. No matter what doubts might plague her, she had gone too far to turn back now. Her only regret was that she would never be able to tell Grandpa Hall about her adventure.

She closed her eyes and tried to picture the old man as she liked to remember him, strolling beside her along the wharf at Boston Harbor, telling her tales of the tall ships and the exotic ports of call he had visited. Jemma tucked her hand beneath her cheek and closed her eyes, but within seconds they were open again.

Hunter Boone was somewhere beyond the fire's glow. She couldn't see him, but she sensed his presence and knew that he was walking the perimeter of the campsite, checking the leather hobbles that kept the ponies from running off, making certain everything was secure before he finally sat down by the fire to take the first watch.

As soon as they had left New Orleans with two Texas ponies loaded with staples of bacon, biscuits, flour, dried beef, rice, coffee, sugar, a bolt of fabric, and some trade items, she knew she had chosen the perfect guide. Hunter was thorough, no-nonsense, and, even if he seemed a bit reluctant, a man of his word. All she had to do was settle back and enjoy the adventure.

But so far, the adventure had proved to be nothing but a strenuous, monotonous trek through dense piney woods and open grassy plains with a taciturn grouch who still refused to string more than ten words together.

He had been grouchy and standoffish since the morning they left New Orleans, and a week on the Trace had done little to improve his personality. No matter what she did, she tended to irritate him, so she tried to keep out of his way as much as possible. Since the only communications between them were his curtly issued orders, she tried to tackle the chores he gave her with as much aplomb as she could muster.

Gathering firewood in the pine forest proved to be the only thing at which she was somewhat adept. Frying bacon without burning it to a charred and blackened crisp, or cooking anything for that matter, had proved too much. Hunter finally insisted on preparing all the meals himself.

Afraid that he would lose patience and leave her there to wait for the next party traveling along, she didn't issue one complaint, even though her derriere continually ached from hours of riding. When the trail proved too narrow and illusive, they had to walk the horses. Her tender feet, insulted by the stiff brown leather shoes, were just as sore as her rear end. Once when she stopped to bathe her feet with a damp rag, Hunter caught her wincing, but he offered no sympathy.

He didn't offer much in the way of conversation at all. She didn't know how a man could hold his tongue for so long. Each and every minute was so full of incredible sights and sounds and new experiences that she longed to talk about them, to ask questions. But since the first day, Hunter Boone had made it more than clear that he wanted no part of her "constant palavering," as he so colorfully put it.

She sighed, a long, weary sound, once again wishing

Grandpa Hall were there to talk to, wishing above all things that he could see her now.

Suddenly Hunter's voice cut through the darkness. "You'd better get to sleep before your watch." His soft-soled moccasins made it impossible to hear his steps as he crossed the forest floor.

Jemma bolted to a sitting position. As she watched him clear the shadows, she realized she never got tired of looking at him. He was like no one she had ever met before. The firelight played over his strong features. Shadows stroked the creases that bracketed his mouth and his hard jawline. When he caught her watching, he looked away, took the long rifle, and set it beside his blanket as he gingerly lowered himself to the ground.

She made a great show of huffing and shifting around, but as usual, he ignored her. Minutes ticked by. The glowing coals throbbed white-hot in the fire ring. Now and again, the wood popped and crackled, shooting sparks skyward to dissolve against the stars.

Unable to sleep, dying for an exchange of any sort, she wriggled around, trying to find a comfortable position on the hard ground. He was directly across the fire, staring at nothing, leaning casually against a decaying log with one knee drawn up and an arm looped over it. Silence stretched like a wide bog between them. She couldn't stand it any longer.

"Mr. Boone?"

No answer.

"Hunter?"

The only sound was the crackle of burning wood.

"Hunter."

"What?"

"I can't sleep."

"Then take the first watch so I can."

She shrugged out of the blanket and sat up, scooping her hair back off her face as she reached for her hat. Every muscle in her body protested as she got to her feet and stretched her arms high.

Making her way around the fire, she stood before him, waiting for him to hand her the rifle. The first day on the trail, he had taken the time to teach her to aim and fire. During the night watch, it was always primed and ready.

"Don't shoot yourself in the foot," he warned. "And wake me at the first sign of trouble."

"Don't you worry."

"I've never had any problems heading back overland, but I've heard plenty of tales."

"What kind of tales?" Her interest was suddenly piqued.

"You don't want to know."

"Yes, I do."

He moved around the fire to the bedroll. "Pirates, Indian attacks, thieves, cutthroats. The Trace is famous for its perils, but as I've said, I've never had a lick of trouble."

Jemma took his place against the fallen log and stared into the darkness. *Pirates, Indian attacks, thieves, cutthroats.* How could he sound so casual about it? She shivered, squinted, and tried to see through the trees all around them, imagining knife-wielding pirates and untamed savages behind each and every one.

"Hunter?" she whispered.

No answer.

"Hunter." Louder this time.

"What?"

"Why didn't you tell me that before?"

"Tell you what?"

"About the pirates, thieves, and cutthroats. All you mentioned were the bears, panthers, snakes—"

"Did you think this was going to be a stroll through the woods?"

"No, but—"

"Don't let it upset you. Like I said, I've always had an easy time of it, probably because I veer off from the Trace and head toward the Mississippi. Makes the trip to Sandy Shoals shorter and safer, but there's virtually nobody around to help if we do hit a patch of trouble.''

A patch of trouble? Jemma frowned. Determined to stay awake during her watch for a change, she tried humming softly to herself.

"I'm trying to sleep over here." Hunter's voice cut through the dark.

"Sorry."

A twig snapped somewhere in the forest in front of her. The sound was so loud and out of place in the chorus of tree frogs and the chirps and ticks of the small inhabitants of the underbrush that she was on her feet in an instant, the rifle trained on the inky black shadows.

Across the fire, Hunter was either already sound asleep or blatantly trying to ignore her. She was afraid to take her eyes off the forest long enough to see if she could gauge the steady rise and fall of his shoulders.

Anything could be out there. Men or bears. Panthers, pirates, or cutthroats. "If you panic," he had warned the morning he taught her how to aim and shoot the rifle, "you're liable to blow a hole through yourself or me. If you see anything, just keep the gun aimed and wake me up."

The instructions were simple enough. She was determined not to wake him without real cause, unless the sound of her knees banging together woke him first.

Jemma held her breath and offered up a silent prayer to St. Francis of Assisi, who had tamed the forest animals. As she stood there poised, gun at the ready, the minutes seemed like hours. A bead of sweat trickled down her temple. When she dared to breathe at all, her breath came quick and shallow. She didn't hear another sound. Finally, she shook herself, cradled the rifle carefully in the crook of her arm the way Hunter had shown her, and sat back down with a sigh. It was just like her, she decided, to make something monumental of a little crunch in the leaves.

Within minutes, the raw excitement had faded and sheer boredom set in again. With the rifle across her lap, Jemma wriggled her toes, flexed her arms, took off her hat, and shook out her curls. She started to hum, remembered Hunter's admonition, and stopped. Her eyelids grew heavy. She rolled her head on her neck.

She didn't recall closing her eyes, but something startled her and she opened them. Much to her chagrin, an Indian stood just within the fire's glow, not six feet away.

He was nothing more than a wavering figure garbed in a hodgepodge of colorful cloth and embroidery, decorated with strings of shells and beads and whistles. A shock of long feathers adorned a turban wrapped around his head. Her gaze froze on the tomahawk hanging from a rope at his waist.

His skin was as bronzed as leathery fall leaves, his eyes deep-set and dark, staring out at her from beneath a heavy brow. He was whipcord-thin and of indeterminate age, although even in the darkness she could tell that his skin was as creased as a well-read newspaper.

Slowly, cautiously, carefully, Jemma let her hands slide toward the gun on her lap, hoping to get a good hold on the stock and trigger before she hefted it and aimed. From where she sat, she figured that if she even came close to hitting him, she was bound to do some damage.

To her chagrin, her guide and protector was still sound asleep.

The Indian continued to stand there in silence watching her, but his arm was moving in some sort of crazed fashion. He kept raising his right hand, pointing two fingers to the night sky. Up and down he pointed, again and again.

Then he took a step in her direction.

Jemma's hands closed around the gun. By the time she had lifted it to firing position, the Indian was waving frantically and the tomahawk had somehow slipped into his other hand.

"Hunter!" She slowly squeezed one eye closed and

sighted down the rifle barrel. "Hunter, it's *really* important this time."

Her paid protector muttered in his sleep and rolled over, presenting his back to her. And to the tomahawk.

"I'm sorry, mister," Jemma whispered as the Indian crept closer and closer.

She squeezed her eyes shut and pulled the trigger.

chapter

5

SHOCKED OUT OF A DEEP SLEEP BY THE SOUND OF A GUN-
shot reverberating in the clearing, Hunter clutched his heart
and bolted to his feet.

Beside the fallen log, Jemma lay flat on her back, the
rifle on the ground between her legs. Instinct drove him.
In one move he skirted the fire and dove for her, sweeping
the area with his gaze. Eight feet away, seated in pine
needles and rubbing his head, was an old Choctaw, his
eyes wide with bewilderment. The feathers that had once
adorned his turban had been reduced to bedraggled stubs.
The red turban itself drooped over one eye.

"Hunter?" Jemma moaned beside him.

The Indian didn't appear to be a threat, so Hunter gingerly lifted the rifle from between Jemma's legs and felt
the pulse point in her neck.

"What in the *hell* happened?"

"I'm just fine, thank you." With a hand on the log, she
struggled to a sitting position.

Hunter kept one eye on the Choctaw, who had yet to
budge. The firelight glinted on the blade of a tomahawk
in the dirt beside the Indian. It was the only sign that the
old man might have meant any harm.

"What happened?" he demanded of her again.

"You failed to tell me that rifle would almost tear my shoulder off when it fired," she grumbled.

"I thought you were an expert marksman. You said you had killed off countless desert hordes in the Sahara."

"This is no time to argue, Mr. Boone. That . . . that savage came at me waving his hands, and when he grabbed the tomahawk, I couldn't get you to wake up. I did what you told me to do. I protected the campsite. Is he dead?"

"No. Just minus a few feathers."

She looked over, saw the Indian seated in the dust. "Oh, no. He's quite old, isn't he?"

"Very."

"I thought he was going to scalp us both."

"You nearly scalped him."

"You told me to fire in self-defense. It was dark." She shot another worried glance at the old man. She got to her knees and beat the dust off of the back of her pants with much huffing and puffing.

The old man was on his feet as well, babbling in Choctaw, frantically making a sign of friendship.

Hunter signed back, offering an apology, then put his closed fist against his forehead and turned his hand round and round, making small circles above his brow.

"What are you telling him?" Jemma whispered, her gaze whipping between Hunter and the Indian.

"I said I'm sorry and told him that you're crazy."

"Well, of all the—"

"Get him some coffee," Hunter ordered as he continued to sign to the old man, who shuffled slowly and cautiously forward, keeping an eye on Jemma as he came into the light of the campfire.

Jemma stood beside the fire, near the coffeepot sitting on the stone ring. She looked as if she were about to cry.

"What now?" Hunter helped the old man sit on the log. He couldn't discern any visible signs of injury, aside from the ruined feathers. He glanced over at Jemma and found her watching the old man lower himself to the log.

"He really didn't look that old in the dark. Is he alone?"

Hunter signed to the Choctaw. "He says he is."

Obviously relieved, Jemma closed her eyes and shook her head. "That's good. I'd hate to have to answer to his entire family."

"The coffee?"

"I'm getting it, but I think *I'm* the one that needs to be served coffee, not him." She thrust her chin toward their exotic visitor. "He nearly scared a year off my life."

"You nearly ended his."

Once they were all holding steaming cups of brew as dark as pine pitch, Hunter asked Jemma to sit quietly while he carried on a conversation in sign language with the old man. At one point, when the man pointed both forefingers and then crossed his hands at the wrists, Hunter laughed out loud and shook his head.

Jemma had taken a seat very close to Hunter. She leaned into him and whispered, "What's he saying?" Her breath was warm against his ear.

"He wants to buy you."

She mumbled something that sounded like, "Not *that* again."

Hunter looked down into her eyes. She was watching the old man warily. "What do you mean, 'not that again'?" he asked.

"It's nothing." She shook her head. "Tell him no and make him leave," she said with a shiver.

"I think I should at least see what kind of a deal he's willing to make." Hunter fought to keep his face expressionless.

"He doesn't even have any *teeth*, for God's sake."

"His name is Many Feathers. At least that's what they called him before you managed to blow apart his fancy headdress. He says he can give you all the corn and sugar you can eat. His farm is very big and his orchard has apples and peaches, too. Would you like to take him up on it?"

"You can't be serious." She was almost in his lap, so close that Hunter felt her shiver.

"I'm very tempted."

"No!"

"I'm only joshing."

"This is certainly no time to make jokes. How do you know there aren't twenty or thirty of them hiding among the trees? How do you know they aren't going to scalp us in our beds when he leaves?"

Many Feathers finished his coffee and extended the cup for another. Hunter couldn't hide his smile. They would just have to humor the old man after Jemma's near-fatal assault.

"He doesn't appear to be headed any place. I think with a little hospitality we can make amends." Then, taking pity on the girl, he assured her there was no danger. "Why don't you bed down and get some sleep? Many Feathers here is liable to try to talk me into selling you all night long. *One* of us should be rested tomorrow."

"I don't think I can sleep. I don't think I'll ever be able to sleep out here again. When I think of the heart-stopping dread I experienced when I looked up and there was that . . . that *man* standing there leering at me, brandishing that . . . that *tomahawk*. Why, I . . . was absolutely terrified."

"Then why are you smiling as if you'd like nothing better than to experience that absolute terror all over again?"

"It *was* as thrilling as it was terrifying," she admitted with a sigh.

"Why don't you just roll up in your blanket and dream about it while I entertain your suitor here."

Many Feathers chuckled to himself, smacking his puckered lips over the coffee while Hunter waited for Jemma to decide to move. Finally, she sat back on her heels and then stood up.

"Don't forget I've paid you good money to get me upriver. I don't want to wake up and discover you've traded me away to this savage.''

''He's as cultured as we are, in his own way.''

She kept a sharp eye on Many Feathers as she backed over to her bedroll. ''You'd have a hard time convincing me of that. Promise, Hunter Boone, that you won't sell me.''

''You really think I'd do that?''

''It's been tried.''

Wondering what she meant, Hunter leaned back against the end of the log opposite Many Feathers, prepared to sit out a long night.

''Look at it this way, Jemma. If you went off to live with Many Feathers here, I doubt the emir's men would ever find you again.''

The next morning, she was in no mood for Hunter Boone's dry wit. The pain in her shoulder was agonizing; the skin beneath her billowing, filthy shirt had already turned an angry purple. She had scratched the side of her face on the log when the force of the long rifle had sent her sprawling. The only saving grace was the satisfaction she got whenever she looked into Hunter's bloodshot eyes. He had spent the night listening to Many Feathers until finally, as the sun began to rise at dawn, the old man got up and disappeared into the piney woods.

The path they followed was tangled and overgrown in places, crisscrossed by divergent foot trails, and often so narrow that they had to dismount and lead their spotted Texas ponies through the maze. Following some innate sense of direction, Hunter never hesitated or even paused to ponder their route.

By the time they had been on the move for a good half day, they heard the now-familiar sound of a river not far away. She prayed Hunter would call an early halt to the day's travel so that he might get some much-needed sleep and she could rest her aching shoulder, but she did not mention the idea aloud. All morning long, whenever he looked her way, he simply shook his head and rode on.

The trees thinned out along the riverbank, affording them a grand view of the largest river they had come to yet. Always before, the waterways had been shallow enough to ford by swimming the horses through or by wading and leading them over, but this was no limpid stream. Muddy water propelled by a driving current cut away at the steep banks and carried heavy debris swirling downstream.

"Where are we?" Not that it would make any difference at all since she had no idea where they were, but Jemma asked anyway in her unending attempt to make conversation. They had reined in at the edge of the riverbank, where he could gauge the current and try to judge the depth of the water.

His only response was to mumble something that sounded like, "I must have been crazy to agree to this," so Jemma thought it wise to make no further comment. She dismounted and leaned against the sturdy horse's side, rubbing her shoulder and staring at the onrush of murky brown water.

"Can you swim?" Hunter asked.

Jemma swallowed hard, about to borrow one of Grandpa's tales about being washed overboard in the Bay of Bengal, until she took another look at the swiftly flowing current and decided the truth would be her best option.

"Not very well," she admitted with a dry swallow.

"Does that mean you can't?"

"That means I might be able to paddle around a bit but . . ." She stared at the rushing water. "I can't swim in that."

"That's what I was afraid of."

"Meaning?"

"We have to cross."

"Can't we go upstream until we find a safer crossing . . . or a bridge?"

He laughed as if she had just said the funniest thing he had ever heard. "*Bridge?* And just *who* do you think might have built a bridge out here?"

"You don't have to be rude about it. It seems perfectly logical to me that some traveler may have come along and built some sort of a bridge out of fallen logs or something."

"Well, no one did, so we're going to have to figure out a way to get you across."

"Could we swim the horses over like we've done before?" They had already made a few river crossings, but nothing like this one. She had dreaded clinging to the stout pony for dear life, and hated spending the rest of the day in wet pants, but like now, there had been no alternatives.

"This river is much deeper than the others. If we swim, our supplies will get all wet. The horses will do better without us. I'll have to build a raft, swim the horses over, and then come back for you and the provisions."

She stared at what seemed to be an impossible crossing, trying to imagine Hunter swimming back across without the aid of the horses, and even worse, picturing herself adrift with biscuits and bacon and sacks of supplies on a flimsy log raft.

"What if you drown?" she mumbled, thinking aloud. "What'll happen to me?"

Hunter cleared his throat. "Well, I imagine a resourceful girl like yourself would manage somehow. Maybe you should have taken Many Feathers up on his offer."

"That's very insensitive of you, Hunter," she said, her temper rising.

"I don't intend to drown."

"No one *intends* to die, but accidents happen."

"I've done this before. Don't worry about me." He dismounted and led his pony over to a clearing, where he pulled out the hobbles and let the animal graze.

"I'm not worried about you," she lied. "I'm worried about me."

Jemma followed him and began taking supplies off her sturdy little mount. She had grown fond of the spotted pony, often coddling it when they stopped for the day and offering wild apples when she found them.

Hunter paused with a pack on his shoulder. "Don't fret, Jemma. Everything will be fine. You set up camp and gather some wood while I start cutting timber for the raft. I'd like to have it built before midday tomorrow."

Jemma watched him go, encouraged by his lack of concern as well as his confidence in her ability to organize the camp. While he combed the banks and began to chop down a tree, she walked along the river's edge until she found an abandoned campsite. She tried to imagine who might have been there before them: rivermen going north, settlers moving into Mississippi and Tennessee from the southeast, Indians who had used these trails for generations. Jemma gathered firewood and started a fire in the stone fire ring beside the river, the way Hunter had taught her.

He was out of sight, but she could hear the dull, hollow throb of his axe against stubborn wood somewhere nearby. She didn't know how he could keep up the pace with such vigor. She was near exhaustion. Rather than wait for him to come back to camp and cook, she decided to start the evening meal. She had seen him cook enough bacon to give it another try.

The sun had slipped behind the trees and the long green shadows of the forest had merged and blended to become darkness when she heard Hunter trudging tiredly back into camp.

"I hope you're hungry," she said without glancing up, proud enough to burst as she began laying strips of crisp, unburned bacon on a dented pie tin. She rummaged around in the bundle of dry goods, came up with the biscuit tin, and piled some soda crackers on his plate.

Jemma held up the offering, finally looking at Hunter. He was half-naked, stripped to the waist. His leather shirt was hooked in two fingers, slung over his back. His shoulder-length blond hair, still tied in a queue, was wet. It curled riotously, with tendrils any woman would envy teasing his brow and temples. His lashes were spiked with water droplets, as was his broad, suntanned chest.

The minute she laid eyes on Hunter Boone's muscular chest, Jemma realized in a blinding flash of insight that everything Sister Augusta Aleria had ever warned about temptations of the flesh and the curse of nakedness was absolutely true.

Speechless for one of the few times in her life, she could do nothing but stare. Forgotten, the plate in her hand began to droop. The bacon slid perilously close to the edge before Hunter lunged and retrieved it.

"What's this?" he said, half-smiling, as he looked at the bacon.

With her senses still in a stupor, Jemma tried to put a coherent thought together. All that came out was, "Bacon."

"Ah. I thought the only bacon you made was black."

"I'm . . . getting better at it. How . . . did you get all wet? Did you fall in?"

"I jumped in. I worked up a sweat chopping logs. We're in luck, though. A little farther upstream, I found an area that must have been hit by a powerful storm. The trees have been felled by the wind and scattered like twigs. Tomorrow morning it won't take long to tie the horses to some of them, drag them to the river, and lash them together."

The man had no idea of how greatly his half-naked state aroused her. He tossed his shirt over a nearby bush and sat down cross-legged in the sandy soil near the fire. His leather pants were soaked; water oozed out of them as he bent his knees to accommodate his plate on his lap. Without looking up, Hunter began wolfing down bacon, scraping up the drippings with his biscuits and licking his fingers.

Jemma's mind raced. Until this very minute, she had thought of him as her guide and protector. He had to be a good ten years older than she, at least twenty-eight—*old* by her standards—but he was definitely a virile man. There was something awesome and frightening in that thought, something that set her nerves on edge. That same something made her tingle all over as she stared at his naked chest and the fire's glow snaked over his bronze skin, gilding the tightly matted blond hair.

Sister Augusta Aleria had definitely known what she was talking about.

Her mouth had gone dry. She tried not to think about Hunter or his bare chest and busied herself with her own supper, filling the plate with thick, well-done bacon strips and biscuits, pouring them both cups of coffee from the metal pot by the fire. Although she tried to concentrate on the task at hand, she couldn't keep herself from pondering what it would be like to deeply kiss a man, to touch him intimately, to lay her hand over his heart and feel his warm skin.

She thought of the kiss he had given her in the Rotgut, remembered his soft lips and felt warm all over. It had been an experience she definitely wouldn't mind having again.

"What are you thinking about?" he said around a mouthful of food.

"What? Oh." She mumbled a soft, unladylike curse as coffee sloshed over the rim of her cup. "I was thinking about kissing," Jemma said without thought.

Hunter began choking, wheezing, and coughing so hard that she started to set down her tin and go over to pound him on the back, but he gasped in lungfuls of air and waved her back down.

"I thought you said you were thinking about *kissing*."

"I did. I was."

He was rendered speechless. Then slowly, from the neck up, color began to creep toward his hairline. He glanced over at his sopping wet shirt where it hung on the bush.

"Kissing," he said softly, pondering the word as if he had never heard it before.

In for a penny, she thought, and plunged ahead. She was on an adventure and intended to experience as much as she could before it was over. Just last night she had almost killed a man. Kissing was a far less dangerous endeavor.

"The nuns at the convent—"

"In Algiers?"

Her gaze quickly dropped to her plate. "Yes, anyway, the nuns at the convent spent inordinate hours talking about the various sins of the flesh. I suppose so we girls would know what to expect. And what to avoid. One nun in particular harped on kissing and . . . well, all the rest, so much that at times, it was all we could think about. Mortal sins, venial sins. Kissing that led to mortal sin. Kissing that was *more* than kissing."

"*More* than kissing?"

"Kissing that led to *other things*."

"Other things?"

He was holding his empty plate on his lap, his green eyes intense. His hair had dried some; the curls were lustrous. His expression was blank, either intentionally or because he was so shocked by the subject that he didn't quite know what to make of her. Jemma suddenly felt like squirming under such close scrutiny.

"You know," she shrugged, gripping her plate. Her voice dropped to a whisper. "*Other things*."

"Things other than kissing?" He set the plate beside him in the sand warmed by the fire.

"Yes. Intimate, unspeakable other things. Things a lady shouldn't even think about, let alone discuss over supper."

"The *nuns* were versed at describing these other things?"

She blinked. "Of course. Some were widows. Some had been fallen women who had repented, given up lives of sin to devote themselves to the church. *They* certainly knew what they were talking about.'' She shifted uncomfortably, suddenly too warm.

"So tonight, in the middle of biscuits and bacon, you just thought about kissing?''

There was no way she could tell him the truth, that seeing his bare chest had led her thoughts astray, that it was his fault for walking around half-naked, leading her mind down such a dangerous path. He had her cornered. The only thing to do was brazen her way out.

"How many women have you kissed?''

"Taking a survey?''

"Something like that,'' she said.

"To be honest, I don't see how it's any concern of yours.''

"No. I don't suppose it is. I was just curious.'' She felt herself blushing, thankful for the darkness.

"I've kissed my share,'' he offered.

She bolted upright, nearly spilling the rest of the coffee on herself. A thought that had not occurred to her before suddenly shot to the forefront of her mind.

"Are you *married*?''

He shook his head emphatically. "No. I'm done with women altogether.''

A shadow darkened his eyes. She could almost feel the hurt emanating from him, and her imaginative, romantic soul ached.

"Someone broke your heart,'' she said softly.

"No. Someone taught me a hard lesson is all. But that just helped me realize who I am.''

Thoughtful, her appetite satisfied after a few bites, Jemma began gathering up the plates and cups. In the morning before breakfast, she would take them to the riverbank to rinse in the still water that eddied in the rushes. She couldn't get her mind off what Hunter had just said. A woman had taught him a hard lesson. She couldn't help but wonder who, how, why.

By the time she had finished clearing away the frying

pan and moving the coffeepot farther from the flames, she was certain he was pining for a lost love. Hunter had slipped his shirt on once again. Jemma experienced a wave of relief, as if the door to a room full of unspoken dark secrets had been opened far too long for comfort. She was surprised to find how disappointed she was that it was closed again.

Hunter sat back down and stretched, then crossed his legs at the ankles. He pulled his hat on, using the brim to shade his eyes from the firelight until all she could see were his lips—finely tapered, strong, masculine, but compelling. And unforgettably soft.

"How many women have you kissed, do you think?" she asked, before the thought was fully formed.

He shoved the hat back onto the crown of his head and stared at her hard.

"Are you crazy?"

"No. I just have a very fertile imagination. The nuns always thought so, at least." She sighed, trying to picture the kind of woman who might have walked out on him. "You've obviously loved and lost. No matter what, you still have your memories. Just think, though. You have suffered, which means you are living life to the fullest. Why, some people never find anyone to love, never even have the experience, good or bad."

"Don't make my past into some great dramatic tragedy, Jemma, because it's not. I'm a loner. Things worked out for the best."

A loner. A man who needed no one. *Perhaps he was like Grandpa,* she reasoned. A man whose sense of adventure was greater than his love of family. A man whose home was the world at large, not just one tiny corner of it. When she thought of Grandpa Hall, she could fully understand what Hunter Boone meant by being a loner.

He was a man who wanted no ties. No future with a family. He wasn't looking to tie a woman down with any marriage agreement, wasn't looking to fill his coffers with her money. His life was his own and he liked it that way.

She understood completely and began to see him in a whole new light. "If you're such a loner, why did you decide to take me with you?"

"I didn't have much choice. It was either bring you along or have you solicit the wrong person and end up in the back room of one of those barrelhouses raped or dead. I knew you were safe with me."

"So more than being a loner, you are a man of honor."

He ignored her observation. "Do you mind telling me the truth?"

The truth? She waited to hear exactly what part of the truth he wanted.

"What were you doing out on the streets alone? Where did you come from?"

"I told you. The ship I was on had just docked. That's the gospel truth, Mr. Boone."

"The ship from Algiers?"

Her gaze slipped away and so did the truth. "Yes." She decided to change the subject. It was far, far safer that way. "Like you, I'm not looking for attachments, either." She sat back down beside the fire.

"Just your father and brother. In Canada."

It took her a moment to remember, and then she quickly nodded in agreement. "That's right."

As they sat there chatting, an idea began to nag at her. It was outrageous. It would require her to be downright brazen, but there was only one way to satisfy the curiosity that had been planted with the kiss he had given her in the Rotgut.

"Since you are a self-proclaimed loner, perhaps you wouldn't mind kissing me again."

"*What?*" He became perfectly still, looking at her as if she had just lost her mind.

"Experimentally, of course."

"*Why?*"

Jemma shrugged and tried to voice her opinion in a logical fashion. ''It has to happen sometime, doesn't it? To me, that is. It might as well be now.''

''*What* has to happen?''

She was afraid his big green eyes might roll right out of his head. She started talking faster.

''Kissing. Let's face it. We've been alone together for over a week. I've found you to be just the man I thought you were. You are trustworthy and a man of honor. You obviously aren't interested in women—''

''Hold on a minute—''

''I mean, enough to want to settle down. You said yourself you are a loner.''

He cleared his throat. ''I am, but—''

''Exactly. You aren't looking for attachments. You can remain clear and objective.''

''About what?''

''Kissing. I want to know all about it. I want you to *show* me the differences. I need to know what to watch out for. I'm a woman alone in the world right now, Hunter Boone, and when it comes to kissing . . . and all the rest . . . well, I'm utterly uneducated.''

''I thought you said the nuns covered it pretty thoroughly.''

''Yes, in theory. I've had no real experience, except for the kiss you gave me in New Orleans.''

''That was for protection purposes only.'' He actually looked shaken.

''So you see. Another aspect of the whole. Obviously, you can remain clear and objective.''

''Objective.'' He shook his head. ''Do you think you can remain objective, Jemma?''

''Of course. Why not?''

''You are obviously very innocent.''

She brushed off the knees of the baggy wool trousers. ''Did you really think I was a whore when I approached you on the street?''

''It crossed my mind. Why are you smiling like that?''

"I'm just thinking about what my father would say if he heard this conversation." She knew Thomas O'Hurley would probably lose ten years off his life. "Will you help me?"

"Kiss you, you mean?"

"Yes."

He sat there looking at her for a long while, simply staring at her across the fire as if either he were having trouble making up his mind, or he thought she had completely lost hers while she was frying bacon. She didn't think she was asking too much. All the man had to do was pucker up and kiss her a few times, stressing the differences in technique. Judging from the way her body had reacted to him at the Rotgut, she suspected he'd already done most everything except slip his tongue into her mouth, which would be the ultimate step before . . . well, before the unspeakable. They would never get that far.

"What do you think?" She was beginning to feel uncomfortable under such intense scrutiny.

"I think you need to move closer if you're serious about this."

She got to her knees and crawled the short distance around the fire until she was kneeling beside him.

"I'm so glad you're willing to help."

"Only because I'd hate to have you stumble into trouble later on." His lips were twitching at the corners again.

"You look as if you're trying not to laugh, Hunter Boone. What do I do first?"

"Close your eyes."

She closed her eyes and puckered her lips. Jemma sensed him moving closer. She had a thought and opened her eyes, only to find him very close, staring very intently.

"I was thinking, perhaps you should tell me what you're doing, right before you do it, so I'll know the difference."

"You'll know the difference."

"Instinctively, you mean?"

"Yeah, something like that." He was smiling again.

"Close your eyes and I'll give you the kind of kiss a man gives a woman when he kisses her for the first time."

"A socially acceptable kiss," she said.

"A first-time kiss."

She closed her eyes. Her heart fluttered like a leaf in the wind. Hunter put his hand on her shoulder and pulled her closer, but not too close. His breath was warm on her face. So were his lips when he touched his mouth to hers. It was barely a touch, more of a stroke, an invitation for more. His lips met hers and pressed gently against her closed mouth. Just as she had in the bar, she experienced a warm, heady sensation that spread like slow molasses through her veins.

Suddenly his lips were gone and the kiss was over. She found herself wanting the closeness to go on and on. She felt cheated of something that had beckoned just beyond that simple meeting of mouths. Slowly, she opened her eyes.

His face was still near, his eyes dark, contemplative. She had to clear her throat to speak.

"What comes next?"

"I'll kiss you the way a man kisses a woman he's known a while. You shouldn't let anyone kiss you like this unless you want him to."

"Should I close my eyes?"

He nodded. She did.

His lips were on hers before she was ready. There was no gentle invitation to this kiss. It began with more intent, with a sense of purpose. His lips were actually *moving* against hers, his mouth pressing harder than that first time. She felt compelled to reach up and slip her arms around his shoulders for fear that she might tip over backwards.

By hugging him, she was able to steady herself, to give resistance to his pressure. It was all very stimulating. She actually felt tingles run through her. Before she knew what to think, she felt his tongue teasing the seam of her lips. A shiver ran down her spine and back up again. She held on tighter, shocked and delighted by the warm, slippery, seductive feel of his tongue as he traced her lips again and again.

He pulled back abruptly this time, so suddenly in fact, that she had no time to let go and nearly fell against him. Hunter steadied her. The smile had faded from his mouth— probably, she suspected, because they had reached the more serious part of the lesson. He seemed to be having a hard time breathing.

"Are you all right?" she asked softly.

"Yeah. I'm ... I'm all right. You need to open your mouth."

"I need to *what?*" Indescribable things were already happening to her. She shuddered to think what might occur if she did as he asked and took another big step.

"Open your mouth."

She knew what he was asking. Sister had outlined the forbidden act of open-mouth kissing in glorious detail. Definitely, the nun had warned, this sort of activity would lead to *other things*. Now Hunter Boone wanted her to actually open her mouth when he kissed her.

She was on the brink of one of life's darkest carnal secrets. She was terrified. She was exhilarated. There was no way she was going to let this moment slip away.

"All right," she said, adjusting her arms on his shoulders. "I'll do it."

"This is the kind of a kiss," he whispered, "that you shouldn't let anyone give you unless you're ready to ... unless you want ..."

"More."

"Yeah. More."

"I understand."

"I don't think you do, but I'll try to show you."

He slipped his hand behind her head, cradled her, and turned her so that his mouth, when he brought it down to meet hers, slashed across her lips. She was so overwhelmed by the force of the kiss that she had forgotten to open her mouth as he requested. When his tongue stroked her lips, she remembered. Shock waves rocked her to the core when his tongue slid into her mouth and teased hers. More than molasses was flowing inside her now. She was melting in unspeakable places.

Her body was drawn to his like a magnet. He was still sitting back against the log. She went from kneeling beside him to pressing against him full length. His hard, muscled thighs were like stone. His arm tightened around her; his hand continued to cradle the back of her head, but she no longer needed the silent instruction to move her mouth against his.

Their tongues swirled around each other. Teased, tempted, tasted. She heard Hunter groan low in his throat. An intense desire to get closer was nearly driving her over the edge of rational thinking. She began to wonder what it would be like to feel his skin against hers and the very thought made her ache all over with a forbidden need.

When she felt his hand moving over her shirt, playing along her ribs, trailing up to the underside of her breast, she quivered with shock and the heat of desire. Oh, how easy it would be to slip over the edge, to abandon herself to this man and let him show her, step by step, what to avoid in the future.

She flattened herself against him, forcing him to cup her breast. This time she moaned, unable to stop the sound when the unbearable pleasure of his touch was nearly overwhelming. She was definitely on the verge of throwing caution to the wind and trying a few *other things* right now.

Suddenly, he was no longer caressing her breast, no longer laving her mouth with his tongue. He put his hands on her shoulders and pushed her back to her knees. She opened her eyes and nearly burst into tears at the sheer, unsettling notion that the lesson was over.

Shaken, she reached up and tried to shove her curls into

some semblance of order. Her breath was coming fast and shallow. Her hands were unsteady.

"I'm sorry," he apologized.

She couldn't quite put two thoughts together and simply stared at him. At his lips, in particular.

He looked down at his hand as if he'd never seen it before, as if it had a life of its own. "I didn't mean for things to go that far."

Jemma opened her mouth to speak, couldn't get a sound out, then closed it and swallowed before she tried again.

"Of . . . of course you didn't. I see now, why Sister Augusta Aleria was so adamant about never engaging in open-mouth kissing. The sins of the flesh." How easy it had been to let her traitorous body lead her astray. It was astounding to realize she wasn't virtuous at all. When she thought of poor St. Apollonia, the aged virgin who had all her teeth broken out, of St. Thecla and all the other virgin martyrs who had fought and died to preserve their virtue and their faith, she was convinced they had never met a man who could kiss like Hunter Boone.

"From now on, maybe you should avoid kissing altogether," he told her.

His voice was gravelly in his throat. There was a very pinched, uncomfortable look on his face. Hunter ran a hand through his hair, drew his leg up, and casually draped his arm across it. She wondered how he could be so unaffected when she felt as if she were about to come out of her skin.

It was a struggle to get to her feet, to leave his side when all she wanted was to have him kiss her again. She wanted to experience the wild tingle, the spreading molasses, the fire, the forbidden heat again and again.

"I'll take the first watch," he offered, but he didn't budge.

"All right." She was back on her side of the fire. More than happy to bed down and think about his kisses without having to watch the camp, she quickly agreed. She was eager to let her mind wander over and over the experience, committing it to memory.

Jemma slipped into her jacket, then crawled beneath her blanket and pulled it up to her chin. Before she lay down, she lifted herself up on an elbow and smiled at him across the fire.

"Good night, Hunter," she whispered.

It was a minute or two before he responded. " 'Night, Jemma."

Kissing.

What in the hell had he been thinking? Rock-hard and aching for release, Hunter watched Jemma roll up like a contented little snail and nestle down for the night. He, on the other hand was left to suffer the result of his foolish attempt to teach her a lesson, and had learned a hard one himself.

He was not as immune to Jemma as he had fooled himself into thinking. Day after day, night after night, he had fought not to become captivated by her impish dimples, her flashing eyes, or that lush, ripe young body just made for loving.

Things had almost gotten out of hand a few moments ago. He shook his head when he realized things had been damn well *in* hand a few minutes ago. Her breasts had felt full and ripe—just the right size, as far as he was concerned. Her lips were tempting and sensually seductive. She was a more than willing pupil. Even though he cursed himself for noticing, a man couldn't help but observe certain things, even a self-proclaimed loner.

He *was* a loner, despite the distractions and obligations that fate had continually thrown in his way. In his heart he always had been. It was his drive for open spaces on the frontier that had led him out of Ohio when his mother died, but that trip had been coupled with duty. He had carved a place out of the wilderness for his brother Luther and Luther's wife Hannah and their children. When Sandy Shoals was established, he had stayed on to help Luther expand the farm to include a trading post and tavern on the river.

His own dream had always been to head further west, to the far reaches where few white men had ever trespassed. Just when the post was beginning to flourish and he was about to set out on his own, Amelia White had arrived on a flatboat headed to New Orleans. When she looked up at him and smiled, he had lost his head and forgotten his dreams. She had been his one great mistake.

Traveling downriver with her daughter Lucy, aiming to make a name for herself as a singer, Amelia had taken stock of the trading post, the tavern, and the admiration in his eyes. When the flatboat swung back into the current and continued on with the other passengers, Amelia and her daughter had stayed behind.

She had never loved him. He had realized that with an embarrassing clarity the day he returned from fighting alongside the other Kentucky recruits under Andrew Jackson and learned she had not only walked out, but had taken his and Luther's hard-earned savings with her. The woman had even gone so far as to abandon young Lucy, her daughter by some long-ago lover.

Now here he sat, staring across the fire at a sleeping Jemma-with-no-last-name. No matter how much time he spent with this girl, he doubted that he could ever fathom the workings of her mind. Her romantic wool-gathering had quickly spun what was nothing more than a tale of rejection and duplicity between him and Amelia into unrequited love; then immediately she had turned the tables and wanted him to teach her about kissing.

Hunter picked up a handful of pine needles and began tossing them, one by one, into the fire. He doubted he'd ever get the truth out of her, but he was more than happy to let her live a lie for the rest of the journey.

It would be easier knowing she could never completely

trust him with her secrets than to become close enough to gain her confidence. All he had to do now was keep from thinking about the way his body had reacted to hers when she was in his arms, keep his distance, and see her upriver. Then he'd be done with it.

After that she was on her own. Someone else could worry about St. Theresa and her damned dimples.

They were up at first light. After a hasty meal of ground corn mush and coffee, Hunter set the ponies to work; they quickly turned surly, offended by the task of hauling fallen logs into the water. He chose a bend in the river where the current eddied slowly and curled back on itself, so that the logs were not lost as soon as they hit the water. He left Jemma nearly waist-deep in river water, howling like a screech owl for him to hurry while she held on to a rope that kept the raft from swinging out into the current.

"Are there any alligators in here?"

He could hear her shouting as he worked the ponies down the riverbank with the last load.

"No. Too far north."

"How do you know? There were hundreds in that lake we crossed outside New Orleans—"

"Pontchartrain."

"How do you know for certain they don't crawl this far north? How do you know there isn't one somewhere nearby working up an appetite? I really don't think I'm the one to be standing here in this water. Do you know how long it's going to take my clothes to dry? Last time we crossed a river it took hours, and these things *itch* in unmentionable places."

Hunter sighed and wished she hadn't brought up the subject of unmentionable places. It had taken him a good hour to get one of his unmentionable places under control last night.

It was going to be another very long day. He negotiated the slight incline, with the slender pine logs slipping down the muddy bank with such force that they battered into the makeshift raft. He was ready to leap in after Jemma, but she threw herself forward and draped herself across the logs.

"*That* was too close for comfort, Mr. Boone." She sputtered and coughed, then shoved her floppy hat tighter on her head and pushed off the logs to gain her footing on the muddy river bottom.

She might be slowing him down, but she was certainly entertaining.

"What next?" she yelled. "Are you taking the horses across?"

He made his horse the lead and tied the rein of Jemma's mount to the back of his saddle. Hunter nodded in her direction. "I'm going upstream before I swim them over to the other side. The current will naturally carry us down a ways. Then I'll hike back upstream, swim over, and guide the raft to the other side."

"And I have to wait here alone?"

"You'll be too busy to get lonely. The raft is secured now, so you can get out and start stacking everything in the middle of it."

"It looks sort of rickety." She was standing with her hands fisted on her hips, totally unaware of the way her damp shirt clung to her very shapely breasts. Her nipples were pebbled against the front of the material, tempting him like two ripe pieces of forbidden fruit. His mouth went dry.

Hunter tore his gaze away before she noticed and stared at the opposite bank of the river, looking forward to a plunge into cold water. Sweat trickled along his hairline and down his temple as he began to guide the ponies upstream.

Half a mile away, he forced the horses into the water. Their eyes were wide with fear but neither faltered, even when the water left nothing but their heads visible. He slid off the lead, pulled on the reins, and led the horses up the opposite bank before looking back to see where he had come ashore.

The current had carried them so far downstream that he could barely make out the bend where he had left Jemma. Hunter stripped out of his shirt and jogged along the bank until he could see their camp and the raft on the other side. He shouted a hallo to Jemma and then kept going until he thought he was far enough upstream to drift down to where she waited.

Without hesitation, he dove headfirst into the muddy water; then, with strong, sure strokes, he crossed the river, letting the current propel him downstream at the same time.

She was waiting beside the raft as he took the last stroke and felt the sandy bottom beneath his feet. He stood on the shoreline with his hands on his knees drinking in deep drafts of air. Jemma hurried over to him. When he straightened, he found her standing there staring at him, her blue eyes wide as gold pieces. Her shirt had dried some, but not completely. He fought to ignore it and kept his eyes trained on her face.

"Is the raft loaded?" He barely managed to gasp out the words.

"It is, but I'm afraid I can't do this." She had her palms pressed together at her waist as if in prayer.

The damp material clung to her breasts, outlining every lovely facet. He swallowed hard.

"I'm afraid you'll have to, Jemma. I can't leave you here and we can't go on without crossing. The longer we stand here jawin', the harder it's gonna be to make yourself do this."

"I have to pray first." She fell to her knees in the lapping water at the river's edge.

He watched her cross herself, press the palms of her hands together, and roll her eyes heavenward. She knelt there for a good three minutes. Hunter glanced at the river. The Texas ponies were hobbled on the opposite shore, but he didn't like leaving them vulnerable very long.

"Finished?"

"I haven't even started yet."

Hunter gazed up at the sky. The wispy clouds that he had noticed earlier seemed to be gathering in on each other. A storm upstream would mean trouble. He looked back down at Jemma kneeling there in the water. "What in the hell are you waiting for?"

"I'm trying to think of a saint who drowned."

He wished to God he could fathom the way her mind worked.

"All right. Why?"

"I try to direct my prayers to one of the saints who can understand my plight and will intercede on my behalf. Do you understand?"

"Not really. Just get to praying."

"I will as soon as I can think of one."

Hunter reached behind his head, gathered the wet hair in his hand, and retied the leather thong that held his queue. As he squeezed the water out of his long hair, he reckoned *he* had to be a saint to put up with this.

"Wouldn't it make more sense to pray to someone who didn't drown, if that's what you're trying to save us from?"

She frowned, giving it serious thought. "A saint who drowned would have more empathy."

"Why don't you just go straight to the top and pray to God so we can get out of here?"

She looked at him as if he were a simpleton. "God, Mr. Boone, has a lot to do. That's why going through an intermediary helps."

"Ah."

Her hands were still folded, palms together, fingers pointing to heaven.

"Put in a good word for me." Tired of waiting, his loins aching even though he couldn't see her breasts since she had fallen to her knees, Hunter waded farther into the river and stood by the raft to check the lines. Finally, he heard her mumbling behind him. When she was finished, she joined him beside the raft.

"Well?" he asked.

"I couldn't think of a drowned martyr, so I prayed to Peter, the fisherman, because he was around boats a lot, and then for good measure, I prayed to St. Christopher, who watches over travelers."

"Could he swim?"

Her perfect brow creased again. "I don't know."

While she stood there mulling over his question, he reached out and checked the ropes that anchored the provisions to the center of the raft. Jemma had done a fine job of tying them. The knots were not recognizable, but they were creative and effective.

"Climb aboard," Hunter said, ready to help her pull herself out of the water and up onto the raft. When she was well situated, he reached around her and began to tie her to the supplies.

"What are you doing?" She squirmed in his arms.

"Tying you to the raft."

"Do you have to?"

"I wouldn't be doing it if I didn't think I had to."

"Are you tying yourself to this thing?"

"I can swim. Besides, I'll be in the water steering the raft across."

"In the water?"

"Like a rudder."

Once she was as secure as he could make her, Hunter took off his possibles bag, the horn that held his gunpowder, and his hat and lashed all of them atop the pile. He then took hold of the raft, carefully positioned himself, and shoved it out into the raging current.

chapter
6

HER HEART WAS POUNDING SO HARD IN HER THROAT THAT it threatened to choke her. Jemma clung to the bundles in the center of the raft, too terrified to close her eyes.

Hunter shoved off and instantly the river had them in its grip, whirling them out into the murky depths. The shoreline sped past; the hickories and maples along the banks blurred and merged as the craft raced downstream. She didn't know how he managed to propel the crude raft toward the opposite shore, but while the current pushed them downstream, they gradually edged toward the northern bank.

Relief washed over her when she spied the ponies, but the raft swept past the grazing animals. Hunter's head appeared and disappeared as he continued to use his body and strength to guide the raft toward the opposite shore. Jemma wriggled to her knees, prepared to help him land. They were almost there. The rope was cutting into her waist, hampering her movement; she feverishly worked the wet knot.

"We passed the horses!" She pointed as she tried to shout over the roar of water.

Hunter, concentrating on his grueling task, could do little but glance in her direction. Jemma waved and smiled.

"What in the hell are you doing?" he shouted back. They had almost made it to safety. He was head and shoulders above water, straining, shifting his weight and legs. His hair was plastered to his head.

"We're almost there. I . . . the rope was cutting into me." She was about to yell that he needn't be so bossy, when she saw him glance away and his eyes widen as he shouted, "Hold on!"

Before Jemma could think—let alone act—the raft crashed into a log lodged in a sandbar. The force of the impact sent her flying over the side, over a huge tree branch that looked like a grasping, skeletal hand. Eyes open, all she could see was dappled sunlight streaking through the murky water. As she tumbled headlong through the churning depths, her arms and legs flailed around like a rag doll's. Her lungs felt as if they were about to burst.

She tried fighting the current that tugged on her oversized clothing and the heavy brogans on her feet. When her head suddenly broke the surface, she barely had time to gasp in a mouthful of air before she was sucked under again. Her lungs burned. Blinding light flashed behind her eyelids. She kept her arms extended, hands in front of her, feeling the water, terrified of crashing into another log or a submerged rock. Images of the countless alligators they had seen farther south intensified her terror.

She was going to die. She was certain of it. Her craving for adventure would be the death of her. Her father would mourn her, never knowing she had perished in a watery grave in unnamed wilderness.

As her death became a certainty, her terror slowly receded, replaced by overwhelming calm. This time she had pushed the saints too far.

She would meet her end with only two regrets: one, that her impulsiveness would cause her father endless grief, and two, that she would die a virgin.

● ● ●

The raft ricocheted off the log in the sandbar and rammed into the shoreline, where it battered into the reeds and lodged on the thick undergrowth.

Hunter dove toward the spot where Jemma had gone under. His every muscle burning from the exertion of guiding the raft, he let the current take him downstream, bobbing up every now and again to fill his lungs with air. He thought he saw Jemma's golden head of curls a few yards downstream, but she disappeared so quickly he couldn't be certain.

His mind raced ahead of the current, offering up flashes of hideous premonitions. Jemma fighting the water, soundlessly screaming, calling his name, expecting him to come to her rescue. Jemma lying on the muddy riverbank, her perfect lips purple, her angelic face ashen, lying with sightless blue eyes turned toward the heavens. She had entrusted her life to him and he had let her drown. He should have warned her to sit still, to leave the rope alone. It was all his fault. He had lost her while her kisses of the night before were still warm on his lips.

He let the river carry him a good mile downstream before he realized that if he didn't make his way to shore quickly, he would end up losing his own life. Exhausted, he finally reached the riverbank and, on hands and knees, pulled himself through the reeds, where he collapsed. His heart was beating so hard he thought it would burst and he would die face down in the mud. Finally, the pounding slowly receded to a dull, aching thud that echoed Jemma's name.

Hunter forced himself to drag his bone-weary body up out of the water. He rolled over on his back and blinked water out of his eyes. Above him spread a cloudy sky shot through with streaks of sunlight. Finally, when he was able to breathe evenly again, he sat up and shoved his hair off his face. The leather thong that had kept his hair tied back was gone. His hair dripped muddy water on his shoulders. His leather pants were heavy with water, slung low on his hips. He glanced at his feet, relieved to see he had not lost his moccasins.

He looked downstream, hoping beyond hope, aware that the chances of finding Jemma alive were slim. There was no sign of her along the bank, so he began walking upstream again, back to the raft and the horses. She could have washed up on the opposite bank, but before he tried to fight his way across, he would search for her along the way, then load the supplies onto the horses and head back downstream until he found some sign or was forced to abandon all hope.

Cursing fate, he blamed himself. Jemma was so vibrant, so full of life. For the entire trek, she had done just what he had asked of her, and admittedly he had pushed her hard. She had met every challenge with courage and few complaints. He should have taken better care of her, should have warned her not to budge during the crossing. All his life he had been responsible for his family, his mother, his brother; later, Hannah and the children, then Lucy. Nothing like this had ever happened to him before.

As he started plodding through the mud along the riverbank, each step he took echoed the heaviness and guilt squeezing his heart.

On hands and knees, Jemma hung her head, heaving and retching until the watery contents of her stomach stained the ground. She gulped down a sob and tried to stand, but her arms and legs had minds of their own. As she sat there violently trembling on the riverbank, it took her a while to realize she had truly survived. She was safely on land and the nightmare—of the muddy water swirling before her eyes, of her fight for air, of praying for a foothold or a chance to break the surface of the water—the struggle was all behind her.

She had lost a shoe and a stocking, but somehow she was safe. She crossed herself and offered up a prayer to both St. Christopher and St. Peter. One of them surely must have helped her reach the shore when she had not an ounce of strength left. She watched the water surge by, and as she gathered strength she speculated on what might have happened to Hunter. If he had been thrown from the raft when she was, he might very well be injured or even dead. The thought chilled her to the bone.

Jemma rested her arms on her knees and buried her face in the crook of her elbow. Hunter Boone was too much a part of this frontier wilderness to meet his end in such a colorless, tragic way. He couldn't be dead. He just couldn't.

But if the worst had happened and he was gone, then she was on her own, without food, shelter, or transportation. Without a guide, she couldn't go on without getting further mired in the wilderness.

She was a fool, she quickly decided. She had acted impulsively, intent only upon having a grand adventure without thinking of the consequences. She had almost lost her life and had perhaps caused Hunter to lose his. No story her grandfather ever told came anywhere near the soul-shattering reality she had faced fighting the river's depths.

Adventure was definitely not all it was touted to be.

Even if he was furious with her, she would give anything to see Hunter right now, even if he cursed the day he laid eyes on her. He simply *couldn't* be dead. Glancing around, trying to get her bearings, she realized she needed to get up and moving or she might miss him.

She reached down and pulled off her remaining shoe and sock and tossed the hateful things aside, thankful to be rid of them. The stocking hit the water and floated downriver. Although she was still shaking like a leaf, her legs held when she tried to stand. She ran a hand through her soaking-wet hair and her palm came away bloody. She stared at the blood, shivered, and then quickly swiped it on her wet trousers. She ignored the cut, afraid that if she stayed there hidden by the rushes much longer, she might miss Hunter. There were miles of riverfront to search.

If she didn't find him—

She wouldn't let herself think of that. Not now. Not when the reality of being stranded alone without supplies or any means of protecting herself was too horrifying to face.

Jemma turned and started up the bank. Her foot slipped on the muddy incline and she nearly sprawled facedown, but caught herself in time. She struggled up again and continued to climb the steep bank until she could pull herself over the top. When she did, she straightened and immediately felt light-headed. She closed her eyes, weaving on her feet.

When she opened them again, her vision was still blurred, but she could make out someone walking toward her.

"Hunter!" She thanked all the angels and the saints. Too dizzy to move, she waited for her vision to clear until at last she recognized the man who had nearly reached her side.

"Oh, no. Not you." Jemma groaned and fainted dead away.

She was gone. St. Theresa of Algiers had disappeared without a trace, swallowed up by the Homochitto River. Exhausted enough to fall out of the saddle, Hunter refused to stop searching the riverbank until dusk. There would be time enough then to rest his weary body—dark, empty hours that would stretch unmercifully, hours filled with the horrible memory of those last few moments of Jemma's life.

Whoever she really was, wherever she was from, her secrets had been swept away with her. There might be someone who cared for her, someone who would shed a tear over her passing, but he had no idea how to contact them. Hell, he didn't even know her last name.

She was just Jemma. His St. Theresa of Algiers.

Hunter blinked and turned his face up into the gently

falling rain. Ridiculous, mourning a girl who didn't know the truth from a gold piece, a girl with a head full of crazy notions and the world's best imagination. A week ago he had not known of her existence. Now, all he wanted was to see her dimpled smile again, to watch her hair glisten in the sunlight, to hear the sound of her voice.

Aching, discouraged, Hunter dismounted. The mucky soil squished beneath his moccasins. The ponies stood unmoving in the rain, their heads down, expressions blank. He rubbed the back of his neck with his palm and then stretched. The muscles along his shoulders were becoming increasingly stiff and sore from poling the raft across the river.

He took up the lead pony's reins and started off again when an odd-shaped black rock near the water's edge caught his eye. He blinked and then stared at the dark brown lump.

It was Jemma's shoe.

He slipped down the bank, slid the last few feet on his rear end and grabbed up the brogan. It was sopping wet, the toe curled up and the heel worn more on one side than the other. Definitely the shoe he had bought at the levee. The leather was cold against his skin.

Cold and empty.

As Hunter held Jemma's shoe, cradling it against him, he refused to believe he had seen the last of her. If her shoe had washed up, why hadn't she? He wished he had listened more closely when she told him about the legion of saints she prayed to. At this point, he was willing to try anything.

The water lapped gently against his feet. He looked down, hoping for a sign, another shoe, anything. A cluster of broken reeds drew his attention. His gaze scanned the riverbank to the right. Rain had gathered in a group of muddy depressions not far away. He leaned closer, confirming the fact that he was looking at footprints. Small, barefooted footprints.

He slapped the shoe against his palm and stifled a joyous shout, fearing he'd spook the horses. Jemma was on dry land. She was alive.

Perhaps she was stumbling around alone and disoriented, but at least she was alive. Determined to track her down, he knew that she was exhausted, maybe even in shock. She wouldn't get far. Hunter bent close and traced her footprint with his fingertips. He climbed the riverbank and stopped dead still at the top. The small prints were intermingled with another, larger set made by someone wearing moccasins. His heart missed a beat. She wasn't alone anymore. The tracks led away from the river toward the piney wood with its maze of Indian and buffalo trails.

Hunter hurried over to the horses, loaded and primed his rifle, and hung it over the lead horse's saddle horn. He strapped his hunting knife to his side and made sure his shot bag was fastened to the belt at his waist. He was ready.

Picking up the reins he stayed on foot, running ahead of the ponies. Head down, he followed Jemma's footprints, searching the trampled, wet ground for signs of her.

"St. Genevieve, you're the only one I haven't called on lately. If you're watching, help me. Please." Jemma hastily crossed herself as Many Feathers, in all his toothless glory, shook his fist to make some point or another before he shoved her inside his crude dwelling.

Jemma squinted and looked around the dark interior. The place was nothing more than a hovel made of stakes shoved into the ground, plastered with mud inside and out—giving it a dank, musty smell that mingled with the smoke from a fire burning low in the middle of the single room.

"And St. Genevieve, please hurry." It wasn't often that she invoked the patron saint of disasters who had saved the Parisians from Attila and the Huns, but she was desperate. Being locked in an Indian hut in the middle of no place left little room for hesitation.

As her eyes became adjusted to the gloom, Jemma noticed a low platform of oak saplings covered with woven cane mats and skins. Obviously the old man's bed, it looked big enough for four. She shivered involuntarily.

"Mister Feathers . . ." Jemma began inching toward the low door, the only opening besides the hole in the roof that allowed smoke to escape. She pointed toward herself. "I go now." She pointed at the door, at herself and at the door again. "I go." She smiled and nodded. "All right?"

He shut the door, which was nothing more than wooden stakes lashed together, and proceeded to stand in front of it with his arms crossed over a bony chest barely visible between the edges of his soiled flannel garment.

Her panic mounted. "I'm still not interested in marrying you, if that's what you're after. Believe me," she said with a toss of her head, "better men have tried. Why, my father—"

He barked a strange, guttural word at her, put his hand on her shoulder, and shoved her farther into the center of the room.

She shoved him back. "Don't touch me, please!"

He pushed her into the mud wall. Shocked speechless, Jemma stayed put, watching as he walked to a pile of furs. Implements for planting were scattered around the place, along with colorful baskets woven of dyed cane. Many Feathers sifted through a basket of goods, finally picking up a leather cord to which various nuts had been tied. Curious, she watched as he tied the cord to his wrist and then another to his ankle. The nuts made a hollow sound when he moved.

Next the old man pulled out a wad of dried bronze tobacco leaves tied together. He walked over to her and rubbed the tobacco against the side of her face and started to trail it down her neck.

"Stop that!" she demanded, trying to slap his hand away.

He tossed the tobacco back into the cane basket.

She heard a shout followed by laughter outside. The village had appeared small, no more than a gathering of five or six wood-and-mud dwellings, but she couldn't be certain how many Indians might have occupied the cornfields they had passed on the way.

Many Feathers was jumping around now, waving his arms, singing and droning some sort of off-key song in his language, rattling the nut bells on his wrist and ankle and glancing over at her on occasion as if to see whether she was impressed by the show.

Jemma crossed her arms and shook her head. Let him dance all night. Let him dance for a month. He was never going to persuade her to marry him.

Was Hunter alive? If so, where in heaven's name was he and how was he *ever* going to find her here?

In the middle of Many Feathers's performance the door suddenly opened, nearly knocking the old man to his knees. Forced to stoop to enter, a younger version of Many Feathers walked into the hut and straightened to an imposing height. Like the old man, he wore a colorful turban of crimson and saffron yellow. His pants were bright red flannel with blue stripes down the inseams, and his shirt was appliquéd in brilliant design. He wore a beaded choker.

As he slung a blanket that held a heavy burden off his shoulders, he pinned Jemma with a dark stare that swept her from head to toe, then entered into a fast and furious conversation with Many Feathers, often gesturing in Jemma's direction.

While the men argued heatedly, Jemma began inching toward the door. Without any notion of what she would do once she escaped the hut, she had her hand on the crude latch and was about to bolt when the young Choctaw slammed his hand against the door and shouted, "Stop!"

Jemma whirled on him. His gaze was shrewd and calculating as he silently sized her up.

"You speak English?" she asked, amazed.

"Is that so strange?" he asked. The coldness in his voice whipped through her. "There are too many of you whites here now. I learn your tongue for my own good."

Jemma shivered. "Who are you? What is this place?"

"Who are *you?* What are you doing here?"

"I'm Jemma." She pointed at Many Feathers, who stood behind the young man, watching silently. "He kidnapped me."

"*He* is my father, Many Feathers. In your language, I am called Soaring Raven."

"He walked into our camp last night and wanted to buy me to be his wife."

The young man barked off a laugh but did not smile. "He intends for you to be *my* wife."

"*Your* wife? That's impossible."

Soaring Raven nodded. "That is what I told him. Who wants a wife with skin the color of the full moon and holes in her cheeks?" He reached out to touch one of her dimples.

Jemma slapped his hand away. "Now that *that's* settled, tell him to let me go."

"Go where?"

"Back to the river where he found me. I have to find the man I hired to see me safely up north." She tried to swallow her mounting panic.

"He is not doing a very good job."

"He was until our raft capsized crossing the river."

Soaring Raven shot her another sullen glance and then began to unwrap a hunk of meat that he had carried in the blanket.

Jemma looked away.

"When you are hungry enough, you will not turn your face away from this food."

"I don't plan on staying that long."

Soaring Raven took a step closer. "No? And where do you go? Do you think this white man who lost you once will be able to find you here?" His gaze raked her from toes to hairline. "Maybe you are too much trouble. Maybe he is happy to be rid of you."

Jemma rubbed her arms. Exhaustion was wearing on her already frayed nerves. Her clothing was still damp. Mud was encrusted in every fiber of her baggy shirt and trousers. She was hungry and tired and at the end of her rope.

She certainly didn't want to think Hunter Boone might be happy to be rid of her, but Soaring Raven had a point.

"He'll find me—and when he does, you'll be sorry." She tried to muster some bravado.

Soaring Raven crossed his arms. "I am already sorry to have laid eyes on you. My father is sometimes a fool in his old age. I do not want a white wife. I would waste all my time beating you to get you to obey."

"Then if you don't mind, I'll be leaving." She reached for the door latch again.

Many Feathers broke into a spate of rapid-fire Choctaw and wild gestures that sent the nut bells ringing hollowly.

"Whether I want you or not, you belong to my father now. Here you will stay until he decides to sell you or release you."

Jemma's heart sank. Many Feathers was smiling his gap-toothed smile. She groaned.

"Come with me. You will do woman's work." Soaring Raven opened the low door.

Jemma tried to tell herself that her situation was only temporary, that she should be relishing the opportunity to learn all she could of these people while she was here. This was more than a grand adventure. This was a thrilling, firsthand look at primitive life.

But she couldn't convince herself of anything of the sort. All she wanted right now was to backtrack the way Many Feathers had brought her and begin searching the riverbank for Hunter.

"I'm not going to do anything until you let me go."

Soaring Raven took her chin in his hand, leaned close, and said slowly and distinctly, "I do not care what you want or don't want. You belong to my father and you will obey him. You will obey me and you will not shame us. If you do, you will be beaten. You are lucky I have not yet cut off all of your hair."

Her hand crept up to her tangled hair. "You can't be serious."

Without another word, Soaring Raven stooped to duck beneath the door frame and stepped out into the sunlight. As Jemma followed him outside, Many Feathers's nut bells thunked mournfully.

Hunter crouched in a stand of trees and underbrush, hoping his vantage point was not laced with poison oak. Hidden on the edge of the Choctaw cornfield, he had a clear view of the settlement. The footprints had led him to the outskirts of the village, and once he realized Jemma had to be there, he doubled back and left the horses hidden in a meadow where they could not be heard or easily discovered.

Six houses sat in a cluster, some with gardens of pumpkins, squash, and fruit trees alongside. He could smell apples rotting on the ground beneath the trees. His empty stomach grumbled. There was a long common house in the center of the village, a dwelling with no windows where the clan would reside in winter.

On a platform high above the cornfield, two Choctaw women acted as human scarecrows, constantly flapping their arms, shouting at the crows and other birds that threatened to steal ripe corn still to be picked. Their colorful red and blue striped skirts stood in brilliant contrast against the azure sky.

Men and women moved easily about the settlement. Beside one shelter, a wrinkled old woman dyed split cane splinters in pots of color made from bloodroot, butternut, and black walnut. Nearby, a younger woman wove the cane into baskets, using the intricate checkerwork design committed to memory from tribal lore.

He glanced over at the log mortar and bit back another relieved smile. Earlier, he had been elated to see a disgruntled Jemma being led over to an upright hickory log that had been hollowed out by charring and scraping. As Many Feathers followed in her wake, she grudgingly trailed another tall Choctaw, arguing and balking every step of the way. The younger man quickly turned her over to the women grinding corn in the log mortar. Shoving and pinching her, the women showed Jemma how to pound kernels into cornmeal with long hickory-pole pestles.

As he watched, Jemma often paused, ostensibly to wipe her brow on her sleeve, but Hunter could tell that she was really casting surreptitious glances around the camp, looking for a way to escape. He wished there were some way to let her know he was nearby before she tried to escape on her own.

Crouching in the undergrowth, Hunter shifted, trying to ease a cramp in his leg. For the moment Jemma seemed safe enough. He hoped she would not do anything to endanger herself before he could get to her. Her shoulders sagged with exhaustion. Her hair was matted and tangled with twigs and grass.

He could see by the determined set of her shoulders that she was not about to let the situation get her down, but even from a distance he could tell that she was pale and exhausted.

Whenever she paused too long to rest or examine the palms of her hands, she earned a sharp rap on the head from one of the women around her. Jemma was no doubt praying, but Hunter knew that even if there was a patron saint of great escapes, if anyone was going to get her out of this fix, it was going to have to be him.

chapter
7

WEAK ENOUGH TO COLLAPSE, JEMMA REFUSED TO CRY.
Her palms were blistered, but she would not give the
women beside her the satisfaction of seeing her shed a
single tear. Nor would she give up hope. If Hunter was
dead, if he never came to her rescue, then she was determined to walk out of this place on her own bare feet. This
was worse than endless hours of embroidery. There was
no way she was going to live out the rest of her days
pounding corn into dust.

She raised the five-foot-long hickory pestle and brought
it down with as much vengeance as she could muster, despite the pain in her hands. Her mind wandered through
her list of saints. The way things were going, it would not
do her any good to overwork anyone.

She decided upon St. Leonard of Noblac, the patron
saint of prisoners, whose symbolic emblems were fetters
and manacles. About to begin a prayer, she realized that
the tinkling of shell bracelets had suddenly stopped. The
women around her had abruptly quit pounding corn.

A chorus of shouts went up. Men, women, and children
had stopped their work and play to watch a tall white man
in buckskins lead a horse into the heart of the village.

"Hunter!" Jemma let go of the hickory-wood pole. It

clattered against the side of the log mortar before it hit the ground. She shook off the hold of the woman beside her and broke free. Her bare feet hit the ground with uneven slaps as she barreled toward Hunter, running with all the strength she could muster. Her heart pounded joyously with each step.

Jemma launched herself at him, threw her arms around his neck, and hung on for dear life.

"I've never been so glad to see anyone in my life! I thought you would *never* get here!"

He pried her loose and set her firmly on her feet. What a truly glorious sight he was, despite the golden stubble on his jaw and his wild mane of unruly hair. He did not smile down at her, but kept his gaze constantly roving over the gathering Choctaw slowly hemming them in.

"Where were you? How did you find me?" Overwhelmed by relief, it was all she could do not to grab him again. "I told that odious man that you would come after me, but he refused to listen." She glanced at the faces surrounding them until she saw Soaring Raven.

Pointing, she said, "That's Many Feathers's son. They are the ones who are keeping me here."

Hunter had not moved since she reached him, nor did he now. Instead, he gently laid his hand on her shoulder. His touch was warm, steady. His calm communicated itself to her. He continued to stare at the people around them. When he finally spoke, his tone was low and firm.

"I'm going to try to get you out of here, Jemma, but you have to do exactly as I say—"

"What do you mean, *try?*"

"There are certain formalities to be observed."

"But—"

He gently gave her shoulder another squeeze. "Trust me," he whispered. His eyes met hers and held her gaze.

He was her only option, her only hope.

"And Jemma?" he added.

"What?"

"Better start praying."

She crossed herself, swiftly and silently appealing to Leonard of Noblac as Hunter stepped forward, pulling her along with him while the small gathering stepped aside. He soon stood toe-to-toe with Soaring Raven.

"I want to swap," Hunter said, making the sign for trade.

"No *swop*!" Many Feathers, standing beside his son, shouted and shook his fist.

Soaring Raven crossed his arms and waited while Hunter made the sign for "trade" again.

"Soaring Raven speaks excellent English," Jemma whispered with a tug on Hunter's sleeve. "Talk to him."

Again, Hunter squeezed her shoulder.

"She is my father's property," the man informed Hunter.

Jemma shot her gaze up at Hunter. "I told you."

Hunter ignored her. "I want to trade for this worthless woman," he said.

"*Worthless?* Hunter Boone, I swear—"

Hunter continued without acknowledging her outburst. "She is nothing but trouble, but I will be happy to take her off your hands."

"If she is so much trouble, why do you want her back?" Soaring Raven countered.

"I made a promise to see her safely north. My honor demands that I keep that promise; otherwise I would gladly let you have her," Hunter explained.

Jemma gasped. "You are actually bartering with him? I don't believe this—"

Hunter slowly turned and pinned her with a stare frigid enough to freeze water. He lowered his voice to a whisper. "This is a hell of a time to start arguing. I thought I asked you to trust me and pray. Now, do you think you can do that and stay out of this?"

She scrunched her eyes into slits and glared back at him.

"Come, we will go inside," Soaring Raven said, turning

to lead the way to his father's home. "I am as anxious to be rid of this troublesome woman as you are, but my father must be persuaded to let her go."

Jemma allowed them to usher her back to Many Feathers's hut. The three tall men surrounded her, towering over her. The exhaustion that had vanished at Hunter's sudden appearance rushed back through her in waves. It took all the strength she could muster to put one foot in front of the other and keep moving.

The sun had sunk low behind the forest of trees beyond cleared fields filled with piles of drying cornstalks. Work had ceased throughout the village as the inhabitants went inside their family dwellings. The air was pungent, tainted by the smoke from the many cook fires. Inside Many Feathers's hut, the air was close and still. The aroma of simmering meat filled the room, and Jemma's mouth watered.

The men sat on the floor near the fire. Hunter acted as casual as if he spent every day of his life squatting in the dirt in an Indian hovel. Jemma started to sit beside him, but Hunter and Soaring Raven motioned her back.

"See to the food." Many Feathers's son nodded toward the pot bubbling over the low fire.

"She doesn't cook," Hunter swiftly commented. "I told you she is of very little value."

Ignoring their English exchange, Many Feathers busied himself with tamping tobacco into the bowl of a stone pipe attached to a soft wood stem. Unlike anything she had ever seen, the pipe was nearly two feet in length. A small carved figure of a wolf leaned against the bowl of the pipe.

Once more Hunter surprised her. As she gingerly lowered herself to a sitting position in the shadows behind the men, she watched as he confidently took the pipe the old man offered, held it almost reverently the way Many Feathers had, took a long drag of smoke, and then passed it on to his right. Her guardian angel seemed right at home, ignoring her completely.

Jemma pulled her knees up to her chest, wrapped her hands around her toes, and propped her chin on her knees. Blisters burned her palms. Her shoulders and arms ached from raising and lowering the heavy pestle, as well as from the blows the women had dealt her. Her stomach rumbled noisily. It was going to be a very long evening.

At least his hunger had been satiated. The sun had set hours ago. Hunter and the other two men had eaten hunched over the stew pot, alternately dipping portions of venison, corn, and squash with long wooden ladles. Jemma got what was left. Stories were told and countless bowls of tobacco went up in smoke. He had traded a cooking pot for a Cherokee stone pipe with a bear fetish on the bowl. Nette would enjoy it if he cut the stem down. He now owned an assortment of cane baskets and in the trade had lost a frying pan, a spoon, and a paring knife. Losing the goods would cost him, but Many Feathers was now certain that *he* was the more skillful trader.

The old man wanted no less than four horses for Jemma and he was not about to be persuaded otherwise.

Despite his desperate need to keep both of the horses, Hunter went so far as to counter and offer one of them in trade for Jemma. He had no idea how far he was from a wilderness plantation or a friendlier Indian settlement. To offer both would have been suicide. At the end of many hours of bartering, Many Feathers's offer still stood: four horses for the woman.

The old man gleefully told Hunter, through signs and translation, that he firmly believed his son would eventually see the wisdom in taking the ugly white woman for his bride. If not, he had shrugged, then he, Many Feathers, just might marry her.

The only good thing that happened all evening was that Jemma stopped staring daggers at all of them and had finally fallen fast asleep curled up on the dirt floor near the door. She wasn't aware of his failure.

Finally, Hunter decided to play his last card. He turned to the small pile of goods he had tied into a canvas tarp. Hidden beneath the bolt of printed cotton fabric he had purchased for Nette was a crock of Luther's best Kentucky whiskey, the only one he had reserved for his trip up the Trace. It was the emergency jug he carried for medicinal purposes, enjoyment, for whatever situation dictated a need for the fiery brew. Hunter was not much of a drinker— dealing with Jemma had put him in the mood for a long swig more than once, but he had held out. He was ready to sacrifice the entire contents of the crock as a last resort.

He pulled out the jug and popped the cork, took a long pull, and dramatically smacked his lips.

"Ahhh." He closed his eyes and sighed with all the drama he could muster, swirling the liquor to let the heady aroma of the brew taint the air. When he opened his eyes again, Many Feathers and Soaring Raven were leaning close, eyeing the jug speculatively.

"Whiskey?"

Hunter nodded at Soaring Raven. "The finest, the smoothest, the mellowest batch this side of Kentucky." Hunter smiled.

"Trade?" Soaring Raven wiped his palms on his thighs and nodded at the crock.

"I'll trade you the whole thing for the woman." Hunter was bone tired, ready to take Jemma and get out.

Many Feathers was torn; it was as plain as the pained expression on his face. He licked his lips, cast a glance over his shoulder at Jemma's sleeping form, and then looked at his son.

"No." Many Feathers shook his head and signed. "Woman or four horses."

Soaring Raven said something to his father that made Many Feathers burst into a spate of Choctaw. The men discussed the matter loud and long, so loud that Hunter was afraid they would wake Jemma, but she merely rolled over. Hunter took another pull from the jug and, as the liquor burned its way down his throat, decided his only option was to get the men drunk.

"I'll trade you half a jug for some tobacco," he said.

Soaring Raven translated and Many Feathers's eyes lit up. The old man's son unfolded his legs and rose to a standing position as blithely as if hours sitting cross-legged on the hard ground had not fazed him—while Hunter thought that if he didn't get up and stretch soon, he might never walk again. Soaring Raven rustled through a basket of dried and tied tobacco leaves and returned with two good-sized bundles and two drinking gourds.

"Two bundles for all of your whiskey," came the offer.

"One for half," Hunter said, biding his time. He took one bundle and filled the drinking gourds with whiskey.

Soaring Raven savored his portion, but Many Feathers lifted the gourd to his lips and didn't stop drinking until the whiskey was gone. He smacked his lips and looked expectantly at his son as he held out the second bundle of tobacco.

"Again?" Hunter pretended to take another long draft of liquor. He shook his head. "You don't like it?" He nodded at Soaring Raven's drinking gourd.

"I know the power of the whiskey. I am more careful than my father."

Hunter took the tobacco and poured them both another round.

"I am sorry we could not make a trade for the woman." Soaring Raven glanced at Many Feathers. "My father has a head of rock."

"He has been a good host," Hunter said, "so I'll give you both one more round of whiskey." His gaze shifted to Many Feathers, whose glassy-eyed stare focused on the whiskey jug.

While the old man slurped down the last of his whiskey, Hunter bundled up the newly acquired goods with the few items he had left. Many Feathers's eyes were already heavy lidded. He was weaving where he sat. Soaring Raven made no move to stand.

"I hope you have more luck than I did getting that woman to work," Hunter said, slinging the canvas full of goods over his shoulder. "To tell you the truth, I'm happy to be rid of her."

He heard a gasp behind him and whirled around. The items in the blanket clanked together.

Awake, Jemma shoved herself to a sitting position and scooped her hair back off her face, blinking up at him with astonishment and fear in her wide blue eyes.

"You're actually leaving me here?" Her whisper was laced with disbelief.

Hunter shifted his load and glanced over his shoulder. Soaring Raven was watching the exchange as intently as he could. Hunter steeled himself to feign detachment.

"That's right. Many Feathers drove too hard a bargain. He wanted four horses for you. You know I don't have them."

Her hands were shaking so hard she had clasped them together in her lap. "But—"

"There's no way I can get four horses tonight, Jemma."

"I just heard you tell him you were happy to be rid of me. I paid you good money to get me upriver, Hunter Boone. I gave you my last gold piece." She thrust her chin up as if daring him to walk out on her. It was a pitiful show of last-ditch bravado, but it didn't alter the fright in her eyes. "You can't just leave me here with . . . them." Her eyes suspiciously bright, her voice broke on the last word.

He walked toward the door, passing close beside her to get there. "Do you remember what I told you earlier? Trust me," he whispered.

She reached out and grabbed his pant leg. Her hand curled around the well-worn leather. "Please, Hunter. I'm begging you. Don't leave me here."

Many Feathers had crawled up on the sleeping platform

and was snoring heavily. Soaring Raven tipped up the drinking gourd. Hunter didn't want to leave Jemma with him any more than she wanted him to, but there was no way he could keep up the charade and tell her as much.

He had to be convincing, had to walk out without a second glance if he was going to get her out at all.

"Let go of me, Jemma."

Her fingers uncurled one at a time. She drew a deep shuddering breath and dropped her gaze to the ground.

"I'll be back," he whispered.

Either she didn't hear him, or she didn't believe him. When she looked up again, the expression in her eyes was bleak. Sitting there in the dirt of the Choctaw hovel, she looked like a fallen angel. With all his heart, he wanted to scoop her up and carry her out.

As he turned away, he prayed that he could rescue her. If not, the look in her eyes would haunt him forever.

Her hands and feet bound by stout cord, Jemma lay in the dark staring up at the ceiling. A lazy stream of smoke drifted out of the smoke hole in the center of the dwelling. Battered by the river and the insults she had been dealt, she ached all over. The hard floor added insult to injury. Across the room, Many Feathers was snoring loudly enough to wake the dead.

Reeking of liquor, Soaring Raven had tied her hands and feet, his last act before he left the hut. Hope flared when she thought he might have been too befuddled to do a thorough job, but although she struggled with her bonds until her hands stung, she could not work free. She finally gave in to tears and let them stream silently down her face as she fought back the sobs that threatened to choke her.

She hated feeling weak and defeated. She refused to cry. Her father had never put up with her tears. Hunter had been unmoved by her plea. She wondered if and when he would come back, then asked herself: Why would he risk his life for her? Even though she had tried her hardest not to hinder him, she was slowing him down. This morning she had nearly cost him his life.

Why *should* he come back for her when she had been nothing but trouble since he'd first laid eyes on her?

Her nose itched. Her cheeks were streaked with unwanted tears. She couldn't do more than rub them with the backs of her bound hands. Forcing her eyes shut, she was determined to try to sleep despite the hard cold ground beneath her and the pain in her wrists and ankles. There was no time to be maudlin, no time to waste crying when she should be making plans. She would need to keep her wits about her. If Hunter failed to come back for her, she would have to save herself.

What seemed like hours later, Jemma heard stealthy footsteps beside her. Her breath caught in her throat. She forced herself to lie still and feign sleep. The fire had died out completely; the room was bathed in inky darkness. Slitting her eyes open, she could barely make out a tall shadowy figure moving toward her. She glanced at the sleeping platform and saw Many Feathers still lying there asleep. As much as she was repulsed by the idea of the old man trying to touch her, she knew she would have a much better chance fighting him off than Soaring Raven.

She interlaced her fingers, prepared to strike out with hands and feet as soon as the Choctaw touched her. She could feel the warmth of his body, smell the hickory-tainted scent of the fire when he knelt beside her.

Curling slightly in on herself, she lay like a wound spring, prepared to combat her attacker. With her eyes half-open, she watched the man lean closer, feeling the slightest waft of air as his hand moved toward her.

Just when she was about to scream, he reached out and covered her mouth and nose, cutting off all but a garbled cry. Fear snaked down her spine as he slid over her, pinning her with his weight. His warm breath hissed past her cheek. His voice was low in her ear.

"Don't make another sound if you expect me to get you out of here alive."

Jemma went limp with relief when she recognized Hunter's voice. Over his hand, she glanced across the room at the sleeping platform. She saw Many Feathers still lying there asleep. Soaring Raven might walk in at any moment and they would both be in jeopardy. She feared her pounding heart would give them away.

Without another word, Hunter rolled off Jemma and began to cut the bonds around her ankles and her wrists. He moved with stealth and silence, the only sounds in the room the *swish, swish* of the leather fringe on his clothing and Many Feathers's rhythmic snores.

He pulled her to her feet. Her legs buckled and she almost went down. Hunter slipped his arm around her shoulders and behind her knees, lifting her as if she weighed nothing. He had left the door ajar.

They slipped out into the night.

A dog curled up outside a hut raised his head and stared at them. Hunter froze. The dog yawned, sniffed, and went back to sleep. Jemma, her arms about his neck, tightened her hold as Hunter carefully made his way through the settlement. He felt solid and warm in the October night's chill, his arms a safe haven. She was tempted to nestle closer, to press her cheek against his shoulder and hide her eyes against his neck.

They reached the edge of the village. There was one last hut to pass. Hunter was moving soundlessly, like a ghost in the night, when the door of the hut opened, taking them both by surprise.

Soaring Raven stepped out and straightened to his full height. Half-nude, he stood there in flannel trousers, the blue stripe a dark slash in the darkness. Hunter gently let her down. As Jemma's feet hit the ground, she prayed her legs would hold her.

She felt Hunter tense at the first sight of the Indian. With a hand on the hilt of his knife, Hunter was braced for attack. Soaring Raven stood there watching them, but made no move to rouse the others. Instead, he crossed his arms over his bare chest and nodded slowly to Hunter.

"Go," he whispered.

"You're just letting us walk out of here? Why?"

Jemma was appalled that Hunter would even take time to question the man. Soaring Raven looked back at the hut he had just exited.

"I have three wives already. I don't need another. Besides, my father and the other old ones don't understand that keeping a white captive will bring your people down on us. Since the war with your English brothers ended, you have many soldiers in need of someone to kill. I would prefer it is not my people.

"Get as far away as you can by morning. My father will insist on a search. If we find you tomorrow, I will not be able to intercede."

chapter
8

THEY RAN AS IF THE HOUNDS OF HELL WERE AFTER THEM, out of the Indian village, into the forest, heads down, feet pounding. Hunter held tight to her hand, half-dragging her along behind him. Pine needles and twigs cut into the bare soles of her feet. Her breath was ragged, searing her throat. Just when she thought her heart would burst, he veered to the right.

"I hid the horses over there." Heading for a stand of trees, he stopped in front of the animals loaded with his remaining supplies. When he grabbed her around the waist, Jemma reached for the saddle horn and Hunter tossed her up onto her mount.

Grabbing the reins of both horses, he mounted up and headed away from the Indian village. How he could see anything, let alone the zigzag path through the trees, was beyond her, but he seemed to know where he was headed. She tightened her hold and hung on.

Jemma spent the rest of the night clinging to the saddle and glancing back over her shoulder, praying that she would not see a Choctaw search party closing in on them. All night long Hunter remained intense, tugging on her horse's reins whenever it balked, traveling along the intricate cobweb of Indian trails and buffalo runs. He crossed streams and backtracked.

As dawn melted the cover of darkness, the new day gained strength. The sky paled to gray and slowly came alive with streaks of light. Jemma began hoping he would stop longer than the usual time it took to swallow water or relieve themselves, but he pressed on at a frenetic pace until midday.

Finally, he forced the exhausted horses into the edge of a clear running stream. He dismounted, unaware of the water that soaked his moccasins and the hem of his pants. He walked back to Jemma and reached up to help her out of the saddle as if it were the most natural motion in the world.

The caring gesture was so simple, so unexpected, that she almost burst into tears.

"I think we're safe now." Hunter carefully lowered her to the ground, pausing for a heartbeat to trace her with his gaze. "Are you all right?"

"I think so."

Shaking from hours of riding, she clung to her horse's mane as Hunter walked away. The cool, rushing stream was a balm to the bruised, aching soles of her feet. When she felt steady, Jemma bent down and scooped up a handful of water, splashed it over her face and neck, and repeated the gesture until she felt cleaner. She cupped her hands and drank, letting the blessedly refreshing liquid spill down her chin.

When she had finally had her fill, she glanced up. Hunter was staring at her, but more than that, there was something dark and dangerous blazing in his eyes. She followed the direction of his gaze and looked down. The front of her shirt was soaked, clinging to every curve and swell of her breasts. Her nipples pressed like hard pebbles against the white fabric. She might as well have been standing there half-naked.

Quickly, she grabbed the fabric of her shirt and plucked it away from her skin, too embarrassed to look up until she heard his footsteps splashing away from her. He had turned his back and was walking toward his horse with long, determined strides.

Still holding the damp material off her skin, she half-expected him to mount up again. Instead, he stood beside his horse with his back to her, staring at a point somewhere over the saddle. His hands were balled into tight fists at his side. His shoulders rose and fell as if he were taking deep, even breaths.

"Are we going to make camp?" She forced the question out, trying to flush the burning embarrassment from her tone. She had seen raw hunger in his gaze and it had moved her. He might profess to be a loner, but Hunter Boone was a man, with a man's needs. His expression was something she would not soon forget, for it hinted at all the dark, secret sins the nuns had warned her about.

It was a while before Hunter responded. Time hung suspended in the dappled fall sunlight. Finally, she saw Hunter move, watched him pat his horse's neck once, lightly, before he gathered the reins and began to lead it along the edge of the stream.

"Follow me," he said over his shoulder, sparing her one quick glance and nothing more. "We'll stay in the streambed until we find a safe place to stop."

They walked in silence until Hunter found a clearing that was on high enough ground to afford a view of the surrounding landscape. Tall grass covered the gentle swells of land and offered camouflage as well as food for the horses. Jemma unloaded her own horse before he had a chance to help her, and then she sank wearily to the ground beside the canvas bundle of the few supplies and goods that were left.

"You'll have to be content with cornmeal mixed with cold water," he told her, unwilling to light a fire to take the chill out of the fall night air until he had put more time and distance between them and the Choctaw encampment.

"That will be fine." She was half-reclining, curled in

herself with a blanket across her shoulders. The edges were tightly drawn across her breasts, anchored in her fist. She carefully avoided meeting his eyes.

Hunter was every bit as circumspect, averting his gaze while the memory of the embarrassing scene at the stream, still so fresh in his mind, hovered unspoken between them. He cleared his throat and forced aside the image of Jemma's ample breasts pressed against the wet, white fabric.

"I can't leave you alone while I hunt for game," he began, concentrating on finding the bag of cornmeal.

"Aren't we out of danger?"

"Probably, but I don't want to take any chances."

"When Soaring Raven stepped out of that hut I thought we'd be murdered where we stood," she told him.

"The one thing the Choctaw don't need since the last rebellion is government troops raiding them." He poured clear water from a buffalo-bladder bag into a cupful of cornmeal to moisten it and began shaping a corn cake.

"Do you think we're safe?"

He looked around at the open landscape. "I hope so. I have a feeling Soaring Raven would try to discourage a search party after a few hours anyway." He finished the task, handed the cake to her, and dusted off his hands. "The Choctaw are the least of our worries now. We're out of bacon. Someone stole all the dried beef and sugar off the horse I took into the village. I had to throw away the flour and rice because water seeped into the sacks during the river crossing. We'll have to depend on what I can shoot. Maybe we'll come to an outpost."

"I need shoes and a hat," she said softly. "I'm sorry I lost the others. Well, I'm not really *sorry* I lost those shoes, but my feet are getting cold and my soles feel like pincushions."

When he looked up, he caught her trying to finger-comb her tangled hair. Outfitting her was the least of his problems. No matter what he tried to concentrate on, his mind

continually returned to the tantalizing image of her standing in the stream with her shirt clinging to her skin.

He'd grown hard at first glance and hadn't been able to
look away until she caught him staring. Her blue eyes had
gone so wide with shock that he still felt as guilty and
embarrassed as if he had been caught with his pants down.
He was just thankful that she couldn't know the intense
longing that had rocked him.

Although his swift reaction to her had been mortifying,
it was not surprising given the time they had spent together
on the trail, sharing not only the boredom and the danger,
but life's most intimate details. Even in filthy, oversized
clothing, with smudges of mud on her face and twigs in
her snarled hair, there was no denying Jemma's innocent
allure. After kissing her and holding her in his arms, he
didn't have to try hard to imagine what it would be like
to have more.

There had been an instantaneous flash of shock in her
eyes when she caught him staring at her breasts. Like a
coward, he had turned away, pretending to concentrate on
the powder horn hanging from his saddle while he waited
for his heated blood to cool.

"Hunter?"

He shook off thoughts that were far too arousing.
"What?" Afraid she was about to mention the scene in
the streambed, his hand stopped midway to the cornmeal
sack.

"Thank you for coming back for me," she said softly.
"I wouldn't have blamed you if you had left me there,
especially after the way I nearly got us both killed."

She spoke so softly, sounded so penitent, that he finally
chanced meeting her gaze. His heart lodged somewhere in
his throat when he realized that the brightness in her eyes
was caused by unshed tears.

"I would never have left you there." He couldn't tear
his eyes away from hers.

"I thought you drowned."

"I thought the same of you and realized I still don't even know your last name. Is there no one who cares about you, Jemma? If you had drowned in the Homochitto, is there no one who would mourn you?"

Her eyes darkened. She looked down at her hands. Once perfect, they were now streaked with dirt, her nails jagged, her palms blistered. Jemma tucked them out of sight beneath her thighs and stared at him thoughtfully.

"Those are strange questions for a loner."

"I have kin in Sandy Shoals who care about what happens to me."

She frowned and appeared thoughtful as she gazed off into the distance, her thoughts obviously far away. "I have 'kin', too."

"Where?"

She hesitated a bit too long. "I told you before. Canada." She didn't sound any more convincing than she had the first time she'd told him about wanting to find her father and brother. If she was running from something, or someone, she still didn't trust him enough to tell him. "My last name is O'Hurley," she blurted quickly, as if afraid she might change her mind. "Jemma O'Hurley."

Sensing her distress, he tried to lighten his approach. "So, you're Jemma O'Hurley, bound for the wilds of Canada, by way of a convent in Algiers?"

She nodded. "Now a former Indian captive, too, don't forget."

She smiled at him for the first time in two days and, despite the fact that his quick, visceral reaction to that smile annoyed him, Hunter felt as if the sun had just come out after a long rain spell. Her dimples teased her cheeks and his imagination. It would be all too easy to unlock the door to his heart, but what then? He didn't want a woman in his life, didn't need the ties that bind or the heartache that comes when they dissolve.

Guarding his heart and his future, he broke the connection and tended to the task at hand. He was silent throughout the modest meal and so was Jemma. By the time he had put away the cornmeal, the tension in the air was almost palpable. He stood up, prepared to walk the perimeter of the camp. Out of habit, he dusted off the seat of his buckskins and straightened his hat.

"Why don't you get some sleep?" he said. "I'll take the first watch."

"I don't know if I can sleep."

"Try."

"You'll wake me if there's any trouble?" She stood up and rubbed her arms. Her shirt had dried. He walked over to where she had left the striped wool blanket and picked it up.

"If there's trouble, you'll hear about it." Hunter opened the blanket and dropped it over her shoulders.

"Hunter?"

"What, Jemma?" The sun was going down, a shimmering ball of flame that set the deep grass glowing as if it were on fire. Sunset backlit her blond hair with shimmering highlights, creating a halo effect. She reminded him of an angel that heaven had misplaced.

He stopped a few yards away and looked back over his shoulder. She was on her knees, smiling up at him as she spread her bedroll out on the ground, looking far too vulnerable and innocent to be halfway to nowhere, all alone with him.

"No matter what happens, I want you to know this has been the grandest adventure of my life and well worth the gold piece."

He ran his hand over his stubbled jaw. It was the first time he felt like smiling all day.

"You mean escaping the emir's men didn't hold a candle to running from the Choctaw?"

Her dimples deepened. "Not when you throw in that river crossing and Many Feathers trying to buy me." She stood up and walked toward him. "And I'll never forget that horrible place, the Rotgut."

"With everything else, I'd almost forgotten about that."
He started to walk off again.

"Hunter?"

"What, Jemma?" He turned around. She walked over
to him, stopping just a few inches away.

"How much longer until we get to Sandy Shoals?"

"With luck, another week, week and a half. Plenty of
time for more adventure, if that's what you want."

"I hope not. I'll say a few prayers."

He watched her run her tongue over her lips. She was
staring at his mouth. He told himself to move. To check
on the animals, make certain all was secure. But he
couldn't budge.

"What will you pray for?" he asked, fighting not to
notice how close she was.

"It might surprise you." Her voice had dropped until it
was barely above a whisper.

"Nothing you do or say surprises me anymore."

Walk away, his conscience shouted. She was so close
he could feel her warmth. Her lips were too inviting, her
trust in him far too great. He was a man, not one of her
long-dead saints. Need pounded through him, urging him
to reach out and take her in his arms.

He kept his hands at his sides, determined not to touch
her. No matter how willing he wanted to think she might
be, she was far too innocent to know what hell she was
putting him through.

"Do you know what I was thinking when the river was
pulling me down?" She asked,

"No." He looked over her shoulder. Night engulfed
them. Above them, the starry sky cupped the land.

"I didn't want to die a virgin."

Her blunt admission shook him. "You shouldn't talk
like that, Jemma."

"Why not, when it's the truth?"

"You might give a man ideas." His head was already
chock-full of them.

"That's just what Sister Augusta Aleria always said."

"You should have listened to her. It's best to avoid trouble."

"You see making love as *trouble?*"

"Not if it's the right time or place."

"But not here, not now?"

"Jemma, you don't know what you're saying."

"I think I do, Hunter. I think I know very well what I'm saying and so do you."

"I think you must have hit your head on something in the river."

"You don't want to make love to me, is that it?"

"That's not it at all. It's just that . . . you put me in an awkward place."

"I've embarrassed you?"

"It isn't right—"

"You think a man should do the asking, is that it? It's a man's world, Hunter, but I think choosing the man who's to take her virginity is the one thing a woman ought to be able to decide for herself."

"I can't do this, Jemma." Dear God, he was actually beginning to shake with need.

"Something in your eyes tells me different, Hunter. Am I asking so much?" When she laid her hand on his arm he felt the touch vibrate through him.

"It's not as simple as kissing."

"Then show me," she urged.

"I don't have the right."

"Oh, yes. I know. The right should be reserved for my husband. I should save myself for someone willing to marry me. What if that man turns out to be someone of my father's choosing, not mine?"

"You haven't found your father yet—"

"But I know him well. What if he chooses someone old and toothless like Many Feathers, or someone cruel, or perhaps demented?"

"Surely he wouldn't—"

"You don't know my father. Why shouldn't the single most important act of my life be shared with someone I trust and admire?" She was angry, beneath the bravado of her outrageous request; he heard her bitterness.

"Jemma, don't." He was afraid her argument was actually beginning to make sense.

"Why shouldn't it be you?"

"You know why. I'm not looking to settle down."

"Nor am I. All I'm asking for is tonight."

He was going to burst and embarrass them both if she didn't quit talking. He wasn't made of stone. Pulling her into his arms, he silenced her with a kiss. One kiss, that's all, he told himself. One kiss and he would let her go, send her back to her bedroll. He kissed her long and deep, drew her sensual body close until she warmed his entire length. She was so soft, so willing.

"All I'm asking for is tonight." Her hushed whisper gave him pause. Was it so much, what she was asking? She knew him, trusted him. She had put her faith in him and her life in his hands since that night in New Orleans. Now she wanted more, without commitment, without thought for tomorrow. Where would they be tomorrow? No one could say for sure.

If nothing else, the past twenty-four hours had taught them both that life is a gift as fleeting, as temporal as a crystal droplet of dew balanced on the tip of a leaf. It was too precious to take for granted, too priceless to waste.

The bite of fall was in the air. Hunter enfolded Jemma in his arms and, without a word, held her against his heart. She was snug and warm in the striped blanket, and yet he could feel her trembling. When she tipped her head to look up at him, he smoothed her hair back off her face. She was silent, as if she knew that he was wrestling with his thoughts, weighing her request.

He cupped her jaw with his hand, traced her lips with his thumb. There was nothing about her that wasn't soft, except for her will, which had the strength of granite.

"Jemma, you make it hard for a man to say no," he whispered.

"Then don't."

"Are you afraid?"

She shook her head, turned her lips into his palm and kissed it. "Not of you."

Every intention he had of refusing her evaporated. He was lost.

She kissed his palm again. The land had grown so dark she couldn't read his expression, but she could feel the hesitation, the war that was being waged inside him.

She knew he wanted her. She had seen as much that afternoon in the stream, but now, most likely he thought she had taken leave of her senses. When he let go of her and took a step back, she wasn't surprised; she only wondered how she would ever be able to face him when dawn's light painted the sky with a new day.

Jemma watched him walk away without a word and felt like a fool.

She turned her back to the hastily set-up camp that was invisible in the sheer black of the moonless night. It was a blessing there was no fire. At least she could hide her embarrassment and chagrin until morning. Cradling her elbows with her hands, shivering, she tightened her arms and hugged herself. Rocking a bit, she stared up at the stars overhead and listened to the hoot of an owl somewhere in the distance as it joined the cricket songs and the *hush, hush* of the breeze that rustled the tips of the tall sea of grass.

Hunter was moving around near the supplies; she could hear him not far away. Wishing she could call back her impulsive request, she was certain he would be anxious to see the last of her.

"Jemma."

She started at the sound of Hunter's voice, foreign against the background of nature's night symphony. Half-turning, she tried to make him out in the dark. He seemed to be kneeling near the canvas of supplies.

"Hunter, I'm so—"

"Come here."

The apology died on her lips. Her heart hammered a bruising tempo. The blanket around her shoulders began to slip. She rescued it, tugged it up, and began dissolving the distance between them as she moved through the dark.

When she drew closer, she found him still hunkered down on one knee. He raised his hand. She slipped her fingers into his warm palm and he drew her down beside him.

"I put the bedrolls together," he said. "For warmth if nothing else. If you've changed your mind—"

"I haven't," she said, suddenly wondering at the enormity of what was about to take place. "What should I do now?"

He took the blanket from around her shoulders, unfurled it, and set it close by; then he reached for the hem of her shirt.

"Nothing. Let me do everything. It's what you wanted."

"And you? Do you really want to do this, Hunter?"

He paused in the act of drawing her shirt up and rested his hands at her waist. "I can't resist, not when it's something I didn't dare let myself think about these past days and nights."

She was not looking for a husband. She knew better than to expect words of love from a man who proclaimed himself a loner. He had only admitted that he could not resist her offer and she did not begrudge him that, for he was only human, but his touch spoke volumes. She felt calm. Quite certain she was doing the right thing. After tonight, there would be no fear of her father bartering away her virginity. No more wondering about *other things*.

His hands were warm and sure as he finished with her shirt, forcing her to kneel before him so that he could pull it over her head. She was bare from the waist up, half-naked and exposed to the night, which in itself sent an unmistakable thrill through her. Boston seemed a lifetime away with its crowded streets, the congested wharf, houses of brick and wood built close beside one another—the stringent, uncompromising rules of society that hemmed people in more than brick or mortar ever could.

She untied the thong at the nape of his neck, ran her fingers through his hair, and shook out the long, heavy mass. Any woman would have envied him this thick blond mane, yet there was nothing feminine about it. She suspected, now that she knew him better, that he wore it long as a sign of rebellion, a symbol of his frontier independence.

He sat back on his heels and pulled her closer until she was kneeling between his thighs. Gently, without a word, he lay his open hands on her shoulders, drew them down her skin, stroking her, leaving a trail of fire in his wake. When his fingers reached her breasts, he gently molded his palms to fit her, closed his hands over her and cupped her, squeezing lightly. She threw her head back and moaned, leaning into him, wanting more.

When he drew his hands away, exposing her heated flesh to the teasing night air, she trembled. His mouth replaced his hands. She gasped aloud when she felt the pull on her breast as he suckled.

"Did I hurt you?" he whispered.

She struggled to think of the word. "No."

He took her in his mouth again, caught her hardened nipple in his teeth and teased it. Deep inside of her, a wild primitive throb had begun to echo her heartbeat. She wanted him to go on and on forever, wanted to melt into him. Just when she was beginning to think that surely nothing, nothing he could do to her could make her feel any more glorious, she felt his fingers loosen the drawstring at her waist. The baggy trousers fell to the ground and pooled around her knees.

Before she could think, his hands slipped around and cupped her buttocks, lifted her and crushed her against him. His mouth slashed across hers, his tongue exploring, delving, teasing. She clung to him. With her arms locked about his neck, she pressed into him, wishing she could crawl inside his skin and know the mystery of him.

''Jemma.'' The word came on a rush of breath, more than a sigh, for there was wonder in his voice. It made her heady with delight.

Hunter rose to his knees. She could feel his hard arousal as he pressed her up against him. The cool, slick feel of his buckskin pants sent a shiver down her spine. He urged her back until she was lying on the bed he had fashioned out of blankets and waited, silent, expectant, aching with need while he shucked off his clothes and stretched out beside her.

chapter
9

IT WAS A NIGHT OF FIRSTS.

She was his first virgin, not to mention the first woman who had ever asked him to make love to her.

Drawing a blanket over both of them, he ran his hand down her side, along her ribs, over the gentle swell of her hip. It surprised him when he realized that his hand shook, that it was important to him that her first time be perfect.

Cloaked in the night, huddled beneath the blanket, he could not see her lovely body, so he committed it to memory with his touch. Her skin was smooth, flawless. Her breasts were lush and ripe, begging to be tasted, stroked, molded to his palm. She lay beside him, willing, anxious to discover, to give back. He felt her hands on him. Wherever he touched her, she mirrored his exploration.

When he cupped the mound between her legs, she gasped, but didn't draw away. Instead, she pressed into him, offering him more. Jemma ran her hand along his thigh until she grazed his throbbing manhood with her fingertips.

At the gentle touch, light as air almost, he shuddered and nearly spilled his seed. His breath caught in his throat and he lay there quivering, taut as a bowstring, fighting to gain control. Closing his eyes, he pressed his forehead to hers until his raging senses calmed.

"Are you all right?" she whispered against his mouth. He nodded, afraid to speak.

"Am I supposed to feel this way?"

Clearing his throat, he finally managed. "What way?" The words came out in a gravelly croak.

"Hot and cold all over. Like I'm about to . . . to fall apart inside."

"Yeah." He began to explore her with his fingers. Gently probing, he was surprised to find her moist, ready for him. His fingers, slicked with her dew, easily slipped inside. Hunter heard her gasp, felt a shudder reverberate through her slender frame.

"Hunter?" she whispered, almost frantic.

"What?"

"I . . . that's . . . oh! I feel so . . . is this . . . normal?"

"Yeah." He began to explore deeper, easing his fingers further, opening her, preparing the way.

She gasped against his lips, rocked against his hand.

"Hunter?"

"*What?*"

"Is this supposed to . . . feel so . . . so very *good*?"

"Jemma?" He strained for composure.

"What?"

"How about you just kiss me and let things happen without all the questions?"

"But—"

He covered her lips with his, thrust his tongue between her teeth, and increased the stroke of his fingers. Within seconds she forgot all about talking. Clinging to him, she dug her fingers into his shoulders, moving her hips to match the rhythm of his touch. He kept up the deep caresses until she began to whimper softly and then moan low in her throat. Finally breaking the kiss, she threw back her head and cried out when her release came.

He held her close as her body rocked with the pleasure of her first fulfillment. Smoothing his hand along her spine, he whispered, "Shh. Shh." Gradually she calmed and lay her head on his shoulder. Her breathing was still ragged. He was aching to slake his own thirst, but wanted to give her the chance to change her mind.

"Jemma?" He shrugged the shoulder she was using for a pillow.

"Hmm?" Her fingers were tracing his collarbone.

"We don't have to go on."

Her voice was lazy, seductive. She drew her fingertips over the rise of his shoulder, along his arm to his hip, feathering her touch across his pelvis.

"We've gone too far to turn back now," she whispered, voicing his own thoughts aloud.

"No, we haven't. You can keep your virginity, Jemma. No one will ever know."

"So far, it's brought me nothing but trouble. I don't want it."

But he did. He wanted it. God forgive him, he wanted to take her with every breath that left his body. He wanted to be her first. He wanted to slip inside that tight warm passage and carry the memory of it with him into the unknown wilderness of his future.

He wanted to give her what she wanted, take what he so desperately needed, and still believe they could go their separate ways with no regrets. She had asked for this night without stipulations. He would take her virginity, but he was determined not to spill his seed inside her. That way, there would be no danger of pregnancy, but he could have her none the less.

It was what the lady wanted. What he wanted.

Just once. Just for tonight.

He pressed her back on the blankets, drew her beneath him, nudged her legs wider with his knee and settled between her thighs.

Again, he touched her with his fingers, opened her, found her hot and ready. He kissed her deeply, cupped her face in his hands, and whispered against her lips, "This will hurt for a moment, but no more."

She kissed him back and slipped her arms around his neck, ready, willing, so achingly sweet.

He wrapped her thighs about his hips and touched the entrance to her honey-slicked depths with the tip of his shaft. When he eased inside her, she gasped, but held him close. Slowly, gently, he edged into her and then withdrew when he met resistance. He moistened himself with her dew before he entered her again. He had intended to go slowly, to repeat the movement until her virginity was breached, but when she suddenly shifted and opened herself to take more, his control snapped. He plunged, driving into her fully. He felt her tear, heard the sharp, anguished cry she tried to stifle.

She lay beneath him unmoving, but not resisting. He sensed that she was waiting for the pain to subside. His breathing was uneven, jagged as he hovered there above her until he could move slowly once more. Along his shaft, her sheath began to pulse, to tease, to quiver. Jemma was panting, moaning against his throat. Slowly, her hips began to undulate against his, demanding he move faster. Once again she was on the brink of release. Her fingers pressed into the flesh of his buttocks, urging him to go deeper, to take more.

He complied, slowly lunging into her until his movements picked up tempo and they were rocking together, climbing close to the precarious edge of fulfillment. Jemma cried out, tightened around him and lost control. Before he could withdraw, his own climax was upon him. Hunter threw back his head and cried out. Unwilling, unable to stop, he came deep inside her.

For a long while afterward, they did not speak. He held her close, knowing that, like him, she was staring up at the stars. He wondered what was going through her mind.

''Hunter?''

''What?''

''What are you thinking about?'' Her question echoed his thoughts.

"Nothing." And everything. She had entrusted him with her life on this journey and he had let his need override his common sense. Not only had he put her in danger while they made love and were vulnerable in the dark, open countryside, but worse, he had not been able to control his lust. Now only time would tell whether or not his seed would find fertile ground in her womb. Time he didn't have to give. Hunter sighed.

Still naked beneath the blankets, they lay on their backs, shoulders and arms pressed together, but otherwise not touching.

"What are you thinking about?" he asked.

"I was just looking up at all those stars, too many to count in a lifetime. It's strange, but I feel a part of it all now, a part of the whole universe. I've never felt that way before."

He found her pronouncement odd, seeing that she had her God and a whole host of saints. Even without all of that, he had always felt a part of a bigger whole.

"You know what else?" she asked.

"What?"

"Lying here next to you, thinking about what just happened between us, I know that no matter what the nuns ever said, I'm certain, without a shred of doubt, that what we just shared had nothing whatsoever to do with sin, or the everlasting torment and fires of hell."

He didn't know what to say. He didn't believe what they had done was wrong, either. They were adults, on the edge of nowhere, far from the restrictions that society imposed, but if the ground had just fallen away, he couldn't have felt any more shaken or unsure. With that one soul-shattering act, he might have created a child. More frightening than that, while he'd held her, his mind had pulsed with visions of clearing the land, of building and putting down roots. Of babies and gardens. Of waking up to new-fallen snow and watching countless sunsets with this woman in his arms.

He had envisioned seductive images that he wanted to avoid dwelling on. Things that had no place occupying the private, guarded corners of a loner's mind.

Letting the conversation die seemed the easiest way out. Hunter lay tense but silent until he heard her breathing deep and easy. Sandwiched between Jemma and his Kentucky long rifle, Hunter slid his hand over to the gun. It was primed and ready in case there was trouble.

Jemma shifted and rolled over in her sleep, threw her leg over his and nuzzled up beside him. Her skin was soft as a duckling's down, far too tempting to ignore. She was sound asleep. Because she would never know that he could not resist touching her again, with a light, gentle movement Hunter laid his hand on her thigh. Sleep would elude him tonight. He contented himself with watching the constellations move across the heavens, vowing never to give into temptation again.

To Jemma, the next two weeks seemed endless. They found a shabby tobacco plantation on the edge of the wood, where Hunter was able to trade fresh venison for thick woolen stockings and a pair of moccasins for her. Closer to settled lands, the last major river crossing they had to endure was accomplished by ferryboat.

As they headed north, the landscape changed dramatically. Grassy open plains gave way to great forests of oaks, hickory, ash, maple, and even cottonwood. Even though fall had painted the leaves and then stripped them from the trees, Jemma couldn't help but think of how wondrously full the forest must look in spring and summer.

Since the night she would forever think of as the end of her virginity, Hunter had become increasingly distant, worse than he had been on the first few days of the journey. He barely spoke more than to issue orders when they made camp. At times she found him watching her closely, speculatively. She knew what was wrong, that he no doubt regretted taking her virginity, but she couldn't find the words to make things right between them.

The night they had shared was never far from her thoughts. A thousand times a day, memories crept back without invitation, haunting her with flashes of sensual recollections, stirring her intensely. More than anything else, she realized she had been naïve to think that she could let Hunter possess her and *not* dwell on such a momentous occasion.

He had been so gentle, so kind. How could she stop thinking of the man who had made her senses sing? How could she not want to repeat the experience again and again? Her heart beat triple-time whenever he looked her way, when their hands met accidentally or their gazes locked. She doubted that he had erased the memory altogether, but he had certainly steeled his heart against it.

He seemed to grow more anxious to get to their destination with every passing hour and pushed on unmercifully. Being hungry and tired had become part of her existence. When she finally questioned him, asking if he was intent on killing them both and the horses, he merely shook off her complaint and said, ''I've been at this too long. I need to get back.''

Now, as they traveled along the bluff above the Mississippi, she couldn't help but notice he had become even more preoccupied than usual. They rode to the top of a knob, as Hunter called the upswells of land, and Jemma fought to keep her gaze from straying his way time and again. She had forced her attention to late asters growing alongside the trail when Hunter suddenly reined in.

''There it is. That's Sandy Shoals,'' he said.

Astonished by the love and pride in his tone, she drew up beside him and stared down at what appeared to be little more than a gathering of log structures of all shapes and sizes. They were almost within shouting distance.

Captivated, she stared at the scene below. Lazy smoke drifted up from the chimneys of two of the larger cabins, lacing the air with the comforting smell of hickory. Huddled above the river, the settlement was surrounded by dense woods on three sides. Here and there, burned-out remains of enormous tree stumps scarred the open land. In one field, half a crop of dried cornstalks had been cut and bundled. Thick ground vines of pumpkins and other squash trailed between the rows. A smaller vegetable garden had been laid out close to one of the cabins.

"Is this the outskirts of town?" She had seen two cities in her life: Boston and New Orleans. Surely this group of cabins, some half-hidden by trees, was not the entire settlement of Sandy Shoals.

"There is no town. Our only other neighbor is my friend Noah LeCroix. He lives a bit farther north, in a house he built on stilts over a lake formed by the big earthquake a few years back. Noah's a half-breed; his mother was a Cherokee, his father a French trapper. He's legendary for piloting river craft over the shoals downstream. Not a boat captain goes through here that doesn't want to hire Noah on to see him through."

It seemed incredible to her that there were no shops or stores, no carriages or cobblestone streets, no sound other than the rushing river, bird songs, and the chatter of a jay in a nearby oak. It was wonderful, an enchanted village that might very well have been tucked away in the Black Forest, a magical place where mystical creatures existed side-by-side with settlers.

"It's not much," Hunter said, his love for the small, crude settlement evident in his tone. Even as he denied its raw beauty, she could see the pride on his face and wondered what it must be like to have carved a life out of the wilderness.

"It's wonderful. Like something out of a storybook."

His gaze swung her way. Although he tried to hide it, she could tell that he was pleased by her words. It surprised her that he cared so much. She wondered if he even realized that he did. A chilly breeze kissed with the promise of winter played with her hair before it moved on. Jemma shivered and tucked the edges of her coat up around her throat. Hunter had nudged his horse into a walk down the gentle slope.

"Where is everyone?" she asked.

"It's time for the midday meal. Nette's probably set out the dinner by now."

"Nette?"

"The widow woman who cooks and takes care of Lucy for me."

Her heart stilled. *"Lucy?"*

"You recall I said a woman taught me a hard lesson? Her name was Amelia White. When she left me, she left her daughter, Lucy, behind."

"Is she your daughter, too?"

"No, not mine. She's fifteen. Nette takes care of her."

She found it strange that such a loner was connected to this place by so many ties. As she wondered about this woman who cooked for Hunter and a mother who would abandon a daughter, her stomach rumbled. Jemma's mouth watered at the thought of an actual meal served at a real table. "I can't wait to take a hot bath," she said, half to herself, but she doubted that something as simple as a bath would take the ache out of her bones and the chill out of her body.

With a few more yards, the Mississippi came into full view.

"Would you look at that?" Hunter had stopped and was staring at the river below them. From this new vantage point she could see the riverbank clearly. What appeared to be a substantially large boat was docked at a landing fashioned of wood. A series of crude, crooked wooden steps wound their way up the embankment.

"A boat?"

"A steamboat," he amended. "First one made it up the river last year. This is the third expedition we've seen."

"You don't sound pleased."

He shrugged. "It means there'll be more people moving in. Trade goods will be moving up and down the river faster."

She thought of what steamboat trade would mean to her father's expanding business and knew what Thomas O'Hurley's reaction would be. "That's good, isn't it?"

"For some. For me, I'm just glad I decided to be movin' on." He didn't meet her eyes as he shifted in the saddle and adjusted the reins. "I imagine Nette and Luther have their hands full right now trying to get everyone fed. Looks like that bath of yours is going to have to wait."

"That's all right. I don't—What are you staring at?"

He was assessing her, his gaze sweeping over her face, her hair, her hands where they gripped the reins. And he was frowning. "Nothing."

"I can tell by the look on your face that you're thinking of *something*. What is it?" It was obviously a thought that was giving him grief.

"You could get up north a lot faster if you're aboard when she pulls out."

"Who?"

"The steamboat."

Intense, unexpected panic swept her, unlike any she had known before. "North?"

"On to Canada. To find your father." He prodded her memory.

Her heart hit her stomach. "Canada," she whispered.

Endless miles of grueling travel. Weeks, perhaps months. Stifling a groan, she wished the world had suddenly shrunk to the size of a pea. She was almost tempted to blurt out the truth—that she must have been addlepated to undertake this trip. She had been bent on adventure, unaware of the costs or the consequences.

She didn't want to think of heading north. Right now she was weary to the bone and wanted nothing more than to plunk down until she felt rested enough to decide what to do. Frowning down at the steamboat, feeling as if it

were some evil force sent to spirit her away, Jemma realized with aching clarity that the very last thing she
wanted to do was board that boat.

Nor did she think she could bring herself to say good-
bye to Hunter Boone just yet.

"I—" She started to object, but he was already on his
way.

Jemma cast another glance at the steamboat and hurried
to catch up. She followed Hunter to the largest cabin—the
one that fronted the river—dismounted, and tied her horse
to the hitching post beside his. When he opened the door,
the deceptive peace outside was shattered by the din of
voices and the press of too many bodies crowded in one
room. Makeshift trestle tables were set up end-to-end, covering nearly every inch of open floor space.

As if they had not eaten in weeks, men of every size
and description sat shoulder-to-shoulder and shoveled
down forkfuls of generous mounds of ham, mashed potatoes smothered in brown gravy, and string beans mixed
with bacon. Two spotted hounds ran back and forth beneath the tables, noses to the ground, hoping for any scrap
that might hit the floor.

A white-haired woman whose lined face told a story of
its own carried a heaping platter of ham over to one of the
tables. Reed-thin, with her hair wound into a bun at the
nape of her neck, she moved with the agility of a woman
half her age, bantering easily with the men as she refilled
their plates, urging them to "eat up, 'cause these are the
best vittles you'll see anywheres."

Two others helped serve the travelers. One was no more
than a girl, with lanky, unkempt hair, wearing a faded
brown dress that was a good five inches too short. Unlike
the older woman, the girl spoke to no one, nor did she
make eye contact. She slipped around the room so quietly,
so unobtrusively, that she was barely noticed.

Jemma was hard-pressed to tell the age of the third
woman in the room, but guessed she might be in her twen-

ties. Her hair was chestnut, her face weather-worn; and she was thin but smiling and cordial to the guests at the crowded tables. She and the older woman had established a routine, one assisting the other when needed, handing platters and bowls back and forth without having to communicate in words. Jemma realized with a tinge of jealousy that she had never been in such communion with another living soul.

There was so much commotion in the room that no one had yet noticed their entrance. Hunter leaned close and said, "I'm going behind the counter to help Luther." He nodded in the direction of a tall blond man who looked very much like him but was of slighter build. It wasn't until then that Jemma realized that the cabin must be the trading post Hunter had mentioned.

Around the walls were rows of shelves lined with various and sundry items, neatly folded piles of blankets, and cooking pots and pans of every shape and size. She recognized barrels of dry staples and stacks of folded fabrics. Hunter's brother was spreading out what looked like an iron trap along the wood plank counter where it could be more easily displayed.

Oddly, when Hunter stepped away from her, she felt abandoned and more out of place than ever. Glancing down, she became aware of her bedraggled appearance. The baggy trousers were stiff with dirt and mud. She was thankful that the heavy wool coat covered the white shirt now soiled beyond redemption. Reaching up, she tried to shove the trailing ends of her tangled hair beneath her hat, but it was so hopelessly snarled that her fingers caught and pulled. Tempted to step back outside and find a stream or even a horse trough where she could wash, she looked up just in time to see that the older woman standing not two feet away had lost her grip on a heavy platter piled high with ham.

Jemma dove for the platter and grabbed it just before it hit the ground. A few pieces of the slippery ham had barely touched the wood plank floor when the hounds ran over, tails high and wagging furiously, and gulped them down without chewing.

Jemma straightened to hand the woman the platter and found the gray-haired lady watching her closely.

"You just now coming in off the steamboat? You almost missed the meal," the woman said. Without looking away, she passed the platter on to a bearded man sitting at the end of the table.

"No, I came in with Hunter."

"*Hunter?*" The woman's gaze swung around the room. When she saw Hunter behind the long counter with Luther, her stare whipped back to Jemma. This time the matron looked her up and down. "Well, I swan. Don't that beat all. I'll bet once you're all washed up you're prettier than a June bug with those dimples and big blue eyes."

Somehow, the woman made being as pretty as a June bug sound like the grandest compliment in the world. Jemma found herself smiling.

"I'm Jemma."

"I'm Nette Taylor. You stayin' on, Jemma?" Nette glanced over at Hunter again.

"Well, I don't—"

The tall, chestnut-haired woman bustled up to Nette. She cradled an empty bowl in her arms. She was reed-thin; her calico dress hung from her shoulders without touching her anywhere.

"We're out of potatoes, Nette." There were questions in the woman's eyes as her gaze settled curiously on Jemma.

"I'm not mashing any more potatoes for this bunch. They've had enough. 'Sides, none of 'em will go away from my table starvin'. At this point they're eatin' out of sheer gluttony and for fear they won't get better where they're goin'." Nette nodded at Jemma. "Hannah, this is Jemma." There was a dramatic pause before the woman added, "She just come in with Hunter."

"Hunter's back? Thank the Lord. When these men are finished eating they're going to want whiskey and supplies, and Luther already has his hands full." She nodded to Jemma. "I'm Hunter's sister-in-law. Luther's wife. Glad to meet you."

Jemma didn't miss the look that passed between Nette and Hannah before Hannah said, "So, you came in with Hunter?"

"Yes. I needed a guide upriver—"

One of the steamboat passengers called out to Nette. She waved in his direction. "Let's get the apple pie passed 'round so we can get these men on their way. We could sure use your help, Jemma."

Jemma blinked twice and looked down at her soiled clothing. Obviously, her ragged appearance meant nothing to Nette or Hannah. The young girl she had seen earlier and assumed was Lucy had disappeared. Hannah was already back to serving the travelers. Jemma took in the boisterous crowd at the long tables and then glanced over at Hunter. He stood behind the counter dispensing shots of whiskey out of a stoneware jug, too involved even to look over and see how she fared.

Nette walked away, obviously taking Jemma's silence for agreement. Jemma experienced a moment of panic. She had never in her life served a meal, never even carried a platter to the table. Used to being waited on, she had no idea how or where to begin, what to say or do, but before she could hesitate any longer, Hannah was walking toward her with a wooden tray crowded with an array of mismatched plates that held golden slices of warm apple pie. Her mouth began to water as she slipped off her hat and coat and set them aside.

"Here," Hannah said, handing her the tray. "Pass these out while I go cut more. And make sure nobody takes more than one piece or there won't be enough to go around."

Hannah left her standing with the heavy tray in her hands. Jemma took a deep breath and, carefully balancing the heavy load, cautiously walked over to the tables. When she began handing out plates of pie, a ruckus went up from the men when they realized dessert had arrived. They were a rowdy lot, talking of little but their experiences on the trip upriver, the impending cold weather, and Nette's delicious apple pie. Although none of them appeared to be what Thomas O'Hurley would have considered a cultured gentleman, no one made any undue remarks to Jemma while she moved among them. They were respectful and grateful for the meal.

When they were finished, one by one the men left the table and began milling around in the section of the large room that was devoted to supplies and other items. Some took the time to pull up a barrel, relax, and enjoy a pipe full of tobacco. Others went straight to the counter for whiskey or to barter with Hunter and Luther over blankets, hardware, gunpowder and shot, and staples. As the travelers left the table, Nette and Hannah began clearing the avalanche of dirty dishes the men had left behind.

Jemma followed their lead and pitched in to help, carrying stacks of empty plates and platters, soiled flatware, and mismatched glasses, mugs, and cups out to a smaller cabin that had been added on behind.

The addition was barely as large as the foyer in her house in Boston. It was attached to the end wall of the trading post and contained its own fireplace, a huge, cavernous affair made of stone and mortar. Water was boiling in large pots on hooks sunk into the fireplace wall; the steam added warmth to the already overheated room. Jemma let the close heat seep into her, a welcome delight after so many days and nights with only a low campfire for warmth.

She set down a stack of dishes beside one of the washtubs filled with warm water. While Hannah went back to the dining room for more plates, Jemma paused a moment to stand before the fire and let the heat and steam seep into her. Pushing stray, tangled curls back off her face, she took a deep breath and then turned away from the fire, intent on going back for more plates.

"You look tired enough to drop. Why don't you amble over to my cabin just across the way and take a little nap? If I know Hunter Boone, you two didn't waste any time coming up the Trace."

Jemma turned around and found Nette, up to her elbows in dishwater, watching her from across the room. Stacked on a crude log table beside her sat what appeared to be an entire pantryful of dishes and soiled utensils. There were huge dirty pots and pans stacked on the hearth.

"How on earth are you going to get all this done?" Jemma shook her head in awe. She had no intention of leaving the woman with all this work.

"One dish at a time," Nette laughed, undaunted.

Jemma smiled and began rolling up her sleeves. "Tell me what to do," she said.

Nette looked at her face closely, and then down at her hands. It appeared she was about to refuse the help, but then said, "Not much to it. You just pick up one of those dish towels on the stack over yonder and when I hand you a wet plate, you wipe it dry."

For over an hour they worked side-by-side, Nette chatting about the wonder of the steamboat. She predicted that steam was a passing fancy and said there was nothing safer and more riverworthy than a nice, sturdy flatboat. Hannah bustled in and out, carrying in more dirty dishes. Nette talked while Jemma wiped the dishes dry, pausing only to change dish towels as needed.

Slowly, the pile of clean items grew, while the dirty ones disappeared into Nette's dish tubs. Jemma didn't realize the full extent of her exhaustion until Hannah called on her to help carry a steaming pot of water over to the tub. As the steam billowed up into their faces, Jemma felt her head begin to swim. When the pot was emptied, she quickly stepped back, crossed the room and leaned against the stone fireplace. Neither Hannah nor Nette had noticed.

"I need to go see about the children," Hannah was telling Nette. "It shouldn't take long. Noah volunteered to look after them while I helped out here." She reached up and tucked a wisp of her long hair behind her ear. To Jemma, the sound of her voice seemed to be coming from far, far away.

"We're nearly done, thanks to Jemma here," Nette said. "No need for you to come back. Stay home and tend to all those young'uns if you need to."

Hannah took a coat off a peg on the wall, slipped it on, and left after a quick good-bye to Jemma, who hadn't left the fireplace. Nette turned her way and paused, studying her closely. "You look white as a sheet. You feel all right?"

Jemma was afraid to speak. Her head was spinning; her knees felt as if they were slowly dissolving. There was a distinct, increasing hum in both her ears.

Nette's image began to blur. Frightened by the strange sensations, Jemma began, "I'm not . . . I don't . . ."

Before she could explain, the room went black.

chapter
10

TOO MANY PEOPLE IN ONE ROOM TENDED TO MAKE HUN-
ter nervous, even if they were spending money that was
going into the till. Riding over the knob earlier and seeing
the steamboat anchored off Sandy Shoals had given him a
shock. He had suspected it was just a matter of time before
steam travel took over the river, but he hadn't realized that
day might be just around the corner. They never saw more
than an occasional keelboat this time of year, so the steamboat crowd had been a surprise, not just to him, but everyone at Sandy Shoals.

"'Nother whiskey." A short, balding, obnoxious man
standing at the counter in front of Hunter tapped his glass
impatiently on the stained wood bar.

"Three-shot limit," Hunter told him as he moved to
pour a glass for a traveler farther down the line.

"I never heard of such a thing," the short man sputtered, his fingers clutching the empty whiskey glass. He'd
already had his share and was showing the effects.

"It's my post and my liquor. I figure I can make whatever rules I want." Hunter wasn't in the mood to argue.
Luther walked up beside him and crossed his arms over
his chest.

"Trouble?" Luther asked. Hunter knew that side-by-

side they presented a formidable front, both of them over
six feet and in prime condition.

"Ask him," Hunter nodded to the short gent.

The man slammed his glass on the counter, craned his
neck to eye each of them in turn, and backed down. "None
at all," he groused. Hunter watched the disgruntled cus-
tomer pick his way through the room.

"When did the steamboat dock?" Hunter wiped down
the wet counter with a damp rag, keeping his eye on the
other men sidled up to the bar. He might sell the best
whiskey in Kentucky, but he couldn't abide anyone abus-
ing Luther's liquor to the point of drunkenness.

"Just this morning. Took a while for Nette and Hannah
to lay out the meal for so many. I even made Lucy come
in and serve, but shortly after you got here and that little
friend of yours began to help, she slipped out back."

Hunter had seen Jemma moving around the tables with
a tray of pie and helping Nette and Hannah clear dishes.
Even when he wasn't looking her way, he knew where she
was and what she was doing.

"I don't know what's gonna become of Lucy," he told
Luther. "She's scared of her own shadow." She'd been
shy even before her mother had deserted her like so much
extra baggage; what little confidence Lucy had was slowly
diminishing.

"Who is she anyway?" Luther asked.

"Who?"

"Come on, Hunter. That little blond dressed like a boy
who sneaked in the door behind you. Who is she?"

His brother was trying to keep his query sounding nonchalant, but Hunter could tell that Luther was curious as
hell.

"Her name's Jemma O'Hurley. That's all I know about
her, except that she paid me good money to bring her
upriver and she's headed for Canada."

"That's *it?*"

Hunter pinned Luther with an impatient look. "That's it, little brother, so quit diggin'."

"She's traveling *alone?*"

"Yep. Says she's trying to hook up with her father and brother in Canada, but I don't believe a word of it."

"Why not?"

" 'Cause she's fed me a full bucket or two of hogwash already. I don't know who she really is or what she's really up to."

"Canada? Then you can put her on the steamboat when it pulls out." Luther was watching him closely.

Hunter kept his reaction well hidden as he scanned the room. Men of every shape, size, and description filled the place, all of them different, all with one thing in common—they were headed up the Mississippi to the Missouri as far as the boat would take them and on to parts unknown. Some were scoundrels, some honorable, but he couldn't tell by looking at them which was which. There wasn't a woman among them.

"Hunter?" Luther prodded.

"What?"

"So will she be taking the steamboat when it pulls out?"

Luther was watching him so closely that it set Hunter's teeth on edge, but more than that, trying to picture Jemma traveling with these strangers—fending for herself, the only woman around for miles, alone, at the mercy of her fellow passengers—was making his stomach turn. He glanced across the room at the fat drunk leaning against a table, spitting as he babbled into another man's face, slurring his words.

"No," Hunter said abruptly, surprising himself. "No, Jemma won't be on the steamboat when it pulls out. She'll leave with a family headed north when one comes through." He wasn't putting the woman who might be carrying his child on a steamboat unescorted.

"It's November now, Hunt. Not many more comin'

through here headed north till spring. She might be here for months if you don't send her on her way."

Hunter swung around, about to tell his brother to mind his own business. Luther was grinning from ear to ear.

"That's what I thought," Luther said.

"I never figured you for much of a thinker," Hunter told him. "Why do you have that stupid grin on your face?"

"I didn't think she'd be leavin' today, not after the way I saw you watching her every move while she served up dessert. You never took your eyes off her longer than a minute. Know what I think?" Luther didn't wait for an answer before he volunteered his opinion. "I think you got feelings for her."

"What I feel is like knocking that stupid grin off your face, Luther."

Instead of taking offense, Luther laughed out loud. Hunter tried to ignore him as he moved down the length of the counter to where a man stood with a pile of dry goods, waiting to turn over his coin.

The back door opened and Nette came running into the room, the front of her faded apron soaked with dishwater. Her white hair, damp from steam and perspiration, stuck to her forehead and temples. She shoved her way through the men who stood shoulder-to-shoulder at the bar.

"Hunter, you better come quick! That little stray you dragged in just fainted dead away in my kitchen."

Hunter vaulted the counter and hit the ground running. Anyone unfortunate enough to be in his way found himself reeling across the room. He pounded into the kitchen, his heart beating louder than his feet on the oak plank floor. Jemma was lying on her side, her eyes closed, her face as pale as a catfish belly.

He reached for her, gently laid his hand against her throat, and felt for a pulse.

"Jemma?" He half-lifted her into his arms, cradling her

head and shoulders in the crook of his arm as he brushed her hair back off her face.

Nette ran in and stood behind him, peering down at Jemma over his shoulder. "She's out like an empty lantern."

"What in the hell happened?" He knew he sounded harsh, but was unable to control himself.

"She was helping with the dishes, walked over to stand by the fireplace and next thing I know, she went white and had a dazed look on her face. Then she dropped."

"Jemma?" Hunter repeated her name, holding her against his chest.

"When was the last time she ate?" Nette demanded of him. "Or slept? She looks plumb wore out, Hunter. If I know you, you beat her into the ground to get here. She's not a man, like you. Did you expect her to keep up every step of the way?"

He had, and he regretted it now, but he'd be damned if he would admit either.

"Get me a wet cloth," he said.

Nette soaked a dishcloth in the bucket of cold creek water and handed it to Hunter. He pressed it to Jemma's forehead and cheeks.

"Just like you not to notice she was bone tired," Nette grumbled behind him, still hovering over his shoulder. She reached out to smooth back Jemma's hair. "Pretty little thing. Don't think she ever did a lick of kitchen work before. She was scared to death she'd break somethin'. Held those old chipped plates and glasses like they was fine china."

Jemma began to stir. Hunter handed the rag back to Nette.

"Jemma?" He spoke softly. Afraid to startle her, he shook her gently. Her lips twitched and her eyelids fluttered. Her lashes were spun gold, thick half moons against her pale cheeks. A smattering of freckles coaxed by sunshine were scattered across the bridge of her nose. They had not been there when he met her.

"Jemma?"

Although she didn't open her eyes, her fingers closed tight around his shirtfront.

"Grandpa?" she whispered.

Nette hooted. "*Grandpa?*"

"Jemma, it's me," Hunter said, giving her another jiggle. "It's Hunter."

Her eyelids fluttered again and finally her eyes opened.

"Hunter?" She focused on Nette, who was standing over his shoulder, then around the kitchen cabin. Finally she looked up into Hunter's eyes. She struggled to sit up. "What happened?"

His relief was overwhelming. He didn't know whether to shake her for scaring the wits out of him or hold her close. Since he was already holding her, he decided to just hang on a minute more until she got her bearings.

"You passed out. Nette here's certain I've been starving you."

Jemma looked up at Nette and offered her a weak smile and a nod. "He has. Corn cakes and water. An occasional rabbit."

"Take her over to my place, Hunter, and make her comfortable," Nette directed. "I'll just make up a plate for her and bring it right over."

Jemma struggled to sit up. Hunter helped her to her feet, but kept his arm firmly around her waist. A loud shrill whistle sounded, long and high.

"Steamboat'll be leaving in a half hour. They're calling everyone back aboard," Nette explained.

"The steamboat," Jemma whispered.

There was uncertainty in her eyes and something more, something he hadn't seen since before they escaped the Choctaw camp. Fear.

She clutched his shirtfront. "You said that it was headed north . . . that I should go . . . and I—" She paused, waiting for him to do something, to say something. Anything.

Hunter shifted uncomfortably, his arm still riding her waist, his hand resting on her hip, where it seemed to belong. His mouth had gone dry. For the life of him, he couldn't think of what to say or do. She had been dead set on heading to Canada, but since New Orleans she had rarely, if ever, mentioned the father or brother she had been so desperate to find.

It was hard to think with her looking up at him with those trusting blue eyes. Perhaps she hadn't thought through the ramifications of the night they had shared in each other's arms. Was she so innocent that she didn't realize she might be with child? There was no way he was going to send her on, no way he could leave Sandy Shoals until he knew for certain. For a few days more, at least, they were ordained to be together.

Before he had time to say anything, Nette said, "You don't mean to put this child on that boat any more than I do, Hunter Boone. Now you just get her over to my cabin and see that she's comfortable. I'll get some vittles dished up."

Hunter let out a pent-up sigh that he didn't even know he'd been holding and looked down at Jemma. She was watching him closely, tentatively, as if she expected him to object. He could feel her trembling.

He bent and scooped her up into his arms, cradling her against him. She was as light as a feather.

"What are you doing?" she said, as she slipped an arm around his neck without protest.

"When Nette gives an order, she expects it to be followed."

The air outside had grown colder, the sky dark and leaden. The first snow of the season would fall before morning. He could feel it in his bones, smell it on the dry fall air.

"I'll miss the steamboat." She looked toward the river, but didn't sound all that disappointed.

Hunter wanted to attribute her lack of enthusiasm to exhaustion, not the haunted look he had seen in her eyes earlier.

"There'll be a keelboat along soon enough. Better that you go with a family than that motley crew out there."

"I don't have any money left to pay for passage anyway," she said as they passed the smokehouse with its distinct hickory smell. "I was thinking about that while I was drying dishes. I was thinking maybe I could work for you . . . so I could save up enough for passage upriver. I'll have to pay my way when another boat comes along."

He frowned down at her. He suspected Nette had been right when she said the girl hadn't ever done a lick of work in her life. At least not of the house-tending kind, anyway.

"Why are you looking at me that way?"

"I can't quite see you slopping hogs or baking pies."

"And why not?"

"I don't know. I don't imagine you had much practice at the convent."

"I can learn."

"About all I've ever seen you do is pray."

They had reached another cabin, this one not as small as the kitchen outbuilding nor as large as the trading post. He lifted the latch and the door swung inward to reveal another one-room affair with rough walls and a loft that covered half the room. Poised in the center near a spinning wheel, looking like a cornered doe with nowhere to run, stood Amelia White's girl, Lucy.

She was tall and thin, her hair of a nondescript brown shade that matched the drab, too-small dress she was wearing. Parted in the center, her hair had been fashioned into a simple knot at her nape. Stray locks straggled from the uneven part and hung into her eyes.

"It's only me, Lucy." He didn't miss the girl's immediate relief.

"Hey, Hunter," she said so softly he barely heard her.

"Turn back the quilt, will you, Luce, and watch after Jemma till Nette comes in?"

He carried Jemma over to Nette's bed in one corner of the room, knowing better than to set her atop one of Nette's prized patchworks as filthy as she was.

Lucy flitted over to the bed, turned down the spread, and backed herself into the corner where she could observe without being noticed.

"I've got to go back and help Luther," he told them, his gaze on Jemma. She looked young and vulnerable and lost sitting there in the middle of the big bed. He felt lower than a skunk's belly for what he had done and wished he had never obliged her when she'd talked him into taking her virginity.

"Sit tight and Nette will be right here. This is Lucy. She'll look after you."

"I'm fine," she told him. He watched Jemma's gaze flash over to Lucy, curiosity plain in her eyes. When he failed to move, Jemma looked up at him again and said, "What are you looking at?"

"Nothing. I've got to go."

He turned abruptly and headed for the door, wondering what in the hell had come over him. After he'd set Jemma on Nette's bed, he felt as if his feet had been nailed to the floor and he couldn't move. Seeing her there in the cabin with her face still smeared with dirt and streaked from the steam in the kitchen, garbed in the filthy, tattered boys' clothing, she appeared so defenseless, so vulnerable, that he hated to leave her.

Shaken, he walked out of Nette's cabin without a backward glance. Head down, he marched back to the trading post, where he found Luther counting the money in the battered metal cashbox while Hannah straightened up the benches at the trestle tables, sweeping under them as she went.

"She all right?" Luther said as Hunter crossed the floor.

Hannah stopped to greet him. "Welcome home, Hunter. How's Jemma?"

"Fine." He wasn't about to say more until he looked up and found them waiting expectantly for an explanation. "She's exhausted and hungry. Nette's going to fix her a plate and see to her."

Hannah propped the broom in the corner and wiped her hands on her apron, then walked over to the table closest to the counter. She sat down on the end of the table and braced her hands on each side of her, wrapping her fingers around the edge.

Hunter looked at his brother's wife, thinking that if he were the marrying kind, he'd be lucky to find a wife as good-hearted and hard-working as his brother's. Hannah and Luther had been married seven years and had four children already. She'd been a bride at sixteen, already pregnant on the way to Kentucky from Ohio. Together they'd seen trials and heartaches, winters of want and sickness, but still, whenever Hannah looked at Luther, her love shone bright in her eyes and her smile.

Yes, if he were the marrying kind and not a loner, he'd want a woman like Hannah. Amelia had been flighty, with a head full of clouds and the body of a siren. She had never even held a candle to his capable, loving sister-in-law, but Hunter hadn't seen that until it was too late.

"Where'd you find this one, Hunter?" Hannah asked. "I thought after Amelia you'd learned about inviting home strays."

"Jemma's not anything like Amelia. Besides, I didn't bring her home to stay. She'll be heading to Canada soon." *As soon as I know she's not pregnant.*

Hannah and Luther exchanged a look that Hunter didn't miss.

"That's the truth," he said emphatically.

"I saw the way you were looking at her, Hunt. Did you notice, Hannah?" Luther asked.

She looked mightily disappointed. "No. I was too busy

running back and forth to the kitchen to see much of anything.''

''I wasn't looking at Jemma in any particular way,'' Hunter told them. ''I barely had time to look up.''

''He spent all his time watching her from across the room,'' Luther told Hannah. ''Even poured whiskey on the counter twice.''

''So you *are* sweet on her,'' Hannah laughed. ''Never thought I'd see the day again.''

''I'm not sweet on her or anybody else for that matter.'' Hunter picked up the cashbox and bent over to stuff it under a pile of blankets beneath the counter. When he straightened, they were both still watching him expectantly.

''I mean it,'' he went on, ''I'm through with women and you both know it. I'm not cut out to live with anybody.''

''Hunter Boone, you're full of peanuts,'' Hannah laughed.

''You intend to live up in the loft of this trading post like a hermit forever? You're only twenty-eight,'' Luther reminded him.

''I'll be moving on soon, off across the river. Maybe down to Texas, but most likely up the Missouri. Plenty of new land waiting to be explored, lots of open space for a man like me. I want to see it all.''

''Oh, Hunter, you can't mean that, not when this place is just starting to flourish,'' Hannah said, unable to keep the disappointment out of her tone. ''You've worked harder than all of us put together. If it wasn't for you leading the way, none of us would have made it this far.''

Hunter felt edgy and uncomfortable. They meant the world to him, Luther, Hannah and the children. In some ways he had done it for them, pushing on through the forest, searching for just the right place to settle on the Kentucky frontier—but he'd been looking to open up a new world for them, not for himself. Never for himself.

He had a dream of exploring, had the urge to keep moving and pulling up roots before they took hold. A wanderer's life wasn't something he could ask a woman to share.

"I've always planned on leaving—you know that. I've just been waiting for Lucy to get a little older, a little more sure of herself. And then there was Nette, with Jed up and dying on her. There was no way Luther could have supported you all, so I stayed. Now that the steamboats will be coming upriver, there'll be plenty of shipping and trade. More folks will move in nearby. You can all take care of yourselves and make something of this place."

"I don't want to talk about you leaving, Hunter. I want to know about Jemma." Hannah crossed her arms and began swinging her feet back and forth beneath the edge of the table.

"Found her in New Orleans, or I should say, she found me. Persuaded me to bring her this far. She even offered me a gold piece—"

"And you took it?" Hannah looked skeptical.

"Took nearly that much to outfit her and buy another horse," Hunter said. "But she doesn't know that."

"She's headed up to Canada?"

"That's what she said, but I don't believe her," Hunter said honestly. After nearly a month on the trail with her, he still didn't have any idea who or what Jemma O'Hurley really was and he told them so, along with her absurd story about escaping from the emir's men and stowing aboard ship in an oil jar.

"She might really be straight out of a convent, if all the praying she does is any indication, but I don't think she's ever been anywhere near Algiers," he finished.

Luther finished stacking glasses on the back wall and walked around the corner of the counter to stand beside Hannah. "Well, whoever she is, she's gotten to you, brother. Anyone can see that."

Hannah nodded.

"I'll tell you the truth, Luther, she's gotten to me all right. She drives me plumb crazy."

Jemma stared at the cabin door after it closed behind Hunter, so relieved that he hadn't bundled her off aboard the steamboat that she had forgotten Lucy was still in the room. When the girl stepped out of the shadows, a tall, lanky waif with deep-set, soulful dark eyes, Jemma nearly jumped up off the bed. When her fright passed, she settled back and watched the girl step closer.

"I'm Jemma O'Hurley," Jemma volunteered, waiting for the girl to reply.

"I'm Lucy White." Lucy stood there with her arms crossed almost protectively over breasts that strained the fabric of her too-small gown. The hem was way above her ankles, which stood out like knobs on her thin legs. When Jemma looked up, she found Lucy watching her. When the girl blushed, Jemma wished she hadn't been caught staring at the inadequate gown.

"Nette's got a new gown all cut out for me," the girl whispered, rubbing one foot over the other. "I know this one's way too short, but she hasn't had time to finish the new one, what with all the cooking and farm work. 'Sides, she likes working on her quilts a lot more than sewin' up a dress."

Her apology only made Jemma feel even worse.

"I'm . . . sure it will be lovely," Jemma floundered.

Lucy shrugged. "It doesn't matter."

Since when doesn't a new gown matter to a young girl? Jemma wondered.

"You need anything?" Lucy was still standing there, an awkward bedside attendant to say the least.

Jemma shook her head. "No, thank you. Nette should be along any moment."

"What happened to you?"

Looking down at her filthy, trail-weary outfit, the stiff

moccasins, and her chapped hands with their broken, ragged nails, Jemma simply shook her head.

"I've been on an adventure," she said, rubbing her temple, "and it was a bit more than I had bargained on."

Lucy appeared to relax some, so much so that she pulled up a chair and perched, rather than sat, on the edge of it, as if she might flee at any moment. Jemma tried to put her at ease.

"I was in New Orleans, running away from . . ." as soon as she recognized the fascination and trust in Lucy's eyes, Jemma couldn't bring herself to launch into the ludicrous fabrication about the emir's men and her escape from Algiers.

"I had to get out of there in a hurry. I saw Hunter on the street and he appeared to be a man who could be trusted, as well as capable—you've seen that big knife he wears and that rifle he carries?"

Lucy nodded.

"So I persuaded him to escort me this far. I told him I was on my way to Canada, to meet my father and brother."

"But that's not the truth?" Lucy was hanging on her every word.

For a moment Jemma thought that Lucy had seen through her, but then realized the girl had merely picked up on the way she had phrased her words. "I . . . yes, I was . . . I am headed to Canada."

Jemma wondered how convincing she could sound when, with all her heart, she wished she had never mentioned Canada. She studied Nette's cabin, which was crowded with a table and chairs, the corner bed, a spinning wheel, and, beneath the only window in the room, a quilting frame. The place was warm and cozy, as tidy as the inside of a well-organized butler's pantry. A basket of shiny apples stood on the table and a fire burned low in the stone fireplace opposite the bed. Adventure be damned.

Jemma wished she could strip off her dirty clothes, crawl beneath the covers, and sleep for a week.

Before she had to evade any more of Lucy's questions, there came a knock on the door and the girl hurried to open it. Nette crossed the threshold. She held a tray with a plate piled high with ham, fresh bread slathered with butter, string beans cooked with bacon, and a tall glass of milk.

Jemma's mouth watered. Nette fussed and fluttered around her, carefully centering the tray on her lap and setting the milk on the stool Lucy had vacated.

"Now, while you eat up, I'm going to have Hunter fill you a tub of hot water and then you're gonna take a nice long soak and go to sleep." She bustled over to the fireplace and hefted a heavy black pot off the hook and was out the door before Jemma could say a word.

"Looks like you're staying," Lucy said softly, watching as Jemma shoveled a heaping forkful of dripping green beans into her mouth.

Swallowing, Jemma agreed. "It certainly seems that way. Do you mind my being here?"

Lucy continued to stare at Jemma for what seemed a very long time. Standing stoop-shouldered, her limp hair hanging in her eyes, the awkward young girl cupped her elbows with her hands as if she had been reduced to hugging herself because no one else ever did. Not even a hint of a smile flickered across Lucy's face.

Maybe she's jealous, Jemma thought. Perhaps the girl was afraid she would usurp Hunter and Nette's time. Jemma wanted to assure Lucy that any worries she had along those lines were unfounded.

She set down her fork. "You don't mind my staying here, do you, Lucy? It'll probably only be for a little while."

Lucy made a high strangled sound. Her throat worked

as she swallowed twice, her brown eyes filled with tears. Her words rushed out in a choked whisper.

"I've been waiting for a friend near my own age for so long, I thought God might have forgotten all about me."

c h a p t e r

11

ALL THINGS CONSIDERED, SHE WAS FED UP WITH ADVEN-
ture.

Scrubbed and combed, fluffed and stuffed full of Nette's
luscious food, Jemma sat in the corner bed feeling more
pampered and fussed-over than ever before in her life. She
pulled the beautiful patchwork quilt up and snuggled under
it, tracing the intricate pattern and near-invisible stitches
with her fingertips. Dressed in a borrowed nightgown of
Nette's, she felt clean, cozy, and cosseted. The white gown
was smocked and embroidered by Nette's own hand.
Jemma complimented Nette first on the quilt and then on
the handiwork on the gown.

"Did it years ago," Nette admitted. "Back then I liked
to sew clothes. Now I make 'em because I have to, but I'd
rather be quilting."

Jemma hadn't seen Hunter since he'd deposited her on
the bed. Nor had Lucy White reappeared since her heart-
wrenching declaration. Luther had come in with a tub for
her bath, toting the heavy pots of boiling water and buckets
of cold while Nette stood over her like a sentry.

"I'll not have you passin' out and hittin' your head on
anything or drowning in that tub," Nette had said. She
became a willing and able attendant, waiting nearby while

Jemma soaked and scrubbed off weeks of grime. The woman bundled up her filthy traveling clothes along with the ice-blue silk dress and cape she had been wearing in New Orleans and whisked them away, promising they'd be as good as new after a long soak.

Tucking Jemma in, Nette set her moccasins beside the bed and told her to rest, assuring her that for tonight she would sleep right there in Nette's own bed because it was closer to the fire.

"I don't want you climbing that ladder up to the loft tonight," she had warned. "Tomorrow'll be soon enough for you to bunk up in the loft with Lucy."

Jemma had tried to protest, but Nette wouldn't hear of it. When the woman pulled up the quilt and gave her a motherly pat on the cheek, a warmth spread through Jemma the likes of which she had never known through all her years with nannies or even with the caring nuns at the convent school. She decided not to argue with the formidable little woman and contented herself with settling back and observing her hostess's comings and goings. Considering it impolite to ask Nette her age, Jemma decided the woman could be fifty or she could be eighty; there was no way to tell. Nette's hair was almost completely white and her face was well lined, but she had the energy of a much younger woman. Rarely did she walk sedately; instead, she bustled back and forth across the cabin at a quick trot.

Tucking herself into a wool coat, Nette had bid Jemma sit tight while she went out to put out the fire in the kitchen cabin and close it up for the night. The fire in Nette's own fireplace crackled cheerily, filling the room with a woody scent. Left alone to reflect, Jemma leaned back against the pillow, tired but feeling much better.

It had been nearly a month since she had exchanged places with the mysterious dark-haired girl hiding in the shadows of the cathedral. She wondered if her father was still in London or if he had sailed back to Boston. If by chance he arrived in New Orleans before he was expected, she didn't want him suffering—not when she was safe and well cared for—at least for the time being. She would have to write him very soon.

Jemma closed her eyes and rubbed her temples, thankful for the respite here at Sandy Shoals. Still, no matter how much she didn't want to leave Hunter, she couldn't very well stay on indefinitely, living off his and Nette's generosity, without doing something in return.

Boarding a river craft any time soon and aimlessly heading off in search of more adventure seemed like a nightmare. After a harrowing month of hard riding, walking for miles, and swimming through muddy river crossings, the idea of staying put seemed the most intelligent thing to do.

If she lived to be a hundred, she would never forget the heart-stopping terror of her near-drowning or the helplessness she had experienced when she thought she might have to live out her life as a slave in the Choctaw settlement. She was sick of dealing with dirt, insects, and all manner of creatures.

The thing to do would be to confess to Hunter that she had been living a lie from the moment they met. Then she would have to swallow her pride and admit to him and to herself that the journey was over. She would ask him if she could stay in Sandy Shoals until she could face the trip back to New Orleans and seek out her father.

That would be the wisest thing to do.

But telling Hunter the truth wouldn't be easy, not after all this time. And leaving here would mean saying goodbye to him, something she definitely wasn't ready to face. The tenor of their relationship had changed, no matter how much they tried to deny it. They had shared something profound, something hot and raw and so elemental that the memory of that night in his arms not only excited her, but made her ache every time she looked at him.

She was a fallen woman and it truly surprised her how

little she cared. In fact, she knew she was more than ready to fall again. And again.

Running from a husband and marriage, she had found Hunter. In his arms she had glimpsed the promise of an adventure greater than any trek around the globe. She had already experienced an escapade filled with the timeless secrets of wonder and passion.

To experience that adventure again, she wouldn't have to travel another mile.

Don't be crazy, Jemma gal. Don't quit on me now.

Jemma groaned aloud in the empty room and tried to ignore the memory of her grandfather's voice. Grandpa Hall's tall tales might have gotten her into this fix, but now it was up to her to get herself out. She thought about starting with a few well-placed prayers, but just then the door opened and Nette bustled in out of the twilight. Trailing close behind her were a boy and girl who looked just like miniatures of Luther and Hannah.

Nette walked directly to the bedside. She reached down and felt Jemma's forehead, then nodded with satisfaction.

"You don't feel like you're running a fever and your color's good," Nette assured her. "You'll be fit as a fiddle in the morning."

The children crowded up close—the little girl hanging onto Nette's skirt, peering at Jemma with shy curiosity, while the boy, a bit older, much bolder, leaned his elbows against the bed and propped his head on his hands. He stared at her as if she were a new bauble on display in the trading post. She couldn't help but notice that he had Hunter and Luther's deep green eyes and light hair. When he frowned at her intently with his fine child's brows drawn together, she thought he took after Hunter more than Luther.

"Why is she in bed so early?" The boy craned his neck and looked up at Nette.

"She's restin' up because your uncle dragged her from

hither to yon and plumb wore her out, is why," Nette explained.

"What's her name?" he wanted to know.

Before Nette could tell him, Jemma smiled and said, "I'm Jemma." She was as curious about him as he was about her.

"Tell her your name, boy," Nette said, ruffling his near-white hair with one hand while she reached behind her skirts and drew the little girl forward with the other.

The boy straightened away from the bed and stood at attention. "Luther Alexander Boone, Junior."

When he finally flashed her a grin, Jemma noticed that his front tooth was missing. "I'm pleased to meet you, Luther Alexander Boone, Junior." She held out her hand.

He gave it a hardy shake. "Folks just call me Junior, leastways they do around here."

"Then I'll remember to call you Junior, too," Jemma assured him.

"These two scallywags belong to Hannah and Luther," Nette told her. "They're the oldest. Got two more babies at home. This here's Callie." Nette smoothed one of Callie's light-brown braids. "She's a big help to her ma already and she's only four."

"Hello, Callie," Jemma said softly, half-afraid she might frighten the little girl staring up at her with wide hazel eyes. Callie popped her thumb in her mouth and gazed at Jemma over her fist.

Nette asked her to keep an eye on them while she hurried out to the "necessary." Jemma didn't have time to warn her that what she knew about children could fill a thimble.

"Can I sit on the bed with you?" Junior was already climbing up beside Jemma when he asked.

"Certainly." She scooted closer to the wall to make room, curious to see what the boy would do next.

"Me, too!" Callie shouted.

Amazed that the girl had suddenly found her voice—

and it was a loud one at that—Jemma watched in awe as a battle for the unlikely privilege of sitting beside her blossomed into a heated argument. Within seconds a shoving match had ensued and threatened to evolve into a full-fledged battle.

"I wanna sit next to her!" Callie tried to wedge her way in between Jemma and Junior, but the boy would have nothing of the sort.

"I was here first!" Junior gave his sister a shove that resulted in Callie bursting into a hysterical spate of tears.

Jemma tried to make herself heard over the shrieking. "I don't think . . . someone could get . . . Don't do that, Junior!"

"Why not?" He was intent on dispensing with Callie by shoving her toward the edge of the bed with his feet while the little girl kicked and screamed, her mouth gaping, her face red as a beet.

Jemma threw back her side of the covers, wrestling with the tangled sheets, forced to her knees in order to separate the two battling children. She tried to reason with Junior while she reached for Callie, who was slipping precariously near the edge of the bed, a whirlwind of arms and legs that still managed to produce shrieks of injustice, the most frequent being, "That's not fair, Junior Boone! That's not *faaaaair!*"

Jemma had Junior by the collar and Callie—who was dangling over the side of the bed—by the upper arm when the door opened.

"Thank heavens you're back, Nette." Relieved, she started to explain what happened, glanced up, and found herself looking straight into Hunter's eyes. He was quickly bearing down on all three of them with a bundle in his arms.

When he reached the bedside, he set his package on the table and moved as swiftly as lightning, grabbing Luther's son by the waist and hauling him up and off the bed before he scooped up the little girl and stood her on her feet beside her brother.

Miraculously, Callie stopped weeping and wailing the minute Hunter touched her. Her face was streaked with tears and mottled red, but she didn't make a single sound except for an occasional hiccuping sob. She did, however, continue to cast dark glances in her brother's direction.

When Hunter turned his gaze on her, Jemma felt as penitent as the children looked. On her hands and knees in the middle of the bed with her nightgown hiked up, revealing her calves and bare feet, she felt herself blushing to the roots of her hair. Not a word passed between them while she managed to right herself and crawl back under the covers. She whipped the quilt over her with a snap.

Hunter towered over the two children like an avenging angel, hands on his hips, feet astride.

"Which one of you wants to tell me what was going on here a minute ago?"

Callie pointed at Junior, who was already pointing at her.

"Junior, you're the oldest. Why don't you tell me what happened?" Hunter urged.

The two were quaking in their sturdy, scuffed shoes, so Jemma started to explain. "They both wanted to—"

Hunter whipped around and snapped, "I asked Junior. He ought to be man enough to tell me what happened."

"I'll thank you not to speak to me in that tone, Hunter Boone," she fired back.

Not only Hunter, but both children were staring at her, Hunter with a fearsome scowl and the children in wide-eyed amazement.

"Uh-oh," Callie whispered.

"She's in trouble now," Luther Junior announced.

No one, it seemed, talked back to Hunter Boone.

Jemma wasn't afraid to stare him down.

"Both of them wanted to sit next to me and before I could do anything, they started shoving and yelling and I tried to pull them apart and then . . . you walked in." She had almost faltered, half-expecting him to dole out to her whatever punishment he had in store for the former combatants.

"Is that all?" He shifted his stance and glanced down at the upturned faces, but the children were mute.

"No." Jemma threw him another challenge. "I'd like to add that I don't particularly like the way you're standing there with your arms crossed, glaring at all of us like a mad dog."

She thought she detected the slightest twitch at the corner of his mouth, but wasn't sure.

"I take it you're feeling better."

"Yes. Much," she told him coolly.

"You're sure?" His tone had gentled. She realized now he had reacted with anger spawned by concern.

"Then scoot over to the center of the bed," he told her.

She had lost her concentration after staring up into his eyes. "Do what?"

"Scoot over to the center of the bed." This time he pronounced each word slowly and distinctly.

"He wants you to sit in the middle," Junior clarified with a gap-toothed smile.

Callie had lost interest and began fidgeting with the hem of her dress.

Jemma made a great show of lifting the covers, sliding over, and rearranging the bedclothes. Finally she looked up at him and crossed her arms over her smocked bodice.

"There."

Hunter turned to the children, who were still staring up at him, awaiting their fate. "Jemma had a hard day. She isn't feeling all that well—"

"I'm perfectly fine," she insisted.

He ignored her. "She shouldn't be crawling around after you two, putting up with all that caterwauling and fighting. I'm going to let you sit by Jemma if you can mind your manners and not act like wild heathens. Can you do that?"

"Yes, sir," Luther nodded, all seriousness.

"Yes, ma'am, Uncle Hunt."

Hunter didn't say another word, but simply lifted Callie, swung her over the edge of the bed all the way across Jemma and planted her on the opposite side against the wall. Callie primly pulled her skirt down over her stockings to her ankles, crossed her arms in imitation of Jemma, and smiled triumphantly at Junior.

"Don't move your feet and get Nette's quilt dirty or she won't let you come visiting again." Hunter plucked Luther Junior off the floor and set him on Jemma's other side.

"Now," Hunter said, straightening and running a hand through his hair, "is everybody happy?"

"We sure are," Junior declared with a big smile at Jemma. "Aren't we?"

"Yep," Callie had taken hold of Jemma's hand and was squeezing it in a tight grip. "You wanna get in, too, Uncle Hunt?"

It was Hunter's turn to go beet-red. Although Callie's innocent question embarrassed her as well, Jemma found herself enjoying his discomfort immensely.

Hunter was saved having to answer when Nette walked in and had no sooner taken off her coat than Luther and Hannah, each carrying a child in their arms, opened the door again and came in behind her. Bundled in a black wool coat, Lucy trailed in after them. Head down, she crossed the room and climbed the ladder to the loft without a word to anyone.

In the hubbub that followed, Jemma was introduced to the Boones' other children: Sadie, who was three, and Timothy, a baby not yet a year old. Seeing the brood gathered together, she wondered how Hannah managed. If the few minutes she had experienced alone with Junior and Callie was any indication of what a day with the four children was like, she thought Hannah was ready for sainthood.

Nette poured coffee and the adults gathered about the

table near Jemma's bedside to spend the only idle hours of a long day to welcome Hunter home officially. Within a few moments, Jemma realized Hunter must have already told his family about how they had met in New Orleans, for no one asked. She was thankful that she didn't have to dredge up the old lie.

Hunter presented Nette with the fabric and the stone pipe he'd traded for in the Choctaw village. Nette laughed at the pipe and said she couldn't wait to try it, but the gift she was fondest of was the printed fabric. Hunter teased her, claiming he didn't know what possessed a sane woman to cut up good material just to sew it back together again. They bantered back and forth for a few more minutes while Luther and Hannah spoke to the older children.

When everything quieted down, Luther shifted the sleeping infant in his arms as naturally as if he were carrying a sack of sugar, leaned back, and looked at his brother.

"So, Hunter," Luther began, "aside from volunteering to bring Jemma upriver, did anything else happen?"

All eyes were focused expectantly on Hunter. Even Junior sat up a little straighter, and Nette, now seated across the room at the quilt rack, paused and peered over the rim of her glasses at him, waiting.

"Nothing to speak of." Hunter glanced at Jemma and then away. He propped his ankle on his opposite knee and shook his foot up and down. Callie stuck out her lip, her disappointment evident.

Hunter leaned back in his chair. When he looked at Jemma and winked, she wondered what he was up to. "Well, there *was* that one close call . . ."

"Tell us, Uncle Hunt," Junior begged. "What happened?"

"Oh, we ran into some Choctaw, is all."

"Really?" Junior's eyes were filled with admiration.

Callie tugged on Jemma's sleeve. "What's a *chalk-tall?*"

"An Indian tribe." Jemma said.

"Did you see 'em, too?" Junior asked Jemma. When he noticed that Callie had a hold of her hand, he quickly grabbed the other one.

Jemma glanced over at Hunter to see if he was going to do justice to the story. He simply sat back and smiled, letting her have the floor. She looked around the room and couldn't resist, not with such an attentive audience.

"I certainly did see them," she said with an emphatic nod.

Hannah, with Sadie asleep on her shoulder, absently smoothed her hand up and down the toddler's back. "Were you terrified, Jemma?"

"Most definitely. Hunter was asleep by the fire and I was on watch—"

From her place at the quilting frame Nette called out, "Hunter Boone! You made that child sit up and take the night watch with Indians close by? What were you thinking?"

Hunter cleared his throat. "I was thinking that if I didn't get some sleep every once in a while that I was going to fall over dead and then I wouldn't do her much good, now would I?"

"Jemma, please go on. You tell it," Hannah urged.

"I was on watch and suddenly, I could just barely make out a shadowy figure standing amid the trees." She lowered her voice until each and every one of them was hanging on her every word. Everyone except Hunter, who was consciously avoiding looking at her.

"I wasn't certain whether or not I was seeing things, so I tried to wake Hunter, but he didn't hear me calling his name."

"Big brother, did you actually take her money for protecting her?" Luther laughed so hard that the babe in his arms stirred and smacked his lips.

When Hunter didn't respond, Jemma continued, her voice low and dramatic. "I wasn't crazy. Slowly, step by step, a man emerged from the shelter of the trees. In the darkness, with the firelight playing over his face and his shadow wavering against the whispering pines, he frightened the wits out of me. So . . . I took a shot at him!''

She paused and waited for their reactions.

''Mercy!'' Hannah whispered.

''Did you kill 'im, Jemma?'' Junior was pulling on her fingers while Callie scooted closer and shivered.

''I didn't kill him, no, but I did some serious damage—''

''To his pride,'' Hunter finished for her. ''She blasted the hell out of some pheasant feathers he had used to decorate his turban.''

Jemma stuck out her chin. ''I scared him a bit.''

''So much so, that I had to spend the night making amends and palavering with him over coffee while you went to sleep,'' Hunter reminded her.

''Then he went away?''

Callie looked so scared that Jemma had to assure her. ''Yes. He went away.''

''He didn't want to scalp you?'' Junior sounded disappointed.

''Actually, he wanted to *buy* me,'' Jemma said.

''He *what?*'' Nette's needle lay forgotten in the stretched quilt.

''He wanted to trade for her,'' Hunter said. ''But I got rid of him and we thought we'd seen the last of him.''

''You thought?'' Luther prodded.

''Didn't see him again until the raft accident,'' Hunter replied.

''Raft accident!'' Hannah cried in disbelief.

Jemma was surprised to see that Hunter was actually able to enjoy himself thoroughly. He baited the family with bits and pieces of information instead of spinning a real breath-holding, heart-thumping yarn like Grandpa Hall used to do. She jumped in before he could string them along any more.

"We came to a particularly wild, raging river, not like the others that we swam the horses over—"

Nette called out again. "Hunter Boone, if I were stronger and you were a mite smaller I would take you over my knee."

"It turned out all right in the end, Nette," Jemma assured her, "although we certainly had some hair-raising moments. Hunter built a raft out of fallen logs. He piled everything on it, including me, and tied the bundles together and put a rope around my waist and told me to hang on. Then he shoved the raft out into the raging current."

"Hunter Boone, you should be shot," Nette grumbled.

"She's here in one piece, isn't she?" he called across the room.

"Go on, Jemma," Luther said.

"Well, the raft hit a submerged log, I guess, and before I knew it, I was flying head over heels into the river—"

"You would have been all right if you'd left the rope on like I told you," Hunter cut in.

Jemma went on as if he hadn't said a word. "I went under and nearly drowned before I was tossed up on the bank a ways downstream. I pulled myself up onto the riverbank—I'd lost one of the shoes Hunter had bought me, but they never fit well anyway—and managed to crawl up the bank on my hands and knees. I saw a man coming toward me and thought it was Hunter. I called out, but it turned out to be Many Feathers, the very same Indian who'd tried to buy me a few nights before. When I realized who it was, I fainted dead away."

She paused again to see what effect she was having on her audience and found them all spellbound. Only Hunter frowned.

"What's wrong now?" she asked.

"You didn't tell me you fainted that day, too."

"I forgot."

"Do you faint all the time?"

"No, just when I haven't eaten a substantial meal for days or when I'm facing captivity."

"He took you *captive?*" Nette had taken off her glasses and pulled a chair closer to the bed.

Something rustled above them and Jemma looked up. Lucy was peering down from the loft, listening to every word. Jemma smiled and waved at the girl and after a moment, Lucy waved back.

"Don't stop now, Jemma," Lucy called down. "What happened then?"

"Many Feathers led me back to the Indian encampment and threw me into his hut. It was as dark and black as the inside of Hades, and it smelled terrible. There were piles of furs and no windows, just a door and a little hole in the ceiling to let the smoke from the cook fire escape. And there was a pot of reeking stew bubbling over the fire."

"Were you scared enough to want to die?" Lucy called down again.

Jemma shook her head. "No. I was furious that I'd let myself get into that situation in the first place." She glanced around at the Boones, young and old, and Nette, and had a change of heart. "Well, to tell you the truth, I was frightened out of my wits. I tried to tell him, in sign language, that I wanted no part of him and certainly wasn't interested in marriage."

Luther barked out a laugh.

"Then he did a strange sort of dance with some nut bells and rubbed tobacco on my face. Actually, I think he wanted to rub it all over me, but I shoved him and told him to stop it."

Hannah gasped.

"Love charm," Luther laughed, looking over at his brother.

"What are you talking about?" Hunter shot back.

Luther patted the baby's back and chuckled. "The man was rubbing tobacco over her because it's supposed to make her attractive, like a love potion."

Jemma looked over and saw Hunter frowning in thought.

"Go on, Jemma," Nette urged.

"Then Many Feathers's son came home. He spoke English, so I thought I could reason with him, but he was as stubborn as the old man." She sighed and paused. "Then they dragged me out of the hut and made me work alongside the other women, endlessly pounding corn. Pounding and pounding until it was pulverized into meal." She held up her hands, "I had blisters the size of the pumpkins out there in Nette's garden."

"How did you get away?" Junior wanted to know.

Jemma smiled at Hunter. "That's the best part."

Hunter couldn't take his eyes off of her. As Jemma spun the tale of his attempt to make a trade for her and then, as she put it, his daring night rescue, he felt a forbidden warmth seep into his heart that he hadn't known for a long, long time. She was propped up on the pillows with a child under each arm, her golden hair so clean and shining it caught the firelight in every curl. Her eyes were bright with mischief as she embellished her version of the rescue and flight; her smile flashed and her dimples teased her cheeks and tempted him. Beneath the delicate stitches across the bodice of the white nightgown, her breasts rose and fell with every breath. He knew what it was to kiss that mouth, to touch those breasts, to hold her close.

He forced himself to look away and studied his family. Luther was smiling from ear to ear; Hannah was as speechless and spellbound as the two children on the bed. Nette had stopped interrupting but was still shaking her head, her lips pursed, alternately staring at Jemma in awe and then glowering over at him.

Jemma had them all in the palm of her hand. She had even drawn Lucy out of her shell. The girl in the loft was lying with her chin on her folded arms, peering down at them.

When he looked at Jemma, she was smiling at him, her eyes sparkling as she told everyone how he had spirited her away from a howling, raving war party of Choctaws. His heart tripped, struggling like a newborn colt, fighting to run.

Thinking about what had occurred the night they had stopped running from the Choctaw, he wrestled with the question of what he was going to do if she was with child. He was tempted to ask Nette if Jemma's fainting might have anything to do with having a baby, but if he did, he may as well stand up right now and shout to the rafters what he had done. If Nette knew, then everyone would know that he and Jemma had slept together.

He caught Jemma smiling his way again and his heartbeat stumbled. He stood up and left the cabin.

chapter
12

EVEN THE BRACING NIGHT AIR COULDN'T COOL HIS BLOOD.

Hatless, Hunter let the breeze off the river blow through his hair and tried to banish the tempting remembrance of Jemma's smile and the lilt of her voice.

He skirted the corncrib, made his way along Nette's carefully tended vegetable garden, and headed past the springhouse on the edge of the cleared land. The night was scented with wood smoke, rich, newly turned soil, and the dry, dusty smell of the crisp fallen leaves that crushed beneath his feet as he walked toward the river. He could hear the flowing water, a constant, soothing sound that beckoned, "Follow me."

The Mississippi never stood still. He loved her for that. She flowed ever onward, changed her course with every new thaw the way a woman changed her mind. She challenged the sandy banks that failed to hold her and moved on like a fickle lover. He knew of those.

For years he had dreamed of being like a river, ever on the move, challenging the boundaries of life, leaving the wilderness changed in his wake. He wanted to see things few white men had seen, watch the sun set on new horizons. But then responsibilities had come to him, held him back, kept him home.

Luther had asked for his help. Luther, who had been determined to find a place where he and Hannah could raise a family and make something of their lives. Luther, who couldn't do it alone. And Hunter couldn't refuse him.

They had met Nette and Jed Taylor on the trip down the Ohio, and Hannah soon approached him with the notion that it would be a godsend to have the older couple living on the homestead. Nette would be there to help her when birthing time came. The older woman's companionship would stave off the loneliness of a young wife used to living near family and friends. Hunter couldn't deny his sister-in-law. The Taylors joined them.

The bond among the inhabitants of Sandy Shoals had been forged as they all worked tirelessly putting back-breaking weeks and months into clearing the fertile ground, carving out a place in the Kentucky wilderness. Hunter worked alongside Luther and Jed, willing to stay as long as it took to see the families settled and prosperous.

The work had proved too strenuous for Nette's husband. Luther had found Jed in the field, facedown in the newly turned earth, fallen behind his plow. Unwilling to be a burden to Luther, Nette knew there was no way she could support herself without help and decided she would have to move back east. But Hunter agreed to stay on until Luther was established enough to provide for her. In exchange, she volunteered to cook and clean and see to Hunter's household needs.

So a bargain had been struck between them, binding him more tightly to Sandy Shoals, holding him on the banks of the Mississippi far longer than he had anticipated.

Living near the confluence of four rivers, Luther and Hunter decided a trading post was sorely needed by travelers and settlers alike, so they enlarged what had been Hunter's own small cabin. Word went out along the river; that first spring, produce began to arrive by oxcart from all over the surrounding area. The venture between him and Luther soon proved highly profitable, but it further complicated his life.

Whenever he looked back, Hunter knew that if he had left Sandy Shoals early on, as he had fully intended, he would have never met Amelia White. He had made the fatal mistake of letting his body do the thinking instead of his head.

Her desertion had added Lucy to the little band dependent upon him. And now there was Jemma with her fabricated past, her enticing smile, and the fact that she might be carrying his child.

What bothered him even more than waiting out the month was the unsettling way he was beginning to feel every time he looked at her. Luther and Hannah had seen something in him today that he had been trying to deny for weeks.

He stared out at the Mississippi, flowing black with moonlight sparkling on her breeze-rippled surface, but all he saw was Jemma. Jemma, settled in the midst of his extended family. Jemma, whose radiant beauty and charm had not only struck him with a burning need to touch and taste her again, but threatened to flood him with a peace and contentment he had never known before, had never wanted to stay anywhere long enough to know.

The stirrings of what he had felt while he watched and listened to Jemma in Nette's cabin had scared the hell out of him. So much so that he'd had to escape.

Jemma felt a wave of disappointment when, out of the corner of her eye, she saw Hunter get up and leave the cabin. Still, her joy was not entirely diminished. Concentrating on ending the tale with a grand flourish, she came to a triumphant conclusion and everyone burst into applause with such enthusiasm that Sadie awoke and looked around the room, and baby Timothy broke into fits of fussing.

In that moment, Jemma experienced something she had

never known before—the delight of sharing laughter, camaraderie, and friendship within a family gathering. With the two children nestled beside her, Luther and Hannah and Nette encouraging her, and even knowing that she had been able to draw Lucy out for a while—she had been given a chance to experience being a part of a whole, to bask in the love of a tightly knit clan.

Hunter's family had welcomed her with open arms and taken her in, no questions asked. They made her feel a part of them, let her join in their laughter and easy exchange. They allowed her to give them the only thing she had to give—her gift of storytelling.

For that one brief hour, that sliver of a lifetime, Jemma had caught a glimpse of something the Boones and Nette took for granted. Hunter and the others had given her a peek into a treasure chest she had never known existed. Now, after all these years, she had experienced the true meaning of family.

She had possessed many things, lived a life buoyed by a wealth beyond any these honest folk could imagine, but this closeness, this bond they shared so easily was something her father's money could never, ever buy.

Her joy was tempered only by the sadness she felt when she realized that the priceless bond of love and family was something Thomas O'Hurley had never known how to give, never even realized she needed.

Nette suddenly announced that Jemma looked tired and needed her sleep, so Luther and Hannah quickly rounded up their brood. Everyone lined up to kiss and hug Nette good-bye, as if they were leaving for months and not just walking a few hundred yards.

Lucy called out softly that she was going to turn in. Nette said she would join her shortly and then hurried around the table, collecting dirty coffee cups and stacking them on the dry sink. Finally, when the fire was banked and the cabin still as a rock, she walked over to Jemma's bedside.

Jemma smiled up at the older woman, whose wisdom and experience shone in her eyes. Nette's open, loving expression inspired the sharing of confidences.

"Do you know why Hunter walked out without telling anyone good night?" Jemma had fought asking, but her own stirrings won out. The evening had been picture-perfect, until Hunter was no longer there to share it.

Nette picked up the new pipe, sat down on the edge of the bed, and glanced up toward the loft. She lowered her voice.

"I reckon he's got a lot on his mind that needs wrestling with tonight. Hunter Boone is as stubborn as a crick rock, but he's got a heart of gold. You know anything about Lucy's ma?"

Jemma shook her head. "I know she walked out and left Lucy behind, but that's all."

Nette traced a diamond-shaped patch of sprigged muslin on the quilt. "Hunter always talked of movin' on after the cabins were built and we had the first good crop in. Then my Jed died, so Hunter stayed on. He and Luther built the post. One day, along come a flatboat headed downriver with Amelia White and Lucy aboard.

"Amelia was a real looker, far too beautiful for her own good. She got one look at the post and the kind of business Hunter and Luther were doing and had her cap set on Hunter before she'd been here a good hour.

"The poor boy didn't know what hit him. One day he was talking about moving on, the next Amelia had moved into his loft and Lucy was living here with me. I didn't object. Why, I could see that little girl needed more love than what her mother was givin' her."

"Was he in love with Amelia?" Jemma felt an odd twist in her chest. A slow ache.

"I can't say, but I know he wasn't thinkin' straight. He quit talking about movin' on, though, and even offered to marry her as soon as a preacher came through because he didn't want to set a poor example for the young'uns, but

Amelia kept putting him off. Then the war came and he went down to Louisiana with the other Kentucky boys fighting under General Adair and Jackson. While he was gone, a boatload of high-steppers came by, gamblers in shiny satin waistcoats and tall hats on their way to New Orleans. When their boat pulled out, Amelia was on it.''

''Poor Hunter,'' Jemma sighed. ''And poor Lucy.''

''If it did break his heart, he never let on. Kept it buried, the way he does most of his feelings. All he ever said to Luther was that everything worked out for the best and that he'd been feeling the itch to move on anyway. But since then he hasn't made mention of leavin'.''

''But he just went down to New Orleans.''

''He went down to sell Luther's whiskey. Said he just needed to get away. I wondered if he might not be looking for Amelia, but nobody would know that but Hunter. Luther thought we might have seen the last of him when he left, but I knew he'd bring the money back. When he come riding in with you this morning, we thought maybe he'd finally found someone who could put his heart at ease.''

Jemma shook her head. ''It's not like that, exactly.''

''Then how is it, honey?''

''I . . . I needed someone to bring me upriver, that's all. Hunter and I . . . sometimes we don't even get along. He's told me he intends to head west. I never thought otherwise.'' She was stammering and blushing and, for the first time that she could recall, at a genuine loss for words. There was a lump in her throat the size of an apple.

''You don't think he could still be in love with Amelia?'' Jemma whispered.

''I don't think what he felt for Amelia was love, but the woman changed him, that's for sure. Whatever innocence Hunter had about women is long gone. I thought it would be a month of Sundays before he let another woman into his life, but here you are, although I imagine he'll fight the notion hard as he can.''

Nette's words explained the way Hunter had acted on

the last leg of their journey. They had been fighting the same intense emotions—feelings that were all mixed up and hard to fathom.

She wondered if he was having any better luck than she.

Nette blew out the lamps and slowly climbed the ladder to the loft. Jemma rolled to her side and cradled her head on her arm, watching the fire's glowing embers. Outside it was cold enough for frost, a good night to have the journey behind her. Here in Nette's cabin, she was warm and toasty.

She ached all over, as if now that the trip was over, her body had given itself permission to complain. She had thought sleep would come easily, but she lay awake, thinking of Hunter. It was the first night since she had laid eyes on him that they would not spend together.

The fire popped and a log crumbled into embers. Jemma rolled over and faced the wall. She closed her eyes and let her mind wander. She thought of all that Nette had told her and let her mind put images together with the details.

Wrestling with the memory of her own days and nights with Hunter, unable to forget what had passed between them, she tried to sort out her feelings. Her imagination ran away with images of Hunter and Amelia. She didn't want to think of him touching the woman in all the ways he had touched her, but couldn't change the direction of her thoughts.

Filled with doubt and indecision, she was at a crossroads, unwilling to move on, uncertain of what to do next. Hunter might not want anything further to do with her, but she wasn't ready to say good-bye. Perhaps if she told him the truth, he would let her stay on until she thought her father might have given up the notion of marrying her off.

Finally, after tossing and turning, she decided that if she was going to get any sleep at all tonight, there was only one thing to do—turn her problem over to someone else. Jemma folded back the covers and slipped out of bed. The wood plank floor was cold and hard as she knelt down beside the bed, a far cry from the plush carpet in her room in Boston or the rich velvet upholstery on her *prie-dieu.*

Resting her forearms on the edge of the bed, she folded her hands, closed her eyes, and prayed.

"Dear Ladies and Gentlemen, thank you all for seeing me here safely. Please keep my father safe, too, and while you are at it, if you could begin to help him see things my way when he returns from London, I would be truly grateful. Bless Hunter and his family and Nette and Lucy. Keep them all safe."

She pressed her fingertips to her lips, thought a moment longer and added, "Grandpa Hall, I want you to understand that I've kept my promise to you. I've had my taste of adventure and now I'd like you to rest in peace." Jemma started to cross herself and then stopped and bowed her head again.

"St. Clare, you ran away from two offers of marriage at eighteen, but at least you knew where you were going. I have no intention of founding a holy order of nuns, like you did, but that's about all I'm certain of at the moment. If you have time, would you kindly put some thought into helping me decide what I ought to do next? I'd really appreciate it.

"And if anyone up there knows anything about getting a good night's sleep, please help me out. Amen."

The ground was covered with a film of frost that sparkled on the fallen leaves and crackled underfoot. Hunter opened the door of the post and stretched, then rubbed his eyes. The morning sky was leaden, low with heavy clouds that would dump snow before nightfall.

His walk through the woods had done little to ease his mind, and afterward he had spent a restless night, tossing and turning in his bed in the loft above the trading post. More than once he had paced over to the window that faced north and stared through the darkness in the direction of Nette's cabin, wondering if Jemma was asleep or if she found sleeping indoors after so long on the trail as confining as he did.

He was about to step back inside and close the door when he heard a commotion that sounded like it was coming from the pigpen. Dismissing it as nothing more than the exuberant porkers welcoming the morning slops, he smiled and stepped back inside, his hand on the edge of the door.

A high-pitched squeal that sounded far more human than piglike started him running. As soon as he rounded the root cellar, he caught a flash of sky blue almost hidden behind a wall of hungry pork. His initial panic ebbed when he heard Jemma shout.

"Get off me! Get away, you . . . you pigs! Ouch! Let me up."

The wheezing and snorting pigs were far too busy gobbling down the mixture of corncobs and scraps to pay her any mind. Hunter ran up to the split-rail fence that hemmed in the young porkers and the old sow, reached over and grabbed Jemma beneath the arms, and pulled her up and over the rail.

For a moment she simply stood beside the fence, staring at the pigs that still swarmed the bucket of slops dumped on the ground and smeared on her skirt.

"What in the hell were you doing in there?"

He saw her shudder. She stiffened her shoulders before she turned to face him.

"Nette sent me out to slop the hogs."

"You aren't supposed to slop *yourself*," he said, shooting a glance at the front of her dress. "And you're sure as hell not supposed to get *in* the pen to feed 'em. If those hogs were a few months older, they could have killed you. You're lucky that mother pig didn't charge you."

"Nobody told me that," she shot back.

"Did you tell Nette you didn't have any idea how to slop pigs in the first place?"

"No—"

"You wouldn't think of telling the truth and asking her for help, would you? If I know you, you probably told her you've been slopping hogs since you could walk. You probably said you were the head hog slopper at the convent in Algiers."

She crossed her arms, tapped her foot, and avoided his eyes by staring at the root cellar not far away.

"Well?" His temper fizzled and died when she looked up at him with her blue eyes swimming with tears.

"When Nette asked me to do this for her, I didn't have the heart to tell her I didn't know how, because then she would have jumped in and done it herself. She's been so good to me already; she . . . she loaned me this dress and now it's filthy and I'm sure she doesn't have another one to spare."

When she paused to look down at the hopelessly soiled gown, tears slipped down her cheeks. She whirled around and wiped them off with the back of her hands, smearing her cheeks with mud.

"It's barely daybreak and I've ruined everything," she whispered.

Hunter reached into the pigpen and collected the bucket. Tempted to slip his arm around her shoulders, he took her by the arm and led her back to the trading post, purposely skirting the front of Nette's cabin. Jemma went along without a word, sniffling and wiping her nose on her sleeve until, by the time they reached the post and he opened the door for her, she had collected herself. The fire was back in her eyes.

"Come with me." He led her up to the loft, lifted a striped wool blanket that was folded across the end of the bed, and handed it to her.

"I'll go out to the kitchen and pour some coffee while you slip out of that dress and wrap up in this." He handed her the blanket.

"Thank you," Jemma mumbled, carefully holding it

away from the front of her muddy gown, waiting for him to leave.

She didn't move until the sound of his footsteps faded on the stairs; then she dropped the blanket and unbuttoned the borrowed gown. Letting the soiled garment fall, she stepped out of it, surveyed the damage to her petticoat, which was minimal, and then walked over to a series of pegs on the wall where he had neatly hung his shirts. There were but three extra. She chose one, slipped into it and was reminded of the huge shirt she had worn on the journey north. Somehow, the familiarity comforted her.

The loft was sparsely furnished. His bed was covered with a quilt that she suspected was more of Nette's handiwork. Beside the bed, Hunter had placed a trunk, on top of which stood a candlestick. She walked over to the bed and let her fingers trail over the intricate quilt patches, up to the pillow. Lightly she skimmed the cotton case, closed her eyes, inhaled.

She drifted over to the window that gave him a view of the other cabins. Leaning against the window, she looked down at Nette's and the Boones' cabins and saw Hannah accompanying Callie to the outhouse in back. Finally, she picked up the blanket he had offered, draped it over her shoulders, and closed it, hiding her bare thighs and legs. Collecting the soiled gown, she rolled it into a tidy bundle and climbed down the stairs to the floor below.

Hunter was just entering the main room with two cups of coffee and a wet dish towel. Jemma, bundled up from neck to toe, sat down at one of the trestle tables and laid the rolled-up blue dress on the bench.

"Here." He handed her the towel and as she wiped off her face and hands, he sat down on the opposite side of the table.

"It's not as bad as I thought," she said without meeting his gaze. "Most of the dirt is on the front of the dress, and a little in back where I sat down in the mud, but it's not soaked through."

He slid a cup of coffee across the table to her. Jemma set down the towel and hugged the coffee cup with both hands.

"I'm glad we're finally alone. We need to talk," he said.

"I'll tell Nette I'm sorry—"

"I know you will." Hunter stretched his legs and crossed his ankles.

Jemma knew that the warm, cozy feeling she was experiencing was not hers to keep. Taking a careful sip of the hot coffee, she waited for him to speak his peace.

"I've made a decision," he said.

She took another sip, looked at him over the rim of the cup, and waited expectantly.

"Circumstances being what they are, I think it would be best if you stayed here for the next couple of weeks. I won't be going anywhere either, until things are settled."

"Settled?"

"Until you know for certain you aren't with child."

She blinked twice. *"With child?"*

"You know what I mean."

"With child?" Dear Lord, she hadn't thought about the possibility of *that* complication, but then again, she hadn't been thinking very clearly for quite a while. Her hand went to her stomach, resting there. Even now, her and Hunter's child might be growing.

"I can see that the idea comes as a shock to you." He was looking at her as if she were thick as a post.

Jemma swallowed. "It does. I never . . . well, I just never thought about it. You mean? That is to say, we only did it once."

"Once is more than enough to make a child."

Her cheeks were afire. She could feel her skin burning and looked down at the table to avoid meeting his eyes. Obviously he wanted her to stay, not because he felt anything for her, but because he felt responsible for the child she might have conceived that night under the stars.

Once she had accidentally dropped a sky-blue robin's egg she found on her windowsill. She had watched it fall to the ground, seen the contents spill out on the ground. Right now she had that same sinking sensation.

"Jemma?" He set his cup down half-full.

She started. Her thoughts had been miles away. "I want to stay." She blurted out the first words that came to mind. "Not because of what you just said, that I might . . . that we might have . . . anyway, I decided last night I would like to stay a little while longer, if you and the others don't mind."

"I thought you were desperate to find your father and your brother." He watched her wrestle with an answer.

She ran her fingertip around the lip of the cup, trying to come up with some reason why she had suddenly lost interest in her trek to Canada.

"Tell me the truth, Jemma. Just once."

Sitting there in the quiet stillness of the morning, the time of day that held the most promise, a time for starting over, she wished she could tell him the truth.

"I can't," she whispered.

She could see it wasn't the answer he expected.

"Hunter, I wish I could tell you, but I can't, not yet. All I know is that I'm not sure where I'm headed anymore or what I'm going to do."

She could hear the confusion in her tone that sounded nothing at all like the brazen girl who had cajoled him into taking her up the Trace with her ridiculous bold talk of rebel Berbers and daring escapes.

"I promise I'll try not to be a burden to anyone. I'll work from dawn until dusk. I'll stay out of your way."

He had grown so still, so contemplative that she was afraid he was thinking of a way to deny her request. Finally, he set his cup aside, folded his hands, and looked her straight in the eye.

"I once brought a woman into our lives and she stole

from me and my family. I don't ever want to make that mistake again.''

His words hurt her deeply, but she didn't argue.

"Promise me two things," he added.

"Of course."

"Don't do anything to upset Nette or Lucy while you're here."

She instantly took offense, then realized that his past directed his present. He really knew nothing about her. "I would never intentionally hurt anyone," she assured him.

"And Jemma?"

"What?"

"Stay out of the pigpen."

chapter
13

"NOW, YOU SURE YOU WANT TO DO THIS FOR ME, honey?" Nette sat at the quilting frame, her glasses riding the end of her nose. She threaded a needle with white thread.

"Of course, I'm sure." Jemma watched her wrap the thread around the end of her needle to knot it. "I may never master pie dough, but I think I can dust without any problem."

Jemma was determined to do her share while she was in Sandy Shoals, and so far she had helped Nette with everything except cooking—which continually proved to be almost as big a disaster as pig feeding.

"Hunter's mighty particular about his things," Nette warned. "Just stick to dusting the shelves and sweeping the floor. That'll be plenty."

"All right." Jemma buttoned up her wool coat and wrapped a wool scarf around her face and neck until only her eyes and nose were showing.

"Try to be finished before he gets back from Noah's."

"I will." Jemma had yet to lay eyes on the elusive Noah LeCroix, the half-breed renowned for his ability to pilot boats through the shoals.

"If any boats pull in, ring the bell outside the kitchen door and Luther'll come runnin'."

"I know, Nette." Her voice was muffled by the wool scarf. She had her hand on the door latch.

"And keep the fire going."

"I will." The shawl hid Jemma's smile. Nette looked after everyone like a mother hen. Jemma loved it.

"If you see Lucy anywhere, remind her that I need her to card more wool so I can do some spinning later." Nette began rocking a needle through the layers of pieced materials and the cotton batting.

"All right." Jemma stood there waiting for the final word before she opened the door and let the cold air into the cabin.

Glancing up from her work, Nette waved in the direction of the trading post. "Well, what are you waiting for, child? Get a move on."

Jemma laughed and stepped out into the cold.

Thanking the saints for her good fortune had become a habit. A fair share of keelboats and flatboats were still headed downriver, but November had brought snow, and even though it soon melted, mornings like this one were still biting cold. The trees were skeletal, the sky gray. Except for an occasional ruckus from the henhouse or a complaint from one of the pigs, it was absolutely still outside. The contrast between mornings in Sandy Shoals and the hustle and bustle of the vendors, carriages, and wagons on the streets of Boston was the same as the contrast between night and day. The peacefulness of the place permeated her soul.

Burying her hands in the sleeves of her coat, Jemma gingerly picked her way through the scattering of snow and ice that covered the ground between Nette's cabin and the trading post. She was determined to linger there until Hunter showed up so she could tell him that his worries were over. Her monthly time had come to her in the night. For the week-and-a-half they had waited, he had avoided being alone with her.

Inside, the trading post was warm and cozy. Hunter had

left a low fire burning in back of the massive hearth. The tables were wiped clean. Everything was in its place. She found the rags under the counter just where Nette had said they would be, along with some oil for polishing and a turkey-feather duster. Jemma took off her scarf and coat, rolled up the sleeves of the blue gown that had survived the pigsty, and went to work.

An hour later she stood atop a ladder propped against the highest shelf in the store. She tossed the dust rag onto the counter behind her and had started down the ladder when the toe of her heel caught in the hem of her gown. There was a rending tear just before she fell backwards. Polished shelves full of trade items flashed past her as she hurtled to the floor with a startled cry.

Jemma heard an angel singing with such heavenly sounds that she was certain she had died and gone to paradise until she realized that her head was pounding. She didn't think there was supposed to be pain in heaven.

When she opened her eyes, the angel was still singing. Stars danced and shimmered on the ceiling of the trading post. She blinked to clear her vision but otherwise lay still, not certain if she could move anything at all, unwilling to try.

Gradually the stars faded and she slowly pushed herself up to a sitting position, pausing when her head began to swim. The angel was still singing, the notes so pure and ethereal that Jemma didn't know whether it was the sound that made her want to cry or the horrid pain at the back of her head. She reached up to feel her scalp and her hand came away bloody.

Jemma couldn't utter more than a squeak at first, but as she sat there on the floor behind the counter staring at the blood on her palm, she finally managed to shout, ''Help!''

The angel abruptly stopped. Jemma heard footsteps outside the post. The back door flew open and someone ran in.

"Jemma?"

"Lucy, I'm down here." Jemma breathed a sigh of relief as Lucy rounded the corner of the counter and ran over
to her.

"What have you done?" The girl tossed aside her thick
shawl and knelt down on the floor beside Jemma.

"I fell off the ladder," Jemma said, unable to keep the
embarrassment out of her tone. "And I think I cracked my
skull open."

Crawling around behind her, Lucy gently parted
Jemma's hair and inspected the wound.

"You cracked your head good. Sit tight and I'll press a
clean rag to it." She pulled a rag off the shelf under the
bar top and held it against the cut.

"Was that you I heard singing?" Jemma fought to keep
her mind off the throbbing ache at the back of her head.
She tested her ankles and bent her knees one at a time.
Everything seemed to be working.

Lucy didn't answer outright. Making conversation was
an effort for the girl, especially when the subject was herself.

Finally, after she had helped Jemma to her feet and led
her over to a bench, Lucy blushed. "That was me singing."

Jemma reached up to hold the compress herself.

"When I came to and heard that voice, I thought I was
in heaven listening to an angel," Jemma said.

Lucy's eyes began to sparkle. Then she smiled one of
her rare smiles. "Jemma, you say the funniest things."
After a moment she lifted a hand to her hair and asked,
"Why are you looking at me like that?"

"Lucy, you are so genuinely beautiful when you smile.
You should do so more often." Jemma was stunned by
the change that had come over the girl.

Lucy was blushing, staring at the table where her graceful hands lay folded one atop the other. "I'm *not* beautiful," she whispered. "Please don't say that."

The cut on her head had stopped bleeding and the throb had receded to a dull ache. Jemma set aside the compress. "Yes, you are. Why, I'll bet with a bit of spit and polish and that new dress Nette's promised you, you'll turn the head of every young man who stops here. And that voice! Lucy, have the others ever heard you sing?"

"I don't want to turn heads," Lucy cried, twisting her fingers together. "I'm *not* beautiful. Not like my ma. And Nette's never gonna finish making that dress, not with her quilt takin' up every spare minute she's got."

Jemma reached out and lifted a lock of Lucy's hair off her shoulders. "I could fix your hair, if you let me. It would be fun—"

A sparkle replaced the pained look in Lucy's eyes. "I never had anyone fix my hair for me."

"This is as good a time as any to start. We're friends, aren't we?"

Since her arrival at Sandy Shoals, Jemma had tried hard to fill Lucy's wish for a friend, but the girl was so shy; she kept to herself most of the time and spent the quiet hours of an evening reading the Bible by firelight. As much as Lucy claimed she wanted a friend, Jemma had almost despaired of ever really getting to know her.

"You know, Lucy," she said, "I'm not a bad seamstress myself. At least, I'm fairly certain I could manage to put a dress together. I used to embroider samplers in . . . well, at home."

"It'd be a heap of trouble for you." Lucy protested, but there was a thread of hope in her tone.

Jemma stood up and waited to see if her head would start spinning. It merely thrummed, so she smiled over at Lucy and took the girl's hand.

"Come on. Let's look through the bolts of cloth Hunter has on the back shelf and find one that will look good on you."

"I don't think we should."

"Why not?" Jemma shrugged.

"Nette already cut out a yellow dress for me."

Jemma looked at Lucy's tangled brown hair and her big, wide, brown eyes. "What's wrong with owning two dresses? You would look wonderful in pink."

"*Two* new dresses? I think that fall might have knocked you senseless, Jemma."

Lucy hadn't budged, so Jemma sat back down. She thought of her armoires in Boston, full of gowns that she hadn't worn in ages. Noticing Lucy's forlorn expression, Jemma asked, "Lucy, what's wrong?"

Lucy shook her head and shoved her hair back off her face, looping it behind her ears. "I can't ask Hunter for material for a dress. I heard Nette tell you all about my ma the night you came here, about how she up and left me with Hunter and Nette and didn't look back. I'm beholden to them for everything as it is. I can't ask for more."

"But—" Jemma knew Hunter was thrifty, but she couldn't imagine him begrudging Lucy a few yards of material and some thread. "I'll ask him for the things we'll need myself. Surely he won't mind."

"Don't you see? It's not that he might mind—"

"Then what is it? Something else is bothering you."

Lucy stared down at her hands.

"We're friends, aren't we, Lucy? Friends share their troubles." The silence in the post was deafening. Jemma waited, hoping she hadn't pushed the girl too far. Finally, she watched Lucy swallow and then lift her soulful eyes.

"I don't want to be like my ma."

Jemma frowned. "What do you mean?"

"Ma is so beautiful that she can get a man to do anything for her. She came here and made Hunter fall in love with her and then up and left. It was that way my whole life, watching her move from one man to another, one place to another, takin' and takin' and never givin' back." She drew a deep shuddering breath. "I never thought she would leave me behind. You know what it's like, bein' left behind, Jemma? Havin' someone think so little of you that they disappear without a good-bye, without any warning at all?''

Not only did Jemma's heart go out to Lucy, but through the girl's heartfelt words she had a glimpse of the pain her own disappearance would cause her father if he arrived in New Orleans earlier than expected and discovered that she had vanished without a trace.

Tears shimmered in Lucy's eyes. ''For a long time I kept waiting for Ma, thinking that she would just be gone a while and that she'd come back for me—''

''Maybe she will,'' Jemma encouraged.

Lucy shook her head. ''It's been too long. She won't come back now.''

At a loss for words, Jemma fingered her wound again. It was tender and still oozing, so she picked up the compress and held it against the back of her head.

''You're not anything like your mother, Lucy.''

''But if you fix up my hair and I start wearin' pretty dresses, then it might go to my head. What if I start thinkin' like my ma, actin' like her? What then, Jemma? That's not the way God intended a body to behave.''

''Oh, Lucy.'' Jemma set aside the compress and put her arms around the girl's thin shoulders. ''You've got too good a heart to change, no matter what you wear, or how you look. Why, you're good to Nette, always doing your chores and helping out, and you take care of Hannah's little ones whenever she needs you. I don't think you have a thing to worry about.''

''Really?'' Lucy sniffed and pulled back.

''Absolutely. Just like that wonderful voice of yours, beauty comes from the inside, Lucy. Not the outside.'' Jemma glanced at the stack of fabric again and smiled. She pulled Lucy over to an open space between the counter and the table, prized the girl's hands off her shawl, and set the knitted blue wool aside. ''Stand here.''

''What are you doing?'' Lucy looked around the room

as if she expected Hunter to pop out of the mud chinked between the logs.

"What any good dressmaker would do—I'm going to see which fabric looks the best on you." She opened a length of blush-pink fabric and draped it over Lucy's shoulder. "*Very* nice."

Lucy smiled. "Really?"

Jemma whipped another bolt off the table, shook it out, and draped it across the girl's opposite shoulder. "Terrible," Jemma mumbled as she pulled off the mustard-yellow cloth and tossed it behind her.

"I like the first one," Lucy said, fingering the pink.

They both started laughing when Jemma wound a length of cloth around Lucy's head like a turban and let the end of the fabric trail down to the floor.

"Do you know that some Africans wear turbans that are a foot high?" Jemma said as she unwound Lucy's impromptu headpiece.

"Have you ever been to Africa, Jemma?" The girl was so sincere that Jemma couldn't even launch into one of her tales.

"No, but my grandfather was a long time ago, and when he told a story, he had the ability to make me feel as if I had been there right along with him. I used to pretend I had been there, too."

"You have that gift," Lucy said. "When you tell one of your tales, I feel like I'm right there in it myself."

"Why, thank you, Lucy. That's quite a compliment."

Lucy took her hand and gave it a squeeze. "Thank *you*, Jemma. I never had this much fun before. Ever. I hope you don't ever leave."

So moved that she was unable to respond, Jemma picked up the cloth that Lucy liked best.

There was nothing to keep her here now. Hunter certainly didn't share her feelings—that much was evident. She almost hated to see the look of relief that would surely come over him when she told him her news. No, Hunter

Boone wouldn't be begging her to stay. In fact, she wouldn't be surprised if he didn't start packing the minute she told him.

"Someday I'll have to leave, but that doesn't mean we won't still be friends. Why, I expect someday a young man will catch your eye and you'll be thinking of getting married."

"I don't know about that," Lucy said. "Nobody ever looked twice at me before, but I did hear that Hannah married Luther when she was sixteen and I'll be that old in a few months."

"You see," Jemma said as she fluffed open a bolt of light-blue wool and held it up to Lucy, gently wrapped it across the front of the girl's bodice, then smiled and stepped back.

"How come you're not married yet, Jemma?"

Caught off-guard, Jemma could only founder. "Well, I . . . that is . . . I just never met anyone I wanted to marry. I . . . up until a few weeks ago, I led a very sheltered life."

"You ever think about it? What it would be like to be married?" Lucy asked.

Jemma paused, considering her answer. "A few weeks ago I thought that it would be a nightmare, too confining, because I'd be forced to stay in one place and give up my freedom. That was before I saw the way Hannah and Luther get along, before I knew what being part of a family was all about. I'm beginning to think that maybe, if you find the right man, marriage can be a joy, not a jail sentence." Most of all, she now knew what it was like to lie in a man's arms, to want to feel him inside her, to wait to hear his step outside the door, the sound of his voice.

"I think about it some," Lucy said, surprising Jemma. "I don't intend to jump up and marry the first man who asks me, if one ever does. But I'll know him when I see him."

Jemma paused, holding a folded bolt of fabric against

her heart. Lucy had never sounded so confident before. "How will you know?"

Lucy suddenly became dreamy-eyed. "I'll look in his eyes and see him looking back at me and I'll get all tingly and warm inside . . . and I'll just know."

Jemma closed her eyes. Lucy had just described the way she felt every time she looked at Hunter.

"Jemma? Does your head hurt? You want to go back to Nette's?"

"No, I'm fine." Jemma put the material aside and looked at the pink fabric in Lucy's hands. "That's your favorite, isn't it? It's perfect."

Satisfied with the choice, Jemma walked over, took hold of Lucy's limp hair, and lifted it up to the crown of the girl's head. Lucy laughed aloud, let go of the fabric, and began to help Jemma.

Standing at arm's length, Jemma had pronounced her friend lovely when she heard the sound of men's voices outside.

Lucy's eyes went wide with panic. Jemma let go of her hair and spun around.

The door opened and Hunter stepped over the threshold, followed by a broad-shouldered man just as tall but of dark hair and eyes. His clothing was a mixture of wool and leathers, like his heritage—a blending of two worlds, Indian and white.

"I'm sorry, Hunter," Lucy mumbled. Her radiant smile had dissolved. She tore the fabric off herself. So nervous that her hands shook, the girl began balling it into a wad.

"I thought you'd be at Nette's." Hunter was staring at Jemma, looking as if he wanted to be anywhere but where she was.

"I came over to do some dusting—"

"She fell off the ladder and busted her head open," Lucy finished.

"She *what?*" He glanced over at the ladder leaning up

against the shelves at the back of the room, and then back to Jemma.

"Did you know that Lucy has a beautiful voice?" Not the least bit thrilled with the turn in the conversation, Jemma tried to change it.

Hunter glanced down at the bloodstained rag. His eyes flashed with anger. In three strides he was looming over her.

"It's nothing but a little cut," she protested.

He took her chin in his hand and gently forced her to look up into his eyes. A frown marred his forehead. He looked mad enough to spit fire as he searched her eyes intently.

"You could have broken your neck." The soft tone coupled with his intensity had her feeling dizzy all over again. *Warm and tingly.*

"I'm fine, really," she whispered, too entranced to look away. It suddenly dawned on her that he used anger to disguise his concern. Even when he was upset, there was no denying what a handsome specimen of a man he was. She lost herself in his eyes. Thanks to his campaign to avoid her, she hadn't seen him in so long that she had forgotten just how handsome he was. She wound up staring at his lips.

As if he knew what she'd been thinking, Hunter abruptly let go of her chin and took a step back. "It doesn't look like you rattled anything any looser than it already was." He picked up the bloodstained rag and stared at it for a moment. "Lucy, take Jemma back to Nette's."

"Really, I'm all right. I'll stay and fold up these things and finish."

"Please, Jemma," Lucy took hold of her arm. "Let's go on back."

Jemma was about to protest again when Noah LeCroix sauntered over to stand beside Hunter, openly curious.

"I'm Jemma," she said, not waiting for an introduction. "You must be Noah."

The tall half-breed nodded but didn't speak.

"Jemma, please." Lucy's hand tightened on her arm.

Jemma decided that Hunter might be able to avoid her this time, but she was going to talk to him later, even if she had to camp out on the doorstep.

Her head was pounding again. "I need to see you alone, Hunter." Her gaze flicked over to Noah and back. "Whenever you have time."

Hunter stood there speechless while Lucy helped Jemma with her coat and scarf. Watching the two of them leave together, he knew that if he lived to be as old as Methuselah he would never understand women.

"If I knew what went through their minds I'd have a woman of my own like that," Noah told him.

"That one's *not* mine," Hunter said emphatically.

"No? You could've fooled me."

Hunter didn't like LeCroix's smile in the least.

"I can't for the life of me figure out why everybody around here keeps acting like there's something between us. Hell, I haven't even seen her in a week."

"On purpose?"

Hunter hated the way he kept getting the feeling that his head had opened up and folks could look right into it.

"No, not on purpose," he lied. It wasn't easy avoiding Jemma, not with her living a few hundred yards away. He'd given up going over to Nette's at night to visit, and had even taken to eating by himself in the empty trading post. Surprised that the self-imposed isolation wasn't sitting well with his loner's nature, he blamed it on Jemma.

"What's she doing here?" LeCroix wandered over to a pile of tins on a table, picked one up, turned it over, and set it down.

"Hiding from something. Trying to make up her mind what to do next, where to go."

"Like you."

"What are you talking about?" Hunter stared at the man

who had fought beside him at the Battle of New Orleans. Noah LeCroix was a recluse who lived alone in a treehouse built over the water on a nearby swamp. He came in contact with folks only when he was hired to pilot boats through the shoals or when he was out of supplies. Hunter envied Noah his life of solitude.

"I been hearing you say for years that you're leaving here, but you don't. I suspect you're trying to make up your mind where to go and what to do next, too," Noah explained.

He was right, but the moon would turn to cheese before Hunter admitted it aloud. Lately he'd thought of leaving just as soon as he knew Jemma's condition, but every time he sat down to make plans, all he could think of was her. He spent too much time wondering who she was and what she was hiding.

"I know damn well what I'm doing," he said, wishing he could sound more convincing, even to himself.

LeCroix walked over to the door and paused beside it. "I do, too," he said. "You're falling in love. Now are you going to get that gunpowder I need or are you going to stand there all day with that scowl on your face?"

An hour later, Jemma opened the door to the trading post again, stuck her head and shoulders inside, and looked around. Noah was gone. There was no sign of Hunter either. Rubbing her hands together, she shivered as she walked over to the fireplace to warm them. She heard a sound overhead and looked up in time to see Hunter step onto the ladder and climb down from the loft.

She slipped off her coat and began to stack the material he had refolded.

"Just leave it." He stood halfway across the room without moving, looking as if he would rather be anywhere else. She felt awkward and hated the feeling. She forced herself to cross the room.

"You said you wanted to talk to me," he said softly.

"You don't have to worry about being responsible for me any longer. I'm . . . I'm not having a baby." She looked at her hands.

"You're sure?" There was no note of relief in his tone, which surprised her.

Jemma nodded. "Yes."

"Well, then."

"Yes. Well, then." She lingered. Looked up. Caught something in his eyes she never thought to see there. Concern. Regret? Impossible.

There was more she wanted to say, so much more, but she knew she was only making him uncomfortable.

"Do you know how much you upset Lucy earlier?" she asked.

His brow wrinkled with a puzzled frown. "She's scared of her own shadow."

Jemma blinked. "She's terrified of you."

"Me? Why would she be scared of me? I've never done her any harm."

"Look at the way you're scowling right now. Sometimes you act like . . . like an overbearing buffalo. You frighten her speechless."

"I don't mean to."

"*I* know that, but she doesn't. She feels obligated to you for everything she has—"

"I don't begrudge her a thing."

"I didn't say you did. I know you well enough to know you'd give her anything she needed . . . if you took the time to notice, which you haven't. She's outgrown her dresses and is too proud to ask for material for another."

His expression had darkened, but he didn't comment. Jemma rushed on. "A kind word to her or even a smile once in a while would mean a lot coming from you, Hunter." She held her breath.

"I'll talk to her," he promised.

Jemma sighed with relief. "Good. I knew you'd understand. And if you don't mind, I'd like to choose some material for a new dress for her. Nette said she'd help me cut one out and get started.''

''Is that all you need?''

''I don't need anything,'' she said softly, staring into his eyes, dropping her gaze to his lips.

''Nothing?''

She could feel a pull between them stronger than any river current they had faced on the journey, and wondered if he felt it, too.

''A kiss,'' she whispered before she could change her mind. ''That's all.''

chapter
14

"JUST A KISS."

She made it sound like so little. As if he would not have to bridge a huge gulf in order to grant her request, as if he wouldn't have to let down his guard and go against every resolution he had made since he made love to her.

Jemma stood there waiting, staring up at him, expectation mingled with hope in her eyes.

"A kiss?" He almost choked on the word. "We've been down this road before."

He knew she was up to something, but for the life of him he couldn't fathom what it was. He broke out in a cold sweat. All he wanted was to drink in the taste and feel of her, to never let her go. His need went against everything he had convinced himself that he wanted out of life. God help him, he took a step closer as if his body and his mind were disconnected.

"I'd like to oblige you, but I can't." He slipped his arms around her. She stood on tiptoe, staring into his eyes. He gazed into hers. Her eyes were bright, blue, beguiling.

"I wouldn't want you to do anything you don't want to," she whispered against his mouth. Her fingers curled around the hair at the nape of his neck.

He closed his eyes. Maybe if he told himself this really

wasn't happening. Their lips met, touched tenderly, opened. She slipped her tongue into his mouth and he almost came undone. Hunter clasped her tighter, held her to him, and kissed her long and deep and slow.

Jemma moaned and clung to him. Finally, when they were both breathless, he lifted his head, reached up and took her arms from around his neck, held her wrists, and stood her a good arm's length away.

"I don't think we should ever do that again."

"Sister Augusta Aleria would say that lusting in your heart is as great a sin as doing it," she told him.

"But a hell of a lot safer. Do you mind telling me what that was all about?" Intent on hiding his arousal, he walked over to a small table stacked with all-purpose awls, hatchets, and small picks, stood behind it, and pretended to be absorbed in rearranging the items.

"I was curious about something."

"I would think your curiosity has been well satisfied already."

"It has now." She wouldn't stop smiling at him.

"And?"

"Do you have a pen and ink and some paper I might use?"

It was the last thing he had expected her to say. Speechless, all he could do was nod. What now?

"I need to write a letter," she said without prompting. "I'd like to send it with the next party that comes through."

He cleared his throat and stepped behind the counter. "I'll bring them over when I come to talk to Lucy."

"That would be wonderful, thank you." She still didn't leave, although she had moved to the door.

She continued to stare at him with stars in her eyes, the way a man dreamed a woman might one day look at him, *if* that man wanted to pay the price of keeping those stars bright and shining. The way she was looking at him made him as uncomfortable as if he'd been sitting on a hot poker.

He stared at her slender, pale hand where it lay on the door latch.

"It's nice to know that that kind of a kiss doesn't *always* lead to other things," she said.

The door closed behind her, shutting him inside the empty trading post with little to do but let his imagination run wild on what delicious "other things" their kiss might have led to if he hadn't had sense enough to call a halt to the whole episode.

Hunter crossed the room and took a jug of whiskey off the back shelf. He poured four fingers into a glass, then walked over to the hearth and stood there with the drink in his hand. He stared down at the glowing red coals.

Since the rainy night they met, Jemma O'Hurley had turned his world upside down; now, to make matters worse, he was forced to admit he was beginning to feel things for her that he had vowed never to let himself feel again. He tossed back the whiskey, felt it slide down his throat.

He was a man with far horizons to pursue. He wanted to explore like Lewis and Clark and Zeb Pike. No sunshine smile framed by a pair of beguiling dimples was going to keep him from his destiny.

A weaker man might succumb—but not him.

Not Hunter Boone.

There was no denying it any longer. Somehow, sometime between New Orleans and Sandy Shoals, she had fallen in love. She knew it as surely as she knew the sun would rise in the morning. What she didn't know was what to do about it.

Staring off into space, Jemma dropped the door to the root cellar dug into the side of a slight rise and picked up the woven willow basket that she had filled with a dozen potatoes. Headed back to Nette's, she let her mind dwell where it wanted to stay—on Hunter.

She was still warm and tingly all over, despite the November cold. If she closed her eyes, she could almost feel his kiss and the way Hunter tasted, his touch, his gentleness. The soft warm glow from the fire burning in the trading post was the same heat he ignited deep inside her. Just as before, his kiss was magic. She would store it with the rest of her memories of him and uncover it as gently as one might observe a flower in a press. Even if Hunter had given the kiss grudgingly, he *had* given it. The memory was hers now, to cherish forever.

She had time to spare before she went back and began to peel potatoes for Nette to use for supper, so Jemma wandered down the path that led toward the forest. She took a deep breath and tipped her head back to see the open sky above the trees. Even the stark, bare branches held a majestic beauty. She could just imagine how they would look in full bud in the spring, then covered with emerald leaves during the summer.

All of her senses were brimming with life. Did Hunter feel the same way? Or was he back to puttering about the bundles, piles, and shelves stocked with goods as usual? Was he watching for river travelers without giving her another thought?

Or was his whole world upside-down?

If she had been confused about her destiny before, she was utterly baffled now. All things considered, she didn't think it proper to pray to any of the saints for help—not even Valentine—not after the way she had felt with her breasts pressed up against him, not while she could still recall the more intimate details of the night they had made love as if it had been just yesterday. Certainly not while she still relished the lingering tingle brought on by his latest kiss.

No, appealing to the saints was definitely out.

She had gotten herself into this quandary; because of its

passionate overtones, she would have to get herself out. She had left home looking for adventure and found far more—the caring, sharing, sheltering love of family, and even more surprising, she had finally experienced the heated, sensual stirrings of passionate, falling-head-over-heels-in-love love.

She hugged the basket tightly and wandered farther, threading her way between the heavy trunks of the maple and hickory trees. The ground was littered with twigs and leaves and decaying nuts. Melting snow still lay in scattered patches here and there, hugging the bases of the north sides of the trees.

She knew now that Hunter might not be able to resist kissing, but did she dare hope that she could ever get him to return her affections? He had confessed to being a loner, but she had since seen another side of him, one that he might not even know—or wouldn't admit—existed. The others rallied around him, counting on his leadership. Lucy and the Boone children looked up to him. Luther let Hunter make the business decisions. Jemma had even heard Nette defer to him on occasion.

Unaware of her footing, she tripped over a root hidden by the leaves, lurched forward, and dropped one of the potatoes. As she picked it up, she realized it was time to head back to the house. Tucking the potato into the basket, she decided that she would watch Hunter and take her cue from him. She could share the discovery of her love for him with no one, not even Lucy.

She decided to head back and quickly realized she had strayed off of the trail. With a shiver, she drew her jacket closer and hugged the potato basket tightly. Determined not to panic, she walked away from the sound of the river, expecting to come back to the trail, but the farther she traveled, the more dense the forest became.

The first stars of the evening were showing themselves against the twilight sky. Afraid she had already wandered too far, Jemma stopped where she was and backed up against a tree.

Surely someone would realize she was missing. All she could hope was that they would look for her before night fell and she froze to death.

She's going to be the death of me.

Hunter walked down the path that led away from the cabins, searching for signs that Jemma might have passed by. A few minutes earlier, Nette and Lucy had arrived at his cabin looking for Jemma, and when he said that he hadn't seen her for a good hour, Lucy was certain the bump on her head had rendered her senseless and that she was deliriously wandering through the forest.

They didn't take kindly to his jest when he told them he didn't think that she was in possession of all her senses to begin with.

He told the women to send for Luther and to stay put, grabbed his gun, and hurried off to look for her. So far he hadn't had any success.

"Jemma?" He called her name, whistled, and shouted, but there was no answer. Forging ahead, he took the path away from the river, cursing the fast-approaching darkness that would wipe out any chance of finding her footprints.

He'd gone a far piece, fighting to keep his panic at bay, when he heard a slight shuffling sound off to his right. Unwilling to come face-to-face with a bear or other predator, he didn't call out. Instead, he crept forward, rifle at the ready, listening intently.

He was two steps from entering a small clearing when, out of the blue, something hit him in the head so hard that his hat flew off and he nearly fell over.

"Shit!" He cursed aloud, forgetting the possibility of bears, and pressed his hand over the spot above his ear where a lump was rising. A potato lay on the ground next to his foot.

"Hunter?"

He spun around and saw Jemma standing just within the circle of trees, a basket clutched in her arms.

"I suppose I should be thankful you didn't have a gun with you," he said as she hurried over.

"Oh my stars, did I hurt you? I didn't mean it, but I saw this dark, hulking shape looming between the trees and I thought . . . well, I thought you might have been an Indian, or a bear, so—"

"So you decided to bean me with a potato?"

"I'm so sorry!" She was fussing over him as if she really had shot him, setting the basket down, reaching up to examine the lump with her fingertips.

Leaning far too close, she brushed up against his arm.

Hunter stopped trying to dodge away and let her fret, using the cover of darkness to hide the fact that he was rising to the occasion of having her so near. Jemma carefully inspected his wound; then, as if she realized he had become still, she paused. Her arm was draped over his shoulder, her body pressed close. She had gone up on tiptoe so she could hold her hand against his head.

He heard the catch in her breath and felt her draw nearer. A quiet hush of expectancy heated the very air around them. Hunter closed his eyes, fighting his need, determined not to fall into the trap of kissing her again, knowing that this time it definitely would lead to *other things*.

But she was so very close. So warm.

"Hunter? Did you find her?" At the sound of Luther's voice, Jemma pulled away and grabbed up the basket.

Hunter started to call out, had to clear his throat, then yelled, "Over here, Luther."

His brother came bounding through the trees and halted a few feet away. "Thank God. What happened, Jemma?"

"Nothing," she said. Hunter thought she sounded very disappointed. "I lost my way and decided to just stay put, hoping somebody would notice I was missing."

"Well, of course we did. Nette and Lucy are frantic.

Let's get you back right away. You comin' or not, Hunter?''

Hunter watched Jemma walk over to his brother's side. She paused to look back at him, and even in the growing darkness he saw her smile.

''Thanks for saving me again, Hunter. I'm real sorry about that potato.'' With that, she followed Luther back to the path.

It was a moment or two before Hunter started after them, wondering who in the hell was going to look after Jemma when he was gone.

That evening after the supper dishes were cleared away, Nette sat at her quilting frame where, straining to see by the light of an oil lamp, she refused to quit before finishing the last of a row of feather quilting.

Jemma sat by the fire combing her hair, her thoughts so jumbled that she had been unable to accomplish much of anything at all. Lulled by the sound of Lucy reading the Bible aloud, Jemma had fallen into a contemplative silence, her mind wandering in and out, her thoughts woven amid the words of Solomon.

Far more familiar with the catechism than with the Bible itself, Jemma wondered if Solomon hadn't provided the inspiration for more than one of Sister Augusta Aleria's instructional sessions.

''A bundle of myrrh is my well-beloved unto me; he shall lie all night betwixt my breasts,'' Lucy read.

While Jemma found herself blushing, there came a quick, familiar knock at the door. She had grown hopeful that Hunter might come by, but so used to his avoidance that she didn't expect him. Especially after both of their earlier encounters.

The door opened and there he was, his face glowing from the cold night air, his thick hair combed as neatly as he could manage and tied back into a queue. He was holding a brown paper bundle in his arms. His glance took in all three women. Jemma felt a rush of pleasure when his gaze lingered on her the longest before moving back to Lucy.

"What finally brings you in out of the cold, Hunter Boone?" Nette wanted to know. She anchored her needle in the quilt, took off her glasses, and stretched.

"I came to see Lucy," Hunter said, taking a second to nod an awkward greeting to Jemma.

"Me?" Lucy set the Bible down on the table and folded her hands. Although she appeared serene, Jemma knew she was quaking inside.

Hunter took off his buckskin coat and draped it over the chair he pulled up to the table. He sat down across from the girl and laid the package on the scarred wooden top, which was almost white from so many scrubbings. He laid his hands palms down on the tabletop. They were big hands, work-worn and scarred by honest labor and long hours clearing the land. They were the opposite of her father's—hands that had never done anything harder than sign business agreements and her marriage contract.

She watched his shoulders rise and fall as he took a deep breath, collecting his thoughts.

"Would you like Nette and me to go up to the loft?" Jemma asked, willing to give him time to talk to Lucy in a more private atmosphere.

Lucy's eyes begged her to stay.

"No." Hunter shook his head. "What I've got to say to Lucy needs to be said and I don't care who hears it." He turned to the silent, watchful girl who sat so still that she didn't even appear to be breathing.

"Lucy, I'm sorry if I've ever given you reason to fear me or to believe that I might think less of you because of your ma," he said.

Jemma could see that the girl was stunned; her eyes shimmered with unshed tears.

Hunter took a deep breath. "I don't ever want you to feel beholden to me or Nette or the rest of us."

"But Ma stole from you—" Her voice quivered.

"You aren't your mother," he said softly. "I know that and so does everybody here." He glanced down at the Bible beneath her hands. "Your mother might not have known right from wrong, but God made you good so you can balance things out. We all think of you as one of us, and we always have. I'm the one who took up with your mother. When she left, we all wanted you here, but I never figured you didn't know that. Until today, I never knew how you felt."

Lucy didn't say a word. She wiped away tears with the hem of her skirt.

Hunter spoke softly, pausing as if organizing his thoughts.

"You're as close as I've ever come to having children of my own. Don't fault me for not realizing you felt the way you did all this time. I was doing the best I knew how. I guess I kept thinking of you as that little girl who stepped off the boat holding on to your mother's skirt, but you're nearly grown. If you need anything from now on, you be sure to ask any of us and if it's in our power, we'll see that you have it."

He shoved the bundle into the center of the table and began to open the string. When he had trouble untying the knot, Lucy touched the back of his hand. Hunter let her do it.

Jemma's eyes were moist with tears. In the corner, Nette watched in silence. Inside was a folded length of the pink fabric that Lucy had admired.

"This is for you," he said, offering Lucy the material. She picked it up and smoothed her hand over it before hugging it to her heart. Her lashes were still spiky wet from her tears but she was smiling at him as if he had just given her the moon.

Hunter turned around. His eyes met Jemma's across the room. "I brought the things you asked for."

It was a night for truths. She set her brush aside and

stood up. He had opened his heart to Lucy and let the tenderness pour out. Jemma walked over to the table and sat down next to him. She felt him stiffen but ignored it. The paper, pen, a box of nibs, and a pot of ink were all bundled together in an open box. She reached for them and smiled over at Hunter.

"I'm going to write my father," she told him. "And let him know where I am."

Hunter leaned back and folded his arms across his chest. He watched her closely, making no comment. Jemma heard Nette stir behind them, leaving her chair. The old woman's rheumatism had hurt her of late. When she moved, her left foot shuffled along the floor. She came slowly to the table, pulled out her own chair, and eased herself into it.

"So, you're writing to your father in Canada?" Nette said to Jemma.

Jemma blushed and glanced at Hunter from beneath her lashes. She toyed with the corner of the paper box and then took a deep breath and let it out.

"My father is in London right now, if I'm lucky. If not, he's in Boston or New Orleans looking for me."

"What about your brother?" Nette wanted to know.

She could feel Hunter's gaze boring into her and chanced another glance. There was a just-as-I-thought air about him.

"I don't have a brother," she confessed.

"But you told Hunter—" Lucy began.

"I lied. Well, actually, I made up a little story in order to persuade him to take me with him so that I could get out of New Orleans."

"It wasn't a *little* story." He amended.

"Yes," she nodded in agreement. "It was quite a tale."

"So, there was no convent escape, no emir, no Berber rebels in Algiers?" Nette sounded heartily disappointed.

"No oil jar?" Lucy asked.

"He told you both?" Jemma was appalled.

"Hannah told me," Nette confirmed.

"Me, too." Lucy added.

"Oh." Jemma would have liked to crawl beneath the table. It was one thing to make up a whopping lie on a dark, rainy night when one's entire future depended on it, but to have it passed on to people who deserved the truth was yet another.

"There was none of that," Jemma confessed. "Except for the convent. I went to convent school in Boston until a few months ago."

"Then what happened?" Lucy wanted to know.

"How'd you end up here?" Nette asked.

Jemma thought Hunter might say something, but he simply sat there waiting for the truth. The look on his face told her he still wasn't certain he was going to hear it.

"My father owns an import company in Boston. He's moving it to New Orleans. In his opinion, it was high time I wed, so he arranged a marriage to a French Creole whose family is quite prominent. Father believed it would be good for his business contacts and that I would be well settled near him. I—" She looked over at Hunter again, then back down at the paper. "I objected, but he played on my sympathy and reminded me that he had never asked anything of me before. Finally I promised I would go through with it."

"But you didn't," Lucy smiled. "You ran away from your father."

Jemma shook her head. "Oh, no. I fully intended to keep my promise, even though my father went to London to settle business affairs and sent me on my way alone, except for one of his bodyguards. The night the ship from Boston docked in New Orleans, I received word that the man I was to marry had been killed in a duel."

"And you were left wandering the docks with nowhere to go," Nette finished.

"Not exactly," Jemma said. "The Creole family wanted

me to go through with the marriage. You see, they planned to substitute a cousin.''

Lucy leaned forward. ''When you got there, the bridegroom was a hideous creature and you refused to marry him. You ran screaming into the night, right into Hunter.''

''She's been around you too long.'' Hunter's gaze was intent, as if he'd never seen Jemma before.

''Let Jemma tell it, child.'' Nette was sitting on the edge of her chair, her elbows on the table, chin propped in her hands.

Jemma took a deep breath. ''I realized I had been freed from the promise I made my father. I knew he wouldn't get back from London for at least two or three months, and even then, he might not get word of what had happened until he reached New Orleans. All my life I had yearned for adventure. I wanted to see the world, embark on a dangerous journey into new lands. I slipped away from my father's man and ran through the streets of New Orleans.''

''Until you saw Hunter,'' Nette said.

''Yes,'' Jemma nodded, looking over at him again. She couldn't help but smile. ''Until I saw Hunter.''

She was looking at him *that* way again. The way a child with a sweet tooth looks at a gumdrop. Hunter felt his blood heat up. At this rate he was going to die of frustration.

''You said before that you thought Hunter looked like he could be trusted and that he could protect you. You saw that right off about him, didn't you, Jemma?'' There was more than a hint of pride in Lucy's voice.

''I . . . I certainly did. Persuading him to take me with him was another thing. That's why I resorted to making up that long, involved story.''

''Now what will you tell your pa?'' Lucy wanted to know.

''I'm going to let him know I'm safe, that I'm well

taken care of." She smiled at Nette. "I'll tell him how I changed places with another girl that night, a stranger who took my place in the carriage headed for the wedding."

"Will he forgive you?" Lucy was still holding the fabric.

Hunter wondered how anyone could be immune to her charm. The mystery was solved. Now he knew why she had run, why she had demanded that he make love to her. She had taken away the one thing her father had the power to barter with—her virginity. But now she had put herself in a worse situation. Not only would her father be furious, but few husbands would want a soiled bride.

"I'm going to let him know that I'll not be home until I'm good and ready. I want to wait until he is over the notion that he can choose a husband for me."

A husband. Someone who had the right to kiss her, to hold her, to take her to his bed. Although it shouldn't have, the thought jarred him.

Her revelation also explained away the expensive dress she had worn the night they met, her smooth white hands, the gold she had given him. He thought of the life she must have led in Boston, a life he could only imagine. She was well educated, used to culture and the best of everything.

Yet she had let him drag her through the wilderness with barely a complaint.

She had fallen in the pigpen trying to help Nette.

She had come to him on behalf of Lucy, to set things right between them.

She had asked him to be her lover, talked him into taking her innocence.

She had almost made him forget who he was and what he wanted. Now that he knew that their backgrounds were worlds apart, he should have been relieved. She would be going back to New Orleans, to her father. She wouldn't be his responsibility any longer.

He should be happy.

But as he sat there listening to Nette and Lucy ask her all about Boston and the latest styles, as they conferred about the cut of Lucy's new dress, he didn't feel relieved or happy.

Not even a little.

chapter
15

SISTER AUGUSTA ALERIA HAD BEEN RIGHT ABOUT EVERY-
thing. Once a girl had fallen into sin, she was doomed. A
life of endless kissing and *other things* was about all
Jemma ever thought of in her spare time.

Seated on her bed in the loft, taking advantage of the
heat trapped beneath the eaves, she finished hemming
the sleeve of Lucy's new gown, tied a knot, and bit off
the thread with her teeth. She shook out the near-finished
dress and held it up to survey her work. The seams were
straight, the stitches even and carefully placed. The simple
gown wasn't dressmaker-quality, but it was her best effort.
All the embroidery she had completed during those long,
quiet hours alone in Boston were paying off. Every time
she began to fret that her skills were lacking, Nette bol-
stered her confidence.

"Lucy will love it," Nette had assured her time and
again. "The girl only sits still when she settles down to
read the Bible. Whatever little mistakes you made will
never show on a galloping horse."

Before she began the pink gown, Jemma had gained
experience by finishing the butter-yellow dress that Nette
had already started. She had worked all month long so that
by Christmas, a week and a half away, Lucy would have

not one, but two new gowns. Jemma began to thread the needle again so that she could hem the other sleeve when she heard the door open downstairs.

"Jemma? Are you here?"

Jemma recognized Lucy's voice when the girl called up to her. Since her talk with Hunter, Lucy had lost much of her hesitance and reserve. Jemma had taught her how to style her hair and now she kept it clean and shining, tied back with a ribbon or woven into a long, fanciful braid.

"I'm right here, Lucy." Jemma quickly put her thread and needle away and folded the dress, hiding it beneath her bed. Lucy knew she was working on it, but Jemma wanted the finished product to be a surprise. She hurried down the ladder from the loft.

"What is it?"

"Do you think you could go over to Hannah's and watch the children for a while? She and Luther are going over to the post to finish up making Christmas presents, and Nette needs my help with the breadmaking. She didn't think you'd mind."

Jemma smiled, happy to think Hannah wouldn't hesitate to ask her to help out. She was proud that they trusted her with the children. "Of course not. I'll go over right away." She grabbed her cape and was out the door in less than a minute.

When she reached the Boones' cabin, Hannah was hesitant to leave. "Are you sure you don't mind looking after them, Jemma?"

Hannah stood in the middle of the main room with her hands on her hips, her brows drawn together in a frown. Jemma waited beside her, looking over at the four children. Luther Junior sat at the table with his head propped on his fists, smiling. Callie was on the bed in the corner, playing with baby Timmy, who lay on his back, gurgling up at his sister. Little Sadie was sitting on the floor pounding on the bottom of an empty pot. How much trouble could such darling innocents possibly be?

"You just take your time. We'll be fine," Jemma assured her. She was actually looking forward to caring for the children.

When the door closed behind Hannah, the toddler, Sadie, threw the pot against a table leg and let out an ear-splitting howl. Jemma slapped her hands over her ears and rushed to the child, afraid the little girl had hurt herself.

"Sadie, what's wrong?" As Jemma bent to scoop her up, the child shook her head yelling what sounded like, "No, mama! No, mama!" at the top of her lungs.

"Mama had to go out for a minute," Jemma said, her hands slipping off Sadie's waist. The girl was crawling beneath the table, so Jemma was forced to go down on hands and knees to retrieve her. She grabbed hold of Sadie's ankles, impeding her forward progress, but couldn't pull her out.

Baby Timmy joined in the screaming, and to further add to the din, Callie was yelling, "Timmy wants you, Jemma!" over and over.

Junior smiled, stood up, and began to drag his chair over to the shelves of food staples hung alongside the fireplace.

Jemma left Sadie wailing under the table and hurried over to the bed, where Callie was bellowing, "Timmy wants you *now!*"

She reached for the bundle of flailing arms and legs and picked up the beet-faced infant. "Shh. Shh, Timmy. Please." Jemma tried holding Timmy against her shoulder, bouncing him up and down the way she had seen Hannah do so many times. The motion only seemed to upset the baby even more.

Jemma peeked beneath the table to be certain Sadie was still there, then turned toward the bed to ask Callie what to do, but Callie wasn't there. In fact, Callie had disappeared.

"Luther Junior, where's your sister?" As she raced to the window, Jemma saw Junior climbing onto his chair. Could Callie have slipped outside without her noticing?

She didn't think the door had opened, but—

"Sadie's still under the table." Junior shouted over the din of both screaming younger children.

"Not *that* sister. Where's Callie?"

"Probably under the bed," he shouted back.

Jemma knelt down—nearly dropping the squirming, screaming Timmy—lifted the quilt, and peered beneath the bed. "Come out of there, Callie." She tried a gentler tone. "You gave me quite a fright."

"No."

Jemma blinked. *No?* "Callie, come out of there right now or . . . or . . . I'll be really upset."

Callie scooted closer to the wall and tightened like a sow bug.

Her knees were aching. Jemma stood up and shifted Timmy to her other shoulder. She turned around in time to see Sadie crawl out from under the table and run headlong toward the door, her arms outstretched, screaming, "Mama! Mama!" as she went.

"Here, Sadie. Not the door," Jemma said. "Come with me." She took hold of Sadie's wrist with her free hand and gently tried to tug the child away from the door. Sadie had pressed herself up against the wood panels like a spider, arms thrown wide, sobbing brokenheartedly.

Jemma took a deep breath and blew the wayward strands of hair out of her face. Timmy's screams had ebbed to occasional bursts and hiccups. She had successfully pulled Sadie halfway across the floor when she glanced up and spied Luther Junior with his hand in a heavy crockery jar that was teetering on the edge of a high shelf.

"Junior, watch out!" Her warning came just as the crock tipped over and fell, thankfully missing Junior, but smashing against the floor and breaking into four huge, jagged hunks. Honey spattered and oozed over the floor.

"Don't touch that," Jemma cried. Callie suddenly appeared from beneath the bed to stand over the broken shards of crockery with her arms folded across her chest.

With wide hazel eyes she stood there staring up at Jemma.

"Mama's not going to like this one bit! Junior Boone, you're in deep trouble," Callie predicted.

Junior jumped down off the chair. "No, I ain't." He bullied up to his sister, his bottom lip out, his arms folded in imitation of hers.

Jemma kept an eye on the two combatants while she edged Sadie closer to the bed. Timmy was almost calm as he watched his older siblings' performance. She put the baby down in the center of the bed, lifted Sadie up, and set her beside Timmy.

"Don't move," Jemma admonished Sadie, who immediately started howling again, but stayed put.

"Callie's bleeding," Junior yelled.

Jemma spun around and saw Callie holding one of the ceramic shards, her lower lip trembling at the sight of the small cut on the forefinger of her opposite hand.

"Luther, get something to wipe her hand with. Callie, come here and let me see." Jemma cradled Callie's hand in hers and led her over to the bed. Sadie crawled over to inspect the drop of blood along the cut on her sister's finger. Callie was sniffling and whining. "Ow, it hurts."

Junior came running back with one of his mother's aprons. "Here." He thrust it at Jemma. "Wipe it with this." He leaned close to stare at the cut. "Is she bleeding to death?"

Callie screamed, a short, earsplitting burst of sound.

"No!" Jemma yelled. "She's not even close to bleeding to death. She's barely bleeding at all. Take this back and get me a dishrag or something and don't step in that honey, Luther Junior, or I'll tell your Mama."

Junior took the apron and started off to do her bidding; then he paused in the middle of the room and smiled. "You sounded a little like Mama, just then."

Jemma wondered how Hannah kept her sanity. She offered up a quick, short plea to St. Felicity, a martyr who had seven sons.

When Junior came back with a wet rag, Jemma pressed it to the tiny cut on Callie's finger. She was holding the girl's hand in hers when the door opened and Hunter stepped in, whipping the door closed behind him to keep the frigid air out.

His cheeks were red with cold, his eyes shining above the muffler around the lower half of his face. He took two steps and halted before he stepped into the honey.

Pulling off the muffler, his eyes met Jemma's from across the room.

"What happened?"

Junior stiffened. His gaze shot to Jemma's.

"An accident," Jemma told Hunter. "The crock fell. I didn't have time to clean it up."

Callie was too preoccupied with her cut to tattle on Junior. Hunter crossed the room and stood over Jemma, watching her tend Callie's wound. Suddenly, Jemma felt her hands begin to tremble. He was too near, watching her too closely. She would rather face another thirty minutes alone with these screaming banshees than have Hunter hovering nearby.

"Callie cut her finger," Junior announced.

"It's just a little cut," Callie informed her uncle. "Jemma said I'm not bleeding to death."

Hunter smiled. "I don't reckon you are."

"Bleedin'," little Sadie mumbled.

"You need any help?" Hunter asked Jemma. She wanted to leap in the air and shout for joy. Instead, calm and collected again, she smiled up at him.

"Everything seems to be fine now, but if you care to stay and watch the others while Luther and I clean up that honey, I would appreciate it."

Baby Timmy had fallen asleep with his thumb in his mouth. Hunter smoothed the little boy's hair back off his sweaty face and gently shifted the infant toward the wall to make room on the bed.

"Come here, Sades," he said, stretching out, planting Sadie on his stomach, where she began bouncing up and down. Callie climbed up beside him, holding her wounded finger in the air like a hard-won battle trophy. She lay her head on Hunter's shoulder and joined him in watching Jemma and Luther as they scrubbed up the spilled honey.

Hunter found the view enchanting. Jemma was on all fours, wiping up the honey-smeared floor with soapy water, carefully instructing Junior, deftly making the boy think he was doing all the work.

When they finished, Junior insisted that they all had to have baths before they could be tucked into bed.

"Are you up to it?" Hunter asked

Jemma had pulled up a chair, slumped down into it, and stared over at the four children lounging on the bed with him.

She shook her head. "How does Hannah do this day in and day out?"

"A labor of love. Besides, she's used to it," Hunter told her, wondering what Jemma would do with a houseful of dimpled children that took after her.

"She's a saint," Jemma mumbled.

"I'll help bathe them," Hunter volunteered, knowing what torture he would have to endure in such close, homey confines with Jemma, watching her every move, listening to the honeyed tones of her voice, drinking in her loveliness. He had denied himself the pleasure of her company for so long now that his senses were singing.

Determination stiffened her shoulders. She rolled up her sleeves. "What do we do?"

"You tell them one of your stories while I heat some water and fill the tub," he suggested as he eased himself off the bed.

He turned and pointed to each of the older children in turn. "You stay put and don't give Jemma a minute's grief while I fill the water buckets, you hear?"

"Yes, Uncle Hunt," they chorused in unison.

"How did you do that?" Jemma whispered as he walked past her.

He leaned close and whispered, "I'm bigger and I look meaner."

An hour later, Junior, Sadie, and Callie were bathed and dressed in their nightclothes and tucked into bed. Hunter decided it would be best not to disturb Timmy, and Jemma quickly agreed. Finally, the washtub had been emptied and the floor mopped again. She poured him a cup of coffee and they sat at the table, reveling in the quiet.

Hunter stared across at Jemma and tried to imagine her in the life she must have led in Boston. He'd been to Philadelphia once, seen the grand homes there lined up row upon row, marveled at the lacquered carriages, admired the fine, tailored clothes of the city folk.

"You ever scrubbed a floor before?" He spoke the thought aloud, before he realized what he was doing.

Startled out of her quiet thoughts, she looked up. One of her dimples appeared in her cheek. "Whatever makes you ask?"

"I was just wondering."

Her finger traced the lip of her coffee cup. "No. I never scrubbed a floor before. Did I do something wrong?" She glanced over at the floor beneath the shelves, presenting him with a view of her lovely profile.

"Perfect," he whispered. Hunter cleared his throat. "You did just fine."

Even in the soft glow of the lamplight, he saw her blush.

"You've done well here, Jemma, getting along, helping out Nette and everyone else." He meant the compliment sincerely. She had affected them all. In a few weeks' time she had drawn Lucy out and given the girl new confidence. She had become Nette's companion and lightened the old woman's heart and load. She was anywhere and everywhere anyone needed her.

Jemma was silent for so long that he thought she hadn't

been listening, but when she looked up at him again, there were tears glistening in her eyes. Her smile was radiant. He watched her reach across the table, move her hand slowly toward his. He held his breath, waiting for her touch.

"I've never been needed in my life, never knew what it meant to really belong. My father . . . well, my father never had any time for me. He hired nannies and tutors and then eventually sent me off to convent school. You can pay someone to work, but you can't pay them to care. My grandfather came to live with us for a time, and we grew close, but shortly after that he died. You and your family have given me something I didn't even know I was looking for when I left New Orleans. No matter what happens, I'll always be grateful to you for that."

He felt his heart stumble when she tenderly touched the back of his hand and had to look away from the intensity in her eyes. She made it seem so right, so easy, this opening one's heart and sharing deep feelings. She was adept at weaving ties that threatened to bind a man, to make him feel like settling down.

The warmth of her hand seeped through the back of his, burning him with her touch, stirring up feelings he didn't want to acknowledge any more than he had wanted to walk into this cabin earlier, knowing she was here, unwilling to stay away. When Lucy told him Jemma was alone with the children, he had hurried right over, not to see if he could help, but because after so long a period of self-imposed denial, he had to see her.

If this kept up, he wasn't going to be able to fight it much longer. Slowly he withdrew his hand, watched her draw hers back and finger the rim of her cup.

It was so tempting, picturing quiet nights like this alone with her. With Amelia, he had never known peace. After the first heat of passion was satisfied, there had been nothing left but the cold ashes of desire. If he let himself go, if he set aside his dreams again and opened his heart to

Jemma, her love would no doubt lull him into a cocoon of quiet serenity. Would he be happy forever? Or would he wake up one morning too old for new frontiers, forced to live with the regret of never reaching for his dream?

"You seem so far away, Hunter," she said softly. "What are you thinking?" The hope in her eyes told him she longed for far more than he could give.

Words from the heart didn't come easy to him. They never had. He was unwilling to let them slip out, knowing it would be impossible to call them back.

"I'm thinking it's time I head back to the trading post and see what's keeping Luther and Hannah."

Avoiding her gaze, he pushed away from the table, stood up, and rolled his shoulders to work out the stiffness there. He had spent a long, cold day checking beaver traps with Noah. He knew it would be far more pleasant just sitting there looking at Jemma, spending time thinking of what could be and what shouldn't be, but it was time to go.

Jemma left her chair, unable to keep from staring up at him.

The light and shadows flickered and played over his strong features. He appeared larger than life, a man no cabin walls could ever confine. What would her father think of him? Thomas O'Hurley respected power, wealth, and influence. Would the fact that Hunter had sculpted a life out of sheer wilderness mean anything at all to her father?

She could not imagine Hunter Boone in any other setting, certainly not in the restricting parlors of Boston or trapped behind a desk at the warehouse. The notion that he might one day don wool and linen and spend his days tallying receipts and accounts was not only absurd, it was appalling. Setting her sights on a future with Hunter would mean giving up the life she had always known.

Their eyes met. Their gazes held and locked. In that

instant she knew that she would follow this man to the ends of the earth if he would have her.

Convincing him that that was what he wanted would be another matter all together.

"Hunter, I want to thank you for what you said to Lucy."

"It needed saying."

"Something you told her cleared up a lot of things for me, too. When you said you were doing the best you knew how, I realized my father was only doing what he thought best. He had no idea what I wanted when he arranged that marriage for me. He had no inkling of my own hopes and dreams. He never asked and I never told him."

"You'll be heading back soon." It was a statement, not a question.

She wanted him to tell her that she could stay indefinitely. More than that, she wanted him to tell her that he didn't want her to ever leave. But of course, the words never came. Finally, she said, "I'll stay until I've heard Father has moved to New Orleans."

He stood there as if debating what to do and then filled the awkward pause. "I'd best be getting back."

She wanted to kiss him. Wanted to throw her arms around his neck, kiss him long enough and hard enough to keep him from walking away. Longing to hear him say that he had missed seeing her, she knew she had to content herself with the knowledge that at least he hadn't announced he would be leaving anytime soon.

Unwilling to risk the short fall from impulsiveness to humiliation, she decided that she would leave the kissing up to Hunter. The next move would be his.

He walked around the table, took his coat off an empty chair, and put it on. She watched him, drinking in his every move. She thought he was about to reach for her when he balled his hand into a fist and took a step back.

"You have that look on your face again," he said.

"What look?"

"The one you get when you're thinking about . . . things you shouldn't think about."

"You know me too well," she said with a soft laugh.

She wanted him to know her better than anyone on earth, wanted him to taste and touch and feel every inch of her.

"Will you be all right until Luther and Hannah come home?"

"I'll be fine," she assured him after a glance at the sleeping children.

He left her then, stepped out into the cold and closed the door quietly behind him. As soon as she heard the latch fall, Jemma went back to the table, sat down and cradled her head in the crook of her arm, and let the tears flow.

chapter
16

CHRISTMAS WITH THE BOONES WAS AN ASSAULT ON THE senses. Jemma sat at a long table in the trading post crowded with everyone—Luther and Hannah and the children, Nette and Lucy, Hunter and even Noah LeCroix. As she listened to the sound of the children's laughter, she wished the night could go on forever. The remains of a Christmas feast littered the table; the aromas of popcorn and cider, cinnamon, pumpkin pie, and hickory smoke laced the air. After entering into a constant flurry of activity that had begun at dawn—cooking, baking, decorating, and secreting brown paper packages into the post—tonight everyone seemed content to linger.

Not far away, the older children sat on the floor playing with the new wooden toys Luther and Hunter had made for them. Dolls, miniature horses, and small wagons piqued their imaginations. There was even a toy flatboat and a keelboat that Noah had carved.

"I'm as full as a tick on a fat dog." Luther laughed and sat back, patting his flat stomach with both hands. It started everyone chuckling.

Even Nette was in no mood to clear the table. "That was the biggest turkey I think we've ever had. Couldn't hardly get her on the spit. Next year, you boys have to hunt down one that's a mite smaller."

Luther readily agreed.

Junior sidled over to Nette. When the boy leaned against her, she slipped an arm around his shoulders. ''Nette, remember you said I could have the turkey feathers so's I could make a hat like Jemma's Indian?'' Junior reminded her.

Across the room Callie cradled her new doll, complete with a carved wooden head and a dress made out of treasures from Nette's scrap basket. Motherhood had not stifled her ability to bellow. ''You said I could have some, too!''

''Hush, Callie, or you'll wake Timothy.'' Hannah was sitting beside Luther. The baby was fast asleep in a cradle near the table. ''Nette won't forget. She doesn't forget anything.''

''Jemma and I'll help you make Choctaw turbans tomorrow,'' Lucy promised. She looked like a Christmas angel who had chosen to spend an evening on earth. Her light-brown hair shone in the firelight. The new pink gown that Jemma had made set off the glow of her cheeks.

After his initial shock had worn off, Noah LeCroix hadn't been able to keep his eyes off Lucy. He had chosen a seat directly across the table from her, the best vantage point for staring. If she had noticed his attention, she wasn't letting on.

Jemma was wearing her own gown tonight, the ice-blue silk she had worn in New Orleans. Hannah had washed, pressed, and mended it for her as a Christmas surprise, but when she had slipped it on earlier, she felt as if a different person had once worn it. She couldn't believe she had ever taken the elegant feel of the expensive material for granted. Although everyone proclaimed her lovely, she felt overdressed and out of place.

As the conversation hummed about her, Jemma was content to sit back and listen, loving every boisterous moment.

Hannah shifted away from Luther long enough to cut

herself another sliver of pumpkin pie. "How did you like your first Kentucky Christmas, Jemma?"

"It was wonderful. The best Christmas ever," she answered without hesitation.

"Oh, posh," Nette laughed. "You're just being kind. I'll bet you have real fancy Christmases in Boston."

A bittersweet ache filled Jemma at the memory of the Christmas celebrations she'd shared with her father.

"Tell us about it, Jemma," Lucy urged.

Jemma looked around the table at the eager faces awaiting her description of the many Christmases she would just as soon forget. Early-morning mass was followed by a midday dinner in the dining room. Dressed in their finest, she and her father would dine at opposite ends of the table, a sea of crystal, china, sterling candelabra, and hothouse flowers separating them.

After dinner he would present her with a pile of gifts to open: more of the same sort of gowns and jewelry that already filled her room. Most often she would make something for her father, something he didn't need or want, and buy him a book out of her allowance. He would fuss over the gifts for a moment and then hand them over to Mrs. Greene and have the housekeeper put them away.

Later, the household staff was called in, presented with Christmas bonuses, and summarily dismissed. Shortly afterward, Thomas O'Hurley would leave to go visiting, as it was his custom to deliver champagne and good cheer to his many business associates in the city. Once or twice, when Jemma was a little girl, Mrs. Greene had let her attend the gay celebration in the servants' dining room. Until tonight, those noisy, crowded affairs had been her favorite Christmases. One Boston Christmas had blended into another—none of them very special. Not one had ever left such a warm glow in her heart.

Lucy was waiting expectantly for her to weave a grand tale.

Jemma sighed. No one wanted to relive such bleak Christmas memories. Most especially her.

"My father and I would spend a quiet day at home. That's all there was to it." She spread her hands wide in a gesture of apology. Everyone was expecting more.

Hunter, who had been sitting apart from the group, stepped out of the shadows. All day long, Jemma had been aware of him watching the festivities but not really joining in. Tonight, he seemed not only to be distancing himself from her, but from the rest of them as well. He had not uttered more than a few words since they had all sat down to eat, and when the meal was through, he had slipped into the background like a haunting shadow.

Committing them all to memory.

The notion shocked her. Could that have been what he was doing, she wondered? Or was he merely in a reflective mood?

"How about a walk, Jemma?"

He stood at the end of the table, holding her green wool cloak in his hands. The invitation shocked and surprised her so much that she simply sat there staring up at him.

"Are you crazy, Uncle Hunt? It's freezin' outside," Junior volunteered. He was immediately hushed by his father and his mother.

"Of course, she'll go." Nette nudged Jemma out of her silent stupor.

"I . . . yes. That would be nice." She let him slip her cloak over her shoulders, feeling a sudden warmth when he put his hand on the small of her back.

What in the world was going on? She couldn't help but wonder why, after avoiding her so consciously, he suddenly wanted to be alone with her. Not only that, but he had just announced it to the whole family.

A deafening silence fell over the table as Hunter led her to the door. The only ones not paying them any mind were the little girls, who were still content with placing their dolls on the toy boats and shoving them across the floor.

Jemma paused to look back before she stepped outside and caught everyone in a frozen tableau, smiling at her and Hunter.

"You seemed uncomfortable talking about Boston," he said without preamble as they stepped out into the night. "I thought you might like to escape."

"Thank you for coming to the rescue again. Did you forget I'm not paying you to look after me anymore?" She laughed and looked over at him, but her teasing hadn't even brought a smile to his lips.

Thankful for the chance to stretch her legs after the heavy meal, Jemma noticed that Hunter had matched his long strides to her shorter ones. The air was dry and cold. Overhead, the stars had put on their most brilliant display for Christmas. With the trees towering alongside the path and the open sky above, she felt as if she were in a roofless cathedral.

Side-by-side, they headed down the snow-covered path toward the river. The sound of the rushing water mingled with the light wind blowing through the trees. She didn't think anything could compare to the magical setting of the dense, endless forest surrounding the cabins on the bluff above the Mississippi. Certainly not Boston or New Orleans.

"It's so beautiful here," she said, thinking aloud. "When I first saw this place I thought it looked like an enchanted village in a fairy tale."

"It's a hard life out here on the edge of the world."

His tone was so matter-of-fact, so detached, that Jemma laid a hand on his arm. "What's wrong?" she asked. "You've been so quiet all evening."

They had reached the end of the trail, where it started down the steps built into the bluff that led to the landing. Hunter paused and stared across the river, taking his time answering, drinking in the sound of the water. Somewhere along the riverbank, a night owl hooted. It was a lonely, mournful sound.

A shiver ran down Jemma's spine.

"I'm leaving, Jemma. Tomorrow morning. I wanted to tell you first, before I told the others."

Her breath caught. She felt as helpless and adrift as she had the day she was flung headlong into the raging waters of the Homochitto. He had made it sound so final.

"Leaving? Where are you going?"

He still wouldn't look at her. "West."

The word said it all and yet nothing. The West was an endless expanse of uncharted land. In most minds it was still an idea more than a place.

"But isn't this rather sudden?" A sense of panic hit her. She clasped her hands together to still their shaking. "You're going to just up and leave? For how long?" She wanted to touch his shoulder, make him look at her.

He shrugged. "For good."

Forever. She would never see him again. "Why, Hunter?"

He turned around. She wished he hadn't. His tortured soul was mirrored in his eyes.

"What about the others?" *What about me?*

"They'll get along. They don't need me now."

She stood there mute, her heart racing.

"There will hardly be any more boats headed downriver until spring. Luther can hire somebody to help put out the crops. We have plenty of men through here asking for work every spring. Thanks to you, Lucy's doing fine. It's not easy to explain, but I've just got to go, Jemma."

He sounded panicked, as if he were trying to convince himself, not her.

She had come too far, discovered too much about herself to let him walk out of her life when she was just beginning to understand who she was and what she wanted. The wind off the river picked up a strand of her hair, threading it through her eyelashes. She brushed it away.

"What if I said I didn't want you to leave?"

"Jesus, Jemma. Don't make this any harder than it has to be."

"But, why *does* it have to be, Hunter? I've seen you with your family. You belong here."

"More and more folks will be settling around here, wanting to build close to the post and the landing so they can ship their crops downriver. Pretty soon there will be towns, roads. I don't like crowds, Jemma. I'm a loner. I've got to be on the move."

She lashed out with anger fueled by hurt. "You might think you're a loner, but you're not. You're a leader who needs people as much as they need you. You *collect* people, you attract them like flies to honey. Nette, Lucy. Luther and Hannah and the children. They wouldn't have come this far if it hadn't been for you. They want you in their lives, not just for what you can give them—"

Hunter turned away and stared out at the dark water. She couldn't give up, couldn't let him go without a fight.

"And Noah. Hannah told me Noah's uncomfortable around most people, that he hardly ever says a word. He won't give folks the time of day, and yet he considers you his friend." She took a deep breath and plunged on, reckless. "What about me? You knew I was lying. You could have left me in New Orleans, turned your back and refused to help, but you didn't. Do you think you can ever walk away from what's inside you, Hunter? From this ability to gather people, to guide them and help them find their way?"

"People have needed me all my life, Jemma. My pa died early and Ma needed me to take over. Then it was Luther and Hannah. Then Nette. And Lucy."

"And me. I'm sorry I've been such a burden." A deep sorrow wrenched her heart. While she had been falling in love with him, he had added her to his list of responsibilities.

"And you. But never be sorry, Jemma." He reached out and touched her cheek, traced her dimple with his thumb—

a gentle, fleeting touch, as if he couldn't bear to linger. "I'm sure your father has a home waiting for you whenever you're ready to go back to it."

"So you don't have to worry about me now, either, is that it? Oh, yes, Hunter. I have a place to live, but it's not a home. Never a *home*. What I wouldn't trade for someone needing me," she cried. "My father needed me like a man needs a new carriage to show his friends. I was a reminder of the time he had with my mother, but his business took her place in his life, not me. I was a memento, a showpiece. He never, ever really *needed* me. Do you know how lucky you are to be needed? To have a family that loves you?"

"Yes. I do. But I know what I feel inside. Here." He placed his hand over his heart. "I've dreamed of this for so long, of going out into the wilderness on my own. I want to make the first footprints across lands no white man has ever seen."

She felt as if she were hanging off a cliff and her fingers were beginning to slip. She tried to calm down and not let panic overwhelm her.

"I had a dream, too, Hunter. I thought I wanted adventure. I wanted out of my old life—but what I came to realize was that I wasn't looking for adventure. I was looking for what you have had every day of your life—a sense of belonging, and love—and I found it here."

"If I don't go now, I'll never go."

Desperation made her panic. "Then take me with you—"

"I don't even know where I'm going." His voice was harsh, his lips grim. He grabbed her upper arms, held her away from him. Some of his hair had escaped the leather thong. The wind whipped it across his mouth and away.

"But I've just found you." A ragged sob caught in her throat. "I've been looking all my life—"

"What are you talking about?"

"You. You and me. Don't you see? I love you, Hunter."

"Don't, Jemma. One night doesn't give you enough experience to know whether or not you're in love."

He may as well have taken her heart in his hands and squeezed the life out of it. He went on before she could tell him that the words were tearing her apart.

"I thought I was in love with Amelia, but by the time she left, I was happy to see her go. I didn't know how to end it and she saved me the trouble."

"You're saying you don't care for me at all?" She had gone beyond humiliation, lost her grip and slipped over the edge. She was falling and needed to grab on to a lifeline. "I've seen something else in your eyes when you look at me, Hunter. Something you aren't willing to own up to."

"I care too much," he said softly. "That's why I have to leave. I can't take your love—which is what will surely happen if I stay. I don't want to wake up some morning knowing I made a mistake, wishing I'd gone after my dream."

She knew all about dreams. She had wanted to follow hers so badly that she had walked out of her old life, never knowing that the respite from her father's world would change her forever. If she went back, she knew she would no longer be content with hours of embroidery, tedious tea parties, social calls, pretentiousness.

Yes, she knew about dreams.

He was right—he had to go. She understood, and still it hurt. All of her anger and desperation ebbed to a dull ache that lodged in her heart.

"Go then," she whispered, turning to stare across the Mississippi, furious at him, at herself, at fate. "Go after your dream, Hunter Boone."

"Jemma—"

She felt his hand on her shoulder and shook him off.

"Don't touch me. Please."

"Walk back with me."

She shook her head no. "I don't want to be there when you tell them. I'll . . . I'll go back to Nette's alone."

"You can stay here in Sandy Shoals as long as you want, Jemma."

"I know that."

"Maybe if—"

"Don't even say it, Hunter." She held up her hand, the gesture a plea, a warning. "Don't make me hope when there isn't any."

"Won't you at least turn around and tell me good-bye?"

She whirled around and let him see the icy tears she had been hiding before she wiped them away. Her hands were freezing, her heart a frozen lump in her chest. She had realized that her dream, and now the very heart of it, was slipping away.

"Tell me you don't want me," she said.

"You know I do. Let me go, Jemma."

"Kiss me good-bye, Hunter. Kiss me one last time so you'll have something to think about out there on your damned frontier."

For a heartbeat she was certain he was going to deny her. She could see him warring with his emotions, see the need flaring in his eyes—a need as deep and yearning as her own. Suddenly, as if afraid he might change his mind, Hunter reached for her, slipped his hands beneath her cloak, and dragged her into his arms. She cupped his face. His cheeks were cold. She welcomed his lips. They were warm. She threw aside restraint and melded herself against his hard length.

His mouth slashed across hers. What he demanded, she gave. What she offered, he took. This was no gentle kiss. This was an all-out assault on each other's senses. As she opened to him, as their tongues touched, circled, delved, and tasted, she committed it all to memory.

She ran her hands through his hair. Her breath was coming hard and fast, like his. She felt him shift his stance, press his hard manhood against her. His hands slid up along her ribs; the heat of his palms through her gown rebuffed the cold night air. When his thumb teased the underside of her breast, Jemma wrapped her arms around his neck. He cupped her breasts, teased her nipples—hard, aching buds beneath the silk. Her need shot through her—lightning-swift need that rocked her and started a sweet, aching pulse between her thighs. She moaned against his mouth.

He tried to pull away.

His breath was as ragged and rough as her own. He reached up, took hold of her wrists, and pulled her arms away from his neck. Standing there in the dark, he held her wrists in his hands and stared down into her eyes. In the darkness, his eyes were colorless, black, haunted by warring needs.

"I've got to do this, Jemma."

"I know," she whispered.

She thought he was going to release her—and started to close her eyes so that she wouldn't have to watch him walk away. Then, standing a foot away, he bent down and touched his lips to hers once more. The kiss was light as milkweed down, as quick as the tick of a clock stealing time. Then it was over.

Jemma wrapped her cloak tightly around her, its warmth wanting compared to his embrace, and left him standing there beside the river.

For the first time in his life, Hunter felt completely alone. Alone with only his dream for comfort. As he watched Jemma disappear down the path, heading toward Nette's cabin, part of him wanted to call her back, to beg her to forgive him and forget everything he had just said. But he would only be prolonging the inevitable.

No matter what she said, no matter how logical her argument, they had to go their separate ways. She was from another world. Sooner or later, the novelty of life in Sandy

Shoals would wear thin; when she was facing the everyday hardships without naïve enthusiasm, she would think differently.

He took a deep breath and waited for the frigid air to cool his blood. He should have known better than to kiss her again, but the hard truth was that he had reached the point where he couldn't deny her or himself any longer. Watching her throughout the celebration tonight, he knew that if he stayed one more day, if he had spent one more hour with Jemma, he would have thrown caution to the wind and taken her to his bed. There would have been no turning back. He would never have been able to leave her.

He should have asked her for the name of a saint who might help get him through the next hour. He wished like hell he could walk away right now, simply disappear into the forest. But first he needed to collect his gear and provisions. And he owed his family more. They loved him. Above all else, there was that.

He had to go back to the post and tell them that he was leaving at dawn's first light. He had to say good-bye, kiss Hannah and the little ones, endure Nette's tears and the abandonment in Lucy's eyes. He had to say good-bye, knowing as he did that there was a very real possibility it would be the last time he would ever see any of them again.

chapter
17

Upper-Missouri Wilderness, March 1817

A dream can be a very cold and lonely thing, not unlike the snow that reflected blue-white beneath the sun as Hunter rode across the open plain, leading his pack mules behind him. He had grown used to listening to the sound of his own breath, watching it fog on the sharp, cold air.

There was a storm coming on. He could feel it in his bones, smell it. After waking up mornings with no real plan except to keep moving and stay alive, he even welcomed the necessity of searching for a place to take shelter.

Squinting against the sun, he studied what appeared to be a thin, white ribbon of smoke against the sky. There were Mandan winter camps nearby; he had passed some of the villages and found the people curious and eager to trade. Hunter headed toward the smoke and finally came to a rise that overlooked a shallow valley chiseled out between two foothills. The smoke rose from a crude chimney made of river rock atop a structure half-planted into the side of a hill.

He called out a loud "Hallo!" but no one returned his greeting. Other than the echo of his own shout reverberating against the hills, and the distant call of a magpie, there wasn't another sound in the valley. He nudged his roan and rode toward the dugout.

Up close, he found that the dwelling was little more than a hovel. Rough pine logs formed the front. The sides butted into the hill, a hybrid of a dugout. Certainly not built for permanence, it had been fashioned by someone with no talent for building. As he dismounted and tied his horse to a nearby pine, he took a good look at the structure. There wasn't one decent corner saddle, the joint where the logs met. Luther, a zealot when it came to building log structures, would have been appalled. There was a feed crib in a lean-to that had once sheltered a horse or a mule, but it was empty now.

Far from eager to have his head blown off, Hunter called out and unsheathed his rifle as he walked toward the cabin. Except for the smoke from the chimney, there was no sign of life. With his hand on the door latch, he shouted again. Inside, someone coughed.

He tried the latch and found it unlocked. Rifle at the ready, he slowly pushed the door open. The interior of the place was not much bigger than the smokehouse at Sandy Shoals. The floor was cold, hard-packed earth. The few meager hand-hewn furnishings inside showed more poor attempts at woodworking. A thin piece of yellow hide covered the only window. Muted sunlight stained the greased window covering, but did little to light the room.

The place reeked of poorly cured furs, unwashed flesh, urine, and death. A bed was shoved up against the far wall. At first glance, Hunter thought it was empty. Then he heard the cough again, a weak, rasping sound. The tired struggle for breath made his own lungs ache in sympathy. The slight rise and fall of the bearskin atop the bed was hardly perceptible.

Despite a low fire, the room was still cold. Hunter crossed the dugout, curious to see what manner of man lay dying beneath the hide. The cough scarred the air again.

"Hello?" Hunter drew closer.

A weak, gravelly voice issued from beneath the hide. "If you've . . . come to kill me . . . be done with it." Between bursts of speech, a man gasped for breath, drinking in air until he choked on it and coughed.

Hunter stepped up to the bed and looked down into the gaunt, skeletal face of an old man whose watery brown eyes were stained with pain. His skin was yellow-gray, his hands as thin as crows' feet with blue veins that stood out like knotted rope. The sleeves of his buckskins were almost black, stiff with filth and age. Everything about the old-timer—his thin wisps of hair, his skin, his clothing—all seemed brittle, as if at a touch he would crumble to ash.

"I haven't come to kill you." Hunter hunkered down on one knee, wincing at the offensive smell.

"More's the pity," the man whispered.

"There's a storm coming in. I was looking for a place to ride it out." Hunter wondered if he could stand being shut up inside the fetid dugout even for an hour, let alone for the duration of a heavy storm.

"Suit . . . yourself."

"Where's your water? I'll get you some," Hunter volunteered after seeing the man's cracked, dry lips. Tobacco-red bloodstains ran from the corners of his mouth, down his cheek. The filthy blanket beside his head was stained with his blood. Hunter wondered how he had managed to keep the fire going.

The old-timer shook his head. "No water. I don't . . . want to drag this . . . this thing out any longer . . . than I have to." He fell into frenzied coughing spasms that brought his wasted frame up off the bed and slammed it down again.

Hunter felt helpless in the face of such pain. Not a stranger to death, at seventeen he had lost his father. A few years later, his mother had been struck down by fever in only three days' time. For either, there had been none of this pitiful, slow wasting. Swift, accidental death was commonplace on the frontier, where countless dangers lurked. He had never thought of a swift death as a stroke of luck before, but this old man's immeasurable suffering was a death sentence he would not pass on to a dog.

"Are . . . you . . . alone?" The old man wheezed.

Hunter nodded, finally finding his voice. "I am. Name's Hunter Boone."

"Any . . . relation . . . to Daniel?"

"Distant cousins."

"Never met him." The old-timer's eyes closed. He lay silent for so long that Hunter felt for a sign of life. "I ain't . . . gone yet, more's . . . more's the pity. M'name's Charlie . . . Tate. Make your . . . self . . . t'home."

When the old man closed his eyes again and exhaled on another fit of coughing, Hunter straightened. He walked across the room and stood his Hawkin rifle in the corner near the door. Charlie Tate had drifted off into the world of pain and sickness that was devouring him.

Taking stock of the squalid room and its meager contents, Hunter decided to put his horse and mules up in the lean-to, unload his supplies, and secure his rig outside. There'd be less chance of his things getting infested with bedbugs and lice if he didn't bring them in.

He picked up a few spindly pieces of wood, all that was left for the fire, and wondered how the old man could have managed to gather them at all. Stepping outside, Hunter welcomed the bite of the cold, fresh air, and filled his lungs, trying to overcome the lingering memory of the heavy stench he had left inside.

Settling the animals and unloading his gear had become so much a part of his daily routine that it took little effort and no thought. He took his line and walked to the little stream not far away. His luck running high, he caught two respectable trout with shimmering rainbow scales, strung them on a line, and carried them back to the lean-to, where he unpacked his skillet.

He laid a fire in the sheltered area between the animal hut and the dugout cabin, boiled water, and stick-cooked his trout. As he picked off the savory white fish, he studied the small space between the two structures, wondering if he could create a sheltered area for himself between them by using a tarp and wood to connect the two. It would be preferable to sleeping in filth.

Hunter had saved some fish for Charlie, though he doubted that the old man could eat more than a bite or two. As he picked up the warm skillet, he wished his conscience would let him avoid going back inside the hovel.

The place was as still as death, the fire nearly out. With the skillet in his hand, he stood over the bed and looked at what remained of Charlie Tate.

"I made some trout." Hunter glanced at the trout in the pan. The black, sightless fish eye stared back at him.

The old man's dry lips moved. "I can't . . . eat. Nothin' goes down."

Feeling helpless, Hunter reached over and set the skillet on the table.

"I been thinkin' . . . ," Charlie gasped. "A . . . man can . . . do a lot of thinkin' when he's dying. Who are you . . . Hunter Boone?"

Three months ago, Hunter thought he knew the answer. Now he wasn't sure if he wasn't so much a loner as just alone. He reckoned the old man wanted to hear another voice, needed something to take his mind off of his pain.

"I'm from Pennsylvania by way of Kentucky. Found a place on the Mississippi for my brother's family. Started a trading post. When it looked like more and more folks would be moving into the area, I felt the need to move on. So here I am."

A ragged breath ripped itself out of the old man's throat. He whispered, "Wanderlust."

"I guess," Hunter shrugged and pulled a chair up beside the bed. "I couldn't see myself putting down roots."

"Couldn't?"

"Can't," he amended. An uncomfortable feeling crept over him, one he wouldn't dare admit to, or even dwell on.

"Go back—"

The words were uttered low, a thread of sound. Hunter leaned closer, held his breath against the stench. "What did you say?"

"Go back be . . . fore it's too . . . late. This life . . . it's fine when you're . . . when you're young and able. But," Charlie shuddered, ". . . what's . . . the point? . . . You gonna follow . . . one more river . . . ride over one more . . . mountain? They all . . . look alike after . . . a while."

The old man's words so closely echoed Hunter's own thoughts of late that he wondered if Charlie Tate was able to read his mind.

"There'll come a time when . . . when . . . you'll get awful . . . tired of . . . hearing . . . your own heartbeat." Collapsing into a coughing fit, Charlie raised a palsied hand to his lips and wiped away bloody spittle.

Hunter rubbed his hands on his thighs and looked around the squalid room. "Save your strength, old man."

A strangled, cackle escaped Tate. "What for? I'm dyin'. . . . What good's . . . my life been, if . . . I can't pass on what . . . I learnt? You want to . . . end up like this?"

Exhausted, the old man lay panting for air. His fingers, with their long filthy nails, raked the bear-hide cover. Hunter looked away, studying the fire that was as inept at fighting the cold in the poorly chinked dugout as Charlie's body was at fighting his disease. Hunter marveled at the workings of fate that had brought him to Tate's door. The old trapper's words echoed the thoughts his soul had wrestled with for weeks. What good was a life of wandering without purpose? He had made extensive notes and maps, but what good would they be to any man save himself?

He had gone into Kentucky with a goal. Exploring the upper Missouri, he had seen wonders of nature that made a man certain there was a God in heaven, but lately he'd

begun to question what he was doing. He found himself
listening for the sound of something besides wind and water, the hoot of an owl, the howl of a wolf. He had wandered for miles and months, trying like hell to get Jemma
O'Hurley out of his mind and his heart, but she had been
with him every step of the way. So, too, had Luther and
all of the others.

"Is . . . it snowing . . . yet?"

Used to being alone with his thoughts, Hunter nearly
came out of his skin when the old man spoke.

"Not yet. But it's fixin' to," he told Charlie.

Charlie's lips worked, opened, closed. He shivered.
"I . . . want to sleep . . . outside," he rasped.

Hunter was almost certain Charlie was out of his mind
with pain, then suddenly, he was afraid he understood what
the man was asking him to do. "What are you saying?"

"You . . . know what . . . I . . . I'm . . . saying. Take me
outside. Let me fall asleep . . . out there. I can't . . . no
more pain." With an effort so great that his forehead instantly beaded with sweat, Charlie brought his hand up off
the hide and reached toward Hunter.

Hunter clasped the skeletal hand, which was little more
than cold flesh and brittle bone. "I'm sorry, old man."

Charlie writhed. He shuddered in pain. "I don't . . .
want your . . . your pity. If your horse went . . . went down,
would you do any less . . . than . . . put him out of . . . of
his . . . misery?" He was desperate, gasping for breath like
a fish flung out on a riverbank. "Can't do . . . this alone."

His fingers tightened almost imperceptibly around Hunter's hand. As if he gathered strength from the human contact, he found the courage to make his plea.

"Didn't want to cheat death . . . until I knew . . . it was
the end. Now . . . it's too late for me to . . . do it . . . myself. I can see him. Waiting. In the shadows. Standin'
there. Laughin'. See him? Let me go . . . with my head up.
Not lying here . . . in my own . . . filth."

Charlie's eyes closed and his head lolled on the pillow.

He was still breathing, the sound terrible to hear.

Hunter stood up, paced the room, glanced now and again into the darkened corners. Death was indeed lurking in the room, waiting to take Charlie Tate. But when? How much longer would the old man have to endure? One day? Two? Ten? His body might not be ready to give up, even though his heart and soul were.

"Take me outside."

He glanced over at the man on the bed. It would be easy to grant Charlie's wish, but at what cost to his conscience?

If Jemma were here, she would pray for guidance, but he had never been one to pray. He knew nothing of any of the saints she was always talking about, nor did he know much about what was written in Lucy's Bible, either. He and God pretty much left each other alone.

Hunter stood at the end of the bed and stared down at Charlie Tate. Even in sleep, the pain tore at the man's lungs. The old trapper had been right about one thing. Hunter would never let an animal suffer this much pain.

He crossed the room, threw the door open, and looked out at the afternoon sky. The wind was blowing heavy, gray clouds into the valley, clouds that would thicken until they obscured the sky and snow began to fall. The old man wouldn't last twenty minutes out there in his condition. Other than cold, he wouldn't feel any pain as he drifted off to sleep.

After a heavy sigh, Hunter closed the door, his mind made up. Conscience be damned. He would wait until the snow started falling, then he'd carry Charlie outside. If God couldn't forgive him for helping old Charlie along, then so be it.

He sat with the old trapper until the snow began to fall, waited for it to thicken, hoping death would take Charlie first and not force his hand—but fate refused to give him the easy way out. Hunter found a jug of whiskey beside a pile of furs, took a long pull off the jug, and let the liquor burn its way down his throat. Charlie was coughing again, moaning between spasms.

Hunter opened the door and then walked over to the bed, took a deep breath, and scooped up the old man and the bear hide. Although tall and long of limb, Tate weighed next to nothing. His eyes were closed. If he was awake, he gave no indication.

On his way across the cabin, Hunter picked up Charlie's tall beaver hat. When he stepped through the open door, biting snow driven by a fierce north wind stung his face. He walked away from the cabin, struggling through the mounting snow until he reached a spot beside the stream that he had chosen earlier. A gathering of cottonwoods and aspen formed a semicircle, and it was here that Hunter chose to set the old man. He propped Charlie against the tallest cottonwood and arranged the bearskin over his shoulders. Gently placing the beaver hat on Charlie's head, Hunter adjusted it until he was satisfied. His own hands were already stiffening with cold, his fingers growing numb. It wouldn't take long.

"Boone . . ."

He nearly came out of his skin when Charlie rasped out a whisper. The old-timer had changed his mind. Hunter was ready to bundle him up and take him back inside. Tate coughed, the sound now audible enough to hear, as if Charlie were winning the battle over by killing the host.

"Bless . . . you," he wheezed. "Now . . . leave . . . me . . . be. And go . . . home."

Before he could change his mind, Hunter stumbled out of the stand of trees, head down against the stinging, icy snow, his vision blurred. The cabin door was a golden rectangle swimming in the distance. He hurried toward it, refusing to think of the man beside the stream, for when he did, he not only thought of Charlie Tate, but of himself and this solitary life he had chosen.

He hurried into the cabin but couldn't close the door. Not with Charlie out there dying, freezing inch by inch, fingers, toes, nose and ears. Hunter hoped to God that everything he had heard was true, that Charlie would drift off to sleep without pain.

Like a madman, he began to pull everything out of the dugout and pile it a few yards beyond the door. Again and again he went back into the filthy hovel, gathered an armload of Charlie's possessions, and struggled through the swiftly deepening snow until he had emptied the place save for the table and chairs and the empty bedframe.

Go back. Go home.

Beneath the bed he discovered a battered, leather-bound box. The find slowed his frantic pace and took his mind off Charlie for a moment. Hunter sat on the edge of the bedframe and opened the shallow, dust-covered box. Inside he found a pile of what appeared to have been letters on parchment so yellowed and crumbled with time that they were little more than shreds. He brushed them aside and there, lying beneath the scraps, was a tarnished, hollow, heart-shaped pendant.

The trinket looked even smaller in the palm of his hand. He held it to the light and admired the scrollwork etched on the surface of the brass. Threads of what was once a black ribbon still clung to the loop. His hand closed around the heart.

Where was the woman Charlie had left behind? Her letters had turned to dust; there would be no way to trace her even if he could. Did she even remember Charlie? Had she gone on before him?

Hunter opened his possibles bag and slipped the heart inside. He couldn't get Charlie's voice out of his head as he went back outside, this time carrying a tin of lamp oil. His foot slipped on the icy, snow-packed path he'd worn between the pile and the cabin. He went to his knees, staring into the dark, toward the stand of cottonwoods. Charlie was out there dying.

He doused the pile of furs, knives, antlers, poorly cured hides, utensils, and ragged worn-out clothes. From his possibles bag, he drew a tinderbox, hunched his shoulders to shield it against the wind, and cupped his hands. Finally a spark flared and ignited the oil. Tongues of flame licked at the pile, flickering against the wind. The fire gained strength as it drank up the oil, and Charlie's possessions began to burn.

Within minutes, the bonfire was huge. Flames writhed and leapt toward the starless sky, melting the falling snow. Hunter watched the heavy smoke and fire dance in the face of the wind. He thought of the places he had been, the things he'd seen out here. As he watched the fire burn, he knew for certain that not one of the wonders of the wilderness would ever match the sparkle in Jemma's eyes, the lilt of her voice and her laughter. Not one vista could compare with the way it felt when little Sadie planted a kiss on his cheek or when Junior looked up and called him Uncle Hunt.

He watched what was left of Charlie Tate's time on earth go up in smoke and ash and wondered what it all meant. He had never felt so alone.

Sandy Shoals, March 1817

"Will *you* marry me, Miss Jemma?"

Jemma stared at the young man standing across the counter holding a battered hat in his hand. His Adam's apple bobbed as he swallowed nervously and waited for her answer. It was all she could do not to laugh—not at his discomfort, but at the ludicrousness of the proposal; it was the second he had made in ten minutes.

"Didn't you just ask Lucy to marry you, Stanley?"

The youth swallowed, and his Adam's apple bobbed. "Well, I did, but since she isn't of a mind to marry me, I figured I'd try you. I know you're a mite older than me, but I don't hold that against you." He crushed his poor, weathered hat to his chest with a shaking hand.

"Exactly how old are you?" He was so earnest that Jemma tried not to laugh.

"Sixteen."

"I am a *mite* older." When she had left Boston, she didn't think she was over the hill.

"So the answer's still no?"

"I'm afraid so, Stanley. You'll have to try the next stop downriver," Jemma told him in all seriousness. "By the way, I think your boat's about to leave."

The would-be bridegroom looked around, shocked to find himself one of the few travelers left in the post.

"Thanks, Miss Jemma. Miss Lucy." The youth shoved his hat on and fled.

Lucy, who now helped Jemma behind the counter while Nette and Hannah served meals, walked up and handed her a paring knife.

"How many does that make?" Lucy watched Jemma make a notch on the inside edge of the countertop.

"Twenty-two proposals since we started keeping count. How about you?"

"Twenty-seven." Lucy laughed, her cheeks ablaze with color.

Jemma handed the knife back. "It never ceases to amaze me that these men think they can just stop and collect a wife on the way downriver like they do their jugs of whiskey. What if they meet someone they like better at the next stop?"

Lucy giggled again. "If they're all as fickle as Stanley, that's probably happened."

Fifteen minutes earlier they had been fending off proposals and selling whiskey and supplies hand over fist while Hannah and Nette kept the hot food coming. It had been an unseasonably warm winter, and since the beginning of March, settlers had been passing through. Not all of them traveled on floating crafts, either. Heavy ox-drawn wagons driven by determined, hardy souls were making their way over land into the Mississippi Valley.

Two new families had settled not far away, clearing the land and raising cabins in anticipation of continued good weather for spring planting. More often than not, Luther trusted Jemma to run the post while he went off to join the neighbors in building or clearing the land in exchange for help with his own planting. It was the first day of spring. Everyone hoped the good weather would hold and that the frost was over.

Noah LeCroix had been around more often since the thaw, hiring on to guide the keelboats through the shoals. Jemma tried to sound nonchalant as she wiped down the countertop and smacked a thick cork into the top of a heavy whiskey crock. "Noah was in here earlier. I saw him watching you from across the room."

Lucy's brow knit. "He makes me nervous."

"He doesn't mean you any harm. I think he's smitten," Jemma said.

"I think so, too, but he's just not the one for me, that's all." Lucy smiled a wistful, faraway smile.

Jemma picked up a broom and walked over to a row of gunnysacks full of dried beans. In their haste to scoop out what they needed, the travelers had spilled a few here and there. As she began to sweep, she thought about what Lucy had just said.

Jemma envied the girl her dreams. For herself, she had plans now, but not dreams. She had written to her father again, letting him know where she was and that she was well and would soon be returning to New Orleans. So far, all of her correspondence had been one-sided. She had no way of knowing if he had received any of the letters that she had copied and sent to both New Orleans and Boston. When they did reunite, things might still be unsettled between them, but she was no longer the same starry-eyed girl who had left home looking for adventure. She knew what she wanted out of life, and her father would have to deal with her on her own terms.

The only thing that was certain was that she couldn't have Hunter Boone.

"What are you thinking about, Jemma?"

Hannah had come up behind her, one hand on her hip, the other holding an empty wooden serving tray.

"Leaving." Jemma couldn't hide her regret.

Hannah set down the tray and leaned against the end of the table. The concern in her eyes was hard to miss.

"You sure you can't wait a while longer?"

"He's not coming back," Jemma said softly, stacking her hands on top of the broom handle. "No matter what you and the others think."

"Hunter loves you, Jemma. We all saw it."

"It doesn't matter now, does it? He's gone. I can't spend my life waiting for him to return. I've intruded on Nette's hospitality long enough." She could finally talk of Hunter and of leaving without tears. They had run out long ago. All that was left was a hollow ache in her heart whenever she thought of what might have been and what would never be.

Hannah shook her head. "You've been a big help to all of us, especially Nette. Why, Luther wouldn't have been able to take off and help those new folk settle in if it weren't for your head for business. You can tally up the accounts twice as fast as he can and I swear you could sell a bear a new set of teeth."

"I come by it honestly. My father's quite a businessman."

"You miss him?" For a minute Jemma thought Hannah was referring to Hunter. Did she miss him? She ached for him. Then she realized Hannah was asking about her father.

"I do," Jemma admitted, but she didn't add that even when she had lived with her father, she spent most of her time missing him. "I hope he's received my letters so that he isn't worried."

"I still think you ought to give it more time. Even if

Hunter has changed his mind and is on his way home, the weather might be holding him back.''

"I was very blunt with him the night before he left, Hannah. If he thinks of me at all, it's probably not with much regard.''

"Honey, have you been thinking of him?''

Jemma took a deep breath and sighed. "Night and day.''

"I'll be willing to bet that he could say the same. I think you're making a mistake leavin'.'' Hannah met her eyes and must have recognized the determination in them. "We won't forget you, Jemma. Look at what you've done for this place.''

Jemma looked around the post. Two of Nette's quilts, a Feather Star worked in blue and yellow and a President's Wreath with green leaves and red flowers, were draped over the edge of the loft, adding vibrant color to the huge room. She had gathered dried twigs and flowers and made arrangements in various bottles for the tables. The shelves were well stocked, thanks to the lists she had made of which items sold best and which didn't. She had learned from Luther how to barter for goods whenever a boat came through so they could replenish the stock on hand. Although the Boones' thanked her over and over for helping fill the gap Hunter had left, she was grateful to them for giving her the opportunity of a lifetime.

"I have to go back,'' Jemma said, wishing things were different—wishing Hunter Boone had not walked out of her life just when she had found him. "I have to settle things with my father.''

"You'll let us know where you are, won't you? We'll watch for your letters.'' Hannah stood up and tucked the tray beneath her arm.

"Of course.'' Jemma assured her.

"Lucy will really miss you.''

There were tears shimmering in Hannah's eyes. Jemma felt her own eyes begin to sting. Out of long habit, she turned away and quickly wiped them dry. ''I'll miss all of you.''

''I better get back to the kitchen or Nette will have done all the dishes by herself.'' Hannah hurried away, wiping her cheek with the corner of her apron.

Jemma pushed the spilled beans into a little pile and then began to sweep them toward the door, wondering if she'd ever be able to sweep Hunter Boone out of her heart.

chapter
18

He'd been a wanderer of the uncharted wilderness long enough to know it was not what he wanted. Not anymore. Not since Charlie. He sold the pack mules in St. Louis. Traveling light, Hunter headed toward Kentucky.

Heavy snows in the northwest had hampered his progress, but finally he was so close to home that he could almost smell it. With two or three days of hard riding, he would be back at Sandy Shoals. Spring had come early; the oak forest branches were heavy with bud. Golden-yellow buttercups, toothwort, and rue anemone littered the ground with a palette of color. Dogwood and redbud were about to burst into bloom. One morning, while following the rivers home, he heard a shout and drew rein atop a gravelly knoll carpeted with bird's-foot violets.

Below him, in a meadow of wildflowers, a small family of immigrants gathered around a wagon with a broken wheel. Another wagon piled high with household furniture and worldly goods stood nearby; the oxen had been turned loose to graze. A woman sat beside an open fire nursing her babe. Not far away, a chubby little boy and a red-headed girl played tag, threading their way through the trees while an old man stood with a watchful eye and laughed at their antics. Hunter thought of Charlie Tate, who had been about the wayfarer's age.

Away from the children's game, a younger man was seated in the shade of a gnarled oak. His blond hair reflected the sunlight streaking through the dappled leaves. The youth couldn't have been more than nineteen, but there was a serene gentleness about him, a certainty, as if he knew who he was and where he was going. In the grass beside him lay a long hickory staff and a knapsack. A Bible was spread open on his lap.

It was a scene reminiscent of so many Hunter had seen over the years, of families banded together, braving hardships, Indians, weather, and the unknown in order to make new lives for themselves. Resignation, determination, fear, hope, and regret were written on their faces.

He doubted there was a seasoned woodsman among this weary band. He felt a nagging urge to ride up to the travelers and offer to help, but if he delayed his own journey, Jemma might leave. He didn't want to chance missing her.

Over all the long, lonely miles back to Kentucky, he had refused to let himself think that she might have already left Sandy Shoals. Not now, he swore. Not when he knew for certain that no matter what he did with the rest of his life, no matter where he went or how far he roamed, he wanted Jemma beside him.

The rivers were running high and fast. Flatboats and keelboats going to Mississippi, Alabama, and Louisiana crowded the waterways. She might have already joined one of the parties headed south. If he didn't hurry, there was every chance that he might never see her again.

He was about to turn away and let the pilgrims fend for themselves until his eyes met and held those of the mother with the babe at her breast. She was rail-thin. Dark, careworn circles smudged the skin beneath her eyes. She looked forlorn and exhausted, but the minute she noticed him there atop the knoll, her weary expression was replaced with surprise, and hope. She lifted the hand that wasn't cradling the babe and waved.

"Damn," he whispered, but he waved back.

His horse's ears twitched when he cursed. Hunter nudged the roan into a walk and headed down the knoll. By the time he reached the busted wagon, the whole family, young and old alike, had gathered to greet him. He dismounted, handed the reins of his horse to the chubby little boy with a dirt-streaked face, and nodded to a man beside the wagon who looked to be about his own age.

"What do you think, mister? Can it be fixed?" The pilgrim's hands were still smooth, the hands of a man who had not ever put in a hard day in the fields. He was kneeling in the dirt beside the busted wheel. His brow was puckered, his lips pinched in a worried line.

"Anything can be fixed," Hunter assured him. "Just takes a little know-how."

Relief flooded the man's features. The woman with the infant walked up beside him. "Can it be fixed, Tom?"

"He says it can." The man nodded toward Hunter with far too much undeserved admiration in his tone. The youth that Hunter had seen reading the Bible joined them.

"I'm Devon Childress, a Baptist preacher, headed down to Texas." He introduced the others as his sister, Diana, and her husband, Tom Evans. Glenda was their infant daughter. The older gentleman was Evans's father, Arthur—or Big Artie, as he liked to be called. Little Artie and Fanny were the other children. Young Preacher Childress was easygoing and mild-mannered, gentle of speech, and, although the youngest of the men, apparently he was the spokesman for the group.

Hunter quickly found himself the center of attention as the travelers gathered around. Questions started flying. Where were they, exactly? How far to the next stop? Was there any homestead land nearby? Had he ever been to Mississippi?

"What place are you headed?" Big Artie Evans wanted

to know. The white-haired older gent looked as spry as a bantam rooster. He wore a brown hat and an outmoded waistcoat stretched taut over the paunch at his waist. Pointing to a map, he insisted on knowing exactly where Hunter was going.

"Sandy Shoals, not far south of here, on the Mississippi." Hunter put his finger on the spot and went on to describe the fledgling settlement and the trading post. He talked about the easy access to the river; the fields of cotton flax, corn, and tobacco; and the fertile soil and woods full of pheasant, wild turkey, and other game.

Diana Evans was still holding the child, standing in the circle of her husband's arm. Hunter's gaze touched on the infant. For the first time in his life, he let himself wonder what it would feel like to hold a child of his own, a child that looked like Jemma, or him, or a combination of both. How would it feel to hear someone call him Pa?

"It sounds like your heart is in Sandy Shoals," the woman said, interrupting his thoughts.

"She is," he said with determination.

"I'm sure that Providence sent you to us, Mr. Boone," the Reverend Childress told Hunter. "We left New York too late in the season and got trapped on the Ohio. The party we were traveling with gave up waiting for the thaw and found land near the river. Collectively, what my family knows about homesteading would fit in a teacup, sir. We know even less about making our way south. We would be beholden to you if you could see us as far downriver as you can."

Big Artie had been eyeing Hunter carefully. "We paid a guide good money to take us to Mississippi," the elder man began, "but one morning he ran off, cash in hand. We don't have anything left to spare."

"If you decide to help, all we can offer you is our thanks and our blessings, Mr. Boone," Devon Childress added.

Hunter shoved his hat back and scratched his head. Two

range hens were roasting on a spit over the fire. The succulent aroma made his mouth water. He tried to avoid looking at Devon Childress, his sister and her husband, and the children standing so close with their upturned faces. He wanted to ignore Big Artie standing there so expectant and hopeful at his elbow. He wanted to deny that he actually did care what happened to these strangers even as it hit him with sure, swift certainty that there was no way he could refuse.

Jemma was right. She knew him better than he knew himself. He collected people. These folks needed him. It was as simple as that. His conscience would never let him walk away, even if it meant getting home a few days later.

Jemma, above all, would understand.

"Will you do it, Mr. Boone?" Diana Evans was swaying to and fro, gently lulling the babe in her arms to sleep.

"I will." With that simple pledge to guide them through the wilderness, Hunter was forced to acknowledge who he truly was for the first time in his life, and in doing so, he experienced a newfound freedom. "On one condition," he said.

"What's that, Mr. Boone?" Preacher Childress asked. The rest of the family waited on tenterhooks.

Hunter dusted off his hands and turned to Mrs. Evans. "I'd like to hold the baby, if you'll let me, ma'am, while you tend to those chickens before they burn."

A collective sigh of relief followed by easy laughter cocooned him like the warm cotton batting in one of Nette's quilts. When she gently handed the baby over, the sleeping infant didn't awaken, but simply opened its mouth twice, like a tiny bird, and then settled back into a deep sleep. Hunter looked down at the baby, cupped one of his hands over the child's scalp, and rubbed the fine, downy hair.

Unbidden, the memory of Charlie Tate came back to him. As he had carried Charlie into the woods to die, he had cradled the old man in much the same way. He'd buried the trapper the morning after the storm, not beneath frozen earth too hard to turn, but under a rock cairn marked with a plain wooden cross.

"You have any children of your own?" Tom Evans's words startled Hunter out of his reverie.

"No. I don't even have a wife," Hunter said as the warmth of the small bundle amazed him. Evans's wife had trusted him enough to leave him and hurry over to the fire to tend the roasting hens. "But I'm fixin' to remedy that as soon as I can."

"So you got a sweetheart, mister?" Little Artie, the chubby boy who had been named for his grandfather, tugged on Hunter's pantleg. His two front teeth were missing.

"I hope so, Little Artie," Hunter said. "I surely do hope so."

Sandy Shoals, April 1817

Jemma stood on the riverbank with Sadie Boone clinging to her neck, surrounded by the family she had come to know and love, all but Lucy, who was crying so hard she refused to come to the landing to say good-bye.

When Callie and Junior started scrambling up the steps to the bluff, Sadie wanted down. Jemma let the girl go. As she watched the child run off after the others, her arms felt empty. Tears stung her eyes, blurring the sight of Nette, who had stepped up to her with a quilt folded in her arms. Jemma recognized it. The Honey Bee was one of Nette's favorites.

"I can't take this," Jemma said, clutching the folded quilt to her heart. "It's one of your finest."

"They're all my finest, child. But it's not anywhere as dear to me as you are. Take it. It's bound to get cold once in a while down there in New Orleans."

"You ready, Jemma?" Noah LeCroix stood waiting to

help her board a huge flatboat tied up between the other boats on the shoreline.

Her stomach turned over. The day she had dreaded so long had finally come. It was time to go. She wanted to run up the crooked wooden steps built into the bluff and hide in Hunter's loft. She would never see the forest fully green with summer's leaves. Timmy would take his first steps without her being there to cheer him on. One day the man Lucy was so certain she would recognize as her special mate would walk in and propose, and Jemma wouldn't be there to share her joy.

Jemma thought of a thousand and one excuses for not getting aboard. Noah stood there silent, his dark, unfathomable eyes watching her as she wrestled with doubt and longing.

She had to go. A week ago, a group of travelers headed up to St. Louis had brought a letter for her from New Orleans. Her father had arrived in the city ahead of schedule, contacted the Moreaus and found her gone. The events that followed, he wrote, were too complicated to put down in a letter. He demanded her return, an explanation, and an apology. She had to go.

Her fate was sealed. She would never see Hunter again, never look into his green eyes, never hear the sound of his laughter or the impatient tone that hid his concern. Never again would she know his touch or taste his kiss.

She was certain of it. If she weren't, nothing on earth could have ever made her leave. Travel up the river being what it was, there was every likelihood that she would never see the Boones, Nette, or Lucy again either.

"Stay, Jemma," Hannah begged. "Write your father. He'll understand."

Jemma shook her head. "I can't. I . . . Don't you see, Hannah?" She glanced over at Nette, who had reached for her hand. "If I stay, I'll just keep watching the river, walking the trail along the bluff waiting for Hunter. Every time someone walks through the door of the post, I'll look to see if it's him—and when it isn't, my heart will break all over again."

She blinked back tears and looked over at Luther. He was helping to load passengers on top of a boat so big and so crowded with people and their possessions that it looked like a floating island with rails and a roof. Fastened on each side of the roof near the bow were immense oars. Taking charge, separating the supplies to better distribute the weight, he reminded her so much of Hunter that it was hard to watch him. Nette was squeezing her hand. Tears slipped out from beneath the old woman's glasses.

"I can't stay," Jemma whispered. "Not when everything I see or touch or hear reminds me of Hunter."

"What if he comes back?" Hannah wanted to know. "What will we tell him?"

"Tell him that I had to go." Her voice broke. Even after almost four months, the pain of missing him was still too raw. She managed to whisper, "He'll understand."

If there was an ounce of hope in her heart, she would have stayed, but the words he had spoken on Christmas night were still too clearly etched in her memory. *"I don't want to wake up some morning knowing I made a mistake, wishing I'd gone after my dream."*

Noah picked up the bundle of clothes she had tied in a length of fabric. To the naked eye it seemed she was leaving with little more than she had come with: a mended silk dress, a worn forest-green cloak, the pants and shirt Hunter had bought for her, the moccasins.

And memories.

Priceless memories crowded into every corner of her heart and mind. Her own memories, not her grandfather's embellished tales. Recollections that would last a lifetime. But above all, she was leaving with a clarity of vision she had never known before. For the first time in her life, she knew who she was and what she wanted.

All that was missing from her life was Hunter Boone, but she had survived the wilderness trek and a winter in

Sandy Shoals. She could survive anything. Even a broken heart.

Noah stepped around her, ready to shove off and pilot the flatboat through the shoals. The other travelers on board were anxious to be on their way to new horizons. Knowing that she dare not say another word, Jemma hugged Nette, then Hannah. Biting her lips to still their trembling, she turned away. Luther was just stepping onto shore. He paused, started to say something, then took her in his arms and gave her a bear hug.

"I wish things could have been different, Jemma." He let her go. All she could do was nod. "We'll miss you, and we'll never forget all you did for us. I couldn't have gotten the crops in if you hadn't been here to run the post."

She found a place to sit atop a barrel securely lashed to the rail. The river was yellow-brown with mud, running swift and high since the spring thaw. She looked down into the swirling, muddy water as the flatboat was pushed out into the current, and had a queasy feeling, along with a flash of memory of falling headlong into the Homochitto.

She should have known better than to travel by water. The Mississippi was flowing fast and high, a churning mass of water and silt. Noah stood in the stern, watching for treacherous shoals, floating logs, or lodged debris. Hunter's friend. In his own way, the half-breed exuded the same kind of confident capability as his gaze swept the water and he shouted directions to the men manning the broadhorns, or oars. A few yards away, Noah clung to a lifeline and hung out over the bow, agile as a cat, his gaze sweeping the angry water, calling out to the oarsmen who leaned on the broadhorns.

As she clung to the rail, fearing for her life, a bundle of meager possessions at her feet, Jemma wished she had stayed. But she knew it was too late for wishes.

Over the bawling of a frightened milk cow in the stern and the excited shouts of some of the other passengers,

Noah bellowed commands at the oarsmen. She watched and wondered at the change in the strong, silent man. As soon as the flatboat left the shore, he had become one with the movement of the boat, the flow of the water. She now knew why he was legendary for his skill as a river pilot.

The boat lurched and lodged, one of its corners caught on a sandbar, perilously close to having its bottom ripped out and sinking everyone's dreams. As forward motion stopped and the craft swayed in the river, one of the women inside the cabin screamed, which set the children wailing.

Jemma was torn, wondering whether she should try to work her way inside to help calm the frightened children or prepare to jump overboard. She had tasted the waters of the Homochitto and had no desire to launch herself into the mighty Mississippi. The woman's shrieks had subsided to mere howls. The children were still crying. The cabin was not that far away. If she was careful, she would get there.

Grabbing hold of a cask and an upright wagon wheel hemmed in beside it, she started for the door of the rectangular box built atop the flatboat.

A crate full of chickens slid off the top of the cabin, hit the rail with a crash and a riot of fitful squawking, and fell overboard into the raging torrent. Crate, chickens, and all were swallowed by the river. Aghast, the terrified passengers watched for some sign of the ill-fated fowl, but not even a feather reappeared anywhere near the flatboat.

Yellow-brown water lapped perilously close to the rail. She told herself to stay calm, that Hunter Boone was out of the savior business and wouldn't be here to rescue her if anything happened. She was on her own.

The men atop the cabin gave a mighty thrust against the oars and once again the flatboat started racing downriver. Jemma looked back and could still see the post, high above the river on the bluff. Her friends were gathered on the shoreline, a small huddle of humanity and love banded together on the riverbank. They were still waving, still wishing her well.

She waved good-bye in return, but could not for the life of her muster enough joy to smile. They rounded a bend and Sandy Shoals disappeared, suddenly, irrevocably.

Hunter's three-day ride had lengthened to six. Preacher Childress and the Evanses had the habit of wanting to stop and set up camp early, not to mention insisting on eating three meals a day. Hauling Jemma up the Trace had been nothing compared to the last few miles of his journey home. It called to mind the trek from Ohio with Luther and Hannah and the others—but at least they had been as anxious to reach their destination as he. Since the Evanses had no notion of where they were going, they saw no reason to hurry.

Frustrated, fighting to keep his temper even and his patience intact, Hunter had almost persuaded himself to leave them with a well-detailed map when Little Artie fell off the back of the wagon and broke his arm. Diana became hysterical, her nerves frayed, her spirit understandably low after a winter on the Ohio River. It took Hunter, Tom, and an hour of prayer and persuasion by her brother to convince her that they had to move on. An entire day of travel had been lost.

Finally, the end of the trail was in sight. Sandy Shoals was less than a mile away. Hunter had been consumed with thoughts of Jemma, of their reunion, of the possibility that she was no longer in Sandy Shoals at all. He didn't want to think about what his life would be like without her, not after his weeks alone up the Missouri.

He left the Evanses behind and headed for Sandy Shoals alone. Preacher Childress followed on a slow-minded mule. Hunter nearly reined in when he passed a new homestead and the cleared land around it. On the edge of the clearing, a hickory stump was still smoldering. A man Hunter had never laid eyes on paused behind his plow to raise his hat and wave. Hunter stared, then gave a quick salute and pressed on. What other changes had occurred while he'd been gone?

A covey of quail burst out of the undergrowth along the trail and startled his horse. Determined that nothing was going to stop him now, Hunter hung on, nearly losing his hat, and kept going.

He passed the path that veered through the woods toward Noah's strange pole house in the swamp. He was almost home.

When he was in sight of the tavern, he could see the smoke pouring out of the kitchen chimney, but no other sign of life. Once he cleared the trees, one glance at the river told him all he needed to know. A flatboat, two keelboats, and a canoe were docked at the landing.

His horse was still moving when he slid out of the saddle and hit the ground running. The winded animal shook its head in protest when he tied it up at the hitching post. He quickly shouldered his way through three men loitering outside the door, discussing the price of tobacco, and stepped inside. The place looked different, cheerful, somehow more welcoming.

Scanning the crowded room, he searched for Jemma but didn't see her. A flash of color caught his eye. He looked up and saw some of Nette's quilts hanging from his loft. They looked nice and cozy hanging there, brightening the room. A card game was going on at the end of one table. Further along, three women sipped coffee and chatted about the abundance of doves they had seen on the way downriver. There were empty bottles with spring wildflowers here and there on the tables.

Luther was serving drinks at the counter while Lucy spoke to a portly bald man after handing him a package. As the man walked away, Hunter wondered what in the hell Lucy was doing carving a notch in the edge of the bar. Her hair was wound up in the fancy style she had taken to wearing before he left, and she had on the pink gown that Jemma had made. Her smile was gone, her eyes red-rimmed and puffy.

Nette, Hannah, and Jemma were nowhere to be seen, but from the aroma drifting in from the kitchen, he knew they were cooking. Lucy was his first concern. He crossed the long cabin, nodding a greeting to anyone who managed to catch his eye.

Lucy was crying. Silent, slow tears ran down her cheeks, but she merely swiped them off with the back of her hand and continued to wipe spilled whiskey off the bar. No matter how badly he wanted to rush off to the kitchen and find Jemma, he needed to see what was wrong with Lucy first.

Jemma would understand.

Lucy didn't see him step up to the bar. He asked, "What are you doing carving up my counter? And why in the hell are you crying?"

The girl looked up, startled. She went white, as if she were seeing a ghost; she didn't move until Luther shouted, "Hunt!"

Lucy laid down the paring knife and darted around the end of the counter toward him. Hunter thought she was going to hug him to welcome him home, so he smiled and spread his arms wide.

She walked up to him, drew back her fist, and punched him square in the gut. The wind went out of him with a loud grunt and he staggered back against the bar.

"What . . . was that for?" He barely gasped out the words.

"*That* was for my friend Jemma. She waited for you, Hunter Boone. Waited until she couldn't stand the hurt you'd dealt her anymore, and then she left."

The words hit him like a bucket of icy water. He found out what it meant when someone said their knees went weak. He grabbed Lucy by the upper arms, held her still. "Jemma's gone?"

Lucy thrust out her chin. "What did you think? That a

woman like Jemma would wait forever? Do you know she's had twenty-five proposals of marriage since you've been gone?''

He let the girl go and had to reach for the counter.

''And?''

''She's left, no thanks to you.''

''Lord, Lucy, don't be so hard on him.'' Luther had come around the bar to stand beside him. He pounded him on the back in welcome. ''Jemma left three days ago.''

Proposals?

''Is she . . . is she getting married?'' *Not to someone else. Not now.* He felt like getting down on his knees, but for the life of him, he couldn't recall one single saint Jemma had ever mentioned.

Luther went on. ''Noah piloted the flatboat she was on and he's already back from where he gets off at the ferry, so by now she's well on her way south—''

They were interrupted by the sound of Nette's voice booming across the room. ''Hunter Boone! As I live and breathe, I never thought I'd see you again in this lifetime!''

Nette headed in his direction with a platter of pie slices, when she collided with Devon Childress as the young preacher cleared the threshold. Plates and pie rained down, drawing the attention of everyone in the room.

''Who is that, Hunter?'' Lucy wanted to know, suddenly rooted to the floor.

''A preacher. Picked up him and his family a ways back. I'd have been here to stop Jemma if I hadn't.'' He couldn't keep the frustration out of his tone.

''You came back for Jemma?'' Nette left the preacher scraping up pie, and walked over to join Hunter and the others.

Hunter nodded to her, not ashamed to openly admit what a damned fool he'd been. ''I did. Did she leave any word for me?''

His heart sank to his gut when she shook her head.

"You broke her heart, Hunter. She moped around here for weeks, then she got a letter from her father, badgering her to go home."

"Home? Home to Boston?" It was half a world away, but no farther than he'd already been. If he had to, he'd go and beg her to forgive him.

"She headed for New Orleans. Her pa's set up his new business down there. Has a new house, too."

"So she left." He closed his eyes.

"It weren't easy for her."

He could feel Nette and Luther watching him, waiting. He looked at Lucy, who was helping the preacher wipe up sweet-potato pie.

"Go get her, Hunt," Luther advised. "Before it's really too late."

Hunter slipped his hand over his possibles bag. Inside lay the tarnished pendant. Just when he thought he knew who he was and where he was headed, fate had pulled the rug out from under him.

"You really think she'll have me now?" He focused on Luther, avoiding Nette's silent censure.

"You'll never know until you ask her."

chapter
19

Clutching her bundle of possessions, filled with pride and foreboding, Jemma stood on the deck of the flatboat in New Orleans, staring up at four-foot-high lettering emblazoned on the riverfront side of a huge wooden warehouse. O'HURLEY IMPORTS. She had found her father without having taken a step on dry land.

"He'p you over, ma'am?" A Negro stevedore stood waiting to assist her onto the dock. Nearly everyone had already disembarked and the men were waiting to unload the livestock.

She nodded and gave him her hand, balancing her bundle as she lifted the tattered hem of her skirt. The trip downriver had been fairly uneventful after the near-catastrophe on the shoals. After Noah disembarked, she had made acquaintance with some of the others aboard. From then on her days and nights on the river were spent in conversation or quiet contemplation as she watched the passing shoreline, thinking of all the dear friends she had left behind.

And of Hunter. Always Hunter.

Knowing full well that she could never forget him, she also knew that she had to go on. The first step toward a beginning would be to make peace with her father. She took the bundle from the stevedore and thanked him. Dodging carts loaded with goods and horse-drawn wagons heavy with crates, she picked her way across the bustling, teeming road that ran along the levee.

When she reached the open double doors of the warehouse, she paused to stare into the dim interior. Crates and barrels were piled from floor to ceiling, separated into aisles to allow passage between them. Tantalizing spices rode the air. Black markings labeled the boxes in every written language, some familiar, others so foreign that they resembled odd scribbling. The sight called to mind Grandpa Hall and his stories of exotic ports of call, adventure, danger, and new sights, sounds and smells.

Jemma smiled. Seeing the boxes gave her no desire to escape to parts unknown. Instead of the old, familiar longing for new sights and sounds, a quiet serenity helped her marshal her courage as she stepped inside the cavernous building to locate her father's office. Not two strides inside, she was nearly bowled over by a harried-looking young man carrying a sheaf of papers as he turned a blind corner.

"Excuse me, miss." He began to apologize until he took in her bedraggled gown, mud-stained moccasins, the bundle in her arms, and her tangled hair. What had been a polite smile quickly faded. "We don't give handouts," he said, shooing at her with the papers as if she were a pesky fly. "Get along."

"I'm not here for a handout." She pulled herself up to her full height and met his stare straight on. "I'm here to see Mr. O'Hurley."

He cut her off. "He doesn't have time for the likes of you. Why don't you mosey on over to Tchoupitoulas Street and try to drum up a little business over there?"

"I'm certain that if you tell Mr. O'Hurley, *my father*, that his *daughter*, Jemma, is here, he'll be more than happy to see me."

The color immediately blanched from the rude man's face. He swallowed twice, mumbled an apology, and took off down an aisle between the crates. She could hear a door slam in back of the warehouse, the sound reverberating in the high, cavernous building. Tapping her toe, she glanced over her shoulder and contented herself with watching the passing crowd outside while she waited for a summons from her father.

"Jemma!"

At the sound of her father's voice, she turned. He was racing up the aisle toward her. The death of his partner and the move had taken its toll. He looked older. His mouth was drawn into a stern line. The creases beneath his eyes had deepened, but he moved with the old familiar determination and energy that had made him such a successful businessman. Dropping her parcel, she started slowly toward him and then stopped a few yards away.

He stood still. His gaze swept her, staring as if he couldn't believe what he was seeing. Bracing herself for censure, she tilted her chin and met his gaze. She expected anger. She expected a scene. She was prepared for anything but watching him open his arms to her in welcome.

It was a moment before she realized he was waiting for her to respond to his warm gesture of greeting. Jemma couldn't swallow around the lump in her throat. With tears blinding her, she ran to her father and, for the first time that she could ever recall, she felt his arms close around her as he held her close.

It was the dream of a lifetime. The smooth, cool satin of his waistcoat was soon stained with her tears of relief. She felt him awkwardly patting her back, murmuring, "There, there now, Jemma. Everything is all right now."

Finally, when her tears were spent, she pulled back and wiped her eyes on her sleeve. "Thank you, Father. I certainly didn't expect you to forgive me so easily." Behind them, startled stevedores and clerks watched the reunion. Jemma lowered her voice. "When I arrived last October and found out Alex Moreau was dead, I . . . decided to take advantage of my reprieve. I truly never intended to be gone so long—''

''Thank God you didn't marry Moreau's grandson. I can't begin to tell you everything, but the girl you exchanged places with was nearly hanged for murdering a young man a few months ago.''

''Oh, no!'' Jemma was horrified to think that something so terrible might have happened to the beauty with the startling amethyst eyes she had encountered that fateful night at the cathedral.

''Yes, but all is well, and she and your would-be groom are living on St. Stephen's Island in the Caribbean. Marrying him would have been the worst possible thing for your standing here in New Orleans. His reputation as a drinker was well known; in fact, they even say he was responsible for his cousin's death. But enough of that,'' he said, hooking his arm through hers. ''Let's get you home and settled. I hope you like the house.''

The laborers around them slowly drifted back to work. Because his words had given her pause, before she took another step, Jemma wanted her future settled once and for all.

''Before we go anywhere, I want you to know that I'm not the same naïve girl I was when I left.''

''I'm sure you've much to tell. When I think of you being exposed to the perils of the journey north, it terrifies me.''

''That's behind us now. I want things to be different between us, Father. I've learned so much about myself, about who I am and what I can do.''

She knew he was too astute not to notice the state of her dress and her hair. She was surprised he had nothing to say on the matter. Surprised and grateful. Still, she couldn't shake the feeling that there was something he was not saying.

"I hope you realize I won't be pushed into marriage, Father. If you still have any notion—"

He responded before she even finished. "I certainly won't make the same mistake I did before," he assured her, straightening the watch fob on a gold chain draped across his vest. Then, with another smile, he called for his carriage to be brought around, took hold of her elbow, and steered her toward the door. He called out to one of the clerks, "I'm taking the rest of the week off."

They were going home together. There would be time to tell him of Hunter, time to explain all she had experienced, of her love for the backwoods "Kaintuck" who had stolen her heart and carried it with him into the wilderness. But not yet. Not yet.

She would know when the time was right. First, she wanted to bask in the warmth of her father's love, to put to rest any doubt of his sincerity. And she wanted to hold the memory of Hunter and her time in Sandy Shoals in her heart for a while longer.

Hunter cursed the summer squall, the river, and the streak of bad luck that had kept him from heading for New Orleans. Standing beside Noah at the bow of a keelboat, he let his gaze sweep the river for debris. Rain dripped off the brim of his hat and sloughed into his collar. His buckskins were soaked, his hair plastered to his back, but nothing could dampen his determination. He was going to find Jemma if he had to track her halfway around the world.

His departure had been delayed a week because Lucy had taken it into her head to fall head over heels in love at the first sight of Devon Childress. After knowing him a day, she wanted to pack up and go south with the preacher to the unsettled Texas territory across the Mississippi. Hunter had immediately declared her too young. They fought bitterly. Her resultant tears and pleading, coupled with his own stubbornness, had kept the situation stirred up until Nette negotiated a truce.

Lucy and Devon promised to wait until Hunter either returned with Jemma or sent his permission in a letter. Devon refused to go on without Lucy. Hunter hoped that after the two got to know one another, the infatuation would cool.

Wind churned the water. Spray from the boat hit the chop that misted the air. Noah, his red shirt and black pants sopping wet, hanging precariously from a guide rope, balanced barefoot on the rail like a nimble-footed pirate. He watched the river, looking for hidden sandbars, pointing out directions to the deckhand manning the tiller.

"There's a cove not far from here where we can take shelter," Noah shouted over the howling wind. "I don't like the color of the sky."

Hunter didn't like the threatening yellow-green underbelly of the sky either. A flash of lightning ripped the clouds and then, a few seconds later, thunder rocked the air around them.

"Go around back and make sure the animals are secured," Noah called out. Hunter hurried to do as his friend bid. When Noah hired on as a pilot, it was an unwritten rule that he took command until he had seen the passengers safely through the shoals.

Hunter skirted the cabin and was already headed toward the stern when the flatboat suddenly rammed into something with a force so great it knocked him off his feet. The frightened screams of two horses aboard, as well as cries of terror from inside the cabin, mingled with the shuddering of the craft. With a horrendous groan, large portions of wood and nails were torn asunder.

All forward motion stopped. Hunter lurched to his feet and struggled against the pitch of the boat. With one glance at the empty bow, he knew that Noah had been ejected into the water. Hunter shut out the desperate calls of the other men aboard and leaned out over the quickly disintegrating bow. He thought he saw a flash of Noah's red shirt in the muddy water, and was reminded of the day he had nearly lost Jemma to the water. He doubted that his luck would hold a second time, but without considering the consequences, he dove.

As soon as he surfaced, he spotted Noah clinging to a twisted log that was being swept downstream. He began swimming in that direction, gauging the distance between them as it began to close. When he was close enough to reach out and grab the log, he realized that the left side of Noah's face was torn open, streaked with blood and rain.

His friend was only semiconscious, barely able to hang on. Hunter draped one arm over Noah's back and held on to the tree with the other. Unable to battle the current with the injured man, he hoped it wouldn't be too long before the log jammed against other debris along the bank.

A macabre parade floated by. Passengers aboard the wrecked keelboat struggled against the current. The body of a youth with barely the first fuzz of beard floated past. Crates and barrels bobbed along, crashing into victims. Some crates had broken open, their contents already vanished beneath the rushing water. Screaming horses struggled to keep their heads out of the water as they swam toward shore.

Finally, one end of the branch caught on a logjam and they stopped in a small eddy. Hunter furiously blinked water out of his eyes and tugged on Noah's arm. When his friend was free, Hunter rolled him onto his back, hooked his arm across Noah's chest, and began to swim toward the bank a few feet away.

It wasn't until Hunter had Noah on shore and could examine the extent of his injury that he realized how seriously LeCroix had been hurt. The left side of Noah's handsome face had practically been torn away, the wound gaping close to his eye, which was mottled with blood. Hunter ripped off his own shirt. He swallowed, plumbing the depths of his courage as he reached for the torn skin along Noah's cheek. Then, gingerly, carefully, he tried to smooth the ragged edges back together.

Noah moaned, but didn't gain consciousness. Once Hunter had bound the man's head with torn shreds of his shirt, he dragged him into a copse of trees and waited for the rain to stop. There was no dry tinder, nothing with which to start a fire. His only hope was to sit with Noah and watch the river. Sooner or later, if and when someone from the ill-fated keelboat made it to shore and found help, then word of the accident would spread up and down the river.

He closed his eyes and thought of Jemma, hoping she was safe and that she had reunited with her father. He cursed himself for ever leaving her, and hoped to God she had made it downriver and had not fallen victim to the Mississippi's whims. He thought of what he would say, what he would do when he found her. As the wind lashed his wet hair against his cheek and the rain stung his eyes, he swore to himself and the Almighty that he was never going to let her out of his sight again.

He had lost everything: his hat, his rifle, his bag of clothes. All he had left was the possibles bag at his waist and the powder horn around his neck. He opened the possibles bag and felt inside for the heart pendant. Relief swelled when he touched it. The trinket he had been carrying to Jemma was still there. It gave him hope.

Noah stirred. Blood was still oozing down his torn face. Hunter felt utterly helpless, afraid to go in search of help and leave his friend to the elements and creatures that dwelled in the forest along the river. If he was lucky, a search party looking for victims would find them soon; but he knew it was a big *if*, especially the way his luck had been going.

Sitting on his haunches, shirtless, hatless, and soaked, he felt a tug on his hand and looked down. Noah had his eyes shut, his face contorted with pain.

"Leave me here." The words were barely audible.

"I'm not going anywhere without you."

"I can't see, Hunt. What good's a man like me who can't see?"

Hunter gazed down at the tall, once-striking man who had been his friend for what amounted to a considerable number of years. They had marched downriver with the Kentucky troops, fought side-by-side at the Battle of New Orleans, battled the elements and the river. Both cursed the fact that the land was being settled faster than they liked. Hunter knew what the loss of his eye would mean to Noah, just as he knew what the man was asking him to do, but there was no way in hell he was going to leave Noah to the elements.

"I can't hear you over this storm," Hunter lied.

"If you play the hero, I'll hate you forever, Boone."

"Ask me if I care."

Noah's hand tightened on his wrist, but there was no strength behind the hold. "Get going. Don't risk losing Jemma again."

No matter how tempting, no matter how much he wanted to be with Jemma, the image of Charlie Tate swirled through his mind. Hunter closed his eyes again, turned his face up to the rain.

Noah was in his late twenties. Still so young. He had a long life before him. No matter what he suffered now, whether he liked it or not, Noah could learn to live without an eye. There was no way Hunter could play God this time. He wasn't ready to lose his friend. He knew he never would be.

Noah had fallen silent, his eyes closed. Hunter checked the crude, wet bandage he had made out of his shirt. The bleeding had slowed.

Thunder rumbled in the distance. Rain beat down through the newly budded leaves. The river raged by.

If Jemma's saints were looking down on him, he hoped they understood what he had done for Charlie and why, and had forgiven him. Surely they wouldn't punish him now by taking his friend. Surely they would watch over

Jemma and keep her safe, and his, until he could find her again.

New Orleans, September 1817

The street in front of the opera house was a sea of vehicles. The night air was close and humid. Ignoring the handsome young man seated beside her in the open carriage, Jemma stared at the fashionably dressed theater patrons on the crowded street, lost in the memory of the night she had met Hunter. Then, too, she had mingled with the mostly Creole crowd, but then she had been on the run, using them as camouflage. Tonight, only her heart felt like running.

André Roffignac shifted on the seat beside her. Recently appointed her father's assistant manager, André was a frequent guest at the house on St. Louis Street and had volunteered to act as her escort on many occasions of late. As they began the drive of a few blocks, André casually draped his arm across the back of the seat until it encircled her shoulders. The move was slow and nonchalant. Most everything André did was executed with a practiced indifference, but after spending time with him, she knew he did nothing without perfectly calculating it beforehand.

Jemma stiffened, not caring whether he noticed. She hadn't really wanted to attend the opera alone with him this evening, but originally her father was to have accompanied them, so she had agreed. Lately, André had become openly familiar, taking advantage of their friendship by brushing against her and casually touching her much too often. He made her feel embarrassed and uncomfortable.

Roffignac was facing her now, the picture of refined elegance with his curled-brim hat, double-breasted cut-away jacket, and high-throated ruffled shirt. Appearances and bloodlines meant everything to him, as they did to most Creoles. It was an attribute her father found admirable. André's dark eyes were soulful and languid, his hands long and elegant, his nails buffed to a high shine.

As far as New Orleans society and her father was concerned, Roffignac was perfect. But to Jemma, he was a far cry from all the things she had loved about Hunter Boone. As it did almost every waking moment, her mind drifted back to the days she had spent with Hunter. She wondered if he missed her, how he was faring, where he was now.

While she was lost in thought, André reached out, picked up the fringed hem of the narrow cashmere stole that was draped over her arm, and rubbed the costly item between his fingertips.

"Did you like the performance, Jemma?"

"I thought it was quite amusing."

"The play has been running for so long that I forget how many performances I've seen, but this is the first time I've enjoyed it so immensely." He let go of the stole and ran his finger over the back of her gloved hand.

She pulled her hand away, not abruptly, but easily, ostensibly to smooth her hair. If she angered André, her father would not be pleased, so she vowed to voice her concerns as soon as she and her father were alone.

They were only two blocks from the house that her father had purchased before her return. Attempting to blend in immediately, Thomas O'Hurley had shipped very few of their furnishings from the East; instead, he had decorated the new place according to what he had seen in the spacious, comfortable homes he had visited here in New Orleans. She found the style austere, the rooms cool instead of welcoming.

The driver kept up a slow, steady pace. Night air scented with jasmine enveloped them. Jemma smoothed her long, over-the-elbow gloves and folded her hands, then took a deep breath and turned to face André squarely.

"André, I know you mean well, escorting me about, introducing me to your friends, but I am so busy helping the nuns at the orphanage that I fear I'm often too exhausted to enjoy late evenings on the town.''

''What are you saying, Jemma?'' His dark, fluid gaze roved over her face.

She shivered, but not with longing. All she wanted at the moment was to be out of the carriage.

''I don't wish to go out for a while, that's all.''

His smile thinned. ''For a while? And how long do you think 'a while' might be?''

Forever. She shrugged. ''Just that. A while.''

She could see he was not pleased, although he smiled and nodded acceptance. His eyes had grown cold, almost calculating. They fell into an uncomfortable silence.

When the carriage clattered through the *porte cochère* into the open courtyard of the house on St. Louis, Jemma felt a surge of relief. The Negro driver opened the door and stood aside as André stepped out of the vehicle, took her hand, and helped her down. They walked up the wide wooden stairway to the second floor, where the living quarters overlooked the walled garden and the street. Flower boxes of trailing jasmine and geraniums lined the balcony. Her father was still up, waiting in the sitting room. He was reading, but set the book aside as they entered.

''How was the theater?'' Thomas O'Hurley smiled from a comfortable overstuffed chair beside a brick fireplace that hadn't been lit in months. Although the threat of summer heat and the yellow fever had passed, the weather was still sultry, the night air alive with mosquitoes. With the doors and windows thrown wide open to allow for any breath of air, the pesky insects were a constant annoyance.

''Excellent,'' André said.

''Fine.'' Jemma forced a smile and sat down on a chair close to her father's. She took her reticule off her arm, worked off her gloves, and set them down on a table beside a vase that held palmetto fans stuck into sand.

Her father seemed to be trying, although at times he was awkward in his new role as a loving parent. She had decided that was only to be expected. Miracles weren't worked overnight. It was enough to know he cared.

The three of them talked amiably for a while, Jemma batting at mosquitoes, lingering long enough to be polite before she said, "I know you two always have business to discuss, so if you will excuse me, I'm going to retire early."

André and her father stood when she did. Exhausted from a day spent teaching reading and embroidery to the orphan girls at the Ursuline Female Academy, she bid them both good night. It wasn't until she was halfway down the hall that she realized she had forgotten her gloves and bag. She made an abrupt about-face and went back to get them. Her silk slippers made very little sound on the woven straw matting, a summer replacement for carpeting. Just as she was about to reenter the sitting room, she concentrated on what André was saying. Her steps froze.

"How much longer do you expect me to play this cat-and-mouse game, *monsieur*? I say, tell her and let's be done with the farce."

When he spoke, her father's tone shocked her. He sounded like the Thomas O'Hurley of old—impatient, cold, as stern as ever. "I expect you to play along until she is ready to accept a proposal. I've told you before, if Jemma suspects anything about our agreement, you can kiss the dowry money good-bye, Roffignac, and you'll never be able to resurrect that pile of ash you once called home."

"Do you think you can keep me dangling forever with the promise of cash? You need me as much as I need your money. How else do you intend to gain further introduction into our society? You Americans are looked down upon as money-grubbing barbarians as it is—"

"*I'm* not the one willing to marry for money," Thomas brutally reminded him.

"My family is old New Orleans, *Monsieur* O'Hurley. Marriages such as this are our way and much accepted. I could contract another bride—and a much younger one at that—on the morrow. Sixteen is a nice, malleable age.''

''For half as much dowry,'' her father shot back.

Stunned, anguished beyond words, Jemma leaned back against the wall, her hands pressed to her breast, her heart in her throat. She felt the blood drain from her face as her head began to swim. With one hand on the plastered wall for support, she slipped back down the hall to her room and then closed the door behind her with barely a sound.

Betrayed. Her father had contracted another marriage with no thought or care for her feelings or opinions. His newfound attitude toward her had all been a farce. He had learned nothing, nor did he realize what she was made of now if he thought she would stand for this outrage.

This time her father had underestimated her. No longer could she be swayed by any pitiful pleas he might put to her. As the shock of discovery began to recede, she grew more furious. Pacing over to the balcony, she stepped outside and stared out onto the street below. Except for the passing of an occasional carriage, it was deserted. The flames in the lamplights fluttered with the slight breeze that had just begun. In the distance, the church bells tolled.

There was deep sorrow in her heart when she realized she had come full circle. But this time history would not repeat itself. Thomas O'Hurley could never be the father she had prayed for. He would never respect her, never see her as a person of worth other than as a possession to use for his own ends. She could not stay and be his pawn. This time, when she left her father's house, it would be for good.

Determined to have it out with him, she decided to wait until André took his leave. She stepped inside, tossed back the mosquito netting that draped the bed, and threw her shawl on the quilt Nette had given her. Her *prie-dieu* and small altar were the only furnishings her father had shipped from her room in Boston. He had deemed them satisfactory, not because of their religious value, but because most Creole homes contained similar altars.

She knelt down, folded her hands, and stared up at the miniatures of the saints. Instead of feeling lost and desperate as she had last year, instead of resigning herself to her fate and praying for a miracle, she experienced a wave of stubborn determination and renewed resolve.

Crossing herself, Jemma bent her head in prayer.

"Dear Ladies and Gentlemen, I know that I have sinned and that I haven't exactly lived the life any of you would choose, but I've always tried to do the right thing and not hurt anyone in the bargain. I'm going to have to leave my father's home and his protection, but from past experience, I know that I can make my own way and that with your help and intercession, I'll be safe."

She crossed herself and stood up, walking back to the balcony. This time she would be prepared when she left. She would have plenty of money, the proper clothing, and a destination in mind.

In the courtyard below, André Roffignac was stepping up into his carriage while his driver stood in attendance. Without waiting another moment, she began to pack.

chapter
20

IT'S NOW OR NEVER.

Hunter decided to step up to the edge of the sidewalk and cross over to the house on St. Louis Street, the place that the workmen at the import warehouse had told him was the residence of Thomas O'Hurley. He had come directly from the waterfront, prepared to knock on the door with hat in hand and a heart full of apology. Fast talking and extra coin had gotten him a room in a respectable hotel above a café in the French Quarter, after the proprietor had tried to refuse him solely on the grounds that he was a "Kaintuck" and would likely cause too much trouble. Now, after leaving his things behind, he felt vulnerable and half-naked without his rifle. His long knife was the only protection he carried.

He drew back to watch a fancy open rig with a Negro driver pass by and then inched back into the shadows when he realized that the woman inside was none other than Jemma. She was comfortably seated beside a handsome gent with coal-black hair and the look of a wealthy, indolent Creole about him. Appearing every inch the daughter of a wealthy merchant, Jemma had never looked more beautiful, or unattainable. Her golden hair had been coaxed into a fashionable, upswept style. Bouncing curls teased her cheeks while a strand of pearls at her throat, no more precious than her ivory skin, caught the moonlight. The darkness muted her features somewhat, but Hunter thought he saw her smile up at the handsome young dandy.

Shaken, afraid to let himself think that she might have already married another, Hunter lingered just outside the pool of light cast by the streetlamp and watched the house. From where he stood, he saw the carriage turn into the courtyard. Within seconds he heard the sound of footsteps on the stairs to the gallery, and when they cleared the high garden wall, he watched Jemma and her escort cross the balcony and disappear inside.

Lurking in the dark like a voyeur, Hunter had almost convinced himself that the young man was not leaving and that he was a permanent fixture in Jemma's life. He lost track of time as he intently tried to watch every window. Soon he was rewarded when he saw a slight, blond figure standing in one at the far end of the house.

Jemma. Time stood still and so did his heart. When she stepped back and he could no longer see her, he began to breathe again. Was she about to climb into bed with the dark-haired man? Had he come too late?

Hunter touched the possibles bag at his waist. Had he been foolish to think he could win her back with a simple declaration of love and the tarnished, battered heart? He sagged against the cool brick wall behind him, refusing to give up hope until he knew anything for certain. Much to his relief, the Creole eventually exited through one of the long French doors and followed the upper gallery to the stairs.

Hunter waited until the conveyance carrying the young man pulled out of the courtyard and rolled away. Then, he stepped off the wooden banquette and headed across the street.

As he approached the courtyard, he half-expected some-one to stop him, but apparently the house servants had gone to bed. A few candles were still burning in the upstairs rooms. He could see a silver candelabrum in one window. His moccasins made no sound on the wooden stairs. When he reached the upper balcony, he headed toward the largest open doors. He took off his hat and smoothed back his hair, wondering if he should have waited until tomorrow.

As he stepped up to the open doors, he could see a man who looked close to fifty sitting in a chair, sipping a drink and staring off into space. Afraid to alarm him and make a bad first impression, Hunter shuffled his feet and coughed softly. He watched Thomas O'Hurley's gaze swing toward him as he stepped into the light. He kept his hands slightly in front of him. One was empty, the other held his black hat. He hoped he looked harmless enough.

Thomas O'Hurley stood up quickly, set the drink aside, and moved swiftly toward the door. Nothing about the man reminded him of Jemma, except O'Hurley's blue eyes. Where she was all smiles and light, this man was stern and openly calculating. His cool gaze swept Hunter, assessing him, weighing his worth. There was instant dismissal in his eyes.

"Mr. O'Hurley?" Hunter smiled.

O'Hurley nodded but didn't return the smile. He kept his voice low, as if he were trying not to awaken the household. "Who are you and what do you want?"

"I'm Hunter Sinclair Boone. From Kentucky." He looked over O'Hurley's shoulder, hoping to see Jemma.

"Is that supposed to mean something?" Again, the cold, dismissive tone a man might use with a servant. Hunter clenched his jaw and told himself that this was Jemma's father. He needed to keep a cool head.

"Your daughter hired me on to take her upriver last year. I came by to talk to her, if I may."

O'Hurley put his hand on the door frame. Hunter had no intention of stepping in without invitation, but O'Hurley obviously didn't know that. He couldn't resist slowly looking the shorter man up and down. If he wanted to get in, he knew that a man of this importer's weight and stature certainly wouldn't be able to keep him out.

"She's already retired for the night. Besides, I'm sure she doesn't want to see you. She's getting married in a few weeks."

Hunter's fingers tightened on his hat. He knew he was crushing the brim, but that was the last thing he was worried about at this point. O'Hurley's announcement put Jemma beyond his reach. Images of Charlie Tate flashed through his mind: the old man, the pitiful cabin, the leather-bound box beneath the bed. The legacy of the battered brass heart had been passed on, but Hunter didn't even have any old, faded letters for consolation. Stunned by the news, he stared around the room, trying to collect himself. The room behind O'Hurley was unlike anything Hunter had ever seen. There were silver candle holders and an elegant crystal chandelier that caught the light and reflected dancing rainbows on the walls. Fancy china plates were displayed in a spindly open cupboard of some kind. A life-sized portrait of a woman who looked very much like Jemma hung across the room from a huge mirror over the fireplace that reflected her image.

The opulence was overwhelming. Why would Jemma give up all this to live in a log cabin in Sandy Shoals? He must have been crazy to think she would welcome him with open arms.

He concentrated on the man standing in the doorway.

"Like what you see, do you?" Thomas O'Hurley sounded far too smug.

"I'd like to see Jemma."

"Any real gentleman knows it's too late to come calling. Besides, I can see you're no gentleman, Boone. My daughter isn't allowed to associate with the likes of you."

She's getting married in a few weeks.

If O'Hurley was telling the truth, there was no reason to stand there arguing. And there was no reason on earth not to believe him. For a split second Hunter almost called her name. Maybe she would respond, but what then? Could he suffer hearing about her pending marriage from her own lips? After all, he had walked out on her. Turnabout was fair play.

Although it broke his heart to admit it, he couldn't really blame her.

Remembering his manners, Hunter mumbled his thanks and started to put on his hat. Thomas O'Hurley stepped outside onto the balcony and, in a low voice, halted Hunter in his tracks.

"You know, Boone, now that I think about it, I do recall my daughter mentioning your name once. She told me she had met a backwoods yokel who didn't know any better than to parade around in filthy buckskins. Said she'd talked you into taking her upriver, toyed with you for a time and enjoyed playing at being a frontier homesteader, but she soon got tired of the charade. You see, my Jemma has quite the imagination, as well as a flair for drama. She also has a very odd sense of humor." O'Hurley looked him up and down, just as Hunter had done earlier. "I'm sure she had one hell of a good time pulling the wool over your eyes."

Without a word, Hunter turned on his heel and stalked off, past the flower boxes, down the stairs. He crossed the garden without thought and found himself two blocks down the street before he even realized he wasn't standing outside O'Hurley's door anymore.

His stomach was heaving, roiling. For some reason, he found it hard to see. His eyes were stinging. He rapidly blinked, pressed a fist to his gut. He walked on without knowing where he was headed, without caring.

Backwoods yokel. He looked down at his oiled buckskins, his moccasins. Maybe he should have bought a coat, a fancy cutaway with tails like the one the Creole with Jemma had sported. Maybe he should have cut his hair before he came calling, found a decent pair of boots—

"Toyed with you for a time. Got tired of the charade."

"I was thinking about kissing."
"All I'm asking for is tonight."
"Tell me you don't want me."
"Let me go, Jemma."
"I'm sure she had one hell of a good time pulling the wool over your eyes."

He walked aimlessly for a time, heading toward the river. Memories tumbled through his mind, pounded relentlessly at his battered heart.

He was an idiot when it came to judging women, but he wasn't about to let it happen ever again.

He wasn't much of a drinker, and he hated to pay someone else for whiskey he could get free at home, but he needed some in a bad way. He stumbled when he reached the end of the boardwalk and stepped into the street; right then he decided he needed more than one drink. He needed to get blind drunk so that the voices in his head would stop.

Jemma had finished packing, weighing her traveling bag after each addition so that she wouldn't end up with more than she could carry. This time she knew what was ahead of her; she prepared well, choosing woolen socks, a coat, three serviceable day dresses, cotton chemises, one cotton and one flannel petticoat, and three pairs of pantaloons. She threw in small items for gifts—earrings, bracelets, and other trinkets that she planned to give to her friends when she reached Sandy Shoals again.

And money. The silver tea caddy that held her allowance money was stuffed full of bills and coins. Whenever she went about the city, one of the servants, André, or her father had been with her. The dressmaker's bills came to her father. She had never really needed to use her funds to purchase anything.

While she laid out a plain brown dress and sturdy street shoes, she thought she heard her father speaking to one of the servants. Good, she thought, it would give her time to take down her hair, braid it, and don a nightgown and wrapper. She wanted to keep him from suspecting anything before she made her escape.

There was no great sadness in her heart, not even when she thought of the poignant moment of their reunion in the warehouse. Now she knew that none of his attentions of late had been real, nor were they inspired by love. He had only been pretending, biding his time until she had wed the man of his choice, a man who could further his own ambitions in exchange for her freedom.

Her father would never, ever change. She knew that now. She would not be fooled again.

Tonight, after she spoke to him, she would go to the sisters at the Ursuline convent and ask them to give her shelter until morning. At first light, she would book passage on a keelboat headed upriver. It would be a long, arduous trip, weeks longer than the voyage down the Mississippi because the boatmen had to pole and pull the craft back up against the current. But time didn't matter to her now.

All that mattered was heading back to Sandy Shoals and returning to the only real home she had ever known, to the place where she had been not only loved, but respected for who she was and what she could accomplish. It was a haven where her worth hadn't been measured by a husband bought with wealth and privilege, but by her own achievements and her will to survive.

She walked over to the *prie-dieu* but didn't kneel. All of the saints were looking back at her from their little gilded frames, all except St. Lucy, of course, who stood there serenely even though she was holding her eyes in what appeared to be a fruit compote. Jemma took a deep breath and exhaled.

"I can't take all of you with me," she said, eyeing each portrait. "I've decided to take only one of you along." The decision was a hard one; she had relied on all of them for so very long.

The virgins were definitely out now, which narrowed her choices tremendously. On impulse, she reached for the miniature painting of St. Michael. She stared down at the colorful image of the beautiful figure weighing souls in the scales suspended from his left hand while wielding a sword in his right. A giant who towered over men, the angel-saint had been portrayed with flowing blond hair.

Upon her return, she had noticed that the image looked like Hunter. She would never own a portrait of the man she had loved with all her heart, but St. Michael came close enough. She hurried over to the bag on the bed, pulled out a chemise, and carefully wrapped it around the painting. If she needed any help along the way, she would appeal to the archangel first.

Ready to face her father, she shoved her bag beneath her bed and stepped out into the hall. Head high, without trepidation or reservations, she imagined the avenging angel walking beside her. She hurried down the hall to the sitting room where the light was still burning. She expected her father to be reading, but he was standing on the balcony with a drink in his hand.

As she crossed the room, he tossed back the liquor and drained the glass. Jemma paused as she watched him turn and reenter the sitting room.

He looked startled when he saw her standing there. She took a deep breath, forcing herself to stay calm. In all probability, this would be the last time they spoke to one another. She had no intention of giving in, or giving up.

Thomas cleared his throat and then smiled a broad, welcoming smile. He walked into the room and set his glass aside. "I thought you'd gone to bed."

"Not yet. I wanted to talk to you first." She wondered why he was acting so nervous. If he suspected that she had overheard him and André earlier, he was trying not to act as if he did. Watching him smile his ingratiating smile, knowing there wasn't the least bit of sincerity or affection behind it, turned her stomach.

"What is it, my dear? You look tired. I think you've been working too hard at the orphanage. I don't know why you want to waste your time there anyway. Most of those young girls' mothers were whores. They are bound to grow up and follow the same path."

"You think so?"

"Of course," he said.

"You don't know much about determination, then, do you?"

"What do you mean?"

"I mean that if a girl truly wants to change her life and her circumstances, she can."

"Not very likely in this day and age," he told her, smiling one of his false smiles.

She wanted to scream, to rail, to throw something, but she held her ground. And her temper.

"I plan to change my circumstances, too."

He looked momentarily uncertain. When his confidence slipped, so did his smile. "What are you talking about?"

"I'm going back to Kentucky."

The shock that registered on his face was no surprise. He paced over to the door with short, quick strides, out to the balcony where he seemed to search the night for something. She wondered why, but didn't dwell on it. He made an about-face and came back inside.

"What in the world has come over you? Do you need to sit down?"

"No. I need to hear the truth. Just once, before I leave."

"What are you talking about?"

"I'm talking about your little bargain with André Roffignac, the one I overheard the two of you discussing earlier. You've done it again, haven't you, Father?"

He tried to hide the fact that she had discovered his scheme. "Now, Jemma. I'm sure we can sit down and discuss this like two adults. That's what you've always wanted, isn't it? For me to treat you as an adult? Come, my dear—"

When he tried to put his arm around her, she shook him off and took a step back. "Don't ever touch me again. I lived a lifetime wishing you would put your arm around me like that; now the thought only sickens me. Your actions are only lies, like your words."

The false smile disappeared. He was so angry that his face turned a bright shade of red.

"So what? So I lied. At least I was giving you time to get to know Roffignac before you married. What's wrong with him?"

"I don't love him."

His cold stare raked her. "Do I need to remind you that you are now nineteen years old? Soon you'll be so old no one will want you. Is that what you'd like? To end up a spinster?" He walked close to her, leaned down. She could smell the liquor on his breath. He looked her in the eye. "Maybe you'd rather choose the convent, is that it? Maybe you'd rather dry up and avoid a man's touch forever?"

She backed up another step, rammed into a library table behind her, and winced.

His tirade went on. "I struck a great bargain with André Roffignac, let me tell you. You should be glad he's even interested."

"You haven't learned anything, have you?" she cried, facing him down, hating the trapped feeling of being forced up against the table.

"Yes. I learned not to make the same mistake I did before. I was trying to give you time to see André's worth, to fall in love with him, but now I'll just have to take another tack."

"You sold me again." She ground out the words. They insulted her tongue. "Let me ask you, Father, would the price go down if André were to learn I'm not a virgin? Would he still be willing to take me off your hands? Does he really need the money that badly?"

He rocked back, as if she had dealt him a blow. "Not a virgin? What . . . what are you saying?"

"Exactly that. I'm *not* a virgin. You haven't anything to bargain with anymore."

"You're lying."

She made the mistake of stepping closer. "I've slept with a man."

He raised his hand and slapped her across the face so hard that it sent her reeling. She smashed into the door frame; her breath left her in a rush. Her legs buckled. Jemma saw stars and thought for a moment that she was going to pass out, but she forced herself to remain standing. Gripping the edge of the open door and the frame, she pushed herself upright.

The Negro butler ran into the room, his coat half-buttoned, his feet bare. Winded from the climb up the stairs, he hovered in the doorway, his eyes wide with fright. "Y'all right, Mistah O'Hurley? Y'all need anythin'?"

"Get out."

Her father was so angry he could barely utter the words. She'd never seen him so livid. Glancing over at the butler, she met his eyes in a silent appeal for him to stay. The man looked at her father and disappeared. She couldn't fault him. If she could have, she would have run, too.

When her father regained enough control, he lowered his voice. "I suppose you gave yourself to the man who took you north—"

"That's right. Hunter Boone. That was his name and I loved him."

"Obviously, this Boone didn't think a thing of using you and casting you off."

The words hurt more than she would ever let him know.

"You know nothing about it. Nothing. It was all my idea. Would it please you to hear I practically had to beg him?"

He was shaking with rage. She pressed a hand to her throbbing cheek and reminded herself to tread carefully or she might very well wind up dead. There was no one to stay his hand; not St. Michael, not Hunter. No one.

"You *begged* that long-haired, backwoods barbarian? You slept with that uncivilized savage in buckskins without a penny to his name?"

Jemma's mouth fell open. She stood there in shock, staring. Not once had she ever described Hunter to her father. Not once had she shared any of the details of her life in Sandy Shoals. The intimate moments were too precious. Instinctively, she had known he would have criticized the world she held so dear, would have ridiculed her dear friends, her adopted family. She had not told him any more than she had to.

"He was here," she whispered. "Hunter was here."

She flung herself at her father, grabbing his jacket by the lapels. "How do you know what he looks like? When did you see him?"

He pried her hands loose, set her away from him. She saw him staring at her cheek, at the mark he had left there.

"You're insane," he told her mercilessly. "I could have you locked up, put away."

"No, I'm not." She shook her head, set her braid swinging against her back. "I never told you what Hunter looked like. You had to have seen him. *When?*"

His gaze flicked to the balcony and back. An instant was all it took. His look said volumes and made her recall the way he had been watching the street before she came in. He had been startled when she walked in. His nervousness was still palpable.

"He was just here, wasn't he?" She ran to the balcony, stared out into the dark night, studied the pools of lamplight on the street, frantically searched the shadows between them. "Hunter was *here* while I was in my room packing."

Too late, she realized what she had let slip.

"Packing?" He charged toward her, skirting the furnishings. She tried to slip past him, but he reached out and grabbed her. The dressing gown ripped at the shoulder.

His hold was strong. She tried to break away by twisting, but it only made him angrier.

"You're going nowhere." He was dragging her off the balcony, back through the sitting room toward the hall. She dug her feet in and nearly stumbled when the woven straw matting buckled and tripped her.

The butler was lurking in the hall, scurrying away from her father as fast as he could go.

"I told you to get out of here!" Thomas yelled. The man disappeared around a corner, headed for the servants' back stairs. "Wait!" O'Hurley called out. The old Negro stuck his head around the corner.

"Send up two stable hands."

"You can't do this to me!" Jemma cried out as he thrust her into her room.

"Watch me."

"Hunter will be back. He'll come back for me."

"Not after what I told him. He thinks you're getting married and that you have no desire to see him ever again."

She felt her world crumble. Not again. Please, God, not again. Too numb to move, she stood there while her father pulled the key out of the inside lock and slammed the door in her face. She heard the lock click. Heavy footsteps pounded down the hallway.

Her father issued curt commands to the stable hands. One was already on the way outside to guard her balcony door. She had seen them on many occasions as they worked in the courtyard stable. It made her uncomfortable to be around them, knowing that they were slaves and that her father owned these men. When she had first arrived and questioned her father about owning slaves, he told her they weren't in Boston anymore and this was the way things were done in the South.

Both slaves were burly men, bulging with well-honed muscle. She would never be able to escape if they were vigilant. She began to pace the room.

Hunter had come for her. It was all she could think of. He was at the door tonight speaking to her father while she had been intent on packing and planning her future.

Hunter had been here. He'd left the frontier and come for her.

She wiped her eyes, walked to a washstand, and lifted the heavy water pitcher. Unmindful of the task, she poured too quickly and water splashed out over the rim of the washbowl. Bending over, she bathed her swollen cheek and wiped her eyes, then wet a towel and pressed it to her injured skin.

Outside, her guard had settled down on the floor of the balcony, his back pressed against the wall beside the jalousied door. Another was stationed in the hall. Could she reason with either? Perhaps bribe one of them?

How much money would it take?

She knew the consequences a runaway slave faced. Would one of them take the chance? She was certainly willing to do almost anything to gain her own freedom.

Her hands shook as she pulled her bag out from under the bed. She would dress; then she would wait. And she would pray. Maybe, despite what her father had told him, Hunter would return. She knew Hunter was stubborn. Once his mind was made up, there was no changing it. Hopefully he would try to see her before he left New Orleans. If not, she would just have to escape and follow him all the way home.

One way or another, she was going to see him again.

chapter

21

EXCEPT FOR ANOTHER LAYER OF DIRT, THE ROTGUT hadn't changed in a year. Hunter leaned against the bar, shoulder-to-shoulder with some of the seediest river scum he'd ever laid eyes on. The crowd would have put him in the mood for brawling even if he wasn't already in a fit of temper. About all Hunter had felt like doing since he left the O'Hurley house was driving his fist into something hard. He downed his third glass of whiskey and surveyed the room.

He had just about settled on a bear of a man at a table in the back of the room who kept shouting, "I'm king of the swamp and king of the river. Any of you think you can knock me down are welcome to give it a try, but I gar-on-tee you won't live to see the sun come up!"

Then, suddenly, the swinging double doors opened and delivered up the same yellow-toothed, mustachioed man who had confronted Jemma the night Hunter had met her. It appeared that the man hadn't even changed clothes in almost a year, for he was wearing the same rumpled black greatcoat and hat.

Hunter demanded one more whiskey, then slammed his glass on the counter and pushed off. His victim was almost to the bar when Hunter whirled and, without explanation, drove his fist into the newcomer's jaw. The man's black eyes snapped open in surprise, then rolled up into his head. Unconscious, he dropped to the floor.

One or two raucous cheers went up around the room, but other than that, no one except a barmaid with melon-sized breasts spilling out of the top of her gown took any particular notice. She crossed the room, heading straight for Hunter with a smile on her face and rouge that looked like beacons on her cheeks. She smelled so strongly of musk that the liberal dousing of perfume she had used only made matters worse.

"I'm looking for a big, strong man like you to help me while away a few hours." Sidling up to him, she draped an arm around his shoulders. His right bicep almost disappeared between her breasts. "How about it, mister?"

She glanced toward the back of the tavern, at the door to the room he and Jemma had once shared.

"I don't think so," he said, trying to extricate himself from her hold. "I was just about to leave."

Boldly, she cupped his privates. "I could show you a real good time."

"Maybe tomorrow night." He pulled her hand away and tugged on the brim of his hat. "Thank you kindly, ma'am, but I'm not in the mood."

"Bastard."

Hunter wasn't there to win friends. He stepped over the man in black, who was still on the floor, and left the tavern, not surprised to note that he wasn't feeling any better.

Outside, Tchoupitoulas Street was crowded with rivermen. Most of the respectable farmers and settlers who had knocked together flatboats to come downriver avoided the area like the plague. Wandering aimlessly, his head slightly fogged with whiskey, Hunter retraced the steps he had taken with Jemma the night they met. Soon he was crossing the *Place d'Armes*, the square in front of the cathedral; then he found himself wandering back up St. Louis Street.

By the time he was a block away from the O'Hurleys' house, he was convinced that it wouldn't hurt a damn thing to hear from Jemma's own lips that she wanted to marry someone else. Then he would have to accept his fate and so be it—but she would have to tell him to his face.

Jemma lingered inside the open doors, watching the silent slave who was still sitting outside her room. Once or twice he nodded off, his chin lolling on his chest. She had grabbed her bag, prepared to bolt past him, but each time he awoke before she could move.

She began pacing the room, trying to think of a way to get him to leave his post. Finally, an idea came to her. André, on one of their excursions, had versed her on the superstitions the Negro slaves had carried with them from Africa. He said that many slaves, especially those new to America, believed in curses and black magic, invoking spirits, ghosts, werewolves, and all manner of good and evil.

With a long series of audible sighs, Jemma made certain the slave outside the door knew she was walking the floor. He would occasionally glance over his shoulder to watch, then look away and stare out into the courtyard. Mustering her courage, she walked over to the door and stared out into the night.

"It's a shame this house is haunted," she said mournfully. "I find it so hard to sleep."

She actually heard the man swallow. "You talkin' to me, missus?"

Jemma looked down into his upturned face. "Yes, I said it's a shame this house is haunted, isn't it? The former owner tried to tell my father about it, but he merely laughed. 'We're from Boston,' Father said." She lowered her voice, mimicking him. " 'We don't believe in such nonsense,' he said." She shivered and rubbed her upper arms, then added in a conspiratorial whisper, "I know it's true, though, because I've _seen_ it."

The slave looked left and right, then back into the darkened confines of her room. "You has?"

"I have. Horrible." She shivered again and began to wriggle her fingers in the air. "It floats above the ground, no more substance than fog."

The man leaned forward.

"He was headless, too," she added as an afterthought.

"No." He shook his head in disbelief. "I lived here over a year and I ain't never seen nothing like that."

"Of course not. Why would the ghost go down to the slave quarters? He stays up here, where he met his end." She nodded, certain she had his full attention. "It seems one of the former owners of this place was killed on his wedding night. His new bride objected to an arranged marriage."

Fighting back a smile, Jemma rushed on, adding actions to illustrate her words. "She put a sleeping draft into his wine and when he was out, she sneaked up on him with an axe and *cut his head off*."

When her hands came down as if she were holding an axe, the slave jumped two feet. Thankfully, he didn't utter a sound.

"Cut it clean off." Jemma slid her finger across her throat. "I've seen him almost every night since I moved in." She sighed and looked out into the garden. "If only I had something, some way to protect myself from these hideous encounters."

"I got sompthin'," he said softly.

She clasped her hands over her breasts. "You have? What?"

"Got me a charm from the voodoo doctor. It'd probably keep a haunt away."

"Oh, please. I'd give anything for some protection from this thing. Did you see the ghost in here earlier?"

He shook his head so violently that she thought he might jar something loose. "No, missus."

Jemma looked over her shoulder and then furtively

urged him to go get the charm. "For both our sakes," she added as a last resort.

"You won't go no place 'til I get back?"

"Of course not. You think I'm insane enough to go out alone on the streets of New Orleans at night?"

She thought of her daring escape a year ago. Knowing what she knew now about the city, she couldn't believe she had survived. Tonight would be different. She knew the way to the convent. It wasn't far. If she stuck to the shadows and hurried, she would be there in a matter of minutes.

The slave hesitated, uncertain. She left the doorway and went to her *prie-dieu*, knelt down, and began a hushed prayer. Sneaking surreptitious glances, she saw him watching her, mumbling to himself. At last, he turned away and started along the balcony to the stairs. Jemma jumped up and ran to the open doors. For a man his size, he was light on his feet and swift, which amazed her.

She flew back into the room. To make the slave think she had gone to bed, she shoved her pillows beneath the sheet, and pulled the mosquito net closed. Then Jemma slipped off her shoes, cradled them in her arms, and grabbed her traveling bag. She hurried out the doors and along the balcony in the opposite direction.

Cutting through the sitting room, she exited on the back balcony on the opposite side of the house. All she had to do was climb down the decorative wrought-iron trellis to the street and slip away.

Afraid the stable hand would return at any moment, she pulled the back hem of her dress through her legs and tied it up with the ribbon beneath the bodice. Then, she heaved her bag over the balcony railing.

Hunter had roamed around so long that the effects of the whiskey had already worn off, leaving behind a horrendous headache. He had reached Jemma's house and, deciding that entering the courtyard might raise an alarm, he

walked around the corner. Before he began his climb up
the iron trellis, he reached out to see if it was secured.

He had one hand on the trellis when a traveling bag
flew over the rail, slammed into the top of his head, and
fell into his arms. His breath left him in a *whoosh*. He
staggered back, shook his head, and looked up in time to
see a shoe plummet toward him. He sidestepped, but it hit
him on the shoulder and bounced onto the sidewalk. Fig-
uring the mate to the shoe had to be on the way down,
Hunter set the bag down and took cover beneath the balcony. He might not know much about women, but he decided it didn't take a genius to deduce that Jemma was
behind the barrage.

Daring to stick his head out and peer upward, he was
treated to the sight of a shapely leg encased in a pair of
frilly pantaloons as it came over the rail. He held his breath
while Jemma felt around for footing and then found it. She
swung her other leg over and started climbing down.

Hunter stepped closer in case she slipped. He didn't say
a word as she made her way down the trellis. When she
reached the ground, he was waiting with her bag and both
shoes in his hands. Jemma turned around, saw him, and
gasped.

"Is this how you really escaped the convent in Algiers?
I never actually believed the story about the tunnel," he
whispered.

She had barely opened her mouth before he dropped the
bag and shoes, whipped her into his arms, and covered her
mouth with his.

Her arms went around him and she held on tight, returning the hot, bruising kiss he gave her measure for measure. His head was spinning by the time they stepped apart.

"For a woman who's about to get married to someone
else, that was some kiss."

"The kind that would definitely lead to other things,"
she said with a smile.

"Are you eloping?"

"Whatever gave you that idea?"

"Your father. The bag."

"Actually, I was on my way to find you. I wanted to hire you to take me to a spot I know of upriver."

"How did you know I was here?"

"My father let it slip. I found out tonight that he had betrayed me again—"

"I saw you with that Creole earlier."

"You were here and didn't say anything? Oh, Hunter."

He reached out and wiped her cheek with his fingertips. "I never saw anyone laugh and cry at the same time before."

She glanced up at the balcony. "We have to get out of here."

"*We?*" He was smiling like an idiot and didn't care.

"We." She paused, staring up at him, the stars above them reflected in her eyes. "You did come back for me, didn't you, Hunter Boone? You aren't going to stand there and give me that speech about being a loner again, are you?"

"Yes, I did, and no, I'm not," he whispered. He glanced up at the balcony. "I take it your father wouldn't approve of your leaving town with a backwoods yokel?"

"Oh, Hunter, I'm so sorry for anything insulting he might have said to you. I really am."

"Don't worry about it. To my mind it just justifies running off with you again. Where did you say you were headed this time?"

She threw her arms around his neck again. "Anywhere you'll take me."

Before Hunter would agree to take her back to his hotel, Jemma had to promise that she would marry him as soon as possible. She asked him if they could wait until they reached Sandy Shoals.

The hotel room in the French Quarter wasn't luxurious, but it was clean and comfortable. The minute she walked into the room and took one look at the bed, Jemma felt an odd combination of shyness mingled with unbridled excitement. Hunter left the door open so that light from the hallway would filter in until he lit the lamp on a bedside table. She waited in the middle of the room until the light flared. Hunter set down her bag, then closed and locked the door.

Eager for him to hold her, Jemma walked over to Hunter, but he held her at arm's length and frowned.

"What happened to your face?" He reached out and stopped short of touching the bruise on the side of her cheek.

"Let's not talk about it." Her eyes stung with tears.

"Your father hit you, didn't he?"

"Yes," she whispered.

"Why?" His eyes went icy cold with rage, his mouth hardened into a determined line.

She folded her hands and took a deep breath. "I confronted him about a conversation I'd overheard earlier, between him and André Roffignac, the man you saw me with. Father had arranged another marriage, without my knowledge or consent. I let him know that I had no intention of going through with it."

"Damn the man—"

"He said something that led me to believe you had been there and he had turned you away. I was furious and so I told him I wasn't a virgin anymore. That's when he hit me. Then he locked me in my room and put guards at the doors."

He was disgusted and mad enough to spit as he tossed his hat on a chair and then shrugged out of his coat. "How did you get out?"

"That's another story. Let's not waste time talking about my father." She was surprised at the trace of sadness that still lingered in her tone. Slipping her arms around him, she attempted to calm his rage. "I'm all right, really."

He ran his hands through her hair, untying the ribbon that held her braid, then loosened her curls and drew them around her shoulders. Bending his head, he touched his lips to hers and she knew such a sweet longing that she wanted to cry with relief.

When the kiss ended, Jemma drew far enough away to look up into his eyes. "I missed you so," she whispered. "I thought that time would help, that I would forget the way your touch makes me feel. I sometimes prayed that the day would come that I would wake up and not be listening for the sound of your voice. I told myself that I had to stop wanting you, that you were out of my life forever, but my heart wouldn't listen."

"Oh, Jemma."

He picked her up and carried her to the bed. While he held her in his arms, she drew aside the mosquito netting and then Hunter sat down and held her on his lap.

"What made you have a change of heart, Hunter? Why did you come back?" She drew the thong out of his hair and tossed it aside.

He gave her a quick kiss on the lips and set her down. Then he walked over to where he had hung his powder horn and possibles bag on the back of a chair.

"I met a man named Charlie Tate up the Missouri." He opened the bag and reached inside. Unable to take her eyes off him, Jemma watched him draw something out of the bag. "He was sick, dying very slowly. He was all alone until I got there. That night I saw myself in Charlie and saw what might become of me if I turned my back on everything and everyone forever."

He crossed back to the bed and held out his hand. In his palm lay a battered, tarnished heart-shaped pendant the size of a gold piece. Jemma reached for it, picked it up and rubbed her fingers over it.

"I found it in Charlie's cabin the night he died," Hunter told her. "Right then, I knew that I had to come back to you. I couldn't refuse the love you had offered, Jemma, not for one more day, let alone a lifetime.''

Clutching the heart in her palm, she tipped her face up to him. He cupped her chin in his hands and bent down to place a gentle kiss of promise on her lips.

"I'm so glad you came for me," she whispered against his mouth. "I love you, Hunter Boone."

"I love you, too, Jemma."

"I don't think I'll ever get tired of hearing you say that."

"'I love you' isn't something you say just once. Now that I've spoken the words out loud, it just might become a habit."

"I hope so."

"I do love you, Jemma. I'm just thankful you're still mine." He straightened, finally able to smile since seeing her bruised face. "On the way back, I tried to think of one of your saints to pray to but I forgot their names."

"They heard you anyway."

"I would have been here in May, but when I started downriver, Noah was injured in a boat accident. I stayed to see that he made it."

"He's all right?"

Hunter hesitated so long that she felt a wave of alarm. Then he said, "He's blind in one eye and badly scarred on the left side of his face. The scar will fade, but the whole thing has made him more of a recluse than ever. I don't know if he'll ever forgive me for saving his life."

"How could you not? You just have to hope he eventually comes to his senses." She stood up and hurried over to where he had left her bag.

"What are you doing?" He drew his shirttail up out of the waistband of his buckskins and worked his shirt off over his head.

"Getting out my nightgown." Jemma tossed items right and left. She came across the painting of St. Michael, smiled down at it, and set it aside.

Hunter came up behind her and picked up the miniature. "Who's this?"

"St. Michael the Archangel." She watched Hunter trace the sword in the painting and stare at the devil lying crushed beneath Michael's feet.

"Looks like he could handle just about anything."

"That's why I chose him when I left the others behind. I couldn't carry them all."

Hunter stood the painting on a table and took Jemma's hands in his. "Will you miss everything you have to leave behind, Jemma? I saw your home: the silver, all the riches—"

She put her fingertips to his lips. "Not for a minute. Now take me to bed. I've been thinking a lot about kissing."

"And other things?"

"Definitely the other things."

He undressed her slowly, taking his time, touching her gently as he explored every curve, every rise and hollow. When she stood nude before him, he ran his hands over her breasts, cupped them and lifted them to his mouth. He suckled one nipple, then the other.

Jemma grasped his shoulders and threw her head back, crying out with pleasure. He kept up the wonderful, maddening torture until she was weak with the heady sensations pulsing through her. Then he took her hand and led her over to the bed.

"Wait," she whispered, drawing away from him, returning to the small table across the room. She turned the picture of St. Michael to the wall before she went back to Hunter's side. He was watching her with a half-smile playing over his lips.

She shrugged. He laughed out loud and drew back the sheet.

Jemma slipped into bed and watched, wide-eyed and curious, while he took off his buckskins. There was noth-

ing beneath them but bare skin. His manhood stood proud
and erect in a thatch of tight curls.

"I knew it," she said with a shake of her head.

"*What?*"

"No drawers."

It was his turn to shrug, hers to laugh.

He slid in beside her and stretched out, pressing against
her. His body was all hard muscle and firm lines, strength
tempered with gentleness. She loved every inch of him.

"I've been waiting for this for so long," she whispered
against his neck. "Sometimes I thought that what we did
before might have only been a dream."

"It was a dream. One that I kept dreaming every night
I was away from you." He slipped his hand between her
legs and cupped her mound. She jumped with surprise
when his fingers touched that most sensitive nub at the
apex of her thighs.

"Does that hurt?"

"No," she moaned against his shoulder. "I . . . you surprised me is all."

"I hope to surprise you a few more times tonight," he
said just before he began to kiss her.

His lips were as soft as she remembered. When he
slipped his tongue between her teeth she shivered all over.
His fingers slowly smoothed deeper into her and then out.
His tongue followed the same rhythm, slow and steady at
first, then faster, delving deeper, demanding that she give
herself over to him.

Before she was aware that she was even near a peak,
she cried out, thrusting her hips higher, forcing his fingers
further inside her. He stilled and cupped her while she
broke and melted.

As the world around her became real again, he stroked
her back, gentling her, molding her against his hard erection. "I want you, Jemma," he whispered against her ear.
"I want to feel you all around me. I want to be inside you,

moving and feeling you move against me. The way it was that night beneath the stars.''

''Yes.'' She rolled onto her back, urging him to come over onto her, to press her down on the mattress. The oil lamp was still burning low. Jemma looked down, saw their flesh pressed together. The sight of his hard body, of her breasts flattened against him, excited her and made her bold. She reached between them, closed her hand around his erection, felt the dewy drop at its tip. She could feel him throbbing against her palm. ''I want you, too. I want to feel you inside me.''

Once more, he kissed her deeply. She moaned and tightened her hold before drawing her hand up along his thick, turgid shaft. He gasped and stilled. ''Don't . . .'' It was all he could manage, but she understood and released him.

Touching his forehead to hers, he remained still, breathing erratically, his heart pounding against her breast. Gradually, he gained control, rose up, and then pressed the tip of his shaft against the entrance to her moist sheath. In that one instant in time, the world could have dissolved around them and Jemma wouldn't have noticed. All she was aware of was Hunter—over her, breathing with her, his skin hot and exciting against hers.

She bucked her hips, urging him to enter. When she moved to lower her hands to his hips, he captured her wrists, drew her arms up and imprisoned her hands against the pillows. Only then did he enter her, slowly, so very slowly that the anticipation caused her agony. She wanted to scream in frustration and cry out, but he kissed her again, catching the sound in her throat.

Then when she craved him so much that she thought she would go mad, he was suddenly moving again, driving into her farther and farther, deeper and harder until she wrested her hands free, clasped her arms around his shoulders and her legs around his hips, and cried out with glorious abandon as he reached his own climax and spilled his seed inside her.

• • •

Jemma fell asleep with her head on his shoulder, but for another hour, Hunter stared up at the ceiling. He traced the delicate skin of her shoulder with his thumb, looped a curl around his finger. He couldn't get the image of her father striking her on the face out of his mind.

Slowly and carefully, he slipped out from beneath her and left the bed, careful to draw the mosquito net back into place. He dressed without a sound, put his knife on, found his hat, and crept into the hall. He locked the door behind him.

It would be hours before dawn, but he practically ran all the way back across the Quarter until he was standing in front of the same trellis Jemma had used to make her escape from her father's house. Within minutes he was on the second floor, inching his way along the hall. He nearly tripped over a slave asleep on the floor in front of a bedroom door. It didn't take him long to find the master bedroom.

Thomas O'Hurley didn't wake up until Hunter had put one knee on the mattress and was leaning over him with the long skinning knife just above his jugular.

"Good evenin', Mr. O'Hurley," Hunter said in a tone as smooth as honey, deepening to a backwoods Kentucky drawl. "I hope you weren't having pleasant dreams."

"What . . . what are you doing here?" Thomas O'Hurley started to rise, but when the cold blade pressed against his throat, he flopped back down on the bed.

"I came to get your blessing."

"What are you talking about?"

"Jemma and I are getting married."

"I forbid it," he sputtered.

"I don't think you're in a position to forbid much of anything right now, do you? Besides, she's already safe from the likes of you. I just wanted you to know that you'll never have an opportunity to hit her again. I'll see to that myself. And if you're smart, you'll take my advice and never hit a woman again.''

''I'll do whatever I damn well—''

Hunter pressed the knife closer. ''What? You're arguing? Why, I'd like nothing better than to kill you, but seeing as how you're Jemma's pa, I'll let you off easy this time. All I'm asking for is your blessing. I'm going to marry your daughter.''

''This is preposterous.''

''Yep. But knowing Jemma, she sets store in this kind of thing, along with saints, and angels.'' He prodded the man's flesh to elicit an answer. ''Your blessing, sir.''

''Take her. Get her out of my life. Do you think I want her around after *you've* had her? She's ruined.''

''That's not quite a blessing, O'Hurley.'' Hunter rubbed the blade along O'Hurley's thick neck.

''Take her with my blessing then. Just get out and leave me alone.''

Hunter relaxed the knife, but not much. ''I need one more thing.''

''Just as I thought.''

''I want you to call off the guard in the hall so I can go into Jemma's room.''

''If you're after money—''

''That's the last thing I want from you, O'Hurley. In fact, the way I hear it, I'm the only prospective groom Jemma's ever had that you didn't have to bribe.''

''What do you want?''

''Take me to her room.''

Hunter let O'Hurley up. Dressed in a rumpled nightshirt, his calves and ankles exposed, the man padded down the hall on bare feet. He sent the slave to bed and ushered Hunter into Jemma's room. While Hunter looked around, O'Hurley walked to the bed, pulled aside the mosquito net and sheet, and saw the pillows.

''I told you I had her already.'' Hunter was standing

near the little altar table covered with candles in odd-shaped glasses.

"What are you doing?"

"Taking these with me." One by one, Hunter took down the twenty-two miniature paintings of saints. He ordered O'Hurley to strip the quilt off the bed. Even in the semidarkness, he recognized Nette's handiwork and recalled the long hours one winter that he had sat in her cabin watching her stitch it together. When the man handed the patchwork to him, Hunter carefully packed Jemma's saints inside.

"Now, you stay put. Count to two hundred. By that time, I'll be gone." Hunter started out of the room with his precious bundle, paused in the doorway and turned around. "I meant what I said, O'Hurley. You ever try to hurt Jemma again, and I'll see to it that you regret it. Believe me, I don't plan to spend the rest of my life looking over my shoulder."

chapter
22

The wedding took place beneath the trees on the bluff above the river.

Devon Childress officiated and, dressed in his finest black coat, he looked every bit the preacher. Lucy stood in attendance, proudly wearing the new pearl earrings Jemma had given her. The girl's eyes shone with love for the young reverend and with her happiness for the bride and groom. Nette put her Cherokee pipe away for the occasion, but continued to grumble right up to the last minute about the rudeness of ''some folk who just show up and want to get married without givin' a body time to fashion a decent wedding quilt.''

After the vows, everyone walked back to the tavern, where Hunter announced to the few travelers in attendance that food and drinks were on the house for the day.

''Are you happy?'' He stood beside Jemma in new buckskin pants and a shirt she had hand-decorated with embroidery during the long keelboat trip upriver.

She smiled up at him and nodded. ''I've never been happier. Everything was beautiful.'' She watched Lucy, who was seated beside Devon at a table across the room. The rest of the family sat there crowded together, laughing and talking. For the first time in a week, no one was paying attention to the bride and groom.

"Lucy sincerely wants to marry Devon, you know, Hunter, and she's not about to take no for an answer." Jemma nestled closer and leaned against him.

"She's too young," he said with finality.

"No younger than Hannah was when she married Luther. You've got to let her go or she'll run away." Jemma turned and slipped her arm around his waist. "You don't want her to end up like me, do you?"

"I want her to be happy."

"Then give them your blessing," she urged.

"But he wants to take her to Texas."

Jemma just smiled and waited expectantly.

"All right. I'll tell her tonight," he said.

"Tell her before the party ends, please."

Hunter sighed, a dramatic, long suffering sigh. "If you say so. But don't think you're gonna boss me around for the rest of our lives."

"Just the first hundred years or so," Jemma laughed.

Luther left the group at the table and joined them, after admonishing Junior not to wrestle with Little Artie inside the tavern. The two boys ran outside and Luther shook his head as he watched them go.

"Congratulations again, brother." Luther raised a tankard of beer in salute.

"Thanks for standing up as best man," Hunter told him.

Luther sobered. "It's too bad Noah couldn't even bring himself to come to the wedding. I know he's up and around, because the other day I saw him from a distance setting some traps down by Hickory Creek."

Jemma looked at Hunter, who nodded. Then she told Luther, "Noah was here. From where we stood on the river, we could see him in that copse of trees directly behind all of you. He was watching from the shadows. At the end of the ceremony, he waved and then blended back into the forest."

Luther shook his head. "It's a shame what happened to him. Just before the accident he was sweet on Lucy, or so Hannah tells me. Noah must be feeling pretty low." Luther took another swig of beer and reached down to keep little Sadie from running into the corner of the table.

"Lucy will be marrying Devon," Jemma told him as the little girl ran up and hugged her around the knees. She bent down and lifted Sadie up onto her hip. "As soon as they can find a preacher."

"Luther, did you remember to bring that bundle I left with you?" Hunter smoothly changed the subject. As far as he was concerned, Lucy could marry the preacher, but he didn't have to like it yet and he certainly didn't want to stand around talking about it.

"What bundle?" Jemma wanted to know.

Luther ignored her. "Hannah had to take Callie home to change her dress after she spilt cider down the front of it. They're bringing it over."

"*What* bundle?" Jemma asked again.

"Sort of a wedding present," Hunter told her.

Sadie was playing with the brass heart hanging from a ribbon around Jemma's neck. "I thought we agreed not to exchange gifts," Jemma reminded him.

"This isn't really a gift," Hunter said, glancing toward the back door. Callie came skipping in with her braids flying behind her. Hannah followed with a bulky brown-paper package. Jemma turned to Hunter.

"What have you done?"

"You'll see."

He reached out and took Sadie from Jemma as Hannah walked over to them. Everyone in the family watched as Jemma went over to the table and set the package down. Across the room, Big Artie was serving liquor at the bar. At another table, five men who'd arrived that morning on a flatboat played cards, oblivious to the Boones' wedding festivities. A few other travelers were looking on, enjoying a free meal.

Jemma pulled the string and opened the crackling paper wrapping. Inside was the Honey Bee quilt that Nette had given her the day she left Sandy Shoals. She ran her hand over the patches and minute stitches.

"Did you make another one, Nette?" Jemma could only stare at the pieced quilt that had required hours of work and planning.

"Nope. That's the same one. Signed and dated on the back," Nette said, her lips closing on the pipe stem as she puffed out a cloud of tobacco smoke.

"I left this behind at my father's house." Jemma turned to Hunter. "How did it get here?"

"Unfold it," he urged.

"But—"

"Go on." He nodded at the quilt. Sadie had lost interest in pulling his long hair and was struggling to get down. He set the little girl on the floor and she ran off again.

Jemma folded back the first layer, then one more. Nestled inside the quilt were each and every one of the paintings of her saints.

"How did you ever get these?"

"Let's just say I went on a little adventure the night you ran away from home—for the last time, I might add."

"But—"

"I know how much they meant to you and I didn't want you to have to leave them behind. Besides, I figure where we're headed, we might need more than just the one saint along the way."

"Where are we headed?" She wrapped the pictures up in the quilt and planted her hands on her hips. "We just got here a few days ago."

Hunter drew her up against him and crossed his arms in front of her. She leaned back while he bent his head and spoke softly against her ear.

"During my travels I found this pretty little valley on the upper Missouri. Plenty of water, good grazing land, and a view of forever. In no time at all, steamboats will be heading all the way upriver and I figure there ought to be somebody there to sell those travelers all the things they'll need. Not much out there but wide open spaces right now, though. What do you think?''

Jemma turned in his arms and kissed him right in front of the preacher, their whole family, and even the strangers in the room. When they parted, most everyone was laughing. She spoke just loudly enough for him to hear. ''I think it sounds like a grand adventure. When are we leaving?''

''After we've taken some time to practice kissing and a few . . . other things.''